HER CURSED BELOVED

"No danger?" He spun her around and propelled her down the stairs. Holding his candlebranch high, he led her to another alcove. A pile of old furniture, rolled carpets and bric-a-brac that had occupied the recessed space lay strewn on the cold stone floor beside it. Cassandra gasped. He watched her gaze flit over the cot that had replaced the collected trappings, and the bucket of dirt beneath.

"In an hour's time, I might be lying upon that down here in the dark, Cass," he said through clenched teeth. "And there I will stay until the sun sets if I cannot bear the sunlight. My symptoms are worsening. It could happen at any time now." He set the candlebranch down on an old drum table and seized her upper arms, pulling her against his hard-muscled chest, against his thumping heart, his turgid arousal forced against her. "Here is your danger," he said. "*I* am your danger."

Blood Moon

Dawn Thompson

LOVE SPELL NEW YORK CITY

For DeborahAnne MacGillivray,
for her friendship and awesome support,
and for all the talented ladies at Gothic
Romance Writers, where it all began.

LOVE SPELL®

March 2007

Published by

Dorchester Publishing Co., Inc.
200 Madison Avenue
New York, NY 10016

ISBN 0-505-52680-8

The name "Love Spell" and its logo are trademarks of Dorchester Publishing Co., Inc.

Printed in the United States of America.

Visit us on the web at www.dorchesterpub.com.

CHAPTER ONE

Cumberland, England, Summer, 1811

Jon stripped naked in the woad field. There wasn't a minute to spare; Cassandra would be waiting at the crypt in the kirkyard. He would have been there an hour ago if he hadn't stopped to feed . . . so he wouldn't be tempted to feed upon *her*. He glanced about. There wasn't a soul to be seen, just the tall swaying woad, its strong-smelling yellow blossoms tinted green by the velvet blue of pending darkness. The tall stalks swayed, dancing in the breeze, whispering their secrets, keeping his, just as they always did. They would be gone soon. Midsummer's Eve; the harvesting would begin. Then he would have to take shelter in the forest when he roamed his land in the north.

In a blink and a blur, he sailed through the air and hit the ground running on four sturdy, corded legs, his thick footpads trampling the woad, bending the stalks, his tall, muscular, barrel-chested body grown taller, thicker, covered with a shaggy coat of silver-tipped black fur. He could make better time as *canis dirus*, the dire wolf, beating a path through the woad on all fours, than he could standing upright, though that was always an option— better time than he could in his normal incarnation, come to that. *Normal.* The word didn't even signify. He would never be normal again.

His vision had narrowed now, just as it always did when he shifted into the shape of the great wolf, and his facial features transformed into an elongated snout. It wasn't because of the darkness. He was possessed of keen night vision in both incarnations. *Small consolation, that,* he thought bitterly, swallowing hard in a vain attempt to break up the lump in his throat. His bared canines were dripping blood carried over from his other self and the feeding that had just taken place. It slid down his long pink tongue, splattering his forefeet with foam and spittle as he ran. But still, the thick, metallic taste laced with salt clotted at the back of his palate. Its rich, toothsome flavor—piquant and mysterious—would stay with him until it was time to feed again.

Maybe she wouldn't come tonight. Maybe all this haste was for naught. It was a pleasant fiction. He loosed a bestial canine whine. If she wasn't there, he would agonize over her whereabouts until he set eyes upon her again, just as he was doing now, running his heart out, burning his lungs dry gulping the cool night air. If only he hadn't needed to feed. If only he trusted himself in her presence when the hunger—the feeding frenzy—was upon him once the sun sank below the horizon each night. Streaking through the woad, he cursed Sebastian, the vampire who had infected him and nearly made *her.* Sebastian would stalk her until he finished what he'd started, until he'd made her his slave like the others. Over Jon's dead body.

Would she have sense enough to climb the tor to Whitebriar Abbey, his inherited manor, when she didn't find him at the crypt? Would Bates, his faithful servant, admit her? Why hadn't he told her to meet him at the Abbey in the first place? He was counting upon the sacred ground in the kirkyard keeping Sebastian at bay. According to legend, full-fledged vampires could not bear crosses or consecrated places—or anything sacred, come to that. How Jon himself still could was a mystery, though holy water boiled when he touched it. But this wasn't legend; this was *real*. Perhaps these things came about gradually in the newly made. Whatever the cause, he was glad of the effect.

He was out in the open now. He had left the woad behind, though its pungent scent still filled his nostrils. Was it something remembered from his childhood, when he'd played in these fields and knew every inch of them, or something related to the here and now? More likely the latter. His sense of smell was always heightened in wolf form. It was almost painful when he needed to feed, stabbing pains shooting through his sinuses until he'd tracked down his prey. At least he didn't have to suffer that now; he wouldn't need to feed again tonight. It was safe to be with Cassandra, to hold her in his arms, to comfort her. He dared not take it beyond that, though he longed to live in that exquisite body, to succumb to the lure of an innocence that had bewitched him from the moment they'd met at Almack's in London that Season. Sebastian might have taken her first blood, but *he*—Jon Hyde-White, third son of the Earl of Breckenridge, who'd had noble aspirations of becoming a vicar and had answered the call to Holy Orders before it all began—was to blame, as surely as if he'd been the one who'd plunged his fangs into that sweet flesh that smelled hauntingly of meadowsweet and lilies of the valley.

Wolf though he was, tears misted Jon's eyes. Padding to a halt in the clearing, he threw back his head and howled into the darkness. The sound trailed off to a mournful wail, lonely and sad. No creature answered it; no woodland voice replied, though birds fled the trees into the clouds at the edge of the copse that bearded the thicket. Across the moor, a light in the kirk at the foot of the tor beckoned, and he bolted toward it, praying he wasn't too late.

Nothing stirred in the kirkyard when he arrived. Surging into human form—if he could still be considered human; he wouldn't dwell upon that now—Jon stood naked, clothed only in the mist that drifted among the crooked headstones like wraiths risen from the dead. The Hyde-White crypt loomed before him, deserted, an upright vault covered in woodbine creepers, fitted with an iron-barred door. It would be open. Since the nightmare began, the vicar, Clive Snow, his mentor and confidant, had unlocked it every night at dusk, and locked it again once the first gray streamers of dawn chased the mist each morning. Just to be certain. In case Jon needed sanctuary from Sebastian, who only roamed the moor at night.

Jon tore open the wrought ironwork, then the door, and stepped inside. His heart sank. The crypt was empty. Cassandra wasn't there waiting as he'd hoped she would be—as he'd *prayed* she'd be. He wasn't surprised. God heard him no longer. Why would God help one undead, and another destined to be? Had Clive Snow damned himself as well by giving them aid—by keeping Jon safe and giving her sanctuary? Was Jon's friend and mentor another casualty of the nightmare? He shuddered to wonder.

Shaking those thoughts free like a dog sheds water, Jon strode inside, the stone floor cold and hard beneath his bare feet. A change of clothes was set out neatly on a stone bench in the corner. He dressed himself hurriedly, tugging on his drawers and buckskin breeches, then the shirt, waistcoat, and chocolate brown superfine frock coat. He would go back for the clothes he'd left in the woad field, but not yet. Not until he'd found Cassandra. Not until he knew she was safe.

He tugged on his turned-down top boots and stamped his feet to settle them inside the stiff though malleable leather. They still felt like the large, padded feet of the dire wolf, and would for awhile. The wolf was his favorite part of the *condition*, as he referred to it. He did love roaming fleet-footed over the moors, with the Cumberland north wind whipping tears into his eyes, combing his silver-tipped fur.

His makeshift toilette complete, he stepped out into the misty darkness and closed the door of the vault. The light in the nearby vicarage beckoned, and he parted the mist with long-legged strides, hoping Cassandra had taken refuge there, and banged the knocker impatiently—once, twice. He raised his hand to grip the knocker again when the door came open in the vicar's hand.

The elder clergyman pulled Jon inside. "Are you trying to rouse the dead?" he asked, leading the way toward the study.

Clive Snow seemed borne down as he trudged the narrow hallway lit by candles in wall sconces. The flickering candlelight picked out the silver in his hair and shone in his articulate eyes, the color of amber, which had always seemed to see into Jon's soul. Jon couldn't bear those penetrating amber eyes boring into him now. There was no time for a lecture; even less for explanations.

He dug in his heels. "Is Cassandra here?" he asked.

"No. Is she supposed to be?"

"We were to meet at the crypt. She was supposed to arrive before sunset, and she isn't there. She doesn't realize the danger she is in, Clive. Sebastian will try again. It's only a matter of time."

"Jon, we must talk," said the vicar, gripping his arm.

"Yes, but not now. I must find her before Sebastian does. He's out there somewhere. I know it—I *feel* it! If he finishes what he's begun, she will be his for all eternity. She will be lost to me forever." He broke free. "I must go," he said, sprinting down the narrow corridor.

"Jon!" the vicar called after him. "We must talk, I say! If we do not speak before the sun rises on another day, you will find the crypt locked when you reach it. I mean it!"

Jon didn't answer. It was an empty threat. If Clive were to lock him out of the crypt while in wolf form he would have no togs to change into when he transformed back. Clive Snow knew that. He would hardly let Jon be caught in the altogether by some member of the parish visiting a loved one in the kirkyard. Only one thought moved Jon then. Where was Cassandra? He had to find her.

"Jon!" the vicar called after him. "Come back here!"

"I shall—later," Jon said, slamming the rectory door a little too loudly as he fled, the vicar's protests ringing in his ears. No. He most definitely wasn't himself. How could so much have happened to change his otherwise ordered life in the mere space of a sennight?

Seven days ago, he'd known who he was and where he was going. His future was charted, impeccably planned.

He was to be vicar of All Saints Parish. The previous vicar and his friend, Clive Snow, was retiring by dispensation from the bishop. It was all arranged. What's more, Jon had met the girl of his dreams, and had been about to press his suit when Clive Snow's missive arrived, asking him to try to locate a parishioner gone astray, to convince the man to return to his increasing wife post-haste. Jon now bitterly wished he'd never received that missive.

Half sprinting, half stumbling, he scaled the tor to the flattened summit where Whitebriar Abbey stood buffeted by the cruel north wind, no less scathing in spring and summer for all these seasons' mildness. Bursting into the abbey, he bellowed for Bates at the top of his lungs.

The white-faced valet—cum butler cum footman, since Jon's *condition* reduced the staff—loped to the gallery balustrade above on his lame leg, his graying hair fanned out behind him in dishabille, his stone-colored eyes wide.

"Oh, sir!" he cried. "Thank heavens! I am at the end of my tether. Please come!"

"What is that racket?" Jon asked, scaling the broad, carpeted stairs two at a stride. Only then was he aware of the din echoing through the mansion above.

"'Tis Gideon," said the servant. "I cannot do a thing with him. He's run mad, I think!"

"What's happened?"

"The young lady's come—"

"Thank God!" Jon cried, his posture collapsing in relief.

"I put her in the blue suite off the west gallery," Bates went on, pointing down the upstairs hall, "and no sooner had I done when Gideon come a-chargin' up here goin' at that door all-out straight. See for yourself, it's nearly in splinters."

"Fetch his chain."

The servant shot out his hand, the dog's chain dangling from his fingers. Jon hadn't even realized that Bates was holding it all the while. He snatched it from him.

"Gideon, stay!" he commanded.

The mastiff's head flashed toward him. Its jaws were dripping foam, flinging spittle, its dilated eyes glazed with the iridescent luster of mindless irritation.

"Gideon, heel!" Jon charged.

The mastiff pranced in place—tail wagging, lips snarling—his head bobbing back and forth between the wounded door and his master, a troop of desperate whines leaking from his throat between growls. Jon rattled the chain, and the dog padded toward him warily, tail between his legs. Reluctance ruled the animal's step, and still there was a silent showing of fangs, culminating in another guttural growl and a rousing bark that more closely resembled a snarl. What was wrong with the animal? Gideon had never snarled at him before.

Jon snapped the chain fast to the collar and jerked the dog to a standstill, handing the chain to Bates. "Take him below," he said. "And keep him there."

"Y-yes, sir. I'm sorry, sir. I cannot control him when he's thus. You are the only one he heels to."

No longer, Jon thought. He gripped the door handle and waited, his fingers working the gilded scrollwork impatiently while the servant led Gideon down the stairs, before he lifted the latch. Once the pair was out of sight, he burst into the room, calling Cassandra at the top of his lungs. She didn't answer, and he streaked through the sitting room, charged through the door to the bedchamber adjoining, and pulled up short. Cassandra was nowhere in sight, but her sprigged muslin frock lay in a heap on the floor under the antique Glastonbury chair in the corner.

Calling her name again, Jon spanned the distance to the dressing room in two strides, but she wasn't there either, and he crossed back into the bedchamber, his eyes upon the daintily patterned frock underneath the chair in the corner. It was *moving*.

Approaching with caution, Jon squatted down and seized the frock, suspecting rats. The shape of something small wriggling inside confirmed his suspicions, and he surged upright and raised his foot, set to crush the rodent beneath the heel of his top boot, when he was stopped by a mewing sound leaking forth. Jon lowered his foot to the floor, then reached down toward the moving frock. Once, twice he drew his hand back before he finally seized it, exposing the head of a little black kitten, whose big green eyes stared up at him like two sparkling emeralds in the candlelight. In fact, the creature seemed all eyes, the way they dominated that tiny face.

All at once, the mewing became sobs, the head expanded, and the soft ebony fur became a streak of molten silver surging toward him in a blurred rush of motion. Then *she* was in his arms. The scent of meadowsweet and lilies of the valley threaded through his nostrils from her sun-painted hair, from her naked skin bared by the tangled frock twisted around her that showed him more of her exquisite body than he was prepared to view. His sex grew hard against her. The tightness began at his very core—the hunger—as he could smell her blood. He could taste the salty sweetness of its thick nectar at the base of his tongue. He fought back the inevitable drool, the lubricant saliva that made the piercing easier. Anticipation quickened his heartbeat. He felt the painful pressure as fangs emerged from his canine teeth—long, sharp, hollow fangs—their manifestation an arousal. *The feeding frenzy!* How could it be? He had just fed.

As if it had a will of its own, his hand slid the length of her soft white throat, feeling for the pulse beneath that smooth, opalescent skin. Blood was racing through her veins, through the artery leaping there. Her very life was palpitating beneath his trembling fingers, inches from the deadly fangs hovering above; it was there for the taking. He groaned and put her from him, tugging the twisted frock back up over the milk-white breasts trembling in rhythm with her sobs.

"What . . . do you think you're . . . about, Cassandra ?" he panted. Reeling away from her, he raked his hair with a trembling hand, taking deep, shuddering breaths, and did not face her again until his needle-sharp fangs had receded. After a moment, all evidence of the condition faded—all, that is, except the thick, hard arousal challenging the seam of his buckskins.

He spun to face her. "What did I just see here, Cass?" he asked through clenched teeth, as if clenching them would keep the fangs from emerging again.

Cassandra reached toward him, but he backed away. "Stay where you are!" he said. "Good God, come no nearer!" The throbbing in his sex dominated his body, echoing in his ears like the thunder of timpani. He had to keep her at arm's length.

Cassandra burst into fresh tears. "I . . . there was a rat," she wailed. "I smelled its blood. It gave me such a hunger. I hate rats, Jon. What is happening to me?"

How he wanted to take her in his arms and comfort her—only that. How he longed to embrace that sweet flesh on any pretext. He dared not. He had to keep his distance. He would not finish what Sebastian had started. There was hope for her if he did not yield to temptation. But it was more than mere temptation, this; it was something dark and sinister and all-consuming that he could barely control. How long before he could no longer keep that control? How long before . . . No! He dared not give those thoughts substance with words—not even in his mind.

"Did you feed?" he murmured, his voice trembling and strained.

She shook her head. "All at once I had paws and claws and silky fur, and the rat was bigger than I was," she sobbed. "I wasn't me anymore. I was a *kitten*, and it *bit* me . . . see?" she said, holding out her hand.

Jon stared at the blood still oozing thick and red from the back of her delicate hand, trickling down her fingers. His own hands balled into white-knuckled fists at his sides. It came again: the tightening, the turgid pressure in the pit of his belly like a fiddle bow string stretched to its limit. The throbbing started at his temples, the terrible pounding commanding his sex until it throbbed to the same shuddering rhythm. He had to taste her or go mad—now, before the blood congealed and lost its flavor; now, while it was still fresh. He snatched the hand and raised it to his lips. If he did this, his hunger for her would be insatiable, his thirst for her sweet nectar as that of a wanderer in the desert in search of life-giving water. She was already in his blood, and had been since before the condition changed both their lives. Were he to lick the sticky blood from that hand—whether he were to take but a taste or suck it dry—she would be in his very soul, and nothing would slake that hunger save that he take her to completion.

Unaware, for he hadn't told her everything, Cassandra made the decision for him. She reclaimed her hand and raised it to his lips. Jon groaned. Seizing her wrist, he took her bloodied fingers into his mouth and sucked them clean—then the wound itself, until he'd swallowed every drop. Afterward, ashamed, unable to meet the non-plussed expression on that lovely face, in those doelike brown eyes, he dropped her hands and turned away in disgust. She had no idea what he'd just done, but he knew all too well that he had sealed their fate. She was no longer safe in his company. He would have to fight the urge to finish her with every fiber of what was left of his being to keep himself from ravishing her body—and worse, ravaging her soul.

"Sit down, Cass," he murmured. "No! Not on the bed . . . in the chair." He waited while she did as he bade and took a seat in the Glastonbury chair she'd so recently hidden beneath. He noticed her wary observation of it as she eased herself down with a cautious slither. "Vampires have the power to shapeshift," he explained. "You have seen me change into the form of a dire wolf. Each of us has our own creature—"

"Mine is a . . . a *kitten?*" she interrupted. "A helpless kitten? Am I to be devoured by rats—or dogs? I heard your hound at the door. He would have torn me to shreds."

"How am I to make her understand when I do not?" Jon cried to the rafters. After a moment he sobered, as much as he could with the sweet taste of her life force lingering on his tongue, taunting him, *obsessing* him. Why had he tasted that sweet nectar? "You are not a full-blooded vampire . . . yet," he went on shakily. "You have the ability . . . but not the power—the strength—to take your creature's proper form, which, I presume, would be some form of cat by this display. Did you have fair warning?"

"Fair warning?" she repeated, a frown spoiling her lovely face. "How do you mean?"

"Did you know before . . . it happened that something untoward was occurring inside you?"

"I did feel strange—as if my bones had turned to jelly. My head felt as light as air, and white pinpoints appeared before my eyes. . . ."

He nodded. "When that occurs again, remove your clothing. You must be naked to transform. To shapeshift clothed, you court all manner of dangers just like this here now when you became tangled in your frock. It could mean your life to be hampered thus before a greater creature. If you were not entangled in the gown, you would have escaped the rat before it bit you."

"Will it always be like this?" she asked, her eyes pleading.

"I do not know," he said, "but I think not in your case, unless . . ."

"Unless what?"

"Unless someone were to finish your making," he said. "I mean to see that such a thing does not occur, but you must do exactly as I say. You did not tonight, and look what happened. You were to meet me at dusk at the crypt—"

"But you weren't there," she cried, "and I was afraid."

"I was . . . detained." There was no need to go into detail. She didn't need to know he'd all but drained a lightskirt in the town square. His conscience still nagged at him for feeding upon the slag, but better her than the woman who now stood before him. No . . . he wouldn't tell her that. "When I arrived there and you weren't waiting for me, I nearly ran mad. You would have been safe in the kirkyard. Full-blooded vampires cannot tread consecrated ground, which is why I wanted you to come there before dark—before Sebastian was abroad to finish what he started with you."

She hung her head. "I didn't go gadding about," she defended. "I hurried here straightaway when you didn't come."

"Which was wise but risky," said Jon. "Sebastian is not barred from Whitebriar Abbey, though he cannot enter unless it be by invitation. Still, he could have lain in wait anywhere between the kirk and here to pounce upon you. He needs no invitation in the open. You must do as I say. I cannot be about the business of putting things to rights while worrying that you will blunder into danger. Bates is unaware of the true nature of our . . . situation, but he has been instructed never to admit *anyone*. How you charmed him I will never know, but you can bet your blunt I will have it out of him before the night is done. Come here tomorrow before sunset. I will instruct Bates to let you in, and stay here until I join you."

She started toward him, but he reeled out of her reach. "No!" he said. "Do not touch me! I want you to climb into that bed and sleep. You have that luxury in the night. I do not. I must be about my business under cover of darkness, when I have the strength I lose at dawn. Bates will let you out once the sun has risen . . . when you will be safe. You can still bear to be abroad in the daylight, can you not?"

She frowned. "I can," she said, "though it makes my head ache, and my eyes! It's like I'm seeing through a curtain of blood."

"Yes. It is thus with me as well. If that symptom doesn't worsen, I hope it will fade in time, please God. If anything should change, however, you must tell me at once. *At once*, Cassandra. Is that clear?" He couldn't bring himself to tell her that if Sebastian had his way with her and finished what he'd started, if she became a full-blooded vampire, daylight would likely kill her. Seven days ago, he wouldn't have credited that there even *was* such a creature as Sebastian. He was still having difficulty accepting it, but he was no longer in denial. This loathsome manifestation was no figment of his imagination; the nightmare was real.

She nodded.

"Good!" Jon said, striding to the door. He gripped the gilded handle. "I must pay a call upon Vicar Snow. Now, lock this after me and go to sleep," he said. "Let no one in until Bates knocks at dawn—not even me. Especially not me. Good night, Cassandra."

CHAPTER TWO

Jon sprinted down the stairs and went in search of Bates. He found the man banking the fire in the coal stove in the kitchen. The butler and his wife, Grace, were the only servants he'd kept on; the rest he had let go when the nightmare began. It was hardly fair to the faithful butler, who had no inkling of the dark depths of the situation, even though the man seemed willing. Jon could hardly tell him the truth entire, else he risk losing the butler as well as his wife, who served as housekeeper at Whitebriar Abbey. He needed them.

"Bates, I thought I told you to admit no one to Whitebriar Abbey," he said. "I think we needs must be clear upon that before another hour passes."

"Ya did, sir, but I knew you'd want me to admit the lass. Did I do wrong, then?"

Jon's posture collapsed. "Yes . . . no . . . Leave that and sit, Bates," he said in exasperation, gesturing toward the stove. How to explain without frightening the poor man out of his wits? But maybe that was just what was

17

wanted—at least it would ease Jon's conscience to go as far as he dared with the truth. "You acted rightly admitting Miss Thorpe, and I want you to continue to do so—she's going to be staying here now. I'm simply concerned that you might admit . . . someone else while acting upon your own initiative. That cannot be. No one must cross that threshold below and enter this house unless I bring them myself, or unless it should be Miss Thorpe coming or going, no matter what they tell you. The person that attacked her still stalks her. I have reason to believe he has followed her here from London. He will seek her out and attempt to finish what he started. He will most certainly come here seeking her. He cannot enter unless you admit him, but he is very cunning. He will try to trick you. You must trust no one now. Making matters worse, Miss Thorpe and I contracted an ailment in Town that . . . seems to be circulating of late, and special circumstances may arise. It's past the contagious stage, so there is no risk to you or Grace. I know how difficult this must be for you, and if you wish to leave like the others, I will certainly understand—"

"Beggin' your pardon," the butler interrupted. "I will never leave you, sir, and I speak for my lady wife, too. She may not have the fancy ways with food that Cook did, but she's a fair hand in the kitchen, and you'll never go hungry."

Jon smiled. "I hoped you would say that, Bates," he admitted, "but you both must search your consciences thoroughly in the matter. Staying here puts you in danger. Not from me—never that—but from outside influences that I do not myself understand and therefore cannot warn you against. You have been a faithful servant in this household since I was little more than a lad. I couldn't bear it if anything happened to either of you and it was my fault."

"I'll be careful, sir," said the butler. "There is one thing, though, beggin' your pardon. The young lady needs someone to attend her—not just to see to her creature comforts. The missus is too hard-pressed with all o' the rest o' her duties since the others left ta lend her hand ta that. If the young miss is goin' ta stay here at Whitebriar Abbey, she's goin' ta need a chaperone, a ladies' maid at the very least. She's compromised as it is. . . ."

Jon almost laughed. Proprieties as dictated by the *ton* were the last thing on his mind. Bates was right, of course, but he had plans for that. It had all happened so quickly. . . .

"I agree," he said, "but for now, we must make do. We cannot have outsiders in as things are. As to the proprieties, I shall see to that. I have a plan. Now then, are we clear upon who gains entrance to the Abbey?"

The butler nodded. "Yes, sir," he said. "No one but the young miss."

"Very well, then—and that includes *animals*, Bates. Admit no stray dogs or cats . . . or any creature. Is that clear? This . . . malady seems to affect animals as well."

"Y-yes, sir," the butler said, his scalp receding as his eyes grew wide.

"See to Miss Thorpe's needs—that she is fed and made comfortable in my absence. There is nothing to fear from her, Bates. She is no threat to you or Grace as she is, only to herself in her innocence . . . and her ignorance of this damnable situation. She must not leave the Abbey after dark. She is . . . unfamiliar with the lay of the land hereabouts. She knows this; just be sure she adheres to it—however needs must."

"Y-yes, sir."

"You are sure you understand?"

"I do, sir."

Whether he did or he didn't, there was no more time to waste over it. He'd made himself as clear as he could without sending the poor gudgeon screaming from the Abbey, coattails flying. He would be more specific with Clive Snow. He had to be. He needed the vicar's protection, and his help.

It was still fairly early. He knew Clive would be waiting. Leaving the Abbey, Jon hesitated on the threshold, sifting the mist with keen eyes able to perceive images as they had never done before: another heightened sense. All was still, and he darted off toward the stables.

Jasper Ott, his stabler, was unaware. Jon would not take him into his confidence. Jasper kept to himself in the stables. There was no need for him to know, just as there had been no need for any of the other servants to know when he let them go. None questioned his excuse that he would soon be residing at the rectory, that the Abbey would be closed up or let now that the bishop had approved his appointment. The fifty-six-day waiting period was almost up, and he would shortly be read in so he could take over when Clive retired. Then there would be no need to keep a full staff at Whitebriar Abbey.

Jon hadn't visited the stables since he'd returned; there hadn't been time. There hadn't been a need, what with running about in the form of a dire wolf, swifter than any horse on the place. Shapeshifting wasn't a viable option now, however. He already had one set of clothing to retrieve from the woad field; there was no need to risk another with a magnificent Arabian stallion such as Orion at his disposal.

The horses seemed restless when he entered. Jasper carried the tack to Orion's stall and began slipping on the animal's bridle. Jon strolled closer, and the horse's whinnies became shrill, its eyes flung wide as it watched him approach.

"I dunno what ails the beast," Jasper gritted out, hefting the saddle. "He's been outta sorts all day."

Jon prowled closer still, but the horse reared in the stall, pinning the stabler against the back wall with its rump as the man tried to tighten the girth. Jon bolted forward, took hold of the bridle.

"Whoa, Orion! Down!" he commanded, but the horse reared back on its hind legs, its forefeet churning, resisting, as Jon tried to lead him out of the stall. Jon kept a close eye upon the stabler, pinned against the wall, for the man had taken a blow from the horse's hindquarters and lost his balance. The other horses' whinnies joined the din, and Jon called upon all his strength to coax Orion away from the fallen stabler.

"He's actin' like he's got a burr under his saddle," Jasper said through clenched teeth, trying to right himself. "I never seen the like!"

"Are you hurt?" asked Jon.

"No," the stabler replied, scrambling to his feet, meanwhile dodging the horse's deadly hooves, which staved in the backboards beside him. "I'm just shook up. Can ya hold 'im, sir, till I get outta here? He's never done like this afore. Why, you raised this animal from a colt . . ."

Jon tugged with all his strength as the crazed Arabian bobbed its forefeet up and down, stiff-legged, then reared and bucked again, its screeches inciting the other horses banging about in their stalls to voice more strident complaints. He could smell the animals' fright mingled with the musky sweat permeating the already overwhelming stable odors of dung and fouled straw. Speaking in soothing tones and looking deeply into Orion's fear-glazed eyes, after a moment Jon was able to lead the animal out of the stall, which was all but rendered to splinters behind, and Jasper Ott skittered out of the way of danger.

"Ya ain't goin' ta ride 'im," the stabler said, incredulous.

"I most certainly am," Jon said, one foot in a stirrup. He hefted his weight into the saddle and kneed the animal. "See to the others," he called as he rode the shying Arabian out of the stable. "Orion is too long idle. A run on the moor should set him to rights."

The stabler called something after him, but Jon didn't hear. It took all his concentration and the Corinthian skills he'd learned in his Town Bronze days to control the animal underneath him well enough to descend the tor to the kirk below.

He knew all too well what ailed the animal. It sensed what he was—what he'd become. First his dog, now even his horse shunned him. He hated himself, hated the evil that had possessed him, abhorred the immortality he was doomed to suffer as a vampire. Most of all, he despised the undead, Sebastian, who had condemned him—him, an ordained man of the cloth—to such an unthinkable existence.

The horse beneath him danced crazily down the tor, bucking, complaining, and tossing its long, feathery mane the whole distance. Tethering the animal at the hitching rail before the vicarage, Jon bolted up the steps and addressed the door with a quick hand banging the brass knocker. Glancing behind while he waited, he saw that the horse had calmed, pawing the ground like a rundown toy, snorting through flared nostrils, exhausted.

The vicar's housekeeper had left for the evening, and it was a moment and several more raps of the knocker before Clive Snow pulled open the door and admitted him.

"I'd all but given you up," the vicar said. "I was just about to retire."

"Forgive me if I've disturbed you," Jon replied, "but 'twas you who insisted upon this interview."

"So I did," said the vicar on a sigh, leading him to his study. "I'm getting old, m'boy." Once inside, he filled two snifters with brandy and handed one over. "Drink this," he said. "You look ghastly, Jon."

Jon replied with a mad, misshapen laugh and sank into the lounge opposite the vicar's desk. "How should I look, my friend?" he added around a rough swallow from the snifter. "Should not the undead look a fright?" He drained the glass. "I used to like the taste of this," he said, twirling the snifter by the stem. "It gives me no comfort anymore—no pleasure. It hasn't the quenching flavor of blood."

The vicar refilled the glass and faced him. "You are not undead yet, m'boy, if I'm reading this rightly," he said. "Where is the girl?"

"She's safe . . . for the moment, at the Abbey. She's going to be staying there from now on. It was foolish of me to think she could stay at Emma Broderick's boarding-house while I sorted this out. After what occurred at the Abbey just now . . ." Recalling how close he'd come to stomping Cassandra to death in her alternate form, he shook his head and bit back the rest of the thought.

He hadn't introduced her to the vicar as of yet. That was supposed to have taken place tonight, and would have done if Cassandra had been at the crypt earlier as they'd arranged. Jon hadn't even had a chance to tell his mentor the whole of it yet. He wondered how he ever could now. It was too bizarre. If Sebastian hadn't followed him to the very kirkyard gates, if the vicar hadn't witnessed with his own eyes the vampire's inability to set foot upon consecrated ground in his pursuit, he mightn't have told his mentor anything at all. Since then, Clive Snow had formed his own conclusions, and confirmed Jon's greatest fears.

The vicar didn't press for an explanation. "You cannot mean to keep her there unchaperoned?" he breathed, incredulous.

"What else am I to do with her, Clive? How else am I to keep her safe from the demon that is stalking her—that is stalking us both? We did not exactly part on good terms, Sebastian and I." It was a facetious remark totally out of character for him, and it raised the vicar's brow.

"What of her family? Surely someone will miss her—come looking for her. What then?"

"By then it shan't matter . . . if you will help me," Jon said, his eyes pleading.

"*I?*" asked the vicar. "What can I do?"

"Much, my friend, if you are willing," Jon replied. "That is why I wanted her to meet me at the crypt, where she would be safe until I could join her . . . so I could bring her here and we could discuss it with you together." He gestured with his snifter. "You'd best have another as well," he said. "I fear you shall need it before this interview is done."

The vicar stood his ground, his amber eyes riveting. "Speak your piece," he commanded. "I want the truth, Jon—all of it. Who is this girl? How did she become . . . involved in this madness?"

Jon set his snifter aside. "Cassandra is the daughter of a

captain who passed on to his reward from wounds sustained on the Peninsula," he said. "She was the paid companion to Lady Estella Revere. I met her in the company of the Reveres at Almack's in April. So help me, Clive, I was smitten from the moment I first clapped eyes upon her."

"Go on," said the vicar.

"She's led a very sheltered life, much of it in an Anglican convent in the Midlands until she took the post with the Reveres. She wasn't suited to the order. She has no one now. Her mother passed just before I brought her here. The Reveres think she's gone home to Cornwall for the funeral."

"So, they do not even know that she is here?"

Jon nodded. "If you will help us, by the time they find out it will be too late to pose opposition."

"Did you . . . cause her affliction? I want the truth, Jon."

"No—I've told you, *no*. Though I may as well have. If it weren't for me . . ."

"All right, let's have it from the beginning," the vicar said, sinking into the wing chair across the carpet. "Where did you meet this Sebastian?"

Jon hesitated. He didn't want his friend and mentor to feel responsible. "In an East End gambling hell searching for Ned Stoat," he finally said. Nothing would be served by a lie.

"And you struck up an acquaintance with this . . . person?"

"Of course not. Ned wasn't there. Sebastian introduced himself, followed me outside on the pretext of pointing out another gambling parlor where I might find him, then did his worst and left me for dead in an alley down by the wharf. I shall spare you the bloodthirsty details. Suffice it to say that there was something about his eyes. When I looked into them . . . I don't know, it was almost as though I had no will of my own."

"Were you conscious while it was . . . happening?"

Jon leaned forward on the lounge and nodded his head, which he'd taken in his hands. "Barely," he said. "I saw him disappear into the fog when three lightskirts came on from the public house down 'round the docks. They didn't see where he left me in the shadows, and I dragged myself back to the street and took a hackney cab back to the family townhouse. I was in no shape to ride, Clive."

"You didn't realize what had happened to you?"

"I was in a fog. I didn't realize anything untoward had occurred until Archer, my man at the townhouse, pointed out the marks on my throat when he shaved me the next morning. Then I vaguely remembered . . . something. It still isn't altogether clear."

The vicar's eyes flashed. "Can you still stand the sunlight?" he asked, giving a lurch.

Jon nodded. "Yes, though it hurts my eyes and gives me dreadful headaches. It's as if I am viewing everything through a red veil. And I'm lethargic during the day. Much like several symptoms Cassandra complains of now."

"Go on."

"You know the rest. The cravings began—the hunger for raw meat running with blood; the insatiable thirst that nothing but thick, warm blood will quench. At first it was small creatures: rabbits, squirrels . . ."

"Have you . . . killed—taken a human life?" the vicar murmured.

Jon shook his head. "No," he said. "Just animals. I have thus far been able to stop short of killing humans."

The vicar's posture relaxed somewhat. "Have any of these symptoms begun to intensify?" he asked.

"Slightly. Do you—"

"I want to know how much time elapsed once you were bitten before that occurred."

"I-I don't recall exactly. Is it important?"

"I'm trying to estimate how much time we have before you will no longer be able to come here for sanctuary if this condition is progressive in you. Have you not wondered why Sebastian could not tread upon this sacred ground while you can?"

"Of course. What are you getting at?"

The vicar hesitated. "You say that the girl is not fully *made*," he said. "I don't believe that you are, either. I pray not. It is either that, or your condition is simply manifesting itself gradually, in stages, and sooner or later you, too, will be denied sacred ground."

Jon's scalp receded and his eyebrow lifted. Was there hope? "My God, is it possible?" he murmured.

"I know not, Jon, I know not. That is why you must be honest with me. You say what has happened to her is your fault. How so?"

Jon hesitated. His mind was racing with more than he could take in. "The Reveres had pegged me for their daughter Estella, not Cassandra, her companion," he said. "The attraction was mutual between Cassandra and myself, and we took to meeting on the sly. No! It wasn't like that, Clive," he hastened to add as the vicar's hands clenched. "You know me better than that. We met in public places. We had ice at Gunter's, took a stroll in Hyde Park—quite acceptable, though at Vauxhall Gardens there are secluded walks that lend themselves quite well to assignations of an amorous nature. It was in one of these that Sebastian found her waiting for me. I was going to tell her I planned to travel to Cornwall and seek her mother's permission to wed her. I had no idea then of the magnitude of my situation. I was detained at White's. I was with one of my colleagues from University, who had been gaming, and there was a dispute over vowels. Twilight had fallen by the time I reached our trysting place. Sebastian had hold of her—he was draining her. I can still see it, Clive. He had her on the ground . . . she was semiconscious. I flew at him, caught him unaware. We fought, and he bit me again in the struggle."

"Did you lose consciousness?"

"No. Neither did she."

"And Sebastian?"

"Others were near. We heard voices and he ran off—disappeared. It was my fault she was attacked. He'd been stalking me. He knew who she was. It was deliberate. If I hadn't told her to meet me there . . ."

"You aren't to blame," said the vicar.

"I am, Clive. She knew I would come. She never would have stayed past sunset but for that. She knew such places are dangerous after dark for a woman alone. She wanted to tell me that her mother had passed and she was returning to Cornwall. I hired a chaise and brought her here. I couldn't let her go as she was, and I couldn't go with her as I am."

"You haven't told me how you think I can help," the vicar said.

"That should be fairly obvious," Jon replied. "I want you to marry us. That will put paid to the nonsense of her having been compromised—not that such a thing even signifies, considering the rest of this. It's ludicrous!"

"What? You actually mean to go back to London for a special license?"

"How can I now, when I have no idea how long I will

be able to go abroad in daylight, as you say? They do not issue special licenses at night, Clive."

"Even if I could perform the ceremony and post the banns, it would be four weeks, Jon, before you could wed. By then, the Reveres would be banging your door down at the Abbey. This, of course, is hypothetical. What you ask is impossible. Why, it would be sacrilege!"

"The Devil take the banns, Clive! I'm asking you to join us—here, in that kirk out there, tomorrow night. Once we are wed, there is naught anyone can do. We cannot be separated—not now, not ever. It is the only way. I cannot abandon her to this . . . whatever it is. That would be unthinkable! I want to protect her, care for her, give her the life we planned. And as to sacrilege, you are guilty of that already, and have been since you gave me sanctuary on holy ground."

The vicar was silent apace. Jon couldn't read his expression. It was often thus; Clive Snow always seemed to be able to read his thoughts, but it was never the other way around.

"Do you realize what you are asking?" the vicar said at last, rising from his chair.

"I am asking a dear friend and mentor for help," Jon said.

The vicar gave a stricken look, then turned away from Jon's eyes.

"You are asking that I take you and the girl into that kirk next door and sanctify the unholy before God. How are you in a state of grace? How long before you may not even be able to set foot on holy ground?"

"I am asking for your help, Clive," Jon repeated.

"Anything. Anything but this."

Jon surged to his feet and began to pace the length of the carpet before the vacant hearth. He didn't feel unholy. He hadn't asked to be rendered thus, though he had left himself open to the evil that had possessed him. If he were guilty of anything, it would be carelessness, recklessness, gross stupidity.

"I love you like a father, Jon," the vicar went on, "and my heart is breaking for you, but you are asking me to seek God's blessing upon evil. To attempt to sanctify such a union upon holy ground would damn us all."

"What am I to do, then? I love her, Clive. I planned to press my suit. I'll be damned indeed if I make a whore of her. That's what you're condemning her to—a life of living in sin."

"The blacksmiths at Gretna Green are bound by no such strictures as those to which I must adhere," the vicar said. "Anvil weddings are performed there night and day, no questions asked. All you need do is declare your wish to join before a witness for it to be legal and binding. It's just over the border, Jon. If you were to leave at sunset, you could have it done and return well before dawn— now, while you can still bear the light of day, should you be caught behindhand."

"I know how far it is to Gretna Green. It is possible, yes, but only barring the slightest setback. Uncooperative weather, a broken wheel, an encounter with a highwayman—all are more probable than possible, mind. And I am a dead man should my current situation change, Clive. Have you forgotten? We do not know how long I will be able to bear the light of day."

"No, I haven't forgotten, which brings up another thing: You must make a secure place for yourself at the Abbey—a dark place, without windows—just in case this condition of yours escalates before we can discover a way to prevent it. Do it now, while you are able to be abroad both night and day. You shan't be able to use the crypt any longer."

Jon flinched as if he'd been struck. "You despise me that much—or is it that you fear me?" he asked. "That horse out there was bad enough. It all but trampled me. Even Gideon bared his fangs at me earlier, but you? I never thought I'd live to see the day that you would turn against me, Clive."

The vicar shielded misty eyes and turned away. "I haven't turned against you, Jon," he murmured. "I'm trying to save you. The tragedy in all this is that you were not just a scholar accepting his lot with the clergy as a dutiful second son. You had a genuine vocation. I saw it when you were but a child."

"You speak of me in the past tense?" Jon murmured. Tears stung his eyes. This could not be borne.

The vicar turned his gaze away. "I never should have sent that missive," he said with passion, ignoring the question. "If only I hadn't . . . I should have let Ned Stoat steep in his own bumblebroth. I thought that, since you both were there in Town, you might seek him out and send him home before his poor wife miscarried for worry over the dust-up that sent him there. I thought it would be beneficial to you both. You would face many similar experiences as vicar of this parish; I was glad of an opportunity to give you some firsthand experience in domestic matters." He gave a lurch. "Oh!" he cried. "Speaking of parishioners, several have sighted what they perceive to be a large dog prowling the moor, and many of the men have taken to going about armed. We both know it's no dog, Jon. You must take care, else you be shot down out there. Only a silver bullet can stop a vampire, but you are not exempt from injury."

Jon scarcely heard. He asked, "How can my access to

31

that crypt in the kirkyard pose a threat to you? You've said yourself you do not think I'm fully . . . made."

The vicar spun toward him. "Not me," he said. "The threat is for *you*. Other aspects of your condition seem to be progressive. What happens if one day you try to reach the crypt and cannot walk on consecrated ground? You'll die—incinerated by the light of day. And anonymity is paramount here. This is a small parish. Someone would see what's going on and rumors would start. *On dits* would abound. As it is, I live in constant fear that one of the parishioners will blunder into you coming or going while they're visiting a loved one's grave. Use your head, boy. It's *you* I'm thinking of. Make a place for yourself at the Abbey, at your home, where it will be safe, where you will be safe from prying eyes."

"I'm going to hunt him down," Jon decided, balling his hands into white-knuckled fists. "I'm going to hunt Sebastian down and destroy him. What? Don't give me that look. He isn't human, he is undead. He preys upon the East End slags. I followed him. I saw where he goes. He has followers. I have *seen* them—odious hangers-on. Evidently, some of those whom he has infected are his to command. He must be destroyed—his minions with him—before the sickness spreads. But for Cassandra, I would have done it already."

"Well, there is another argument for your not having been fully made," the vicar said. "Here you stand plotting his destruction. If you were made, how is it that you are not his slave? You—both you and your woman—have been infected, but to what extent remains to be seen. If my suspicions are correct, it isn't only Cassandra who is in danger. You are as well."

"How? I don't understand."

"Were you wearing your official church togs when you went into that den of iniquity?"

"Yes. Why? What has that to do with any of this?"

"It has everything to do with it. Unless I miss my guess, this Sebastian did not mean to make a vampire of you. He meant to kill, and would have done so if he hadn't been interrupted."

"But why?"

"The greatest prize for any necromancer, demon, or vampire is to corrupt one of the Lord's anointed. To kill a member of the clergy is the greatest achievement such creatures can hope to attain—the most valued offering to lay before the Devil himself. This creature is eons old, I'd stake my life upon it, and you are no match for him. He will be driven now. He will not rest until he has taken your life—his ultimate triumph—and turned your Cassandra into what he is—*undead*—to become his concubine, his consort. God help you both."

Jon swallowed, hanging on his mentor's every word.

"I will help you in any way that I can short of sacrilege, m'boy," Clive went on, "but what you need to do is seek out someone with more knowledge of this abomination than I possess. Your very life could well depend upon it." Getting up stiffly, he lifted a tome from the bookshelf beside his desk and opened it.

"What I told poor old Bates . . . how I explained all this was true enough, then," Jon mused to himself.

"How is that?"

"I excused the condition as some sort of malaise Cassandra and I had contracted in London—there is always some malady loose. Town's inevitably rife with one disease or another, and I assured him neither he nor Grace were in danger of contagion."

"Just so," said the vicar. "Who told you that you had become a vampire?"

"No one told me, Clive. I came to that conclusion myself before you first used the word, though I can still scarce believe it. We only touched briefly on such phenomena at university, under the guise of superstition and folklore. Precious little was served up in the way of theology, I'm afraid. We were supposed to take on that mantle when we swore to uphold the thirty-nine articles of the Church. The only theology we were taught was glossed over in the philosophy part of the curriculum. You know that—that hasn't changed since you were there. As long as a man can do sums, knows his history, and hasn't been branded for theft in the prisons, he is deemed fit enough to preside over a living. More's the pity."

"Hmmm," said the vicar, thumbing through the tome. "Ah. Here it is. As I said, I am not qualified to mentor you in this. You need someone more versed in the phenomenon than I. You shan't find that here in England, which is probably why this Sebastian has been able to infiltrate our populace so easily. He will infest here, then move on to other shores before we realize what has come among us. You need to seek help where this insidious affliction began." He pointed to a map on the page before him. "Moldovia, a landlocked principality between Romania and Ukraine, just west of the Carpathian Mountains. According to this, the Orthodox clergy there are well versed on the topic of those they call *vampir*. These are the council you must seek. They have insights none here in England possess."

Jon surged to his feet and studied the map in the open book on the vicar's desk.

"It is a long voyage to reach the Baltic Sea," the vicar

continued, "and an arduous overland journey along the Polish border to Ukraine, then south through the Dkula Pass to this priory." He pointed. "Though I am sure any religious house in the region would do."

"What of Cassandra?"

"You must take her with you. She cannot remain here with none to protect her."

"This is another reason to marry us. By the time I've gotten her to Gretna Green and then booked passage, God alone knows how far this sickness will have progressed."

Clive cast him a look so devastated that it drove away Jon's eyes. "Don't waste a minute's time," the vicar said. "You have the advantage. You can go about in daylight while Sebastian cannot. You must book passage at once—tonight. I shan't lie to you: There is no known cure, but if there is any help to be had, these Moldovian holy men will know of it. According to what is written here in these pages, they have dealt with such for centuries."

"The arrangements will have to be made in daylight hours if we are to keep our plans from Sebastian," Jon said. He began pacing the length of the Aubusson carpet like a caged animal. The inner restlessness was beginning again, the insatiable hunger gnawing at his belly, chipping away at his resolve. He was powerless to prevent it, and it was getting worse. He had fed but a few hours ago. He had never needed to feed more than once a day since the nightmare began. "If I attempt to go about under cover of darkness making such arrangements, I court all manner of mischief," he went on, his speech staccato yet thick, through gritted teeth, as he fought the mounting bloodlust. "I am followed, Clive—stalked. I feel that creature's eyes on me even now, here in this holy place. He is nearby . . . waiting. Yes, what arrangements I make must be made after the sun rises, when there is no danger of him discovering my plans. I must go."

"It is happening again," the vicar said, discovery in his voice. "Jon, do not wait for the dawn. Collect the girl and go. You do not have any time to waste."

"First, I shall do as you suggest, make a dark place at the Abbey, just in case. I may need it before we sail." He didn't tell Clive that he had tasted Cassandra's blood, that he dared not trust himself in her presence when the feeding madness was upon him; he could not tell him. "I am not liking these changes. They are coming too quickly. At dawn, if I can still bear it in the light, I shall leave for Gretna Green with Cassandra. We must be wed before I take her on such a journey. She is an innocent, Clive, and I love her. I will not make a whore of her." He paused bitterly. "Then I shall book passage, if you're sure there is no other way."

The vicar put a hand on his shoulder. "If you paid attention to your philosophy studies at university you are aware that, according to legend, those whose faith is deep-rooted, when infected with vampirism, are the ones who cannot bear the presence, sight, or touch of religious articles . . . or to tread consecrated ground; atheists and agnostics are not repelled by symbols of our faith at all. Some say this is a spiritual manifestation, others credit it to a psychological and intellectual reaction that has naught to do with faith. If we are to credit this assertion as fact, Sebastian was a righteous man before he was turned. If this is so, he will stop at nothing to corrupt you, simply because you are what you are—the image of his former self, an image he can nevermore embrace and now must conquer. What troubles me is that you, too, are a righteous man, Jon, which is why I fear for you on consecrated ground. What gives me hope is that your faith and resistance to the vampire lure is evidently stronger than this creature's ever was, because you can still stand here in this holy place." He smiled sadly, and heaved a ragged sigh. "You ask if I am 'sure,'" he went on, "that there is no other way. You stand before me, a living manifestation of something I have never believed existed outside of folk-lore. I am certain of only one thing: There is no help for you here in England." He closed the tome and handed it to Jon. "If there is any hope at all, here is where it will be found, and I pray with all my strength that you find it. Do not lose hope. Or faith."

Jon gripped the book. He could feel the vicar's strength flowing through his fingers gripping its thick binding, like a stream of pure, cool water. The power tingled against the flesh of his palm, while unease gripped his belly in a fist of iron. The sensation was not unlike that which he'd felt just before his finger, immersed in a font of holy water, set the water boiling. The odd thing was, the boiling water had not burned his fingers. Neither did this holy man's touch. He hadn't confided that bit to Clive Snow, nor would he now. It wouldn't be long. Spiritual or psychological, it didn't matter. The door was closing on him, on his former self.

Clive Snow released the book, and Jon tucked it under his arm and turned to leave. He dared not stay. Something untoward was happening inside him. He must escape it before it was too late.

"One more thing," said the vicar to his back, turning Jon around again. He nodded toward the book. "We do not know how much of the lore laid down in that tome applies. It says in there that vampires . . . once they can no longer stand the light, must sleep upon soil from their homeland. Some are said to spread it in coffins, others strew it underneath their beds. Do not take it from consecrated ground, else it one day reject you. Take some from the Abbey—just in case—and do not set foot on that ship without it."

Jon nodded. "Will I ever see you again?" he pleaded.

The vicar looked him in the eye. "I hope so, but I think not, young son," he said. "Godspeed. And may the Lord have mercy upon you both."

CHAPTER THREE

Cassandra yawned and stretched awake, misty-eyed. The bed was soft, made with feather mattresses and quilts of eiderdown, but still she couldn't sleep. Too much was weighing on her mind. A sennight ago she was rendezvousing with Jon in a secluded lane at Vauxhall Gardens to tell him her mother had passed on, and that she must return to Cornwall. There hadn't even been time to grieve properly. Her tears were not solely for her mother; they were for her whole circumstance, which nagged at her conscience. She had never been a watering pot. If she must succumb, her mother deserved all of her tears now.

She had always been strong and brave in dire circumstances. Now Cassandra was terrified. Just the other evening, while watching from the window of her room at the boardinghouse as Jon took his leave, she'd seen the tall, dark-haired, silver-eyed man she loved—the man she longed to spend the rest of her life with—change into the form of a huge black wolf before her very eyes and bound off into the night. He was infected, too. What did it mean? Was it a permanent condition? Would she never be herself again? *Herself*. Cassandra Thorpe did not know who that was anymore.

She had heard of things such as this, mostly in made-up tales meant to frighten children. Surely vampires weren't real—but the creature that had attacked her was real enough. She would never forget his ugliness: the chalk-white skin veined with blue, stretched over bones whose shape was clearly visible through the skin; the red-rimmed iridescent eyes, black as sin, that she dared not look into, for they foxed her, sunken into hollows so deep he resembled a cadaver; the teeth, protruding—the yellowed fangs, like a viper's, long and curved, stained pink with the residue of stale blood. She shuddered, remembering his thinness, how he was draped in the impeccable style of the season, from beaver hat to polished Hessian boots. For all their style, the togs hung awry on that emaciated frame. He'd seemed so frail, and yet was possessed of greater strength than she had ever encountered.

That was what had stunned her. It had taken her by surprise. He took her to the ground as easily as he would have tossed down a broom straw. Though she fought him like a tigress, she could not prevail against that strength—against the strange, hypnotic magnetism of those obsidian eyes. She could not prevent the greasy fangs from penetrating her flesh. She would never forget the feel of his bones through the superfine coat, so brittle and stiff, as if they had no flesh upon them. She shuddered, recalling the fetid stench of his breath, the cold slime of his drool, like acid dripping on her skin, the paralyzing pain of those needle-sharp fangs at the moment of penetration, when the blood thundered in her veins, pounded at her temples, shuddered through her thumping heart, roaring in her ears. If Jon hadn't come when he did . . . she couldn't imagine what would have become of her.

Her heart was racing now, just as it had then, as she relived those moments that had changed her life forever. She threw back the counterpane and swung her feet to the floor. Padding to the window, she peered through the musty draperies at the tor below, silvered in the moonlight. It was still some time until dawn, and she was wide awake. Above, the out-of-round three-quarter moon shone down through a hazy halo in the summer sky. It didn't seem real. Nothing seemed real.

She turned away from the window. The house was still. Bates and his wife had doubtless long since retired. She'd promised Jon she would remain in her room until daybreak, but what harm to browse through the Abbey while no one was about? What better time to acquaint herself with her new home, for this was where she would live once she and Jon were wed, wasn't it? He wouldn't be coming back to the Abbey yet. He would no doubt be closeted with the vicar until the wee hours. Without giving it a second thought, she took up the candlestick, turned the key in the lock, and stepped out into the cool, dank hall.

Ancestral portraits lined the gallery walls, their subjects glaring at her as she passed. She hadn't bothered to slip on her shoes, and the carpet, a series of Persian runners, felt strange beneath her feet—so tactile it was almost painful to tread them barefoot. Touch was another of her heightened senses. She followed the paisley-patterned runners to the broad staircase carpeted in a Persian design that effectually matched them, and descended to the first floor.

In the east wing, set off to the left behind the staircase, a door fitted with green baise over the panels marked the entrance to the servants' quarters. Avoiding that, she turned right and proceeded to put her head in various rooms along the hall, one more elegant than the next from what she could tell with naught but candlelight to recommend them to her scrutiny. Before she came to the end of the corridor, she'd identified the library, study, sitting room, salon, parlor, and drawing room. The dining parlor, morning and drawing rooms, and the breakfast room were off the east wing opposite the servants' quarters, which made sense, since the servants wouldn't have far to go to serve the meals—especially useful since there were only two servants in residence.

Restless and bored with her solitary explorations, Cassandra was about to return to her chamber when another door on the right side of the staircase caught her eye as she made her approach. This one was not lined with green baise, and she tugged it open and stood in a little foyer on the brink of an archway that led to a narrow staircase hewn of stone. Her breath caught in her throat as she started to descend. A faint flicker of light showing below flared in the pitch blackness, casting tall shadows on the wall. She blew out her candle and flattened herself against the wall in a little alcove set back from the landing where the staircase turned before continuing downward. Voices funneled up the stairwell, and a scraping sound that set her teeth on edge. She was trapped. She dared not climb back up without the candle to light her way, and she certainly couldn't climb down and be caught out. Holding her breath, she hugged the shadows and waited. Oh, why had she blown out that candle?

It seemed like an eternity before she caught sight of

the figures who cast the shadows: Jon and Bates. Her heart leapt again. She should try to creep back the way she'd come. But it was no use. The echo of their footfalls ringing on the stone underfoot was carrying toward her. *Please don't let me swoon, not here—not now!* she prayed, as a sudden light-headed feeling came over her.

"Ain't nobody goin' ta disturb ya down here, sir," Bates was saying. "The missus never comes below; the rheumatism in her knees prevents her."

"I'm sorry for her rheumatism but glad that she will not frequent this part of the Abbey," Jon said. "I shall be going abroad soon, but until I do, I shall depend upon you to see to it that I am not . . . disturbed when I am down here—neither by Miss Cassandra nor Grace, nor you, either. When I am closeted here it is as if I am not at home—to *anyone*. Is that clear?"

"Y-yes, sir."

"I cannot stress that enough. It is a great responsibility, Bates. I have to be at ease that you are clear upon it. I know it is much to ask, but your efforts shan't go unrewarded."

"Yes, sir. I am so sorry to hear that you will be leaving us. Will it be a long absence this time, then?"

"I . . . am not certain. We shall talk before I leave. I will outline your duties, and provide for your wages in my absence."

They had reached a turn in the staircase, were coming into view, albeit in brief glimpses. Cassandra shrank back farther into the shadows. She could see them, so they could see her if she wasn't careful.

"What of the lass, sir?" Bates was saying.

"I will be taking Miss Cassandra with me," Jon replied, taking note of the butler's raised eyebrow. "All proprieties will be met, Bates, I assure you, but until we leave she must be kept safe from danger. I cannot stress enough that you must keep the doors locked night and day, and admit no one except the vicar, should he come by. Open the door to no one else."

"Yes, sir. You just leave all that ta me and the missus. I've already put a bee in her bonnet. You have naught ta fear over that."

"Shhh . . ." Jon whispered.

Cassandra's heart leaped in her throat. He sensed her presence. Of course he would; his senses were heightened as well. How foolish of her to think she could hide from him. She held her breath. They said no more that she could hear. It seemed an eternity before Bates passed her by. He hadn't seen her lurking there, so maybe, just maybe . . . But no. Bates reached the upper landing and passed through the door. It had no sooner banged shut than a hand reached into the shadows and closed around her wrist. Cassandra uttered a strangled gasp as Jon reeled her out of the deep dark of the recessed alcove and into his arms.

"What are you doing down here?" Jon said. "You are supposed to be safe in your chamber." How could he impress upon her the importance of adhering to his directives without frightening her half out of her wits? Maybe it would be best if he did alarm her.

"I . . . I couldn't sleep," she said. "I thought I'd browse about . . . become accustomed to the Abbey while no one was abroad."

"You could have done that in daylight," he said. "Here I think you're safe in your chamber and you are prowling about, blundering into all sorts of peril in the dark in an understaffed house. Who is to come to your rescue if you trip on that frock—or worse yet, transform into a kitten again—and tumble down these stairs all tangled up in it as I found you earlier, hm?"

"I haven't blundered into any danger," she defended, pouting. How charming she was when she pouted, her creamy cheeks splotched with red. He stroked her honey-colored, sun-streaked hair with his eyes. He didn't dare stroke it with the fingers he'd balled into white-knuckled fists. He was aroused at the sight of her—and something more, something dangerous that had been coming on him since he left the vicarage. Anger was his only defense.

"Oh, no?" He spun her around and propelled her down the stairs. Holding his candlebranch high, he led her to another alcove. A pile of old furniture, rolled carpets and bric-a-brac that had occupied the recessed space lay strewn on the cold stone floor beside it. Cassandra gasped. He watched her gaze flit over the cot that had replaced the collected trappings, and the bucket of dirt beneath.

"In an hour's time I might be lying upon *that* down here in the dark, Cass," he said through clenched teeth. "And there I will stay until the sun sets if I cannot bear the sunlight. My symptoms are worsening. It could happen at any time now." He set down the candlebranch on an old drum table that had also been evicted from the alcove to make room for the cot, and seized her upper arms, pulling her against his hard-muscled chest, against his thumping heart, against his turgid arousal. "Here is your danger," he said. "*I* am your danger. I have not fed again. I should not even have to until tomorrow night, but the hunger is upon me once again regardless, and there isn't time for me to do so now and return here to this damnable dungeon before the sun rises should I need to do so—unless I drink from that sweet throat of yours." He stroked her with a trembling hand. His lips were only inches away from the vein he felt throbbing at the base of her neck. She gasped, clearly in fright, twisting against the sudden strength that compelled him, a strength he could barely control.

"Don't!" she cried. "You are scaring me, Jon! My God . . . don't!"

Putting her from him roughly, Jon staggered back, raking his hair with both hands. "Scaring *you?*" he panted. "You have no . . . idea. *I* had no idea until this moment what I am facing. You must do as I say, Cassandra. Never doubt me. Never question."

Cassandra's hands flew to her lips. Were those tears glistening in Jon's eyes? They triggered her own. All at once he groaned, and she was in his arms, clinging to him, accepting his kiss, until the pressure of his fangs flagged danger. She pulled back, searching his face. His eyes shimmered with a glaze, like those of a cat set to pounce upon its prey. Fangs fully exposed, he loosed a howl like nothing human Cassandra had ever heard and reeled back from her.

"Is that enough danger for you?" he gritted out. "I licked the blood from your fingertips. I have *tasted* you, Cassandra. I will never be satisfied until I do so again. You are in more danger from me than you are from Sebastian—because I love you, because it is all that I can do to keep my hands off you without all the rest. Making matters worse, I cannot let you go for fear he will have you, and if you are to stay with me, we must marry. You *will* . . . marry me as we planned?" he urged.

"Yes, Jon," she murmured.

He took her in his arms again. "You are compromised,"

he said, "and I am about to run mad. We leave at dawn for Gretna Green, if I can still bear the daylight. Now, I beg you, go. Go to your room and stay there until I come for you. Once the sun has risen, if I do not come it will be because I cannot bear the light of day. In that case, you must stay in your room until I come for you when the sun sets. If that occurs, we shall just have to take our chances driving to Scotland by night. I didn't want to travel after dark—Sebastian will be abroad after nightfall. He's out there somewhere, close by. I can smell him, like mildew and decay—like death itself . . . waiting. Either way, you must be ready to leave as soon as I come for you. We will stop at the boardinghouse to collect your things on the way." And all at once, he let her go.

Cassandra stared, her tears streaming down her face, watching his fangs reach their full measure, watching his glazed-over eyes shimmer with mercurial layers of luminous silver.

"Go!" he cried, stripping off his frock coat. "Run, damn you, Cassandra, while you still can!"

Her eyes wide and a cry upon her lips, Cassandra stared as Jon yanked back the sleeve of his Egyptian cotton shirt and sank his fangs deeply into the flesh of his forearm. The scent of blood threaded through her nostrils. It hit her like cannon fire. She licked her lips in anticipation, watching the dark red rivulets stream down his arm from the wounds. The sight aroused her, and she took a step nearer.

Howling like a wolf, Jon reeled out of her path, skirted her approach, and staggered toward the alcove, leaving a spotted trail of blood behind on the gray stone floor. Her eyes were riveted to it.

"Run, I say!" he demanded, his voice echoing through the dank lower chamber. "What I have just done will not deter me for long." He turned and made a quick lunge toward her. "Go quickly! Lock your chamber door and do not open it until the sun is high! Go!"

Tears blurred his image. Snatching up her candle, Cassandra lit it from his and fled up the crudely hewn stairs. His bestial howls echoed in her ears.

Had he frightened her? Jon prayed so. Blood was leaking from his forearm, so he snaked his handkerchief from his waistcoat pocket and bound it tightly. The self-inflicted wound would only slake his hunger temporarily, while pain canceled his desire. Once the shock subsided, the feeding frenzy would come upon him again—surely a hundred times stronger since he had disturbed his blood flow without satisfying his feeding lust.

He began to pace the length of the room. Could she have reached her chamber yet? Would she do as he bade her and lock her door? He could smell her blood. It was all around him—in him—the maddening scent ghosting through his nostrils until he could bear no more. Every instinct in him demanded he follow and beat upon her chamber door until she admitted him. She would—he knew she would. He'd held that sweet flesh in his arms. She wanted him just as he wanted her.

Barely two hours remained before dawn. He would never stand it. The feeding frenzy was too strong. Besides, if he didn't feed now, when the sun rose he would be twice as lethargic for not having slaked his thirst. There was only one thing he could do; he stripped off his breeches and drawers, then his boots, waistcoat, and shirt, and bolted naked up the staircase, through the door, and out of the house into the star-studded darkness. Another howl spilled from his throat as he sprang into the air and came to earth in a shimmering streak of silver-tipped black fur and sinew, running on all fours, his jowls plastered with foam.

No, he would never make it to the village on two feet in time to feed and return to the Abbey before dawn, and there was no time to struggle with his frenzied horse, but the dire wolf could easily travel the distance and then some, with plenty of time to spare. In a mad stupor of mindless oblivion, he howled again, and then he raced down the tor toward the cluster of thatched-roof cottages west of the kirk at the bottom of the hill.

The bloodcurdling howl brought Cassandra to the window. Below, in the light of the low-sliding moon, the dire wolf came into view. Fresh tears welled in her eyes. She had sent Jon prowling the night for a victim to feed upon. He would find some lightskirt working the seamy side of the village, he would all but drain her dry. Then Cassandra would be safe . . . for now. He would drag himself back to his alcove in the bowels of Whitebriar Abbey and sleep until dawn if all went well; in the dark until nightfall if it didn't. But why? How? How was this possible? Not knowing was the worst of it.

This didn't seem real—none of it seemed real, and yet it was. What made it so bizarre was that they were trying to maintain some semblance of a normal life in the midst of the dark evil that had come upon them. *"You've been compromised."* His words echoed across her mind. What foolishness. Her reputation didn't even signify now, and yet . . . some semblance of propriety knitted the whole together. Without that ingrained shred of sensibility, there would be madness. It was passing strange.

Cassandra turned away from the window with a shudder; a squealing sound in the corner of her bedchamber directed her attention there. Candlelight picked out the hunched gray form of the rat that had eluded her earlier. She smelled its blood. Yes! It was one and the same. She would resist the urge to shapeshift this time, now that she knew what that entailed. Instead, she stalked the creature, busily nibbling at crumbs of bread she'd dropped from the fare Bates had provided at the dinner hour. All sensible thoughts fled her mind. Making matters worse, she could still smell Jon's blood; she had since he sank his fangs into his forearm.

All at once, her fangs started to descend. She was the predator now, with eyes only for her prey, the unsuspecting rat. She licked the drool from her lips, crept along on tiptoe, and pounced.

CHAPTER FOUR

The plan was to return to the woad field, transform, and collect the clothing he'd left there earlier, so he could dress and feed before he returned to the Abbey. Cassandra was safe, now that he had put distance between them, and he was running free. Why did his heart ache so? There was no relief from it. Even as the dire wolf it ached. Ironically, it was his human side—that facet of Jon, the man that lived inside, still untouched by the evil, still untainted by the vampire's kiss. How long would it live so? If only he knew. When he was the wolf, he saw himself as Jon, the man, through a distortion, as a separate entity. He heard his thoughts as if they were coming from an echo chamber. When he was himself and the feeding frenzy was upon him, it was as if he were two people under the same skin, shadow-selves always together though worlds apart. And when the bloodlust overcame him, the pinging in his brain echoed in his sex, bringing it to life in an unstoppable frenzy, leading him closer and closer to the ultimate climax—a sexual rhapsody of carnal desire and lust after the very essence of life. The thirst was only to be slaked by sexual consummation at the precise moment of the making ritual.

Jon didn't even know how such a ritual would take place, only that when the time came it would be involuntary, like everything else in his strange condition. He also knew he had to fight against it, and against Sebastian's lust for the same consummation, that passion to "complete" Cassandra.

Pondering those thoughts on the bleak periphery of his shadow-self deep inside *canis dirus*, Jon failed to see the hunter raise his pistol. He failed to hear the crack and boom of thunder as the ball exploded from the chamber, riding a burst of blood-red flame. It was as if time stood still until the missile impacted, causing him to break his stride, lifting him into the air with a howl that reverberated through man and beast.

He came down hard with a thud in a cloud of yellow woad spores riding the north wind. The unforgettable pungency spiraled through him to his very core: deeper than the wolf, clear to the memories of his childhood, when the woad field was his secret place, his adolescent escape from the invisibility that was his lot as a second son. That is, until the scythes robbed him of it every Midsummer's Eve, when the farmers cleared the field. That and the scent of blood—*his blood*—was enough to set him on his feet, albeit scrambling. Where was he hit? In the shock of that terrible instant he couldn't feel pain, but he could see, through a blood-red haze, the hunter plowing toward him through the woad. The deep-throated rattle of a snarl poured from him as he sprang, driving the man down, sinking his fangs deep into that throat.

Soon, the hunter's hands fisted in his fur fell away. Still the wolf drank—not too much, just enough to satisfy his craving without killing the gudgeon. Until that moment, Jon had not known that he could feed in wolf form. Was this a power he had always possessed, or was the condition changing again, heightening, taking him deeper and deeper into darkness? If only he knew what he was facing. That he didn't, that was the worst of it.

Having slaked his bloodlust, Jon fell back on his haunches, panting. The man stretched out beside him had lost consciousness. He would wake in a daze, just as Jon had done when Sebastian fed upon him. Raising his head to the heavens, Jon howled into the night, never thinking that if there were other hunters he might attract them. He was beyond thinking. If ever a wolf could be deranged, he was that wolf now. Pain was coming in waves rippling along his left foreleg. Following an animal instinct older than time, he lapped with his long pink tongue at the blood oozing down, leaking a canine whine.

All at once he raised his head and sniffed. Something foul rode the air—something fouler than the woad; he was downwind of it. Hackles raised, his wound forgotten, Jon scrambled up on all fours, slinking toward the place where he'd left his clothes earlier. Could he even change back as he was? The scent grew stronger—not a human scent. A fresh growl rumbled up from deep inside him. That wasn't wise. Whoever it was could follow the sound. He snorted. What did it matter? The entity that stalked him now knew where he was by instinct, by scent—the scent of his blood, leaking faster now that he'd put the pressure of his weight upon it by loping through the woad.

His clothes were in sight, a crumpled heap of yellow-dusted finery reduced to rags in the dampness—at least that was how they looked to his wolf's eyes, glazed over with pain. Again, he sniffed the air. The scent was stronger now. Only then did Clive Snow's words jog his memory: *Sebastian was evidently once a righteous man before he was turned. If this is so, he will stop at nothing to corrupt you.* Then, sadly, too late: *Several parishioners have sighted what they perceive to be a large dog prowling the moor, and many of the men have taken to going about armed. We both know it is no dog, Jon. You must take care, else you be shot down out there.* Why hadn't he recalled that sooner?

Jon stood his ground and turned—feet apart, hackles raised—his glazed eyes sifting through the darkness for the image of whoever, whatever it was stalking him. His night vision was infallible, but the stalker presented no image, though the woad before him bent and flattened as the invisible feet approaching tamped it down.

Sebastian! It had to be. Strengthened now, just having fed, Jon lunged at the invisible entity, but his snarling mouth closed upon empty air. A great bat soared out of the woad field and disappeared off into the wood.

A warning? A biding of time? Or was it that the creature knew he could not win? Jon couldn't imagine that. He put no store in such a guess, and the true answer soon presented itself: The sky was lightening! The faintest streamers of gray were diluting the clouds to the east. *First light!* Leaking a whine, Jon surged to his full height in a silvery rush of displaced energy, and stood naked to welcome the dawn. *Yes!* He could still bear it. But where had Sebastian gone? There wasn't time for him to travel far, even in bat form. More than likely he had found some dark sanctuary and was somewhere close by . . . waiting.

Wincing, Jon glanced down at his left arm. The

wound wasn't deep, but blood was pouring from it nonetheless. The pistol ball had grazed his biceps. There would be a trail. He would leave his scent for Sebastian to follow. Come nightfall, the vampire would hunt him down. The creature's heightened sense of smell would be able to detect the scent for days, unless rain came to wash it away. Not much chance of that, judging from the brilliant sunrise.

All at once his memory was jogged again. Cassandra would be waiting at the Abbey. There was no time to lose. Tearing a strip from the hem of his shirt, he bound his wound, cinching it tight with his teeth, and dressed himself. The hunter lay just as he'd left him, sprawled on his back in the field, but something caught Jon's eye as he came abreast of the man. There was no blood upon him—not a drop—where he had been smeared with it before. Jon squatted down beside the man. Cold chills gripped him. How white the hunter was in the ghost-gray light of dawn—as white as a cadaver. He *was* a cadaver. Jon groaned, feeling for a pulse in the man's throat. There was none. He was dead, but Jon hadn't killed him; Sebastian had finished what was started.

It was daylight now, and Jon was himself again—as much himself as ever he could be anymore. Groaning, he murmured a prayer over the hunter's body. Was it sacrilege to do so? It didn't matter. It was who he was—who he *really* was, underneath the evil that had possessed him. There was nothing more that he could do for the man, and so he staggered to his feet and sprinted through the woad field toward the tor.

To all outward appearances, Jon and Cassandra were a typical couple en route to their anvil wedding as the coach tooled over the North Road through the forest, speeding them toward the Scottish border and Gretna Green. They'd gotten a late start. Between the delay while Grace doctored Jon's wound and Bates packed his trunks, and the side trip to the boardinghouse to collect Cassandra's things, it was nearly noon before they set out. Now there were still at least two hours until dusk, yet all around them an eerie green darkness pressed up against the coach like a gossamer veil, letting precious little light filter through from the sky above.

Outside, the whip cracked incessantly. Jasper Ott had his orders. Each time it snapped through the air, Cassandra gave a start. Her nerves were shattered. Jon had come home wounded and wouldn't say what had happened to him, only that it wasn't serious and that they had to wed and leave the country without delay. That it had something to do with Sebastian was evident. Otherwise, he wouldn't be so obsessed with covering as much ground as possible during the day. The scent of his blood in the close confines of the coach was torture. Would it always be thus?

Jasper Ott lit the coach lanterns well before twilight. It was impossible to tell the actual time; no glimpse of the sky was visible through the fragrant bower of interlaced pine branches that formed a vaulted ceiling overhead. Time and again, Cassandra caught Jon gaping through the isinglass window as the coach sped along in the artificial darkness. He seemed to be staring at the treetops. Finally, curiosity got the better of her.

"What *is* it?" she said, laying a hand on his arm as he inclined his head to look again. "What is out there?"

"Nothing . . . I hope," said Jon, giving her hand a gentle squeeze.

"Something, I think," she replied. "You aren't being fair. I can face anything so long as I know what it is I am facing. You keep me in the dark and I am vulnerable. Have I not proven myself . . . coming on this mad journey with you in total ignorance of the situation? You need to tell me what's happening, Jon."

He heaved a mammoth sigh. "If only I knew what we are facing," he said. "I am assuming that Sebastian cannot be abroad during the day as we can. But I'm not entirely certain of it. There is so much I am not certain of, I hesitate to broach the subject for fear of frightening you unnecessarily—"

"Better that than having me blunder into danger unaware," she interrupted. Could he not see that?

"Last night, I was shot in the woad field," he said, ignoring her gasp. "I fed from the hunter who shot me, but I did not kill him, Cassandra. Sebastian did. I'm certain it was he who stalked me in that field, and finished what I started. When I lunged at him, he shapeshifted into a bat, and flew off as the sun rose. That's why I'm praying we only need fear him at night."

"Yet you fear . . ."

"That he might be following us?" he said, finishing her thought. "Yes. I left a trail of blood behind me, needless to say. He has latched onto my scent. I was hoping to reach Gretna Green and have our wedding behind us before dark—for more than one reason."

"W-what are the other reasons . . . ?" she murmured, almost afraid of the answer.

He pulled her close, in the custody of his good right arm. "It is our wedding day," he said. "Granted, it isn't the sort of wedding day I'd planned for us, but that cannot be helped, Cass. The other reason is that I want to make love to you. But it won't be safe after dark. You know what happens to me after the sun sets—you've *seen* it. I lose my powers during the day, so then we might chance it . . . or once I've fed. Oh, I don't know . . . Clive believes Moldovia is the answer. He believes that if there is help to be had, we shall find it there. It is a dreadfully long journey over land and sea, and there are no guarantees. At the very least it is a place to start. I cannot hope to help us without the knowledge and tools to do so. I will not settle for this—for either myself or for you. If needs must, I will go to the ends of the earth to find a way out of this nightmare, Cass. I *swear* to you."

Cassandra pulled him close. "My . . . 'powers,' if you can call them that, fade with the dawn as well," she murmured. "I grow weak with lethargy."

"We cannot go back," he said, cupping her face in his hand. "The man who shot me will be found, and Clive will surely think that I have killed him when he sees where and the way he died. And there's something else . . ."

"What?"

"I fed from him *in wolf form*. I did not know such a thing was possible. It has never happened before. My condition is changing, Cass. Either that, or I am just now realizing the scope of it. Other . . . peculiarities might surface. I do not know what will be, and while I want you with me so I can protect you . . . I may be putting you in graver danger than either of us could possibly imagine."

She seized him, clinging to him with all her strength. "Don't leave me, Jon!" she cried. "My God, don't leave me!"

"I will never leave you," he said with passion, lacing his

fingers through her hair. "But you wanted to know what is happening. Now you do. Better now, before we wed, than afterward. I will not deceive you."

Cassandra said no more. Sadly, she watched him lean back toward the window, scanning the blackness for some sign of a bat. He seemed so like himself in some ways, like the Jon she knew. She watched the flickering light from the coach lamps play upon the mahogany-colored hair waving about his broad brow, about his earlobes. She saw it shimmer in those silver-gray eyes like dancing mercury, and watched it collect in the thumbprint cleft in his chin. The heady scent of pine seeped in through the closed coach windows. She inhaled deeply, praying that the soothing scent would chase the fever racing through her veins, the insatiable lust for blood that, contrary to Jon's belief, was growing stronger in her, not fading as he had hoped. It was best that he didn't know. The scent of his blood overpowered the rest. It had replaced his natural scent, though she remembered leather and lime laced with musk—clean, of the earth and the wood. She would never forget, though all she could smell now was the enticing aroma of blood, thick and dark and mysterious, wafting toward her from his wound, albeit bound. She tried to steel herself against the lure of it—against the lust. If fighting these terrible urges would keep them at bay, she would fight with her dying breath. It was a place to begin, and she was resolved.

An hour later, they stood over the anvil across the Scottish border at Gretna Green, and they spoke their vows, declared their desire to wed before the blacksmith and his wife. Jon decided to stay the night in one of the little cottages provided for the newlyweds, just in case. Though he had thus far seen no sign of Sebastian, he took no comfort in it. He sensed the creature's nearness, smelled the corrupt stench of death that flagged his presence. If there were to be a confrontation, let it be now. Let it be here, before the creature guessed their plans and followed them farther. Besides, the horses needed rest and tending. He could smell their musky, lathered sweat. Jasper would see to that at the coaching inn, where he would spend the night. And, God help him, Jon needed to feed. This was only the first lap of their journey. They still had miles to go before they reached the estuary at Blyth in Northumbria, where they would book passage on a ship that would carry them east, beyond Denmark to the Baltic Sea and the easternmost Polish border, where they would begin their overland journey.

More than anything else, Jon longed to scoop his bride up in his arms and set her down upon the bed. He longed to lie down beside her, to taste her honeyed sweetness, but already the bloodlust had begun, and he was having second thoughts about the wisdom of consummation. It wasn't meadowsweet and lilies of the valley wafting toward him from her skin, from her sun-painted hair; it was the pungent lure of blood that sent shivers down his spine, that hardened his sex and quickened his heartbeat until it thundered to the same rhythm as her own. Instead, he carried her over the threshold, laid her down on the bed, and stepped back out into the moonlit darkness, warning her to stay.

Half hidden in the clouds, the moon shone down, silvering the pines at the edge of the clearing behind the cottage. There wasn't a breath of a breeze. All was so still, the land around him seemed like a painting. He raised his head and shut his eyes, calling upon his heightened sense of smell to show him some creature. Human quarry wasn't likely in such a remote setting—a deer perhaps? There should be plenty of roe deer in the Scottish forest, but curiously there was nothing. Not even the twitter of a bird sounded in the night. The bloodlust was unbearable. He had to feed soon. He couldn't go near Cassandra again until he had, and even then . . .

He breathed in the pine-scented air deeply, and his quicksilver eyes snapped open wide. Chills snaked down his spine. Hackles raised, he prowled toward the edge of the wood, drawn like a magnet, one shuddering step after another. A flapping sound in the uppermost branches drew his eyes. Something black descended, fluttering, expanding. It took form before his eyes.

Sebastian!

All his fleeting hopes that they had escaped the creature withered and died as Jon faced the tall, cloaked figure circling him in the moonlight. The vampire seemed to float, his motion mesmerizing. He must not look into its eyes; that was what had doomed him in the first place. Instead, Jon fixed his gaze a little to the right of those compelling eyes and fought their magnetic pull, his breath suspended, teeth gritted, cold sweat running down his face for the labor.

The emaciated figure seemed surreal. The latest London togs hung on that cadaverlike frame the way a child playing dress-up might appear draped in her mother's clothes. The creature floated closer. *No!* Jon would not look into those eyes. They dominated the face, glowed red in the moonlight. All Jon could think of was Cassandra, unaware in the cottage behind, awaiting his return. What if she were to disobey his directive and come looking for him? What would happen to her if he were to succumb to the predator circling him for the kill in this lonely Scottish clearing?

It was cooler in the higher elevations, and Jon was wearing his greatcoat. Reaching into his pocket, his fingers closed around the pocket pistol he'd carried since they left the Abbey. Without a silver bullet, how much good it would do against such a creature he had no idea, but he had no other weapon to employ. He drew and cocked it, provoking a burst of blood-chilling laughter from the vampire.

"You think to use *that* against me?" Sebastian tittered. He swept his arms wide. "Do your worst! The noise will bring the girl, and I will have you both. Go ahead! Fire!"

Jon's finger caressed the trigger. Dared he chance it? He wasn't given time to decide. Like lightning the vampire rushed him, and though he didn't even see or feel the contact, the pistol spun out of his hand and landed several yards off in a patch of tall grass and prickly thistles.

"Fool!" Sebastian gloated. "Did you think you could escape me?"

Jon backed toward the woods—anything to put distance between them and the cottage, and Cassandra waiting there unaware. Calling upon his keen senses, he sniffed the air and employed his night vision. No, there was no other entity near. Sebastian was evidently acting alone, and Jon continued to back into the forest, a close eye upon the vampire advancing.

All at once, the creature disappeared. In an instant he reappeared behind Jon, laughing at his staggering surprise as he spun around. Jon turned twice more, and each time Sebastian disappeared and reappeared, thwarting his strategy as he'd done before.

"Do you see how useless it is to oppose me?" the vampire asked. "And while I do so enjoy playing with you, it grows tiresome. You are my creature. I have made you what you are, and what I have made, I can destroy."

"You have not made me yet, Sebastian," Jon said. The gurgling sound of a stream at his back caught his attention. Inspiration struck. If boiling holy water wouldn't burn his skin, perhaps he still possessed the power to bless it. If that were so, he might just have the weapon he needed to fight the creature. He was hardly in a state of grace, but maybe, just *maybe* . . . It was worth a try, and he stepped across the stream at its narrowest and squatted down, a close eye upon Sebastian, coming closer.

The vampire snorted. "What?" he said. "Surely you cannot believe that old wives' tale about vampires not being able to cross water?" He plunged one foot into the stream, dispelling the myth.

Jon's muscles clenched. He hadn't even heard that tale. There was so much he hadn't heard, and so much that he *had* heard was contrary to the truth of his situation thus far. He dared not trust anything except his instincts. And by all accounts, they were screaming: *Now! Do it now!* He plunged his cupped hands into the cool, clear water of the running stream, scooped some up, and murmured a blessing over it. Almost at once, it began to boil in his hands, though it did not burn his skin.

Sebastian jerked his Hessian out of the stream and took a step back. "Eh?" he grunted. "What is this, then?"

"If you were once what I am now—a man of the cloth—you know what this is!" Jon triumphed. Surging to his feet, he stomped through the stream and threw the boiling, steaming water full in the vampire's face.

With a cry unlike anything Jon had ever heard, Sebastian spun. A whirlwind grew that lifted dead leaves and pine needles from the forest floor and sent them flying in all directions. The vampire's dark image was reduced to a squeaking, flapping flurry of fur and sinew, and he soared off into the trees, bat wings slicing through the still night air in a rowing motion, to disappear beyond the outer darkness into whatever underworld gave him sanctuary. Jon had banished the creature . . . for now. That he would be back Jon had no doubt—but that wasn't likely tonight.

That he could bless the water was no great feat; a layman could do that as long as he had faith enough to believe in the blessing. Had his calling saved him, or was it simply that those powers of his former self had not yet been rescinded? The condition did seem to be progressive. He would know more when the boiling holy water burned him. For now, it was enough that he had won a reprieve. He dared not count upon more.

He stared long after the bat had spiraled out of sight. Only then did the voices of the forest, conspicuous in their absence, return. Birds ruffled the pine branches, chipmunk and squirrel skittered over the pine needles underfoot. Behind, a twig snapped, calling Jon's eyes to the author of the noise. A large roe deer had stepped up to the stream to drink. Jon stood very still. He had to feed; he could not return to Cassandra until he did. Whether it was the hour or the excitement of his encounter with Sebastian, the feeding frenzy was upon him with such a voluptuous swell that only gouts of blood would slake it. He felt the pressure as his deadly fangs began to descend. His heartbeat quickened. He had the deer in his sights—eye to eye. He had the power to mesmerize it. Its blood wouldn't be as satisfying as a human's, but the animal was large and there was the consolation that there would be no remorse in draining it dry. Such deer were plentiful, after all. This would simply be one less beast for the hunters to weed out.

With a silent snarl, he sprang. The attack drove the deer to its knees. It was his. There would be nothing left for Sebastian to drain afterward. Jon fed, and having done, he retrieved his pocket pistol from the thistles and strode back to the cottage.

CHAPTER FIVE

Dressed in her muslin nightshift, Cassandra was pacing before the bed when Jon entered. She flew into his arms. He had just fed; she could smell the blood on him, yet no trace of it remained, and his hair was wet, the rich mahogany waves slicked back from his handsome face.

"There is a stream in the wood," he said, answering the question in her eyes. "I washed afterward." But there was another question she had, and he answered that also. "A deer," he said.

Something untoward had happened. She knew it—sensed it. She could smell it on him. She might not be as deeply infected as he, but her senses were alarmingly heightened. Leaning back, she searched his eyes. They shone like silver in the candlelight.

"Was it . . . *him?*" she murmured.

Jon stared down at her for a long moment without speaking. He seemed to be weighing what to tell her. Well, she wouldn't settle for less than the truth. Not now, not ever. They were married. Although it was all so new, and in the worst possible circumstances, she would have the truth—even though she knew his motive was to spare her. They were in this together. When would he know she didn't need to be spared? She needed to be trusted.

He nodded, but turned away.

"You cannot hide these things from me, Jon," she said. "I knew it the moment you entered the room. Will you not trust me?"

"It isn't a matter of trust. I do not want to worry you."

"Well, I *am* worried. If there is danger, we both face it. There is strength in numbers—even in this number."

"Will you submit to a little test?" he said.

"What sort of test?"

"You have no fear of holy relics. I want to see how you react to holy water. It could be vital to us both, Cassandra."

"Very well," she said. "Where shall we get some?"

"I will make it," he replied.

Cassandra stared, slack-jawed. This was the last thing she'd expected him to say. "I . . . I don't understand," she murmured.

Jon took her hands, led her to the bed, and sat her down on the edge. "As I feared, Sebastian followed my scent," he said. "He was waiting outside. My pistol was useless against him. He disarmed me in a trice. Then, all at once, I remembered the holy water."

"What holy water? You aren't making any sense."

"I'm making more sense than you know. One of the first changes that came upon me after Sebastian . . . fed upon me was that, when I put my fingers in a holy water font, the water boiled up around them—yet it did not burn me. I never even told this to Clive."

"Go on," she murmured, hanging upon his every word.

"Sebastian was stalking me in the wood outside when I

came upon the stream. All at once it occurred to me that if I could stand the touch of holy water, I might still be able to bless it. It worked. I repelled him, Cass. I want to see how you react to it. If you can bear it also—as I assume you can—it will make an excellent weapon for both of us against Sebastian, and against others like him until I can meet with the holy men of Moldovia and they can council me on alternatives. Are you game?"

"There's water in the pitcher there," she said, pointing toward the dry sink, where a pitcher filled with water and a basin stood.

Swallowing, Cassandra watched while Jon splashed some of the water into the basin and blessed it. Then, motioning her near, he dipped his fingers into the water. She gasped as it began to boil. Yet it did not seem to burn him, though steam rose from the rolling bubbles.

"Y-you want me to put my hand in *that?*" she cried. She was incredulous.

He nodded. "How else are we to know? If my suspicions are correct it will tingle a bit but feel cool to the touch, just as it does to me."

Cassandra shot out her hand and retracted it again thrice before easing her fingers gingerly into the water. To her surprise, the water did not burn her, though the heat of it suddenly cracked the basin and she jumped back as the ceramic broke with a loud crack, spilling the water at their feet.

Jon took her in his arms. "Thank God!" he murmured.

"What does it mean?" she said. "How can you . . . How did it . . . ?"

"I do not presume to know, nor do I know how long the phenomenon will last, but while it does, we will arm ourselves with it, and use it if needs must without hesitation.

I have an empty wineskin in my trunk. I shall bless the rest of this and we will carry it thus until we can find suitable vials." He stroked her cheek with the back of his hand and slipped his other arm around her. "This is not how I planned our wedding night to be," he murmured.

"None of it is your fault," she said. "We are together. Nothing else matters."

He scooped her up in his arms and carried her to the bed. Her breath caught as he knelt beside her. Stripping off his waistcoat and shirt, he tossed them down, never taking his quicksilver eyes from her face. His moves were more feral than human then, and he slid the nightshift down over her shoulders, exposing her breasts to his gaze. Her heart began to hammer. She was certain he could see it shuddering beneath her skin.

This was no novice bending over her. This was definitely a lover of some skill, called late to his vocation. That did not shock her. The man was in his mid-thirties, after all. At twenty-two, and situated with such an auspicious family as the Reveres, she was no stranger to Town life. She had seen many such men during her employ with the aristocrats—second sons knocking about Town in a quandary over their future. More than one had tasted the pleasures of the flesh before he traded Beau Brummel black-and-white for vicar's togs and settled down to preside over a living in some remote parish. The *ton* was rife with *on dits* about this gentleman or that. Jon's name was not excluded from that company, though there were no serious scandals connected with it. There was something to be said for that, since the *ton* did love a juicy scandal.

She, on the other hand, could boast of no such experience. There had been gentlemen, of course. One could not travel in the Reveres' circles and not attract members of the opposite sex; but she was still innocent. She had never met the man she could visualize spending the rest of her life with until Jon.

Deep inside, her sex throbbed as his fingers tantalized her aching breasts, bringing her nipples erect. Her eyes were closed when he took one in his mouth, and she groaned at the touch of his silken tongue curling around first one hard bud and then the other. He had taken her by surprise. Writhing to his rhythm as he teased them, she couldn't help but groan. Her senses were heightened, every nerve ending raw, sensitive to the slightest touch. Her sexual awareness was no exception. His fingers burned a fiery trail along the curves of her naked body. Where had her nightshift gone? When had he shed his inexpressibles—his boots? As if in a daze she rode the sweet torture of sensation those skilled hands set loose upon her body. Nothing existed then but the two of them. In that moment of sexual awakening, there was no Sebastian, no bloodlust, no feeding frenzy. These were two souls hopelessly in love, and this was their wedding night—until two passions clashed head-on and exploded at her very core.

He had fed, but she had not. Fresh blood was seeping through the linen bandage girding his biceps. It was driving her mad, and she fought with all her strength to steel herself against the lure. Had he noticed? How could he not? His mouth closed over hers, drawing her eyes away from the temptation, his hot tongue sliding silkily between her teeth, drawing hers after it. *Faith! Don't let the fangs descend!* she prayed.

His skin was scalding. It was as if he had burst into flame and set her afire beneath him. His engorged sex, thick and hard, leaned heavily against her thigh. She could feel its pulsing throb, quickening her heartbeat, heightening her hunger. When his fingers slipped between her legs, she arched herself against them, fisting her hands in his damp hair, her breath coming in shallow spurts as his fingers delved deeper and brought her to the brink of an ecstasy she never dreamed existed. The passions he had stirred, coupled with the fever of bloodlust he had aroused, was more than she could bear. Every pore—every cell in her body was on fire for him.

Shuddering, involuntary waves of silken fire coursed through her belly and thighs as his fingers, gliding on her wetness in slow, tantalizing strokes, rubbed gently at first, until a quick stab of pain made her breath catch as those skilled fingers stretched her virgin flesh.

He hesitated. "If it is too painful, I will stop."

"Not painful, no," she murmured, clasping him to her. "I . . . I never imagined it would be like *this*."

Nonetheless, he slowed his rhythm. There was a strange, dark look about him, as if he were seeing right through her. Had she spoiled it? It didn't seem so, the way his member was swelling against her thigh. Still, something was wrong.

"I shan't break, Jon," she murmured, leaning into his caress.

Suddenly, his eyes were wild, hungry things. Where had the silver gone? Dilated with desire, they stared down like two glowing onyx stones, hooded and shining with mist in the candle glow. Driving her hand to his groin, he wrapped her fingers around his sex and groaned as it responded to her touch. Riding the sound, it was as though she had left her body—as though she floated somewhere out of herself watching their naked embrace from above.

Like ripples in a stream when a skimming stone breaks

the surface, bursts of icy fire took her from head to toe. Shuddering with pleasure, she murmured his name again and again in involuntary spurts that matched the rhythm of the fingers that stroked her. Why did her voice sound so thick, echoing in her ears in the tiny room where there should be no echo? The pressure against her canine teeth replied to that. The fangs! Granted, they were not fully formed and could not extend far, though they felt as if they could. Had her climax brought them to the surface? It was happening again . . . oh, it *was*—wave upon wave of unstoppable sensation riddling her swollen sex, tingling through her belly and along her thighs as she clung to Jon in mindless oblivion of all but his dynamic body, hardened like steel against her.

All at once he swooped down and took her lips with a hungry mouth, but the kiss was short-lived. Fangs impacted fangs, and Jon pulled back, dazed. Cassandra gasped. How could this be? He had just fed. But it was. His fangs had descended, their needle sharpness gleaming in the candle shine.

He froze stock still; only his sex heaved against her. She held her breath as his hand slid the length of her arched throat, hovered over the distended veins pulsating beneath the skin. The blood echoed in her ears, pounded through her temples until she feared her brain would burst. He lowered his mouth. It was barely inches from her throat. His sex leapt in her hand, swelling—pumping as he moved against her fingers. The deadly fangs were hovering, a hair's breadth from her skin, so close she dared not swallow for fear he would dive down and take her blood. Was he going to feed?

"No, Jon . . . don't . . ." she begged feebly. Her hand froze on his member.

He stiffened as though she'd struck him. Crimping her

fingers tighter, he undulated against them. All at once his groan became a cry so terrifying it nearly stopped her heart, and he plunged into her grip, releasing the pulsing rush of his seed, meanwhile sinking his fangs deeply into the white-knuckled fist he'd clenched in the eiderdown pillow alongside her head. Soon the back of his hand was running with blood.

It was more than Cassandra could bear, and she seized his wrist and drank from the puncture wounds. Jon's eyes were wild, crazed things snapping toward her. He jerked his bleeding hand away. A bloodcurdling snarl spilled from his throat as he rolled to the side, sprang from the bed, and streaked toward the door. But it wasn't Jon Hyde-White who burst through it into the night. In a silvery blur of skin and fur, sinew and bone, he transformed into the dire wolf and hit the ground on all fours, streaking toward the wood.

Howling into the moonlit darkness, Jon stood on his hind legs and spun toward the cottage behind. Yes; she had closed the door he'd left flung wide. It wasn't likely that Sebastian would be abroad again tonight, but there were no guarantees of anything in these circumstances. Hadn't he just proved that? Hadn't he just nearly fed again, and on Cassandra, with the deer's blood still fresh on his palate?

He knew the deer would not be enough to satisfy the bloodlust. He should have waited until dawn, when he would have been himself again, when there would have been less danger of what had nearly happened just now occurring.

His forefeet came crashing to earth on another howl. He had nearly finished what Sebastian had started. There in that dense pine forest, tears streaming down from his glazed wolf eyes, he made a vow that if it took his dying breath, he would send back to hell every vampire he could lay his hands upon—even if he must number himself among them—but beginning with Sebastian.

He sped through the trees, zigzagging back and forth with no purpose but to run off the feeding frenzy before he returned to his bride. If it took the whole night, he would not return to her until there was no danger. She had tasted his blood, just as he had tasted hers. After this, neither would be satisfied until they were satiated with each other. They lived inside each other now. It was bad enough that he had succumbed to temptation and feasted upon her. That she had done the same to him was incomprehensible. How had he let her? It had happened at the height of his climax, or he never would have.

Her powers were escalating. He had to reach the priests of Moldovia in record speed—if they could even help. There were no guarantees. It was to be a long and arduous journey, according to Clive Snow—too long and too arduous, judging by what had just nearly occurred. But there was nothing for it. There was no other avenue open to them.

He ran until his heart felt ready to burst through his barrel-chested wolf's body. Reaching the stream, he plunged into it—shallow though it was—drinking his fill and bathing his throbbing paw, still bleeding from the self-inflicted wound. The deer still lay where he'd brought it down, a grim reminder. He stiffened. How would he feed upon a long sea voyage? Once they reached the Polish border, there would be plenty of opportunities—human and animal—but aboard ship . . . This didn't bode well.

All at once something rustled in the treetops, calling his attention. Scarcely breathing, he waited, leaking a low, guttural growl. Nothing untoward met his eyes. If it were Sebastian, he would hardly swoop down—a mere bat against the gigantic wolf he was—and chance an attack. Flaunting his posture, Jon pranced up and down the center of the stream, as if he dared the vampire to do just that.

It wasn't until some time later, once he'd worked out the strategy for their journey, that he loped back to the cottage on his sore paw. His keen hearing still picked up the rustling sound even though he'd left the forest behind. Then, as he reached the cottage door, a flock of some winged species in flight ghosted across the moon, and he shrugged off his concern, surged back into human form, and entered the cottage.

He was hoping Cassandra would be asleep when he returned, but she wasn't. She had put on her wrapper, and now sat curled in a wing chair beside the vacant hearth. Her head snapped toward him as he entered. He was warmed by the relief in her beautiful brown eyes, so like a doe's sparkling toward him. She had set out his dressing gown on the bed, and he shrugged it on. No; he wouldn't go too near. The sight of her sitting there with the candlelight picking out the gold in her hair, gilding her flushed face, and showing him the curves beneath her all but transparent gown and negligee, was enough to arouse him all over again. Keeping his distance from her had been difficult before. It was going to be impossible now that his life had been lived at the touch of her hand, though not in that exquisite body. Yet, *how* it had lived! What would it be like to bury himself in that willing flesh, to savor her innocent abandon, to make her truly his own? He dared not think about that now. He'd done the right thing in holding back. He'd made up his mind not to consummate the marriage, at least until after they'd consulted with the priests of Moldovia and knew exactly what they were facing. Looking at her now, so luscious, so ripe for the taking, he feared that resolve was going to be easier said than done.

"Are you angry with me?" she murmured.

He strode to her side, took her tiny hands in his, and raised them to his lips. "Of course not," he said on a sigh. "You cannot help what you did any more than I can. We will find a way out of this, Cassandra. If it is the last thing I do, we will find a way."

"When you stormed out of here, I thought . . . I—"

"I dared not stay in your presence, Cass, with the feeding frenzy upon me, and you . . . like you were."

She averted her eyes. "You're right. I couldn't help myself," she said, low-voiced.

"No more than I could, my love," he said. "I needed to get away and think—to form some semblance of a plan for our journey. I do not want to alarm you more than I must, but since you wish to be informed and I agree that you ought, suffice it to say that this was not a random thing. Sebastian will not stop until he has killed me and made you what he is."

Cassandra gasped, and he went on quickly. "My vocation apparently makes me a vampire's greatest conquest. Killing me will make him stronger. In your case, he means to make you his slave for all eternity. From what I've learned from my university studies—which, by the way, only credit vampirism as myth—he must not only drain you dry of blood, you must drink of his blood also, after which you will die and rise a full-fledged vampire, just as he is. Undead. If he ever confronts you, do not look him in the eye; it will render you helpless. He has the power to mesmerize. That is how he corrupted me. I had no idea what I was facing, that my university myth had come to life. In my ignorance, I let him paralyze my mind."

"You needn't worry," she said. "I certainly shan't court his company."

"Hah! Neither would I, and yet I found myself in his company earlier, didn't I? Never mind, just remember what I've said. Here is what I've planned. We shan't take the brougham to Blyth to book passage. I mean to send Jasper home with it. I shall place my bandage inside. With any luck, the scent of that blood will lure Sebastian in the opposite direction."

"But . . . you're bleeding still," she said.

"Not by half of what I was. It is only a graze, Cassandra. Believe me, Jasper will get the lion's share and he won't even know I've placed it in the coach."

"Won't that put him in danger?"

Jon shook his head. "It's my blood Sebastian wants, Cass—mine and yours. He'll be furious when he doesn't find us there, and will hie off after us. I shall also warn Jasper to be wary of strangers, and to keep to public places. As for us, it's a long distance we must travel to reach the estuary at Blyth. With a fast coach and four, if we leave at dawn and make no stops, we should arrive by dusk. Morning comes quickly. Close your eyes and rest, my love. You need a good night's sleep. God alone knows when you'll get another." He took her hands and drew her to her feet.

"Aren't you coming to bed?"

"I will prepare the holy water, and watch beside you awhile," he said. "I heard a rustling noise in the forest just now, high up in the boughs. That is where I last saw Sebastian, where he flew after he transformed into a bat. I heard it again just before I came inside. It might be nothing, but we cannot afford to take chances. Holy water will not destroy him, but it will keep him at his distance—if we're lucky, long enough for us to book passage and get away. Go to sleep, Cass. With any luck, tomorrow at this time we will be riding the high seas, well on our way toward putting all this behind us."

CHAPTER SIX

The hired chaise tooled off toward the border as the first cold rays of dawn crept over the horizon. It reached the estuary at Blyth in time for them to sail on the evening tide upon the fastest ship in port, the *North Star*, a three-masted barque whose cargo was somewhat suspect. That mattered not a whit to Jon. Whether smuggling, priva-teering, or carrying treasonous refugees was its mission, the stealth surrounding the ship was appealing. The cap-tain, one Elijah Hawkes, was amenable to taking on pas-sengers no questions asked for a price. Jon's clerical garb worked in his favor, and Hawkes didn't even question that he had enough blunt to have the first mate ousted from his cabin aft so that he and his bride could make the voyage privately and comfortably. If these sailors were thieves, they were honorable thieves: they settled their passengers in and afterward for the most part ig-nored them.

That they were making the voyage in summer spared them much of the dirty weather they would have faced during other months, when the notorious North Sea, laced with deadly pack and floe ice, kicked up snow-swept gales and bitter winds that stirred the towering seas to foam and froth; but it wouldn't spare them all of it. Three days out, a squall blew up complete with water-spouts and hellish winds that drove the barque before them all but horizontal in the water. All hands among the crew except the cook and ship's doctor were called on deck, which made it easy enough for Jon to slip below to steerage when the bloodlust came upon him. Cassandra was limited to the rats she abhorred so in her natural state. These Jon provided when she grew too weak to hunt for them herself. Whether it was ordinary seasickness that plagued her or there really was something to the tales that vampires could not cross water without falling ill, he did not know. The effect was devastating. Jon, however, was not affected. That Cassandra could not keep regular food down made matters worse. She rarely left their bunk, and Jon rarely slept in it. Animal blood was not sufficient to satisfy the bloodlust hunger. Recalling what had happened after feeding upon the deer in the Scottish forest, he would take no chances, and more of-ten than not he spent his nights in steerage among the cattle. He would not put Cassandra to the hazard again.

The storm raged for two days and nights, with the salt spray dousing the ship's lanterns, and the eerie blue glow of St. Elmo's fire snaking up and down the naked spars. The crew was a superstitious lot, and murmurings that the strange phenomenon was a sign of evil rumbled among them. But these were for the most part unedu-cated men, and Jon put no store in their fears. He'd learned of such phenomena at university, and knew that the strange blue lights were caused by atmospheric conditions, were the handiwork of Mother Nature, and could be explained away as lightning. St. Elmo's fire paled before the *real* evil in their midst, of which the seamen were in ignorance. Jon would not enlighten them.

As quickly as the storm came up, it dissipated with the dawn. The crew scurried over the decks, clearing away the debris and doing makeshift repairs. The sheets were untied and the unfurled sails, bellied and snapping in the wind, propelled them eastward through the Baltic at a steady clip. And so it went until they reached Gdansk.

The minute the ship docked, Cassandra began to rally. The sun had just set when Jon took her arm and led her up on deck to wait for their trunks to be brought from the cargo hold. But when the first mate unlocked the hatch and lifted the iron ring to raise the cover, he fell back with a shout that ran Jon through like a javelin. A swarm of squeaking, flapping bats soared through the hatch in a great black cloud, streaming past them over the ship's rail, through the ropes and spars and ladders, past the bulkhead, weaving in and out among the pilings to disappear in the bleak shadows of imminent darkness inland.

Meanwhile, the gaping crew members gathered around, swatting at the last of the stragglers, the first mate's rasping bark proclaiming all the while that he'd gone into the cargo hold a dozen times since they'd left Blyth and seen no bats, nor had he any idea how they'd come aboard. Cassandra cried out as one grazed her cheek, and she buried her face in the folds of Jon's multi-caped traveling coat as another's claws caught in her hair strafing past.

"Oh, Jon!" she cried. "Sebastian—could he be among them?"

Soothing her with gentle hands, Jon watched the last

of the bats exit the hold. "Not among them," he said. "Unless I am very much mistaken, he *was* them, or rather they were he. I have been reading the tome Clive gave me when we parted. It tells of such as this."

"I do not understand," she sobbed. "How could it be?"

"The stronger undead, those who have prowled the world for centuries, are reputed to possess the power to transform not only into one creature, but into a veritable army of rats or a swarm of bats at will. He flaunts his power—a very clever demonstration."

"Several of them . . . they . . . he *touched* me, Jon," she said, shuddering in his arms.

"He has marked you for making. We must be even more careful. Stay close to me, and do exactly as I tell you. It could mean your life, Cass."

"But how has he come here? You sent the brougham back to the Abbey with your scent upon it."

Jon sighed. "If you remember, I told you I heard a rustling sound in the wood, and then again just before I reentered the cottage. I'll wager he eavesdropped and overheard me telling you my plans for the voyage. It doesn't matter how he knows, only that he obviously does. He is a vain creature. He evidently could not resist flaunting his cleverness in our faces. But overconfidence will not serve him well; now we are warned. Come . . . we shall find an inn and stay the night. Hereafter, at least until we've put some distance between us and that creature, we sleep by night and travel by day, when he cannot be abroad to follow. We must proceed with utmost caution. He will have minions here."

Cassandra stirred. How strange it seemed to sleep in a bed after the long sea voyage, pitching and rolling with the swells that moved the *North Star*. She had staggered like a lord in his cups leaving the barque. What must the innkeeper have thought? Jon lay beside her, sound asleep. It seemed the sleep of the dead, for he made no sound. But he was not dead. She could feel the warmth of him through her nightshift, the pressure of his corded thigh leaning heavily against her. Strange . . . she had always been alone when the dreams came. She knew it was a dream. Her eyes wouldn't open, and yet it seemed so real—real enough that she lowered her feet to the floor and stood to prove the point.

How light she was. She seemed to float, responding to a gentle tapping noise sounding back in echo. Something was tapping against glass. The sound seemed to swell all around her, like the rising waves of the sea. She shuddered, remembering. That was when the dreams had begun—in the first mate's cabin on the *North Star*. She hadn't told Jon about the dreams, they would only worry him. They were just *dreams*, after all.

There was only one window in the room—a small round opening set high in the eaves, where the roof tiles outside shaded it. It was fitted with a grill of ornamental ironwork, and shuttered on the inside. Jon had latched the shutters before they retired. What a beautiful window. She had never seen the like; such a pity to cover it. It reminded her of the portholes belowdecks on the barque, though they had been square. She raised her arms to lift the latch, but it was out of reach. The tapping grew louder, more urgent, and she began to moan, standing on tiptoe, stretching, reaching . . . but the latch was set too high.

All at once she felt herself lifted. Her eyes snapped open wide. She was moving, but her feet had left the floor. Jon was carrying her! Slowly his image came into focus. How handsome he was, gazing down through those hooded quicksilver eyes. But his mouth was hard-set, and the muscles along his jaw had begun to tick.

"What are you doing, Cassandra?" he asked, setting her down on the counterpane. "The window must stay shuttered—you know that. What were you about just now?"

"Someone knocks," she said, pointing toward the shutters. "Don't you hear it? No . . . how could you? This is *my* dream."

"It is not a dream," Jon said, foraging inside his traveling bag. After a moment, he took out the wineskin filled with holy water and a handkerchief, which he saturated.

"Of course it is!" she breathed. "It always is . . ."

Jon stood frozen in place, the handkerchief in his fist dripping steaming water on the bare wood floor. For a moment he stood rooted to the spot, then he strode to the window. He was tall enough to reach the latch. Cassandra watched, her brows knit in a puzzled frown as he passed the saturated handkerchief over the odd round shutters, then looped it through the latch and tied it securely. Only then did he turn to face her. His silvery eyes were blazing. Anger lived in that stare . . . and something else, something she couldn't read.

All at once a squeaking sound on the other side of the window crescendoed into a rasping screech, then grew distant. Jon sank down on the edge of the bed and gathered her into his arms. How strong he was. How safe she felt in his embrace, though she was not, and unless they could find help in Moldovia among the holy men there, she never would be.

"I heard it, too, Cassandra," he said. "It was him, and if you could have reached those shutters and had not wakened in time, you would have let him in. He has mesmerized you. He owns your mind when he wills it. He commands, and you obey."

"B-but it is such a small window, and so high! Why, it's set beneath the overhang. How could he—"

"Have you so soon forgotten the bats?"

She gasped. She had. Had the creature erased them from her memory? All at once she was terrified. The connotations all but paralyzed her brain.

"How long have you been having such dreams?"

"They started on the ship," she said, trying to remember.

"Did you sleepwalk during the dreams as you did just now?"

"I . . . I don't know. I don't think so. Oh, Jon!"

He soothed her with gentle hands, though his demeanor hadn't changed. That was more terrifying than it would have been had he taken her to task, scolded her, admonished her—anything but this intense, stricken look. She turned her eyes away.

"Where was I when you were having these dreams?" he asked.

"You often left me at night," she said. "You slept elsewhere much of the time—"

"Because I could not risk myself in your presence when the bloodlust came upon me," he interrupted.

"I imagined I heard you calling me, though it didn't really sound like you at first, but then . . . you asked me to rise up and let you in—"

He seized her upper arms and shook her. "You didn't . . . ?"

"N-no!" she cried. "I couldn't. I would have, but the ship—it tipped and rolled in the water so severely, I had to tie myself down with the bed linen to keep from falling out of the bunk. I nearly did once. Even if I could have risen as you bade me, I could never have stood without an arm to lean on. At times the ship was nearly lying on its side in the sea. I couldn't keep my balance. It was dreadful!"

"That wasn't me calling you, Cassandra. It was Sebastian. If you had let him in as he demanded, he would have drained your blood until you died but not died, and you would have risen to number among the undead as he is. In the open he can have you in a trice. But if you are enclosed inside a house, a room, a chamber—if there is a door, some barrier between you, he cannot enter where you are unless it be by invitation. Do you see how vulnerable you are to his wiles? You would have let him in just now if I hadn't stopped you. He would have had you and killed me. Now do you finally see what we are facing? No matter what, you must resist him!"

Tears spilled down her cheeks. "It sounded like you," she sobbed.

"He evidently has the power to change his voice, to mimic others. I do not know. I have not read the entire book that Clive gave me. There hasn't been time, what with trying to stay one step ahead of the creature and dealing with our symptoms. I am trying to separate the wheat from the chaff in the tome. It treats things I have always thought were myth as fact, which is why I am in hopes that these holy men will be able to help us."

"You are angry with me," she said.

"I am out of sorts, yes, but not angry with you. It is the animal blood. It does not agree with me. I need human blood to sustain me until I can find a way to stop the cravings altogether."

"The tome the vicar gave you," she said. "Does it not

offer a solution?" She had to know, though she feared the answer.

"It mentions several things, but none that I might try without the priests. One remedy involves an herb I've never heard of, and the other a ritual so bizarre I would not dream to attempt it without holy sanction."

"Is it a very long journey to Moldovia?" she asked.

"Longer than the distance we would travel from the tip of Land's End in Cornwall to the uppermost reaches of the Scottish Highlands," he replied.

Cassandra swallowed. "Oh," she said. "It will take at least a sennight, then. I had hoped—"

"At the very least a sennight," he interrupted, "depending upon the terrain we must travel and how often we stop along the way. I have never been in this part of the world, but several of my colleagues at university were Romanian. Homesick, they shared tales of their land. They spoke of steppes and forests and valleys, but much of the terrain we must travel through is in the mountains, whose passes are carved high and narrow in the rock— treacherous roads, if you can even call them roads, and Sebastian will be there with us in one form or another, whether he makes his presence known or not. And then there are his minions. We can trust no one here, Cassandra. We were not safe on the ship, and we were unaware. We are less safe here on land, and though we *are* aware of danger, we have no idea of the nature of the danger we are facing. I cannot stay awake the whole distance to Moldovia to keep you from answering the vampire's call. You must be vigilant or we are both lost."

Cassandra was silent apace. She couldn't bear his closeness. The scent of his blood was always a torment. Yet his earthy, masculine scent threaded through her nostrils as well, and she breathed him in deeply. That clean blend of citrus, musk, and leather was the first thing that drew her to him when they'd met at Almack's. She closed her eyes and she was there again, gazing into those mercurial eyes hooded beneath their sweeping lashes, captivated as he bowed over her hand. She lived again the thrill of his lips on her gloved hand, of his caressing fingers on her arm leading her toward the dance floor, quickening her heart, shortening her breath.

With a sinking feeling in the pit of her stomach, she relived the ache in her heart when Lady Elizabeth Revere jerked her out of Jon's grasp and wound his arm through her snippy daughter's instead, and the mortification that ensued when Lady Jersey took her aside to define her place in no uncertain terms. She never thought she would see Jon again after that, but he'd found a way. *Love will go where it's sent*, her grandmother always said. Did he still love her? He hadn't touched her—hadn't made love to her since their wedding night, and even then he hadn't consummated the marriage. Would he ever take her now? Would she ever feel his magnificence inside her? How could he make love to her after this?

"Do you not want me anymore because of . . . ?" she said in a small voice. "I wouldn't blame you if you didn't."

He stiffened as though she'd struck him, and tilted her face until their gazes met. His eyes were wild feral things searching her face. Cassandra held her breath. She'd never seen that look before.

"Want you?" he said, gravel-voiced. "It is all I can do to keep from ravishing you, Cassandra. I cannot take you as I wish, not until we've settled all this. Suppose you were to conceive. Can such a thing occur as we are? We don't even know that! And if it did, what would our offspring be? You want children . . . so did I, but what would our child be? Do we dare take the chance to find out? You think all this isn't killing me—tearing my heart out? I ache to live in your exquisite body. And to lie next to you in this bed and not touch you, not hold you? I am running mad for want of you."

"Then, why?"

"You know why!" he gritted through clenched teeth. "Aside from all the rest, you are in far more danger from me than you are from Sebastian because I am here with you. I've tasted your blood—"

"As I have yours," she interrupted him.

"Yes, and that makes it worse." He stroked her face with the back of his hand. "What if I cannot stop? What if this accursed disease takes over and I finish what Sebastian has started? What if I cannot help myself? I would rather die than cause you harm. Want you? My God!"

Gathering her close, he swooped down and took her lips with a hungry mouth. Her breath caught as his silken tongue glided between her teeth, between the budding fangs that she hadn't been able to retract since he took her in his arms. Did he notice? She couldn't tell, succumbing to his deep, ravenous kisses.

Capturing her hand, he drove it down to his sex, crimping her fingers around the thick, hard shaft, his riveting silver eyes dilated with desire. "Does that feel as if I do not want you?" he panted against her lips, meanwhile raising his hand and sliding it along the length of her arched throat. When it reached the gathering ribbon at the neck of her sheer muslin nightshift, he slipped it down over one shoulder, exposing the breast beneath. His lips hovered there, his hot breath puffing on her skin and sending waves of shivers snaking along her spine in anticipation of his skilled tongue descending.

Her heart was pounding so violently, her whole body shuddered with the vibration. She could bear no more. Arching her spine, she reached toward him, clasping him around the neck, pulling him closer still until, a hair's breadth from her hardened nipple, he resisted.

Groaning, he seized her arms, put her from him, and staggered to his feet. Tears misted her eyes, and her hands flew to her lips. She stared at the needle-sharp fangs that had descended from the canine teeth in his handsome mouth. He loosed a bestial howl. When he raised his fist to sink those fangs into his own flesh again, she seized his wrist in both her hands.

"Don't!" she cried. "My God, Jon . . . don't do that again. I *beg* you. Don't."

"What else am I to do?" he asked. He let out a mad, misshapen laugh. "I've precious little flesh left upon these arms and hands that I haven't bitten to avoid biting *you*, 'tis true, but what other alternative but pain have I at my disposal to cancel the bloodlust? What else but pain will stop the feeding frenzy? I don't dare leave you to feed elsewhere for fear you will open that window . . . or this door here"—he waved his hand toward it—"and blunder into danger or death at that creature's hands during one of your 'dreams.' You should have told me!" He dropped his head into his hands. "Want you?" he sobbed. "Bloody hell, Cassandra."

She held her peace. Whether it was the anger or exhaustion or both, she didn't know, but after a time his fangs receded. He got up from the bed and staggered to a Chippendale chair in the corner—as far away from her as he could range himself, she realized with sinking heart.

"It is still an hour or two until dawn," he murmured, raking his hair back from his damp brow. "Get some sleep. We leave at first light, and God alone knows what we will be facing."

His fangs had wholly disappeared, and she gestured. "H-how did you . . . ?" she murmured.

"I prayed," he said, but no more.

CHAPTER SEVEN

Had he gotten through to her? Jon didn't know. Not knowing what to expect was killing him. Just when he thought he understood his malady, something would happen to show him how very little he knew. The one ray of light lay in his vocation. Evidently, despite the evil that now tainted his blood, there was still power in his faith. How much power, he didn't know, but it was enough to give him hope, and that drove him.

It was decided that Jon would sleep as best he could by taking naps in the chaise during the day, when it was safer for Cassandra to be without supervision. Then, he would watch over her through the night while she slept, whether they stopped at an inn for the night or just to eat, refresh themselves, and change horses. It seemed a workable plan, though if Jon had his way they would drive straight through. The allure of her sweet presence alone was enough to set his loins on fire, the condition notwithstanding. The sooner they reached the holy men of Moldovia the better.

The nights were the worst, when the bloodlust was upon them both. Human blood was not an option; there was no opportunity. Jon dared not leave Cassandra alone while he went in search of a subject, but most of the inns had grazing sheep that by nature brooked no opposition. It was not a wholly satisfactory option, because he'd had precious little else but animal blood since the journey began, and the effects of that were taking their toll upon him in more ways than one. He was becoming physically sick, to say nothing of irritable, and it was with great relief that they approached the Carpathian Mountains on the eve of the last day of their journey.

Jon's instinct was to drive straight on, but the coachman flatly refused to chance the Dkula Pass at night, especially since a storm was threatening. Dry lightning was already spearing down over the mountains in the distance, and the dense cloud cover wouldn't let the misshapen three-quarter moon shine through to light the way.

Leaving the coach to be attended by the hostlers, Jon and Cassandra entered the common room of the White Stag Inn. The evening meal was venison stew and brown ale. They could still eat regular food, though they seemed to take little nourishment from it—more by the blood they consumed were they sustained. This was especially true of Jon, who had fed upon animals the whole journey. The flesh of the species he'd drunk from was abhorrent to him now. Making matters worse, the animal blood did not satisfy for long, causing him to prowl for food more often, which meant leaving Cassandra periodically despite his resolve not to leave her unguarded.

Luckily, this was not so for Cassandra. Satisfied with small creatures, her needs were met more easily. They were so nominal, in fact, that he tended to forget them, what with the rest of the thoughts weighing upon him. She never complained.

This night was no exception, and after their meal he saw her to their room, then left her to feed, so she would be safe in his presence while he watched over her through the night. That was the worst for him: the pull that made him a mortal threat to the one person on earth he most longed to protect.

Having duly warned her for the hundredth time of the dangers she faced—especially now, on what they presumed to be Sebastian's home ground—he left her on her honor to admit no one and stepped out into the lightning-struck darkness in search of a likely animal.

His intention was to keep the inn in sight, just in case. That Sebastian was still stalking them he had no doubt; he'd felt the evil presence the entire length of the journey—especially now, when they were so close to an end. Surely the creature knew their intent. That the stalking seemed more urgent now gave him hope there was something to the supposition that the priests of Moldovia held the key. But the storm was coming closer, the lightning snaking down over the plains in white-hot flashes. Thunder accompanied it, frightening the sheep that, instead of seeking shelter from the storm in the barnyard or close by the stables, began to stray in the direction of the very thing they feared.

"Stupid creatures," Jon grumbled, for they would draw him out into the open where the lightning's glare made him very visible. The rain was imminent, and he swooped down upon a likely subject and proceeded to drain the animal dry.

He had barely straightened from the dead sheep when a bloodcurdling racket coming from the area of the stables nearly stopped his heart. Above the din, a woman's screams rivaled the thunder.

Cassandra?

Other voices carried, too—angry, accusing voices. Cassandra screamed again. Wiping the blood from his lips, Jon bolted toward the sound, his knees threatening to give way beneath him. Scaling the hillock north of the inn, he scanned the scene below with narrowed eyes, and in the rain that had begun to fall, cold chills raced along his spine, puckering his scalp and suspending his shuddering heartbeat. Cassandra was surrounded by an outraged group of men and women, their number steadily growing. Some were wielding what appeared to be clubs or wattles. But for the lightning picking out her sun-painted curls, he could barely see Cassandra for the press of bodies converging upon her.

Half running, half stumbling, Jon raced down the hillock, slip-sliding on the slick wet grass, crushing the blades, releasing their oils until the strong, breath-stealing scent rose up and flared his nostrils. His heart hammering in his breast, he raced toward what had escalated into an ugly mob, and the surly brool—a low, sinister murmur—rumbling through the gathering crowd raised the fine hairs on the back of his neck. Cries of *revenant* and *vampire* leaked from the people, riveting him so severely he had to swallow the heartbeat that had risen in his throat.

Elbowing his way through the crowd, doling out shoves with little regard for how those in his path were dispersed, Jon reached Cassandra, backed against the stable wall, and he seized the arm of a peasant woman set to lower a branch upon his bride where she crouched over the dead rat she'd been feeding upon. The rain had washed most of the blood from Cassandra's face, but enough remained to show him what had obviously occurred. Disarming the crone, he threatened the others with the branch, holding it high, carving wild circles with it in the rain-swept air, meanwhile raising Cassandra to her feet.

"Stand back from my wife!" he demanded, swiping at random as he parted the crowd with long-legged strides and led Cassandra away. "Stand back, I say!"

Out of the corner of his eye, he spied the chaise they had come in speeding northward, the coachman wielding his whip over the heads of fresh horses. Their trunks were still lashed on top. All that remained of their belongings were in the small valises they had carried to their room, also lost to them now. There was nothing to be done. Getting away from the angry crowd was all that mattered. Jon carried his currency on his person; at least they had that. Still wielding the branch, he continued to fight his way through the sea of incensed locals, who crowded closer despite the lightning streaking across the hills and the rain falling hard on a slant from ink-black clouds.

"Vampires!" a woman's shrill voice accused. "They are vampires!"

"Revenants!" a gruff voice echoed from deep in the crowd. "Don't let them get away!"

Other accusing voices rose above the racket, and Jon pulled Cassandra closer. "Hold on to me," he murmured. "We must escape, there are too many. And the coach has left us."

"I am so sorry, Jon," she sobbed.

"No," he said. "This is not your fault—it's mine. If I hadn't left you . . ."

Several of the threatening clubs came swishing through

the air too close to be brooked, and Jon began swinging his branch in earnest now, with little regard for those in the way. Suddenly, something wet was flung in his face. It steamed upon contact, though it did not burn him. *Holy water.* All at once he remembered the wineskin filled with holy water in their room—another thing lost to him now.

Screams rang out from the crowd as steam rose from the hurled water. It didn't seem to matter that it had no other effect; the phenomenon of the steam was enough to cause a panic, and clumps of turf and mud lobbed at Jon and Cassandra created a new press, though the peasants now kept their distance as they hurled. Their accusations proven, the mob began to fall back en masse, though their irate shouts of *"Vampire! Revenant! Nosferatu! Vampir!"*—as well as other words Jon could not understand in his limited knowledge of the dialect—continued.

They were soon running south, out of range of the lantern light seeping from the inn and stable. Only the lightning betrayed them in random flashes. The mob was no longer in pursuit, but Jon took no comfort from that. He and Cassandra were found out, and an army of vigilantes would surely follow. They were hopelessly outnumbered. All he could think of was putting as much distance as possible between them and the danger they'd just fled. But then, what of the other dangers? They were out in the open now, and unarmed. If Sebastian were about, he would not need an invitation to attack. Jon had no idea how far it was to the Dkula Pass, or to the priory they sought on the far side of the Carpathians.

Cassandra must have been thinking like thoughts, for she was the first to speak, when at last he slowed their pace. "Our holy water!" she cried, her breath coming short.

"I can make more holy water."

"The book! The tome the vicar gave you . . . Oh, Jon!"

"It cannot be helped. I've read most of it while watching over you during the night. It is a small loss, considering. Right now we need to put as much distance between ourselves and that mob back there as is humanly possible. I am praying that the storm keeps them at bay until we find some suitable shelter until dawn, when I can see where we're going." He took her measure. "You're soaked through," he said. Stripping off his greatcoat, he wrapped it around her shoulders without missing a step, then continued on, a close eye over his shoulder for any sign of pursuit.

"Whatever possessed you to leave our room?" he asked. "You were safe there."

"I heard the rat scratching at the door," she said. "I smelled its blood. The bloodlust came upon me. Before I knew what I was doing, I had opened the door. You *know* what a fever the craving causes. The animal scurried away toward the backstairs, and I followed—stalked it. I thought of nothing but feeding then. My vision narrows when the feeding frenzy comes upon me, Jon . . . someone must have seen me follow and catch it. All at once I was surrounded! They had clubs! They would have beaten me to death if you hadn't come when you did."

"Shhh," he warned, steering her toward the edge of a wood, where the pine branches would spare them some of the punishing rain that seemed to be following. "We may not be alone. Save your strength. We must keep moving. We shall press on as long as you are able."

"There must be more like us here," she observed, low-voiced. "They were *ready*. All those clubs . . . They were armed in seconds—as if we were expected!"

"According to that tome, these are a very superstitious lot. I heard them call out *revenant*. Those are the dead come back to life to collect the living. Peasants open graves here and drive stakes into the corpses of those whom they suspect, pinning them to the ground. They cut off their heads and turn them backward to confuse them should they rise. I am not surprised that they were prepared for us. We are very fortunate to have escaped . . . if only for now."

It was hopeless to continue on foot over such terrain and in such conditions, but Jon dared not tell that to Cassandra. Hoping for some crude sort of shelter at the worst, or the home of a local squire at best, he urged her on as the narrow mountain pass rose up and loomed before them through the teeming rain. After a time, the storm passed over, and the moon shone through the clouds in all its misshapen glory, its pale rays glistening on the wet blackberries growing in profusion along the edge of the wood, upon which they nibbled along the way. The rich, succulent juice of the ripe fruit was like balm, soothing their parched, dry throats.

The wild berries seemed to cheer Cassandra, and Jon did not hinder her. This was little enough to allow—anything that would ease the tension. He'd heard rustling in the upper boughs almost since they'd escaped the inn. Whether she had or not, he wasn't certain. He didn't mention it. With any luck, it was a squirrel or some bird they'd awakened while trespassing in its domain. Either way, he was glad he still had the pistol in the pocket of his greatcoat. He was glad he'd resisted the temptation to use it to frighten the mob earlier. It would have been useless against such a number, and he would have wasted his only ammunition. At least now he had one shot against whatever enemy threatened. He groped the pocket of his coat draped around Cassandra for reassurance, slipped the pistol out, and wedged it beneath the waistband on his breeches. Yes, it was safe. He would be very careful how he used it.

He had just begun to relax his guard when the familiar sound of wagon wheels crunching on wet gravel pulled him up short, extracting a breathless cry from Cassandra. Spinning around, he faced a large cart lined with straw, its driver a well-built man of indeterminable age, his dark hair lightly silvered at the temples. Judging from his attire and olive complexion, he appeared to be a Gypsy. He seemed to have materialized out of nowhere, emerging from the direction from which they had just fled, out of a ghostlike mist that had risen over the ground after the storm. That alone made him suspect in Jon's eyes, and he shoved Cassandra behind him when the man reined the feather-footed, dappled gray horse in alongside them.

"Come," said the Gypsy, sweeping his arm wide. "The road is not safe at night."

Jon stared, taken aback that the words were in English.

"You cannot travel the pass afoot in the dark," the man went on. "You will not live to see the dawn."

"You were one of them . . . back there," Jon accused, jutting his chin, fully aware of Cassandra's pinching grip upon his arm.

"I was at the inn, yes," said the Gypsy, "and yes, I saw what happened, but I was not one of them." Reaching into the cart, he raised a valise from the straw. It was singed black in spots.

Cassandra gasped. "Your traveling bag, Jon!" she cried. "It's been burned."

"Where did you get that?" Jon demanded, taking a step closer.

"I took both it and the lady's from the pyre the blacksmith made to destroy them."

"Why?" said Jon.

The Gypsy shrugged. "Because you will have need of them," he said simply, struggling to control the horse. It had begun to rear and shy and paw the ground.

"Who are you?" Jon asked. Well aware of the reason for the horse's complaints, he gave it a wide berth. "How do you speak our language?"

The Gypsy spoke gently to the horse's unease, and flashed a smile that did not reach his eyes. "I am called Milosh," he said. "And my people lived for many years in England. Come . . . more dangers than you know of haunt these parts."

"How do I know—"

"You do not," the Gypsy interrupted. "But there is no time to lose. Come."

Still Jon hesitated, and Cassandra leaned close. "No, Jon," she whispered. "I'm afraid . . . Tell him to just give us our bags."

The Gypsy flashed another half-smile and dropped both of their traveling bags on the ground. "Young lady," he said, "I have more to fear from *you* than you have from me. Others follow. You will have a far greater chance to escape a dreadful fate with the distance this cart can put between you than you can hope to achieve afoot. Those who live hereabouts take their mission in earnest. They cut the heads off vampires and stake them to the ground with wooden spikes through the heart. They dig up the dead bodies of suspected revenant, and burn vampires alive." He nodded behind. "You doubt me? Look there. What do you think those torches are for?"

Jon glanced behind. Sure enough, a sea of bobbing torches lit the steppes where the inn stood. They were moving toward them.

Jon tossed the bags back into the cart, lifted Cassandra up, and climbed in beside her. Tearing his bag open, he searched for the tome the vicar had given him, but it was not among his belongings. Neither was the skin of holy water. He heaved a sigh, shutting the bag again.

"I could not save the book," said the Gypsy. "It is the reason for their pursuit. Finding it after the young lady fed upon the rat has sealed your fate. They know why you are here—what you seek. They burned it. In the melee, I was barely able to save the bags." He cracked the whip over the horse and the animal bolted forward.

"Why are you doing this—helping us this way?" Jon asked as the cart lumbered along. "Gypsies do not usually mix in such matters. They keep to themselves."

Again the Gypsy smiled. "I am what you aspire to be," he said, "and what you will become. A vampire hunter."

CHAPTER EIGHT

"We seek a priory—any priory," Jon said. "Several were mentioned in that book." The Gypsy had taken them deep into the forest, and Jon kept his hand poised over the pistol wedged beneath his frockcoat, casting meaningful glances toward Cassandra, whose face had gone as white as the moon.

"The holy ones there will not help you," said Milosh. Jon could no longer see the torches following. The Gypsy reined the horse in alongside a trickling stream and continued, "We are safe here . . . for now. The villagers will not enter this wood in darkness—and with good cause. But that is to our advantage."

"What do you mean, the priests will not help us?" Jon said, having heard little beyond that. It was the sole purpose of their journey. He refused to accept that they had come all this distance for naught. "Of course they will help us."

Milosh flashed a patronizing smile. "Did your clerical togs spare you just now?" he said.

"Perhaps they did not recognize Jon's clothes for what

they are," Cassandra put in. "The holy men in these parts dress differently, I'm sure."

The Gypsy's dark eyes flashed toward her, and Jon gave her hand a warning squeeze.

"Young lady," Milosh said, "I can show you the graves of many a priest whose vestments did not spare him. No one is incorruptible here, and members of the clergy—*any* clergy—are prime targets for the undead." His dark eyes snapped toward Jon. "I should not need to remind you of that—'Jon,' is it?"

Jon nodded, giving a start. He had totally forgotten the amenity of introductions. "Jon Hyde-White," he said, "And the young lady is Cassandra, my wife."

The Gypsy acknowledged him with a deep nod.

"Please do not take our hope away," Jon went on. "The contents of that tome they burned brought us all the way from Scotland seeking help."

"The only thing it has done is mark you both for death," Milosh said flatly. "It has betrayed you—just as the holy men you seek will betray you. Believe me, the book is no great loss."

"But surely, men of God—"

"There are only two kinds of men here in Moldovia," the Gypsy said, raising his hand to flag the interruption. "The undead, and those who hunt them."

"And you are the latter?" Jon asked warily.

"I am both, like yourself," Milosh replied. Stunned, Jon clenched his fists, and Cassandra gasped beside him, her eyes wide. "Which is why I recognized you so easily, and why I came to help you, if I can, or rather . . . if you will allow."

"H-how?" Jon stammered. This was not at all what he'd expected, and his tone betrayed his surprise.

"Vampires have identifying marks at different stages of their making." He gestured against his own face. "The blue veins there beneath your fair skin give you away. If you were fully made, they would be much darker. Your lady wife's are hardly noticeable . . . yet." Jon studied Milosh's face for similar marks, and the Gypsy smiled his half-smile. "The veins do not show so easily beneath my olive skin, which works to my advantage. That is why I seldom go abroad before nightfall. In your homeland, where such a thing as vampirism has not obsessed the people, such marks would go for the most part unnoticed—or attributed to other, more familiar . . . more acceptable maladies."

"How did you become a victim?" Jon asked, a close eye upon Cassandra, who clearly did not trust the Gypsy—especially now, since he had confessed to being what they were. He would have laughed at the presumptuousness of her attitude if the situation weren't so grave.

"The undead Sebastian and his minions took my wife and unborn child from me," Milosh explained, tugging at his mustache. "I was bitten trying to protect them. In my ignorance, I failed, and had to give them peace in a most . . . repulsive way—the way that mob plans to give you peace, though with these your 'peace' is of no consequence. Their purpose is to protect themselves. That pyre the smithy built was not only for your paltry traveling bags; he would not have wasted precious kindling over those alone. Once they had clubbed you senseless, your bodies would have been fed to those flames. And that is a kinder justice than some of their other methods."

Cassandra hid her face in the folds of Jon's neckcloth. She was trembling helplessly, clearly terrified—but perhaps that was for the best, Jon reasoned.

"Your lady wife is not long infected," Milosh observed. "Her . . . inexperience has nearly cost you both your lives."

"The . . . 'infection,' as you call it, is new to both of us," Jon said.

"Would you care to tell me how it all occurred?" asked the Gypsy.

Water splattered upon them, shaken from the uppermost branches by a fugitive wind that had risen. The forest was so dense, Jon couldn't see the sky. It seemed a strange place for a stranger conversation—especially since he no longer had the skin of holy water to defend himself if things should turn sour. Still, Milosh had been forthcoming with them about his own situation, and he had helped them, after all. Before he knew what had happened, he'd told the Gypsy everything.

There was a long silence.

"There is no cure," the Gypsy reminded them at last.

"I know that," said Jon, "but there has to be *something*, some help for it."

"There is," the Gypsy said, "but as I said, you'll not have it from the holy ones. It is a well-guarded secret, and though they know of it, we Romany are the only ones who hold the key to open that door."

"If that is true, how is it that you 'had to bring peace' to your wife and child in such a horrific manner?" Cassandra queried. Jon's eyebrow inched up a notch. She had been so quiet for such a length of time, he had almost forgotten she was there. "What?" she said, answering his expression. "Have you forgotten that when I am not in the grip of bloodlust I am capable of rational thought?"

Jon raised his hands in a gesture of concession, almost amused at her bristling over such a point in these bizarre circumstances. Loving her all the more for her courage and perseverance, he made no reply, though she gave him ample time to do so before continuing.

"Hmmm," she said. How fetching she was when angry, her doe eyes flashing, her pouty lips pursed so provocatively. If the moon were visible, he was certain it would have picked out the irresistible red patches that always colored her cheeks when she was in a taking, and he would have come undone. As it was, cloaked in the eerie green darkness, what little he could make out of that beloved face aroused him. "If there were some help to be had," she went on, tossing her golden curls, "why could you not help them?"

"It was too late," the Gypsy said, his eyes downcast. "There is no help for those whom the vampire fully makes, those who die once he drains them and then rise again to serve him throughout eternity. Help is only to be had for those infected but not made—those like yourselves . . . and like me."

"And you have had such help?" said Jon, fascinated, though wary still.

The Gypsy nodded. "I have . . . but it is not for the faint of heart," he warned, his eyes upon Cassandra.

"My heart is not faint, sir," she said. "Just breaking. . . ."

"How far is the nearest priory?" said Jon. What the Gypsy was saying was intriguing, but he wanted to follow his original course. They hadn't come all this way to take the word of another infected just as they were. He couldn't imagine the Church denying them help were they to beg. It was unthinkable.

The Gypsy stared at him long and hard. "Follow the stream," he said at last. "It will lead you through the forest to the foothills. There you will find a priory."

Jon nodded. Climbing down, he lifted Cassandra down as well.

The Gypsy laid a hand upon his arm. His touch was riveting. Was it only that it was unexpected, or was it something else, something connected to the condition they shared? Whatever the case, Jon's spine was riddled so violently with chills the bones audibly popped.

"You cannot go on foot," Milosh said, climbing down also. "Take the cart."

"You are that certain it will return to you once we fall into the trap you've laid for us?" Jon said, voicing thoughts he'd never meant to speak aloud.

The Gypsy smiled. "I've set no trap—I've sprung one," he said. Stripping off his garments, he began tossing them into the cart. "Once you see how you are received, you will return the cart and Petra here eagerly enough. But this you must find out for yourselves. Besides, though making holy water is no chore for you, we shall need holy oil for what is to come. Fetch some while you are there."

"How do you propose I do that?" Jon asked, his fisted hands braced upon his hips.

"You will find a way," the Gypsy returned. His drawers were the last of his clothes to sail through the air and land in the cart. He stood naked, and Jon turned Cassandra's head away, though there was scarcely enough light to see clearly.

The Gypsy sprang toward the forest. In the blink of an eye, his shape changed from that of a muscular, dark-haired man to that of a large white wolf with a gray-tipped spine. It was a silvery streak of blurred motion that brought him crashing to earth upon all fours. A melancholy howl escaping its throat, the animal sped off and disappeared into the deep dark among the trees and junglelike tangle of vines and foliage.

Jon fingered the Gypsy's clothes, which were still warm in the wagon. "Is that what it looks like when I change shape?" he murmured, half to himself.

Cassandra nodded. "What do you make of it . . . of *him?*" she said.

"That he was telling the truth," he replied, gravelvoiced. "Or at least he believes he is."

The lantern hanging from the cart gave off no more light than a firefly, but in what it spared, Jon took his wife's measure. Despite the rain, traces of blood still stained the front of her sprigged muslin frock, as well as splotches of the mud that the peasants had flung at her. Her face was smudged with dirt as well, and he took up her traveling bag and handed it over.

"Refresh yourself beside the stream," he said, "and change clothes. You cannot go as you are. I shall keep watch while you do."

"What about that wolf?" she said. "What if it comes back?"

"While I have no doubt it will stay near, I do not think you need fear it. I do not presume to understand any of this, but we have to trust something—someone. Let us begin with Milosh, hmm?"

She did as he bade, but her demeanor showed him all too clearly that she was not convinced. Truth be told, neither was he, but they had to play the hand they'd been dealt, and the last thing he wanted to do was overset Cassandra by adding his doubts to hers.

Looking on, he stood mesmerized by the sight of her as she stripped off her torn, soiled frock and began bathing her face, arms, and chest in the cool water of the stream. How exquisite she was in the eerie light, reflected from what source he couldn't identify, unless it was moonlight bouncing off the glistening ripples riding the stream where the dense canopy of boughs let it through. Nevertheless, it sparkled in her honeyed curls and gleamed from the soft, wet swell of her breast above the thin underwaist. She was pure gold.

Jon's sex sprang to life, turgid and throbbing. How he longed to seize her, to lay her down on the cool green moss along the bank of the stream and bury himself inside that exquisite body. How he longed to feel those tiny hands fisted in his hair, caressing his sex, feel those arms clasping him fast, feel the petal-softness of those dewy lips welcoming his kiss. A soft moan escaped him as his lips parted in anticipation of just such a kiss. But then there was something else: the pressure of fangs obscuring his canine teeth slowly descending in rhythm with the contractions gripping his belly, seizing his loins with the thudding pulse thrumming through his veins. The bloodlust! Would it always be thus? Would he never be able to make love to her the way she was meant to be loved?

Reeling away from the sight that had aroused him, he clenched his teeth as if to drive back the fangs. All he achieved was piercing his lower lip with the deadly things. Finally they receded. He loosed a different sort of groan, shuddering with despair. Finally, his shallow breathing became deep. His heartbeat sought a calmer rhythm. Pain relieved the hunger again. At least there was a way—albeit a drastic one, and in this case accidental.

Snatching his greatcoat up from where Cassandra had left it draped over the side of the cart, Jon began slapping the dust and dirt from it relentlessly. This was just what he needed: something to take his mind off the beautiful woman whose closeness was a threat to them both. Carrying the coat to the stream, he saturated his handkerchief in the cool running water and sponged the mud from it. He scarcely remembered being hit so many times with handfuls of ooze as they fled the inn.

"Let me help you with that," Cassandra said, reaching for the coat. He hadn't heard or seen her approach. Dazed, he stared at her through eyes glazed over with rage and desire, but his breathing was deep and controlled. How lovely she looked in her clean white muslin frock and indigo spencer. Not the most practical choice, but that couldn't be helped. The traveling bag she'd taken it from was only large enough to hold one change of clothing, and their trunks were probably halfway to Gdansk by now.

"No," he blurted, a little too loudly. Did it sound as harsh to her as it did to him? He wasn't angry with her. It was himself he hated then; but if it did, so be it! He had to keep her at a distance for both their sakes, and he wrung out the handkerchief, passed it over his hot face, and shrugged on the coat. "It will have to do," he said, more civilly. "Come. There is no time to lose if we are to reach the priory before word spreads."

Cassandra gasped. "What have you done to your mouth?" she asked. "How have you hurt yourself?"

"I bit my lip," he snapped. "It's nothing."

He helped her up to the seat in the cart, hid the Gypsy's clothing beneath the straw, and climbed up beside her. Her eyes were full of questions, but he would not encourage them now. Snapping the whip, he gripped the reins and gave the lane ahead his full and fierce attention.

* * *

They reached the priory situated exactly where the strange Gypsy had told them they would, in the wee hours before dawn. Cassandra was exhausted, though she wouldn't let on to Jon. He would only worry, and there was nothing to be done about it. Making matters worse, her longing for Jon was overwhelming. She knew the reason he was keeping his distance; he'd made that chillingly plain. Nevertheless, she longed for those strong arms around her, that corded, muscular body holding her so close she could feel every throbbing nerve in him. Would he ever hold her again? Would she ever feel him inside her, feel his living flesh inside her, bringing her once again to that excruciating ecstasy he had awakened in her on their wedding night but not completed, leaving her unfulfilled? There was no time to ponder it. They had arrived.

Instead of driving the cart around to the stable yards, Jon tethered Petra at the edge of the stream in the pine grove, out of view of prying eyes, and proceeded with Cassandra on foot.

"Suppose he was right," she said.

"These are men of God, Cassandra. They will not turn us away."

"I am not worried about them turning us away. Suppose they are of the same mind as the peasants who set upon us?"

"Of course we shan't be so foolish as to tell them it is ourselves we've come about—not after what occurred at the inn. We are simply seeking information because of incidents that have happened at home, and because we heard that they have solutions to a problem of which we in England have no knowledge and are at a loss to deal with."

"Still . . ."

"The only thing we need fear is that there are none

among them that speak English," Jon said. "My knowledge of Eastern European dialects is sorely lacking. Stay close beside me and follow my lead. This is why we have come, Cassandra."

Even though it was still at least an hour before dawn, light streamed from some of the lower windows. Of course the priests would rise early. There was even a light in the adjoining chapel, which was where things would begin, so Jon steered her in that direction.

Several Orthodox priests were preparing for matins when they entered, but none spoke English. One, however, led them into the priory proper, and took them to wait in a well-appointed though sparsely furnished anteroom, probably for someone who could understand their speech.

It wasn't long before two black-robed clerics joined them. The elder of the pair, who introduced himself as Father Gurski, was the only one who spoke English. His companion, Father Kruk, seemed to understand the language but either did not know how, or did not choose, to speak it. He did, however, scrutinize them more thoroughly, or so it seemed to Cassandra, often speaking low-voiced in what she assumed to be Romanian. She found it hard to meet this priest's dark-eyed gaze; there was something unsettling in it.

"My rector at home referred me here," Jon said. "He gave me a book. It was lost on the journey. *Legacy of the Undead*—written by one of your own, a priest from one of the priories hereabout. I . . . I forget his name."

Was that a patronizing look? Cassandra wondered. Father Kruk was whispering in the elder's ear again. Father Gurski seemed unmoved by whatever his colleague said. Yes, that *was* a patronizing smile he'd fixed in place . . . and something more. What did it mean?

"You must know of it," Jon urged.

"I know of it," the elder agreed. "You have come a long way on the strength of a few words in an old tome."

"Many are . . . infected, and we are ill equipped to deal with the condition. Too old and frail to make the journey, my priest and mentor sent me instead."

"And your lady? Was that wise?"

"We are just newly wed," said Jon. "I could not brook such a lengthy separation."

"Despite the danger?" said the elder.

"I insisted," Cassandra cut in.

"She was in more danger at home than she might find here," Jon said. "Believe me, there was no other choice."

"Hmmm," Father Gurski replied. "There is no cure, if that is what you seek."

Jon fought back annoyance. "No, I am aware that there is no cure, but surely there must be something—some means of arresting it. Many are infected. The vampire Sebastian has corrupted many in Carlisle alone! Why—"

"Sebastian, you say?" the elder interrupted. "What does he look like, this Sebastian?"

"He looks like death," said Jon. "He wears the fashions of the day, but the clothes hang on him. He himself is no more than skin stretched over bones. Yet he is possessed of great strength and the power to cloud the mind. He also has the power to change his shape into that of a bat."

"*Sebastian,*" the priest murmured, making the sign of the cross.

Jon nodded. "It sounds incredible, I know, but you know the name?"

"We know it, but we rarely speak it aloud," said the priest. "It is one of many names he is known by. So *you* are the cause! We were well rid of him—of his menace, of his evil. We had enough just dealing with the minions he left behind." He surged to his feet. "And now you have brought him back to us!"

Jon's posture clenched. "We have come to rid ourselves of the evil among us," he said, "and to seek some means of help for those this creature has infected."

"Evidently you have done so!" the cleric said. "He plagues your land no longer. His ancestral home, Castle Valentin, sits high in the Romanian side of the Carpathians. In darkness for centuries, light now shines from the windows again. In the night, at the top of the treacherous mountain pass, the castle was all but invisible, forgotten, passed into the mists of recorded time—but no longer! He has followed you, young son. You have brought him home! Why are you so vital to him, hmm?"

"Because he knows I am his enemy, committed to destroy him."

There was silence while the priest considered—dark, deep, palpable silence, as cold as the grave. Father Kruk leaned close to the older priest. Though his lips moved, no sounds were discernible. Father Gurski's eye movements alone were testimony that he heard what his colleague spoke. Now and then his own lips tightened, keeping time with whatever Father Kruk was telling him, and at the end of it, the elder priest nodded.

Outside, the sky was lightening. Were these wary Orthodox clerics waiting to see if their guests could bear the dawn? Something was amiss. If only Cassandra could read it. If only she could read Jon's expression. He looked as though he was about to explode. His handsome mouth had formed a white, lipless line, and the muscles along his angular jaw had begun to tick. Though she squeezed his arm, and his muscles tightened beneath her fingers, his demeanor did not change. Should she speak up or hold her peace? Father Gurski made the decision for her.

"There is no help for you here," he said at last.

"And if I pledge to destroy Sebastian—what then?"

The priest's cold smile did not reach the rest of his face, and Cassandra's heart sank. "Come," he said with a wide sweep of his arm.

Leaving Father Kruk behind, the elder priest led them through a series of winding passageways over gleaming terrazzo floors that rang with the echo of their footfalls and up a winding staircase that spiraled freely into what seemed an endless ascent to a belfry. Jon helped Cassandra up on the platform, where two bells and ropes and wooden supports crowded the narrow space.

Again the priest swept out his arm, pointing through the arched aperture. "Look!" he said.

Only a small lip at the bottom of the opening stood between them and a sheer-faced drop to sudden death. Cassandra fisted her hands in Jon's greatcoat sleeve, holding him back from going too near. Following with her eyes the direction the priest's rigid arm indicated, it took her several moments to realize what she was seeing. All at once, she gasped. First light flooded through the mountain pass in a stream of rose and yellow and violet, and picked out the towering shape of a castle situated on the uppermost peak of one of the western slopes. It seemed to have been hewn out of the mountain itself, set back on a little shelf against the rocky mountain wall. She gasped again.

"Castle Valentin!" the priest said. "You are no match for that. You were no match for him in your homeland. He is a hundred times stronger here in his. Go home, young son. You are not welcome in Moldovia. You have done quite enough damage here as it is."

CHAPTER NINE

"Now I understand why the villagers at the inn were so well prepared," Jon observed, helping Cassandra into the cart. "I couldn't countenance it before, but now everything makes sense. *Sebastian*. He is far more powerful than I imagined if these here are afraid to speak his name."

"Do you think the priests know what happened at the inn?" Cassandra asked.

Jon shook his head. "They couldn't know this soon," he said. He gave a humorless laugh. "But they will before the sun sets again, I have no doubt—and will regret sharing holy water and oil with us. The shortsighted gudgeons," he added in a mutter.

"What are we going to do?" she asked, as he climbed up beside her. A rustling in the cart behind wrenched a cry from her, and they both turned to face Milosh, who poked his head out from under the straw, where he had obviously been napping.

"If you are planning to storm the castle, you will need help," the Gypsy said. "And my cart."

"You aren't going to gloat over our failure?" Jon asked.

The Gypsy shrugged. "What would be the use in that?"

"You might have spared us a wasted trip."

"I did try to warn you, if you recall. But you are of the sort that must see for himself, Jon Hyde-White." He gave a sly wink. "And also, if I hadn't let you go, we wouldn't have the holy water and the oil, would we? They certainly wouldn't have given it to *me*. We're not exactly on the best of terms, Father Gurski and I."

"You cannot seriously be thinking of going up that mountain?" Cassandra cried to her husband, bristling.

"I must," said Jon. "I was in earnest when I said I would kill Sebastian. It must be done in daylight—unless . . . ?" He turned to Milosh.

"Quite right," said the Gypsy. "He is an old creature, is Sebastian. He was made centuries ago. That name strikes terror in the hearts and minds of all who dwell in these mountains—especially the priests. He was once one of them. He cannot bear the light of day, but he will have minions protecting him who can—just like you and your lady wife, and like I can."

"Could we even reach the castle before sunset?" Cassandra queried.

"Not if we stand here the whole day," Milosh said, burrowing deeper into the straw. "Follow the road to the pass. Take the left fork. The road narrows to no more than a path. It is a sharp incline. Stay to the middle. It has not been much traveled for ages, least of all by cart or carriage. No one hereabouts would brave the place. The edge will be undermined by years of foul weather, and to hug the rocky wall you risk a landslide. The way is steep and difficult but not impassable. Go on, then."

"You said there was help to be had for our condition . . . that you have availed yourself of such help."

"I have."

"Do you not need to . . . feed?" asked Jon. The animal blood he'd consumed earlier had not been enough to satisfy him. His belly roiled, empty, but the sun had risen, and with it the lethargy that prevented feeding. It would be a long, painful day embarking upon such a difficult mission with the bloodlust upon him, and with Cassandra so close. The minute the sun set . . . No, he wouldn't think about that now. But what of Cassandra? Her feeding had been interrupted at the inn.

"I do not," said the Gypsy, jarring him back to the present moment. "I haven't 'fed' in centuries."

"If you are as we are, how is that possible?"

"All in due time, my friend," the Gypsy replied. "It wants the blood moon to solve that mystery. We have awhile yet before that event. Now, we must scale that mountain. You had best be about it."

"Walk on!" Jon called to the horse, meanwhile snapping the ribbons. The animal bolted forward.

They hadn't gone a furlong when the weight in the cart was suddenly lifted. Jon and Cassandra both turned in time to see a great white wolf bound out of the vehicle and disappear among the trees that lined the road, traveling in the same direction as they were headed.

"What do you make of it?" Cassandra asked.

"I do not know what to make of any of it," Jon replied. "How can he shapeshift in daylight? I cannot, and you have never done. How is it that he doesn't need to feed if he is as we are? I do not understand at all."

"And what did he mean about the blood moon?"

Jon shrugged. "I do not know. I've heard of that . . . something to do with a lunar eclipse—an atmospheric condition that makes the moon appear blood-red. We learned of it at university, and I have seen it once or twice, but I have no idea how it applies to us."

Cassandra was silent apace, and Jon studied her face in furtive glances. The priests were right, God help him: It was madness to have brought her on such a journey. If he had known for sure Sebastian would follow, he never would have. He'd convinced himself that he had no choice, but deep down he feared that trying to protect her might inadvertently have brought her to greater harm than he could ever have imagined.

Could Milosh, the strange, self-confessed half-vampire, be trusted? Whether he could or he couldn't, the Gypsy held the answer they sought, and Jon would have that answer no matter the cost. Which meant keeping Milosh close. Things were not going the way he'd planned, but maybe . . . just maybe . . .

Reaching the foothills alone took more than half the day in the rickety cart. There, a smattering of dwellings too sparse to be called a village was nestled in the valley at the foot of the peak that housed the castle. That was still a long way off. It would be madness to attempt such a treacherous climb with the sun descending; it would be full dark before they ever reached the summit. They would need to seek shelter for the night and begin the ascent at sunrise.

That they were abroad in daylight should have awarded them some measure of acceptance from people, but it didn't. It was chillingly plain that every stranger was suspect to these people. They shared an evening meal of what could only be described as a sausage stew and rich brown ale at a public house, then were shooed on their way by the wary publican before they'd scarcely finished eating. Inquiries as to lodging bore no fruit. It was soon clear that they were not welcome to stay anywhere in the vicinity—not even for the night, though it was just as well. They both needed to feed, and the memory of their last occasion attempting that in a public place was all too fresh in both their minds.

The sunset was spectacular. Jon had never seen the like. Fleecy cumulus clouds drifted over the mountain peaks as though impaled upon the rocky spires. Here and there, a gray cloud drifted over the white—a summer shower at a higher elevation? Evidently, for a rainbow of great beauty bowed through several tufts, and the air smelled clean and rain-washed funneling down the mountainside. Meanwhile, hues of rose, blue-green, and amber lit the white clouds' underbellies, and the underbellies of snowy-white waterfowl that had fled inland from the Black Sea and were taking shelter from the storm that had just passed. Jon watched the birds ride the zephyrs, gliding upward and sailing behind the highest peaks to disappear from view.

"How could evil exist amid such beauty?" Cassandra murmured. "It takes my breath away."

Jon frowned. "The clouds hide the castle altogether now," he observed, squinting into the blazing sunset. Then, all at once, it wasn't beautiful anymore. The flaming clouds appeared blood-red, reminding him that soon he must feed. Bloodlust surged within him, twisting his gut as if gripped in a human fist.

"Will we be safe in the open forest through the night?" Cassandra murmured.

"I'll not lie to you," said Jon. "It is not the ideal situation. As I've said, at an inn or in a shelter, Sebastian would need an invitation to enter. He needs none in the open. That is how he caught us both before. And perhaps it isn't only Sebastian. There are surely others. We have no idea what or who we are facing here."

"What of Milosh? Where did he run off to?"

Jon sighed. "I honestly do not know," he admitted. "He seems an amiable chap, and he has helped us, Cassandra. But his motive is suspect. I find that rather . . . ambiguous."

"Are we to wait for him? Suppose he doesn't return?"

"At dawn we press on whether Milosh has returned or not. He will find us eventually. We have his horse and cart, after all—and his clothes back there in the straw. He won't stray far." He scanned the immediate terrain. The sun had set, and with it every door, every window had been closed, and every shutter barred against the night. No lights blazed inside the few dwellings scattered nearby. All was in darkness—utterly still. It was as if the whole community held its breath for fear of drawing the creature Sebastian's attention.

"The sun has scarcely set, and look," Jon said, pointing. "Not a soul stirs. Not a light flickers. Not a sound breaks the silence. We needs must take cover, and quickly. And we must feed. I cannot bear it. The animal blood I have been taking scarcely satisfies. My hunger brings a kind of madness. I will not think clearly until the craving is appeased, and I must be clear-headed now, for both our sakes. This is not how I envisioned the journey. I was so certain that the priests—"

A suspicious flapping in the boughs above called both their eyes toward the sound. Overhead, the branches moved as if something had sprung from them. A sudden whiff of pine threaded through Jon's nostrils. In any other instance it would have been a welcome scent, soothing and evocative; now it flagged danger, and he took Cassandra's arm in one hand and the horse's reins in the other and started toward a string of darkened houses.

"Come," he said, "it is not safe here."

"Where?" she cried. "These people will not admit us."

"No, they will not, but perhaps their livestock will. I saw a barn . . . beyond that haystack there. There will be animals, and if there is a door we can bar we shall be safe enough—safer than here in the open."

Indeed there was a barn: a large one. The door was hanging half off its hinges, but it had a latch. Inside there were plow horses in their stalls, cows, goats, sheep, and chickens—far too many to attribute to one owner. It was obviously a shared barn that served the whole sparse community. The ideal place to unhitch, feed, and water their horse and spend the night.

No sooner had they entered than a swarm of bats streamed down from the rafters, soaring past them out into the night. Terrified, Cassandra rushed into Jon's arms. Unprepared for that exquisite impact, every nerve in him reacted. His loins lurched toward the soft thighs pressed against him as his manhood came to life. His hard-muscled chest clenched against the tightness of her breasts, full and round and malleable in contrast to his male strength. She leaned into the pulsating pressure of his sex and he was undone. The horse forgotten, he crushed her close, threading his fingers in the silk of her hair and taking her lips with a hungry mouth.

It was beyond bearing—beyond stopping. Her tiny hands fisted in the back of his frock coat, drawing him closer; the moan in her throat resonated in his. She was aroused. Her budding fangs grazed his tongue. The pressure as his own fangs descended shot him through with waves of passion hitherto unknown to him. This would be slaked by only one thing. He dared not feed from that swanlike throat—dared not succumb to the demands of his corrupted flesh that begged for the blood he could taste, that he had already tasted—but this need would not be appeased until he had drunk his fill of her, until he had completed her.

Whatever shred of sanity was spared him, whatever scrap of his former self still remained was what he called upon then. He knew it would be thus. He knew the minute the sun set the frenzy would begin—this frenzy that was shockingly sexual, this frenzy that ruled his mind, his loins, his very essence and the seed of his body.

Freeing his member from the seams that it challenged, he yanked up the skirt of her white muslin frock, wrapped her legs around his waist, and staggered over the straw-strewn floor until he'd backed her against the barn wall. Every instinct, every nerve ending in him begged for him to take her, to thrust himself deep inside her with mindless abandon. The look in her eyes—half-closed in anticipation, his name on her parted lips, reaching, expectant of his kiss—set his soul on fire. It would be so easy to take her. It was what they both wanted.

Instead, he leaned the bulk of his hardness into the perfect vee between her thighs and ground himself against the soft cushion of her sex. Clinging to him, Cassandra moved to the rhythm of his undulations, her body leaning, reaching, begging him to enter her, her head bent back in blatant invitation, enticing the fangs that would pierce the thrumming veins in her throat and release the blood Jon felt coursing there.

All at once her hands fisted in his hair, drawing his head down closer and closer to the curve of her throat, to the swell of her breast, which he had exposed in his frenzy, as she called his name again and again, keeping time with the palpitations of his sex grinding against her. Drawn to the hardened bud, his lips encircled it, his fangs a hair's breadth from the vein clearly visible just under the surface of that alabaster breast in the moonlight streaming through the wounded door at his back. Her body reacted. Her breath caught. His name spilled from her throat again in rhythm with the contractions he felt riddling her now, riddling *him*, until his throbbing climax paralyzed his brain but not the bloodlust.

She was not safe with him now. These urges were too great—greater than they had ever been. A climax would not bring release from that. It demanded satisfaction, and—his head reeling, pounding, throbbing with pent-up passion—he eased her down, a bestial howl on his lips, and reeled away to the back of the barn, where he fell upon an unsuspecting goat and drained it dry. Behind, he heard the chickens' frantic clucking as Cassandra skittered among them. She, too, had to feed. After a moment, the flapping, clucking racket grew distant and finally stilled. Overhead, a great barn owl Jon hadn't even noticed screeched, then spread its wings. It flew out through the gaping barn door, nearly grazing him as it glided by.

He would have to do something to secure that door. It was open again. And if an owl could get out, a bat could get in. Staggering to his feet, he dragged himself back past the stalls to where he'd left Cassandra, only to pull up short, his ragged heartbeat suspended as if caught in his throat.

Cassandra was gone.

CHAPTER TEN

Jon ordered his clothes and ran out into the darkness. The sky was aglitter with stars, beautiful and calm in stark contradiction to the chaos clawing at his raw nerves from the inside out, his numbed brain scarcely able to permit the thought, much less accept it. *She is gone.*

Screaming her name at the top of his hoarse voice, he plowed through the chickens now milling aimlessly about the barnyard, causing some to test their wings in awkward flapping failure rather than risk being trampled by the madman come among them. Feathers drifted everywhere. One bird lay dead and mangled. He smelled its blood before he saw it.

Again and again he called Cassandra's name until his voice broke. Staggering into the wood he loosed a cry that woke other birds and sent them pouring from the trees in all directions. Bounding through the blue-black haze deep into the forest, he staggered from one ancient tree trunk to another. His way was lit by fractured shafts of misshapen moonlight that filtered through the foliage and provided keys through the vines and bracken, gorse, woodbine, and pine scrub in his path and beyond. Mold and pollen spores displaced from the forest floor by his careless footfalls rose up, took flight, and sifted down around him like snow. The heady scents of pine and mulch and mildew rose in his nostrils, choking him.

Cassandra's scent was not among them. Nothing but the irate screech and hoot of an owl somewhere close by yet out of sight replied to his desperate cries in the shape of her name—for his cries were palpable, having shape indeed, and form and substance. It was no use; he lumbered back the way he'd come, praying he would somehow find her back among the animals in the barn.

Many more besides the chickens had strayed through the open barn door by the time he reached it. There would be hell to pay in the morning, when the villagers woke to the task of rounding up their goats and sheep, chickens and milk cows wandering the foothills—not to mention discovering a dead goat and chicken bled to the last drop. He dared not stay and face that, but he dared not leave, either, in case she returned. His addled brain was mulling that over as he burst back into the barn only to pull up short before Milosh beside the cart, tugging on his breeches.

"Where . . . the bloody hell . . . have you been?" Jon panted, sucking in the stench of dung and musk and barn smells with each word. The Devil take his heightened senses!

"Fine talk from a vicar," said the Gypsy, stuffing his blouse inside his breeches and shrugging on his suspenders.

"Almost a vicar," Jon shot back. "No more. It's sacrilege to say it."

"Get shot of those togs then; they'll earn you no favor here. Those whom you will deal with hereabouts shall know what you are without such trappings. They see inside you—into the soul they lust for taking."

"What I *was*," Jon snapped. "I have disgraced my office."

"But your calling has yet spared you much. When you are calmer you will see it. There is no time now for sparring. You seek your lady wife. You will not find her here."

"You know where she's gone?" Jon spoke through clenched teeth, both his hands fisted in the front of the Gypsy's blouse with little regard for the flesh beneath. He shook the man roughly. "Where? Damn you, man—*where?*"

The Gypsy pried Jon's white-knuckled fists away with frightening strength. "Where you cannot follow until dawn," he replied.

"The castle?" Jon cried, fully aware that he was beyond deranged. The Gypsy hardly deserved strangulation for this predicament. Nonetheless, he seized Milosh's shirtfront again. "Answer me, damn you!"

The Gypsy nodded. "I was just returning from there," he said. "As a wolf, I can go many places that I cannot go in human form—just as you can. I went ahead to scope out the danger, to know exactly what we are facing. I wasn't near enough to attack. He came out of nowhere, astride a horse—a phantom devil horse if ever I saw one, sleek and black, with feathered feet and a great black plume on its head . . . the kind the horses wear in funeral processions. The kind that pull the *coach da mort*—death's equipage. In a blink, he scooped her up as she ran after a chicken, and then they were gone. There was nothing I could do."

"Well, there is something *I* can do," Jon said. Shoving the Gypsy aside, he sprang for the door.

Milosh seized his arm. "You cannot go there now," he said. "It would be suicide. It is what he wants you to do. It is *you* he wants, not Cassandra. She is just the lure, the bait that will bring you. And he does not want to 'finish' you, Jon, he wants to kill you."

"He wants us both," said Jon, "and has done from the start. He never would have gotten to her but for me. He stalked me, knew my haunts, knew what she meant to me and that we met at Vauxhall Gardens—knew who it was he was taking when he took her down. He planned this!"

The Gypsy shrugged. "That may well be, but she is safe enough for now. He has a stable full of female creatures he has made. I have seen them: beautiful beyond imagining, soulless, empty shells of female perfection—hollow-eyed disciples, trophies of his bloodthirsty reign upon this earth. No, believe me, he has taken her to the exact purpose of insuring what you are about to do. She is just another filly in his stable. You must wait until dawn. You cannot hope to prevail against him in his domain, upon his own ground, at night. You will die, and then where will your Cassandra be? I know that of which I speak, and I will help you, but you must wait until the sun rises upon that mountain."

"So, is it my soul *you* lust after taking, Milosh?" Jon said. "Is that why you would dissuade me from going—to keep me for yourself?"

The Gypsy gave a start. "You think—"

"I do not know what to think!" Jon interrupted. "For all I know you could be in league with Sebastian. You could be one of his minions."

"I wish he could hear you say that," Milosh replied with a humorless chuckle. "But yes, it is time that I reveal myself. I have not lied to you, Jon Hyde-White. I am as you are—vampire turned vampire hunter, both in the same shell of a body. I salivate over staking Sebastian, shearing off his head, making an end of him for all time for the atrocities he has unleashed upon this land—upon me and mine—but I cannot do it alone. I have tried many times and failed." He strode to the wagon and swept the straw aside. "Have you not looked here?" he asked, raising a wooden spike in one hand and a mallet in the other. He threw them back down again. "What? Did you think they were for you? Hah! Do not flatter yourself."

"I did not look at all," Jon snapped. "I took you at your word, but there is something . . ."

"That 'something' is that the minute I saw you, I knew that between us we could finish the demon. That is why I helped you—why I help you still, though you do not know a whit about gratitude."

"Why me and not some other? Surely there are plenty of men with tainted blood whom you could enlist in your plan."

The Gypsy's hand shot out, and one stiff finger flicked Jon's clerical neckcloth. "This is why!" he said. "You have no idea of the power it holds—your 'calling.' Power against the vampire, against the revenant, and the undead. With my cunning and knowledge of this land and its people and your power—a power you have not yet even begun to tap, that you have no inkling of—we will succeed. But not if you do not put your trust in me."

"I want to know why you no longer need to feed," said Jon. "I want to know how you can still change shape, and in daylight. I want to know—"

"You are not ready to know!" the Gypsy interrupted. "Else I would have told you." He scathingly tapped his chest with a finger. "I will tell you when the time is right—when the blood moon is near, and when I decide you are ready for that rite of passage. You have much to learn, Jon Hyde-White. You are as green as the grass that grows on the steppes."

"Then you must begin my tutelage on the way," Jon said. "Unless you are afraid? Now stand aside! I am going to that castle."

Her worst nightmare become reality, Cassandra feigned a swoon, lying facedown across the saddle blanket in front of Sebastian as the horse galloped up the narrow trail that led to Castle Valentin. There was no saddle. Aside from the bridle and reins, and the tall, black, funereal plume the animal sported on its sleek head, it wore no other tack or trappings.

There was no use to struggle. She was no match for the vampire. Why he hadn't finished what he'd started with her already, she couldn't imagine. She must avoid his eyes and bide her time. Jon would come for her. But . . . that was what Sebastian wanted, she suddenly realized. She was the bait that would bring him, and he would surely give in and follow.

Her mind was racing. If she could survive until daybreak, there was hope of escape. She had no weapon to use against the vampire; the holy water and oil were still in Jon's greatcoat pocket. She would have to use her wits against this centuries-old demon from hell—this damned undead who had taken her first blood and would not rest until he had made her what he was. Praying that her seeming compliance would give her an edge, she all but shut her eyes as he dismounted at the castle, and went limp in his arms as he carried her inside.

A sense of utter cold rushed at her the minute they entered the towering double doors that would have been at home in a dungeon. Her eyes barely open behind the fringe of her pale lashes, she took note of every twist and turn in the empty corridors through which he carried her. She didn't see another person anywhere, but that did not mean they weren't lurking somewhere out of sight.

Torches in wall brackets shed the only light. Spaced a good distance apart, they caused tall shadows on the ceiling, on the walls and floor, which did indeed seem to have been carved out of the very mountain itself from the resemblance in both color and texture. A narrow staircase not unlike the one she'd traveled at Whitebriar Abbey spiraled down into deep darkness, and they headed down it to the lower regions. How would Jon ever find her here? There was a way to leave her scent for him to follow, but it was a dangerous way because it would also be noticed by Sebastian. She had to act now, before they'd gone too far below.

There was nothing for it. Praying that Sebastian had recently fed, she bit into her lip until it bled, then spat the blood out when he hefted her higher over his shoulder and rounded the last bend in the stairs. He seemed not to notice, just carried her deeper still into the bowels of the castle.

Finally they reached a large, circular chamber with alcoves around the perimeter. There were plenty of inhabitants here: rats. Dozens of the fat, brown, hunched-back creatures with long, ridged tails skittering over the cold stone floor every which way as he evicted them with his careless footfalls, lowering her down in one of the alcoves. There, he clamped antiquated manacles about her ankles and left her wall-shackled among the milling rodents.

Lying stock-still as the rats crawled over her body was the hardest part of her deception. Every instinct demanded a scream. She could feel it building in her throat, like a hard lump of something too large to be swallowed down, despite that the smell of their blood threatened her with the feeding frenzy. She eyed them hungrily. Some were as big as cats.

Cats! It was as if a lightning strike had awakened her fogged brain. She hadn't shapeshifted since that first time at Whitebriar Abbey, and that had been an involuntary occurrence, brought on by her hunger. Could she do it on her own, willfully? She scarcely gave it any thought. Scrabbling to her feet, she tossed down her spencer, wriggled out of her frock as Jon had told her to do before shapeshifting, shut her eyes, and visualized her animal incarnation.

Black at first behind her closed eyes; the image slowly turned to gray, then amber, then blood-red. Light-headedness came upon her, and white-hot pinpoints of light that threatened her consciousness stabbed at the image taking shape in her mind. Still she kept her eyes closed, though every instinct in her cried out for her to open them. Then, when she thought she could bear no more, a feeling of weightlessness came upon her. In a surging streak of silver light, she shrank and spiraled down into the shape of not a kitten but a sleek black cat, one whose hind legs slipped easily out of the human-sized manacles.

Yes! She had evolved. Large enough this time to hold her own against a rat, she scattered the group with a hiss, then bounded up the spiral staircase and through the archway into the castle proper. With her heightened sense of smell, she was now able to detect the blood of the creature that had nearly made her his consort. Her head held high, one front paw suspended, she sniffed the stale, fetid air that reeked of death and decay . . . but Sebastian's scent was not among the rest. As she was the color of the shadows, melting into them, she crept along in search of either the exit or a hiding place he could not reach. He would not leave her unguarded for long. With that thought to drive her, she slunk along in the deepest darkness in search of just such a place.

CHAPTER ELEVEN

"Do you carry *all* your belongings in this cart?" Jon said, picking through the garments in his traveling bag beneath the straw, while Milosh unhitched Petra in favor of a faster horse from among those tethered in the peasant barn. "Have you no community . . . no band to follow, like the Travelers we have at home?"

"I am outcast," the Gypsy said. "This cart is my home."

"I should think you would be applauded for the work you do."

"Men fear what they do not understand. Is it not the same in your land?"

"Unfortunately, yes. But people in my homeland have no experience with this. That is why we have come. I brought Cassandra with me fearing for her safety if I left her behind, vulnerable to Sebastian. I had little idea he would follow us so far."

Taking the Gypsy's advice, he was exchanging his black attire for the buckskins, Egyptian cotton shirt, and conventional neckcloth he'd brought along. It wouldn't do to venture into a nest of vampires announcing his calling, not when clerics were so prized.

Having done, he shrugged on his greatcoat and felt the pocket to be sure of the holy water and oil. Then, scarcely giving the Gypsy time to climb up, he vaulted onto the seat, snapped the ribbons, and the cart lurched forward again toward the pass.

Unburdened horses would have been faster, but they couldn't sacrifice the cart, and even though the new animal was more fleet-footed than Petra would have been, it was well past midnight and into the wee hours when they approached Castle Valentin.

They would not drive right up to the portal. Instead, they left the cart in the shelter of a narrow rocky ledge nearly a furlong below the mountain's summit, and continued on foot. They hadn't gone far when all at once tall shadows crossed their path, stretching across the width from rocky wall to sheer-faced edge—the long-legged, bushy-tailed shadows of a pack of wolves. But there were no wolves, only their shadows milling ahead in the moonlight and creating an eerie barrier.

The Gypsy's hand upon his arm pulled Jon up short. "Ambassadors of welcome," he said. "No, don't!" he whispered, holding him back. "He knows we are come. Do not step into those shadows! They will devour you."

"There is nothing there! How can shadows devour anything?" Jon asked.

"What made the shadows?" Milosh asked, still gripping his sleeve. "Just because you cannot see it does not mean something isn't there."

Jon reached for the holy water.

"No! Do not waste it. Use your powers."

"What powers?"

Milosh stared. His eyes were like two coals gleaming in the night, his lips a solid, stubborn line beneath his twitching mustache. "Your *gifts*, then, if the word better suits," he murmured through clenched teeth. "Jump over them."

Jon stared. "How can I jump that?" he argued. "Those shadows are three deep. I would need wings to—"

Before he could finish, Milosh crouched down, then leapt into the air. Jon stood slack-jawed, watched him soar over the wolf shadows and come down again a good distance beyond on the other side, landing, knees bent, arms folded across his chest, like a Russian dancer.

"That is how!" he said. "You have gifts you do not even know of, Jon Hyde-White—now, jump!"

Following the Gypsy's example, Jon crouched, sprang, and, to his utter astonishment, soared over the disembodied wolf shadows before falling to earth again somewhat less gracefully alongside Milosh.

The Gypsy's eyebrow inched up a notch. "Your form lacks something in the way of finesse, but it will do. *Look.*"

Jon stared, and the sooty black wolf shadows shriveled before his eyes and disappeared with a burst of blood-chilling howls trailing off into the night.

"W-what just happened here?" he murmured. "No man can jump that high. . . ."

"No man, yes . . . but you are not just a man any longer, you are *vampir*. You have no idea of your capabilities. You cannot be cured of them, so use them to your advantage."

Jon swallowed, staring toward the place where the shadows had blocked their path. Nothing remained but moonlight silvering the gravelly ascent. Cold chills raced the length of his spine, undermining his footing. Speech-less, he stared at the Gypsy.

"Remember what you have just done," Milosh went on, turning him back toward the looming castle with a firm hand on his elbow. "Sebastian Valentin has the strength of at least twenty men. You will need all of your 'gifts' before 'tis done."

"There are more . . . ?" Jon murmured.

The Gypsy only laughed.

Casting more than one furtive glance behind him, Jon stumbled on, his knees still tingling from the leap. He and Milosh seemed to trudge on forever, until finally the turreted castle towered over them, standing four stories high, carved in slate-gray rock and fortified with battlements and flying buttresses. A faint glimmer of light flickered within. The source couldn't be near these arched windows with no more breadth than arrow slits; the illumination was too diluted. Splintered rays beamed through the little amber-colored circlets in lead casings, throwing auburn puddles on the drive, if the path could be called such—it was so narrow that a coach would not have been able to turn around without risk of toppling over the precipice into the cavernous abyss beyond. Peering over the edge, Jon couldn't see the bottom; it was steeped in mist. He could not resist dropping a sizable rock over the edge. Leaning after it, he waited for the sound as it hit bottom, but there was none. All at once, a hand fisted in the back of his greatcoat dragged him back.

"You cannot jump *that* far," the Gypsy chided. "Come, we are expected. I can smell him. He is baiting us. If we can hold our own until daybreak, and can find his resting place, we can collect your lady wife, make an end of Sebastian and this travesty, and get on with the real business at hand."

"Which is?"

"Completing your initiation in the noble art of hunting vampires," the Gypsy said. "You have no idea of the scope of the work that awaits you. Come . . . we mustn't keep him waiting."

Casting a last thoughtful glance over the mountainside, Jon followed the Gypsy, their bootheels crunching on gravel the only sound during their approach to the towering double doors. From somewhere off in the forest that hemmed the ridge along the rocky wall, an owl's mournful hoot announced their presence.

"She is near," Jon said. "I have her scent. Very near. It is strong of a sudden . . ."

"You have mastered that gift, have you?" Milosh whispered wryly. "I have had her scent since we left the cart below. You will hone your skills. You will have to if you are to live to do the work. Yes, this initiation may well be your greatest test. Look sharp and pay attention."

Melting into the shadows that hemmed the castle's cracked and broken curtain wall, they inched toward the doors. Jon said no more. His concentration was upon Cassandra's scent.

All at once a swarm of bats swooped down from the battlements. In a steady stream they poured from the wounded crenellations and soared past where the two men had flattened themselves against the wall, then soared off into the abyss in a flapping fit of squeaking frenzy, their wings sawing noisily through the hot, still air.

Jon gulped. "Was Sebastian among them?" he queried.

The Gypsy shook his head. "Not likely," he said. "That was nothing more than another show of his capabilities—

a vampire glamour, meant to dazzle and intimidate. He taunts us . . . Come. Unless I miss my guess, the doors will be open."

Jon inched closer. He gripped the great iron rings and the doors fell open with one tug. The stale, fetid stench of death and decay rushed forward, and something more: rats—dozens of them, streaming past him onto the drive, a sleek black cat in their midst.

"Another show of force?" he asked, glancing behind. He looked again. The drive was vacant. Milosh was gone, his clothes in a heap against the castle wall. Then he saw the wolf—a real wolf now, and not a shadow; Milosh's wolf, white, with a silvery streak down its back. It pounced upon the cat, clamping its jaws shut on the scruff of the animal's neck, like a mother cat might do securing its kitten, then bounded off down the steep drive toward the ledge where they'd left the cart. The creature dangled limp, as if paralyzed, from his jaws.

This was no time for feeding! *Feeding?* Milosh didn't feed. Jon's heart sank. Could all that have been bluster? Was the enigmatic Gypsy no more spared the feeding frenzy than himself? Was the cat to be his dinner, despite the care he had taken to extract it? There was no time to make sense of that now. Cassandra's scent was overpowering, and he stepped over the threshold into what he presumed to be the Great Hall, which was so dimly lit he could barely see the wooden beams, grand ornamental columns and buttresses of carved wood supporting the vaulted ceiling overhead, replete with elaborate plasterwork.

His heightened senses were screaming. Easing the vial of holy water out of his pocket, he pulled the stopper with his teeth and held it at the ready as he parted the still-flowing sea of rodents. The first things that captured his attention were shadows. Reminiscent of the shadow puppet plays he'd seen performed in Drury Lane, whole scenes played out upon the walls. The shadow shapes of wolves roamed over one. Sebastian's emaciated form in ill-fitting clothes was unmistakably slinking across another. The creature was surrounded by female worshippers—there was no other word to describe the demeanor of the partially clothed figures cavorting about him in lewd postures.

Jon's heart nearly stopped. Was Cassandra among them? He forced himself to look. *No.* Air rushed into his lungs again. He wasn't even aware he'd been holding his breath.

Growing taller, the shadow shapes seemed to pulsate obscenely, but just as the wolves on the drive had been, these were only shadows, with no clear corporeal substance. As quickly as they had come, they slithered away like snakes to disappear in the darkness in the direction he was traveling. What did it mean—that the images were mere illusion, or that the wolves, the gyrating females, and Sebastian were there in the flesh, but invisible to him in all but shadow? There was no time to analyze. He flung holy water on the walls where the images had appeared, and staggered back as hissing, spitting steam rose from the splashes.

Screams and howls and blood-chilling laughter echoed through the musty halls, pulling him up short, but only for a second. A brief glance behind showed him no sign of Milosh, and he continued down the hallway, his eyes looking in all directions, half expecting Sebastian to materialize before him with every cautious step. Cassandra's scent was stronger here—not only her human scent, but

the scent of her blood. It was all around him—in *him*—
drifting through his flared nostrils. It was in the very air
he breathed. Her fragrance alone aroused him.

A broad archway loomed before him, and beyond, a
spiral staircase steeped in shadow led below. Snatching a
torch from one of the wall brackets, Jon held it high and,
taking silent steps, climbed down to a large chamber
wreathed with alcoves. One by one, he thrust the torch
into each, progressing slowly through what seemed to be
an antiquated dungeon. Each recessed space was outfitted
with various rusted iron restraints. After stepping into
the third as he progressed, he jumped back. It was occupied. A young woman—all eyes, as pale as milk, her fair
skin crosshatched with a tracery of feathery blue veins—
gazed up at him, moaning. She was shackled to the wall
by the wrists, her bare breasts gleaming in the torchlight
as she strained against the tethers.

Jon searched the floor for some means to free her. "Do
not fear," he said, "I will set you loose." He spun around
and held the torch high. "Are there others?" he asked. He
needn't have spoken. Several more similarly tethered figures on the opposite side shrank from the blazing heat of
the torch as he thrust it toward them.

"H-help me!" the blonde girl pleaded.

Jon returned to her, still searching for some means to
break her chains.

"C-come nearer," she said. Jon bent closer. "Nearer,"
the girl groaned.

But as he moved within range, she lunged, fangs exposed, with full intent to sink them into his chest.

Jon fell back out of reach and scrambled upright, mind-
ful of the torch that had nearly spiraled from his grip. Sebastian's creatures—all of them—their moans and cries

and blood-chilling laughter rang in his ears. A spurt of holy water from his flask sent the blonde skittering into the corner hissing like a snake. He should have known! He would have to harden himself against his compassionate nature if he were to survive here.

Cassandra's scent was overwhelming. Was she among them? Deliberately he forced his right foot in front of his left and staggered around the perimeter, his heart hammering against his ribs. Anticipation of the horror he would surely find—his Cassandra, become one of these, lost to him forever—nearly drove him insane.

He passed three more alcoves before he came to an empty one. No, not empty; something lying on the floor caught his eye. Ignoring the racket the vampires were making behind him, he dove for the scrap of white muslin cloth and blue spencer. He raised the cloth to his nose and inhaled deeply. *Cassandra.* And there was a spattering of blood upon it. He called her name, and it sounded back to him in an echo from every recess, every nook and corner. Standing in the center of the chamber, he reeled in circles, observing the voluptuous females shackled in their alcoves on beds of straw. They were beyond redemption. These were Sebastian's creatures, companions he had made for his eternal pleasure, and those of whom Milosh had spoken. Young bodies housing entities eons old—he smelled the age of them, as old as the grave, and saw into the empty shells that once had housed their souls.

So, this was his new calling—to bring peace to such pitiable creatures as these, whom Sebastian and his ilk had cruelly deprived of their eternal rest? Reminding himself that they were not human but the damned undead until he, or someone like him, sent them to their reward, he strode around the room touching his torch to the straw beds beneath them. Then, stuffing Cassandra's frock into his greatcoat pocket, he made the sign of the cross over the entire circumstance. Viewing the carnage one last time through tears that suddenly blurred his vision, he turned his back upon the sight and the screams and the leaping flames, and bounded up the staircase.

Was this what he would one day have to do to Cassandra to save her soul and give her peace? Would he have to set her afire, stake her to the ground or cut off her head, the only proven methods of killing a vampire? Would he be able to do it if needs must? The screams of these flaming undead he left behind in the bowels of the castle would stay with him for the rest of his life. He couldn't think about them or he would run mad. The godly and ungodly elements in him were tearing his soul apart, rending and shredding it. Then, with a sinking heart, he realized that any one of the poor creatures below could have finished Cassandra, turned her into the evil entity they themselves were. And how many more lurked in wait? He had to find her.

What time could it be? How long before the dawn drove Sebastian back to his grave? Where *was* his grave? How many of his minions were still able to tolerate the daylight, just as Jon was? He had nearly reached the archway above. Billowing clouds of black smoke raced after him like a raging sea. The stench of moldy straw and burnt flesh flared his nostrils and narrowed his eyes, but the fire would burn itself out in time, when there was nothing but stone left to feed it.

A bestial howl like nothing human he had ever heard stopped him at the landing. Before him Sebastian's shadow appeared—arms raised, greatcoat flared—but it was not Sebastian. Again, it was just a shadow, with no manifestation of the creature that cast it. Rage ruled its bearing, no doubt due to the carnage below. Jon thrust his torch forward with one hand and his holy water with the other, meanwhile teetering on the edge of the top step. Where was Milosh when he was needed?

"She is mine, *holy one*," Sebastian's voice sneered, booming out of the shadow. "You will pay for your work here this night!" Another howl knifed through the silence, then a rush of air like a flesh-tearing wind that ruffled Jon's hair and extinguished the torch in his hand. All at once, the shadow faded and the true creature emerged. It towered over him, eyes glowing like live coals, its head challenging the vaulted ceiling: a massive being two stories high with the upper body of a bat, whose unfurled wings spanned the width of the Great Hall, and with the legs of a man whose grotesque feet in place of toes grew talons. Hideous leathery scales caked with gray-green mold sufficed for skin, and were stretched so tightly over the creature's frame that the sinew, cords, and muscle tissue were visible underneath.

Instinctively, Jon thrust the last of his holy water at the creature, but it laughed, and with one swipe of its wing knocked the flask out of his hand with such force it spiraled off toward the doors flung wide at the end of the hallway.

"You will need more than the piddling few drops left of that to bring me low," the creature thundered. "Fool! You are no match for me!"

Behind, the indigo night had turned a paler hue. A ground-creeping mist had risen. Ghosting over the threshold, it reached them in seconds, drawing the creature's rheumy eyes.

"Perhaps not," Jon triumphed, "for you are no match for *that*." And he hurled his burnt-out torch toward the open doors.

Another bloodcurdling sound poured from Sebastian, whose head snapped around, following the torch's flight toward the doorway. The whole castle seemed to shake from the vibration. Then, in the blink of an eye, the vampire shriveled and was gone.

Jon spun every which way, seeking its direction. It had vanished into thin air. Dawn approached, fish-gray with mist. Behind, the clouds of black smoke had ceased to funnel up the narrow staircase; only trailing streamers remained.

Bits of ash rode the beam of first light that the morning laid at Jon's feet, pouring through the open doorway. He snatched up his empty, dented holy water flask from where the vampire had knocked it, jammed it into his greatcoat pocket, snatched up a fresh torch and staved through the castle, calling for Cassandra at the top of his lungs.

Whether Sebastian's remaining minions could not bear the light of day or had fled from him, Jon didn't know. He saw no other creature, though he searched the castle from the Great Hall to the battlements. He left no chamber unsearched, no door unopened, no crevice unprobed. Another staircase hidden behind a door in a recessed alcove at the back of the castle took his notice while coming down from the turrets. Gingerly, he made a silent descent, his torch held high. This was not a spiral staircase like the other. It was narrower, roughly hewn out of the castle wall, and it led to a subterranean crypt, where coffins rested on the mildew-slimed floor—a dozen of them.

One by one, Jon threw the lids back to find undead creatures—women mostly, naked or draped in flimsy grave clothes. The last coffin was empty. *Sebastian's.* Wherever the creature was, it was too late for him to reach it now. He must have others. Without batting an eye, Jon set it afire, and all the other coffins, steeling himself against the keening din of the creatures' screams as the fire woke them to their deaths.

Bounding back up the stairs, he pulled up short. Milosh's cart stood in the Great Hall, where the Gypsy had driven it in through the double doors.

"Cassandra is not here," Jon groaned.

"I know," the Gypsy said, climbing down.

"How the devil could you know? Where in hell have you been, Milosh?"

"Looking after your best interests."

"What? You hare off to feed upon the first creature that crosses your path and leave me here to deal with this alone? I saw what that creature really is. He revealed himself to me." He ripped the dented silver holy water flask from his pocket and brandished it in the Gypsy's face. "This is how much sway holy water holds over him! Is this your idea of a proper initiation? And you told me you no longer have to feed, yet I saw you make off with that cat. You lied!"

The Gypsy swaggered toward the back of the cart and raised a wide-mesh net sack. A hissing, spitting cat was inside, as black as ebony, its huge green eyes glazed over with an iridescent shimmer in the torchlight.

"*Cas-san-dra,*" Milosh enunciated, his lips crimped in an exasperated scowl.

Jon stared at the cat clawing at the Gypsy through the mesh, its fur standing on end, its long bushy tail swishing through the air.

"I-I saw you carry her off," Jon stammered. "I thought . . ."

"I couldn't leave her unattended in that cart with Sebastian's minions roaming about, and I dared not bring her back inside—she had clearly gotten away without Sebastian knowing. I had no choice but to leave you to your own devices."

Jon's beleaguered mind reeled back to the first time Cassandra shapeshifted. She had transformed into a kitten. This was a grown cat. Was she evolving? Cold chills riveted him to the spot. He recalled finding the little black kitten inside her frock lying crumpled on the floor in her chamber at Whitebriar Abbey. How had he not remembered that, when he had found her frock and spencer in the dungeon below? He must be going mad.

"Do not move from that spot," he said. "Now that I know she is safe, I must finish what I've started here." Spinning on his heel, he darted toward the landing leading to the upper regions.

"Wait!" Milosh called after him, setting the complaining cat back inside the cart. "Do whatever you must do quickly. She may not be as safe as you think. There may be a problem. It's been too long. She should have changed back by now. . . ."

CHAPTER TWELVE

While Milosh waited, Jon careened through the castle, from the Great Hall to the battlements, touching a flaming torch to every tapestry and drapery, every timber, column, buttress, balustrade, and scrap of wood—anything that would burn—until flames leapt from the windows and smoke filled the halls above as well as below. Last to be set ablaze were the great double doors, once they'd passed through.

"There is much stone that will not burn," Jon said, staring up at his handiwork, "but Sebastian will sleep no more inside the walls of Castle Valentin. I have burned his resting place."

"This is his homeland. His earth is everywhere. You stand upon the very soil you set afire in that coffin. Believe me, he will find another place to sleep."

"And evidently has already done. But he will not have *this* one. The frescoes, the plasterwork—all gone. The flames will undermine the rest, and much of what remains will be reduced to a heap of slag once the rains come."

"He will retaliate," the Gypsy warned. "You know that. We will have to sleep by day and be alert by night from now on until we finish him."

"Until *I* finish him," Jon corrected. "Sebastian is mine."

The Gypsy took another path, descending the mountain that led them in a more easterly direction. It was a steeper descent, with a thick pine forest at the bottom that seemed to stretch for miles and bearded another peak in the majestic Carpathians. Milosh was an excellent horse handler, but he was clearly struggling with the animal on the treacherous grade, and Jon shielded his eyes from the blinding sun in an attempt to get his bearings.

"Why are we going this way?" Jon wondered aloud. "We're apt to tip over at this pace on such an incline."

"We can hardly go back as we came," said the Gypsy. "It will be chaos in that valley now, and I have the peasant's horse, don't forget." He shrugged. "I will return it after dark, and have my Petra back, but for now, we must put some distance between ourselves and *that*." He gestured behind, where great clouds of ink-black smoke that had belched from the castle had obscured the mountain peak, and where long tongues of flame still spat out of the windows. "There will be much rejoicing in the village," he went on. "Then they will be careless, and more among them will be savaged. He is not destroyed so easily. How many of his disciples did you find in that place?"

"There were seven females in the dungeon, and a dozen more in the crypt. I . . . burned them all."

"They were not human, Jon," Milosh assured him. "You have given them peace—guaranteed at the hands of a righteous man. You have freed their souls. Do not reproach yourself. This is your calling now. It is what we must do."

Loud meows were coming from the sack in the back of the cart, and Jon reached behind to stroke the cat through the mesh. That earned him a deep puncture wound as it sank its fangs into his hand between his thumb and forefinger. He sucked in his breath. Yanking the hand back, he scowled at the animal.

Milosh laughed. "You are fortunate," he said, exhibiting his lacerated hands and forearms. "You have only one little bite. I suffered her claws. She is not happy."

"Suppose she cannot change back?" Jon asked. "There has to be something we can do."

"How long does it usually take?"

"I have only seen this once," Jon said. "As soon as I reached her, she changed back—but the woman wasn't a full-grown cat on that occasion, just a kitten."

"Ummm . . . perhaps when Cassandra is calmer. I have left her plenty of room in the sack."

Jon fell silent apace. He had so many questions, and this enigmatic Gypsy held the answers. More than anything, he needed to confide in someone he could trust.

"Do you consider that I have had enough of an initiation to be trusted with the truth?" he finally asked.

"I will share what information you are ready to absorb," the Gypsy agreed. "Granted, you have had an impressive indoctrination, but you have much to learn before I entrust you with all the answers you seek. In due time, my friend . . . all in due time."

"But that is just it: Time is running out. Cass is as she is because of me. I must give her the means to survive should something happen to me. At first I hoped I'd arrived in time to spare her the infection. Sebastian had just begun to feed when I drove him off. Clive Snow, the vicar I was to replace—the one who gave me that tome—shared some insights with me. From our talks, I presumed—or rather *hoped*—that Cassandra's symptoms would fade in time, since they were so slight, but I fear they are escalating." He glanced at the cat behind, still voicing its complaints. "Just the fact that when she first transformed she took the form of a helpless kitten, and now look! Does this mean that her infection is worsening? Can such a thing occur?"

The Gypsy hesitated. "I explained already, that book your mentor gave you is no great loss," he said at last. "What it did not tell you would fill volumes. There are no rules to follow. Nothing is set in stone, and each case is different. How the vampire's kiss affects one person is entirely different from the way it affect another."

"I was afraid such was so. But I am right. She is getting worse. . . ."

"She is getting stronger," Milosh corrected him.

"What is to be done? There must be something."

"You have made her your bride. You and she are one. You must be one in this also."

"I do not understand."

"You have tasted each other. Bloodlust will compel you until you make her one with you in the blood . . . until you feed from each other."

Jon gave a start. "That is the one thing I am struggling to avoid!" he said. "I cannot go near her once the sun sets, not unless I have fed, for fear of feeding upon her. It is driving me mad—that, and the fear that Sebastian will finish what he has started and make her as one of the creatures I torched in that castle just now. Now you expect me to finish what Sebastian started? No, never! That is madness—obscene! You would make a ghoul of me? I may have shed my vicar's togs, but I am what I am inside no matter what I wear—a man of God. That will not change, not even if He turns His back upon me."

"You wish to know the secret that has made me as I am? She must know it, too. If you are to be together, you must embrace the rite that it entails together as equals."

Jon shook his head wildly. "No. I could never," he insisted. "What if I should take too much blood and she dies? She would rise undead and I would have to destroy her. No!"

"Try to comprehend!" Milosh snapped. "You cannot do better than to make her what you are. Your bite cannot finish her making, because you are not fully made. Take her and she will be no more or less than you. You cannot give her what you do not possess. Leave her as she is, to grow stronger, and Sebastian will win. It is why he bides his time. He does not need to force the event. It will come to him by default, and he will conquer without putting forth the slightest effort. He, too, has her scent. He, too, lusts after her blood. And when he takes her—and he will, I promise you—she will become as *he* is. Once that occurs, it cannot be reversed. She would be as those you burned in the castle. Of all things suspect in this madness, this one thing is guaranteed." He shrugged. "But, if you would rather not . . ."

"Why is this not so of me?" Jon said. "It was Sebastian who infected me as well."

"Ahhh, yes, but I told you, none of this is set in stone. Pay attention! I do not like repeating myself. It wastes time. Each individual reacts differently to the vampire's kiss. That is why it is so difficult to destroy them. What works with one will not work with another. You rightly call your plight an *infection*; the makeup of a victim's body has much to do with the results."

Jon shook his head and brought his fisted hand down hard on his knee. "No!" he said. "I will not sink to that level."

"You can and you will. You must. If you do not, Cassandra's infection will increase until one day she will take you. There will be no way to prevent it. The bloodlust is unstoppable. It is stronger than the drive to live, the drive to preserve oneself. As I said before: if you would face the blood moon, you must do so together—as equals—because as you are when you take that rite, so you will remain for all eternity, so long as you are faithful to the ritual."

"How could you even ask it?"

"*I* do not ask it, Jon Hyde-White. I am trying to help you. I do not want to see you suffer what I have suffered . . . what I will continue to suffer until my dying day."

Jon stared. The Gypsy's eyes had darkened. Though he concentrated upon the treacherous grade they traveled, it was as if his spirit was elsewhere. It was a moment he was loath to intrude upon, but he needed answers.

"What happened?" he asked.

"How old do you think I am, Jon?" said the Gypsy.

Jon shrugged. "Forty? Fifty? It is hard to say."

"I became a vampire and ceased to age in the Year of Our Lord fourteen-fifty-three—after forty summers," Milosh said. "I knew Sebastian Valentin when he was Orthodox Auxiliary Bishop of Moldovia . . . long before he was corrupted. He did not make me. We were both made by the same creature, which I later destroyed."

Jon's jaw dropped. Could it be possible?

"I told you once that Sebastian killed my wife and child. In a way, he did, but I also told you it was my hand that sent them to their reward."

"So you said."

The Gypsy nodded. "I have not told this to another living soul," he continued. "I only tell you now to spare you what I have suffered, because you face what I faced then, and I see you on the verge of making my mistake."

"Please, go on," Jon murmured.

"Sebastian . . . infected my wife, and, like yourself, I arrived in time to save her from becoming one of his disciples. She was as your Cassandra—her condition worsened while mine did not. Like yourself, I could not bring myself to do the thing that had to be done. To make short of it, by not taking her myself, which would have prevented him, I left her vulnerable to Sebastian's evil, and he took her instead . . . finished what he'd started, made her his creature. It then fell to me to give her peace. I loved her . . . very much. She was carrying my child, when I . . . when . . . That was over three hundred and fifty years ago, and I still cannot speak it."

Jon swallowed, waiting through the silence as the Gypsy's words trailed off. Nothing he could have said would have eased the moment. When Milosh spoke again, it was with a tremor in his deep, resonant voice.

"It was then that I vowed to hunt down and destroy all the undead," he went on. "It became an obsession with me. My people were outcast in those days, driven from our homeland. For centuries it was so, and we migrated to the East for a time to the land of our roots to avoid persecution. It was there, from the holy men of Persia, that I learned of the Blood Moon Rite, and I embraced it. It was after this that I broke from my tribe. I had to; so will you from your peers. They will age, but you will not. I told you there is no cure, but I am living proof that there is help. I only wish I had known of it before. Well . . . there is nothing to be served in fondling regrets."

"Considering all that you have told me of your vow to stalk and destroy the undead, how is it that you haven't destroyed me?" Jon asked. "Aren't I a threat?"

The Gypsy flashed another smile that did not reach his eyes. "You are a righteous man who will not hesitate to hunt down and destroy vampires, even though you are yourself infected. You proved that at the castle. Your power will be greater than mine because of your calling. I must protect that. However, your lady wife must be taken in hand. I know Sebastian. He toys with his victims, but he soon tires of the amusement. In her innocence, she will blunder into danger, and she will be lost to you forever. Together, you and I can rid the land of many evils. Think on it . . . but do not take too long. None of us is safe here now, not once twilight falls and that demon wakes amidst a home and concubines reduced to cinder and ash. You must drink of her blood, and you must do so soon."

Did they think she couldn't hear what they were saying? Gudgeons, the pair of them! So, she must be "taken in hand," must she? She should have bitten the Gypsy's hand! How dare he make presumptions? Why didn't her husband defend her? Had she not just escaped a nest of vampires all on her own? Had she needed either of them to help her do so? Had she not just pranced right past him in the company of rats unnoticed? She swished her bushy tail, the hairs standing out along the length as if she'd been struck by lightning. Calm—she must stay calm if she were ever to transform back into human form.

She swished her enormous tail again and hissed at both men. The thick rope hurt her footpads. Milosh was right; he had given her plenty of room to shapeshift—it was a large sack—but there were modesty issues. Was Jon too dense to realize she would not change back in front of the Gypsy even though she had "plenty of room" to do so? She was naked, after all.

Jon had placed the frock she'd left behind in Sebastian's dungeon in the cart beside her. First one paw and then the other shot out as she tried to snag it with her claws. It was no use. Even if she could, she would never be able to pull it through the mesh; it wasn't wide enough. She voiced a loud complaint, followed by a guttural growl—not very ladylike, but very effective. It seemed to get Jon's attention. He looked back.

It was dark in the wood. Ancient trees crowded together let precious little light reach the forest floor. Darkness more green than blue made it seem that night had fallen, but it couldn't be night; now and then a glimpse of azure sky when the breeze parted the uppermost branches testified to that. The cart wheels crunching fallen pine needles and mulch made a calming sound, while releasing pleasant-smelling oils that perfumed the air. How soothing it was to breathe deeply. How bizarre that such a place existed in the midst of evil.

"Stop the cart," Jon said. "I've an idea."

"Eh?" the Gypsy grunted, reining in the horse.

"I want to try something." Jon climbed down. "Would you leave us for a moment—walk off a ways? Perhaps it isn't that she cannot transform, but rather that she will not change before you in her nakedness."

"Ah!" Milosh blurted, as if a candle had been lit in his brain. "You could have a point." Climbing down also, he tethered the horse to a sapling, sketched a bow, and strode off into the trees.

Had he read her thoughts, or had he come to that conclusion on his own? It didn't matter. Cassandra curled on her side, yawned, stretched, and surged to her full height in a silvery streak of motion that backed Jon up a pace. It was difficult, for she became lethargic in the daytime. Perhaps that was why she hadn't ever been able to shapeshift when the sun was high: Nothing had been so vital that she put forth the effort before.

His fingers worked frantically to untie the sack, which she now filled. Then, all at once, she was in his arms; those warm, strong arms. They were trembling as he showered her face, her hair, her throat with kisses, his hands roaming her body, probing, searching.

"Where are you bleeding?" he whispered, crushing her so close she could scarcely breathe.

"I am not," she said.

He snatched her frock, exhibiting the blood spattered upon it. "What is this, then? It is yours—your blood, your scent. I know it. It is part of me now."

She thought for a moment before she remembered. "Oh!" she cried, as recognition struck. "I bit my lip until it bled to leave my scent for you to follow." Were those tears gleaming in his quicksilver eyes?

Jon lifted her out of the cart, snatched her frock, and helped her into it. "I thought . . . I feared—I didn't know if you could change back," he stammered, crushing her close again. "You weren't harmed? He . . . he didn't . . . ?"

"No," she said. "It was you he wanted. I was the bait to bring you. Jon, I heard your conversation with the Gypsy just now. If I am willing—"

"We will not speak of that!" he interrupted her.

"But . . ."

"No, I say," he growled through clenched teeth. "Enough. What he and I spoke of is not an option." Turning toward the deep woods, he called to Milosh, who strode back out of the undergrowth and swaggered toward them. "We will not speak of it again," he went on, low-voiced, lifting her back into the cart. "Now we must away, while we still have the daylight to do so. God only knows what the night will bring."

CHAPTER THIRTEEN

Stormclouds brought the twilight early. Blending with the bilious remains of smoke still belching from the castle in the distance, they lent an eerie pallor to the imminent darkness. Milosh led them farther into the forest, to where a little mountain stream sidled through. There, all but hidden in the dense undergrowth of bracken, gorse, and ground-creeping vines, stood a small, derelict shelter so buried in the foliage it was nearly invisible.

"It was once a cottage used by shepherds," Milosh explained as they pried the woodbine away from the door. "But that was centuries ago, before the forest grew so tall and thick and close to the mountains. Our people used to camp here in later years. No one comes here now, except for me on occasion. It's quite a shambles, I dare say, though I have kept it up, after a fashion, over time. A board here, a roof tile there—I haven't been by in ages. It is not wise for such as we to stay too long in the same location. I have many haunts hereabouts. You will have yours also. Whatever life you knew before exists no longer.

The vampire hunter is himself hunted by his prey. It is a lonely existence. You are fortunate in that you two have each other, but in this one way there is no safety in numbers—especially where the heart rules the head. Distractions are deadly. You must never let down your guard."

"Is it safe here?" Jon queried, taking in the shabby, scarcely held-together appearance of the interior of what appeared to be a one-room cottage.

Milosh smiled his half-smile. "There is no safe place for us, Jon Hyde-White," he said. "But this is your schoolroom, I am your teacher, and that is your first lesson. How well you do we shall see once the sun sets."

"I will need to feed," Jon reminded him. "So will Cassandra."

The Gypsy nodded. "That is the only problem with this location. We are isolated, and you have too long fed upon animal blood. While there are plenty of deer and smaller animals in the forest, the nature of your . . . infection truly demands human blood. How long has it been since you have had any?"

"Not since I left England," said Jon.

The Gypsy shook his head. "Too long," he said. "You will grow weak and suffer all sorts of complications if you do not have what you need soon. We will have to address that." He nodded toward Cassandra. "And your lady wife?" he asked.

"I have never tasted human blood—that is, except for the time that I tasted Jon's . . . but only a little."

"Good!" Milosh said. "Then small animals will still suffice for you." He cast stern eyes toward Jon. "You—I have already given you the means that will help you until the blood moon," he said. "You need to give it thought."

"We will not speak of that," Jon said again, unequivocally, casting a wary sidelong glance toward Cassandra. "Kindly do not bring it up again."

The Gypsy raised his hands in defeat. "As you will. But you shall be alone together. I will not interfere with your privacy here," he said. "As I have mentioned, the cart is my home. Once it is dark, I will unhitch it, return the horse to the village on the other side of the mountain and have my Petra back. But before I go, I will wait while you feed."

"Cassandra should feed first," Jon said.

"I agree," the Gypsy returned. "The minute the sun sets Sebastian will be awake at the castle. She is no match for that demon. Neither are you yet, come to that, but that is a moot point at present; whether you are or not, you must be, if you take my meaning. Go with her into the forest while she hunts, then return her to me to keep watch while you feed—on deer, I suppose. Afterward I will ride to the village. If all goes well, I shall return by midnight. Then we shall talk."

Jon gaped. "Are you in no danger, then, that you can be abroad among vampires—especially now, when retaliation is a certainty?"

"I shan't deceive you: I am just as vulnerable to vampires in my state as you are in yours—or as you will be once you embrace the Blood Moon Rite. It is a deadly dance we hunters perform, like moths to the flame in our quest. Make no mistake, there is *always* danger of being set upon and drained to death. One must hone one's skills. But that lesson is still to come and there is no time to teach it now, so take no chances in my absence and let no one cross that threshold—no one but me. The undead come in many forms, Jon Hyde-White. Trust no one here now, least of all your own judgment."

Then the Gypsy settled down to wait for them to feed.

* * *

An hour later, Milosh was gone, and Jon and Cassandra were alone in the sparsely furnished cottage. A chair, a table, and a straw pallet were grouped around a crumbling hearth filled with fallen bricks and debris. Outside, soft rain was leaking through the trees. The only sound was the music of raindrops landing with hollow splats and trickling down what remained of the chimney.

Cassandra was exhausted. She hadn't slept in so long that she'd forgotten when last she'd closed her eyes. Now was when she needed to sleep, so that they could be abroad during the day, while Sebastian and his minions were driven to their resting places, but there were just too many things that needed to be addressed. Seated on the edge of the pallet, hugging her knees for balance, she studied Jon, who was pacing the distance before the all-but-collapsed hearth. Milosh had left them the cart lantern and tinderbox—resting on the tabletop alongside the flask of holy water Jon had replenished from the stream outside, it cast his tall shadow about the walls, where a tracery of vines creeping in between the gaps in the old boards had fortified the wood and all but covered them. Damp ivy, woodbine, and honeysuckle mingled with the heady scent of pine perfuming the rain-washed air. In any other circumstance this would have been conducive to sleep, but not tonight.

"What exactly does he mean about the blood moon?" she asked, having decided to begin with that.

"I do not know," Jon replied. "There hasn't been time to discuss it."

"He must have told you something."

"Only that there is some sort of rite that must be performed at the rising of the blood moon that will help us . . . that will make us as he is. We would no longer be slaves to the bloodlust. Though we cannot be cured, the ritual would free us to the extent that we could hunt down and destroy these creatures. He has yet to divulge the particulars."

Cassandra gave things some thought. Why would he not look at her? His eyes, shining like mercury in the lanternlight, stared into the vacant hearth. What rage drove him? He was gritting his teeth. It gave a jutting set to his jaw, where the muscles had begun to tick in a steady rhythm. How handsome he was, even in anger. She longed to reach out and touch him—only that, just a gentle touch to soothe whatever it was that gripped him. But while her fingers ached to do just that, she laced them together and hugged her knees harder instead.

"You are angry with me," she said, low-voiced, avoiding those mercurial eyes. Out of the corner of her own she saw his head flash toward her.

"How could you think it?" he murmured.

"I can see it in your eyes. I have displeased you. If I hadn't run out after that chicken—"

"You think . . . ?" He heaved a sigh. "I am not angry with you. I am angry that the feeding frenzy commands us. We are not ourselves when it comes upon us; not our real selves. You cannot be faulted for what is not in your power to control. This . . . insanity is for me to resolve, and I am trying to find a way to do that. I do not dare leave you alone, and I do not dare be alone with you. The sight of you, the *smell* of you—your very essence is driving me mad, Cassandra. It is with me, *in* me—the softness of your skin, the sweetness of your scent. I cannot take a breath without inhaling you, whether you are near or far. I ache for you and cannot take you. It does not matter

171

that I have just fed; when I touch you, the bloodlust comes upon me. I cannot trust myself to hold you in my arms, to make love to you. . . ." He let loose a bitter laugh, raking his hair back ruthlessly. "*Angry* with you? Hah! If it were only that simple!"

Cassandra surged to her feet and started toward him.

"No!" he cried, sidestepping her advance. "Come no nearer! My God, haven't you heard me?"

"I heard *him*, Jon," she said, stopping in her tracks and giving up all pretense. "Milosh. I heard every word. Do you not hear and see and know what goes on around you when you shapeshift? He said that you should finish what Sebastian started—that I would become no worse than you now are. I do not see why, if I am willing—"

"No!" he thundered. "If you heard that, you also heard something else. I cannot be distracted now. We cannot be at cross purposes here or we are lost, Cassandra. We must do what we came here to do, learn what we came here to learn so that we will be able to help others who are infected, and we must run to ground and destroy the creatures who threaten us. You must help me, and to do so you must keep your distance. Come . . . no . . . nearer. . . ."

"What are you saying?" she sobbed. "Will you never touch me again, never consummate our marriage? Will I never feel your arms around me? Your kiss? Speak to me, Jon. What is to become of *us* in all this? You cannot mean you will never make love to me. That is madness! What of the family we planned before all this began? Is there no hope of that now? Can we talk about it at least?"

"Not now," he said. "I cannot make love to you—not as long as it will put you in danger. Perhaps after the blood moon, after I have destroyed Sebastian . . . I-I do not know. I do not know anything except that I cannot embrace you now. I dare not, and if you love me, you will not tempt me. I will not have you on my conscience any more than I have already."

Tears blurred his image. "If I thought you meant to put me from you after we wed, after we have lain naked together, after you awakened me to pleasures I didn't even know existed, only to leave me unfulfilled with no hope for a future—I would let that creature finish me. I cannot live without you, Jon, not now, *not ever*."

She could not meet his anguished stare. They were within arm's distance of an embrace. He was clearly fighting an instinct to seize her. His hands were fisted and white-knuckled at his sides. His scent drifted past her nostrils: salty, clean, of the earth; laced with musk, with leather and lime and his own male essence; evocative, intoxicating. It aroused her. He was aroused, too. He made no move to hide it—or the fangs that had begun to descend, distorting the shape of his sensuous mouth. He was about to take her in his arms—would have done, she was certain, and she would have let him—if a knock at the door of the cottage hadn't turned them both toward it with a lurch.

It was a slow, steady knock, low down on the door, unceasing and methodical, as if delivered to the tick of a metronome. The hollow sound sent shivers racing along Cassandra's spine and raised the short hairs on the back of her neck. This was not Milosh's hand rapping so solemnly.

"Help! Help me! Let me in. . . ." It was the desperate voice of a child. The mere thought of a child abroad in the forest in the rain with the undead about set Cassandra in motion, and she bolted forward.

Jon did reach out then and seized her arm, jerking her to a standstill. He shook his head slowly, a finger over his lips, and whispered, "No! It is a trick. Hear how it knocks? It is undead!"

"It is a *child*," she whispered, resisting. "Can you not hear its voice?"

"Our foe makes no distinction between man, woman, or child, Cassandra. Let that creature in and you let in a vampire."

Again the knock came, and Cassandra tried to pry Jon's fingers from her arm to no avail. "What if you are wrong?" she argued.

"If I am wrong," he said, "then we do it no favors welcoming it here! Have you forgotten what *we* are? Either way, we cannot let it in!"

"Let . . . me . . . in . . ." the child's voice echoed, begging between sobs.

"Is there no way to be certain?" Cassandra pleaded.

Jon hesitated. "Do not touch that door," he warned before letting her go. Snatching the flask of holy water from the table, he tiptoed to the door and waited. The knock came again, and he jerked the door open a crack and flung some of the water in the face of what appeared to be a small girl, whose mournful wails quickly became shrill cries of pain. Steam rose everywhere the holy water touched her, and the child flashed fangs, her eyes glowing red, and recoiled from the threshold hissing and spitting like a viper.

Jon slammed the door, but not before Cassandra glimpsed other shapes moving doggedly among the trees—and something else. She gasped, and the sound caught in her throat. The child who knocked had disappeared! Was she a vampire glamour? Jon threw the bolt and leaned against the door only to vault away from it, for other knocks vibrated the wood. Cassandra reeled back and fell upon the pallet, her head in her hands. The knocks were no longer limited to the door. The cottage was surrounded.

"Now do you see?" Jon asked.

"What are we going to do?" she sobbed.

"There is nothing we can do," Jon said, "but wait it out. They cannot enter without an invitation."

"But the walls are shaking!" she cried.

"Shhhh, be still!" he cautioned. "These are Sebastian's minions. We have not escaped him. Milosh was right: He toys with us as a cat toys with a mouse. Do not let them hear you. They have sharp senses just as we do. Keep your voice down and try to stay calm. They will smell your fear. Milosh should be returning soon. He is accustomed to such as this. Ye gods, I believe he expected it! Why do you suppose he warned us not to let anyone in? I only wish there was some way I could warn him . . ."

Jon blew out the lantern, sat down beside her, and took her in his arms. His body was as rigid as stone. He had steeled himself against the lure of her closeness and was clearly struggling with it in a bold attempt to comfort her. But she needed that closeness; she was struggling with her own demons. She was *like* them, these creatures in the wood. Albeit to a lesser degree, she was nonetheless as they were, driven by the same cravings, the same insatiable bloodlust. The distended vein in Jon's throat was so close. She nestled her head against it—against the pulsating rhythm of his blood thrumming against her skin, listening to his life force. She could smell the blood in him. It was in *her,* and when aroused it rose to the surface, calling her, overwhelming her, tormenting her, demanding consummation. It was calling to her now, igniting the fever, making her heart race. Her budding fangs descended.

They were longer now than they had been in the past, long enough to feed. A surge of adrenaline all but crippled her. She ran her tongue across their hollow-pointed tips. No, she wasn't imagining it. Her condition was worsening.

All at once Jon's posture clenched. Did he know? Did he feel it, too—her danger? He must. How could he not?

He eased her back on the pallet and surged to his feet. Stripping off his greatcoat, he spread it over her. His hands were trembling as he tucked it close about her neck, and she snuggled into the superfine fabric. It was warm from his body heat, infused with his scent. She drank that in deeply, a soft moan escaping her throat as she burrowed down into a fetal position and pulled it closer still.

"Try to sleep," he murmured, pacing like a caged lion. "I need to think, and you are a colossal distraction that I can ill afford if I am to get us out of this nightmare."

"Don't leave me, Jon," she murmured, not knowing why she said it. She knew he never would. Not deliberately. Her fear was that in his fervor to destroy vampires he might inadvertently do something cavalier that would separate them.

He stopped pacing. She could barely see in the darkness, even with her enhanced vision, for the moon hidden behind the dense cloud cover spared no reflected light to filter in between the cracks in the boards, but she clearly heard his footfalls cease extracting painful groans from the ancient floorboards.

"What foolishness," he said. "How could such a thought even enter your mind?"

Her bitter laughter replied. There were tears in the sound, but none physically spilled. She was beyond tears now.

"I need to *think*," he said, as if he hadn't heard or extracted the meaning from that wordless reply. "If it weren't for worry over what would happen to you if I failed, I would go out there and make an attempt to put an end to that lot straightaway. Sebastian must have minions everywhere. The trouble is, we are still what we always were, Cassandra, we're . . . well, never mind. I'm thinking out loud. Pay no attention to me or to that out there. Go to sleep. All will pass with the dawn. There will be much to do then, and between the lethargy that the sunrise brings and the sheer exhaustion of not having slept, you will not be up to it."

Outside the knocking came and went in waves. Cassandra didn't fear it any longer. She was safe, cocooned in Jon's warm coat, wrapped in a cloud of his scent. Somehow, she slept.

CHAPTER FOURTEEN

"I thought I would go mad for want of doing something—anything," Jon said. "I couldn't unless I left her alone. Nothing has changed. It is just as it has been from the start, when I elected to bring her with me. What else could I do to protect her, to ensure her safety? I could not leave her, could not abandon her to God alone knows what. How could my conscience have borne it? And so I brought her, and still I cannot leave her alone, for fear . . . You are absolutely certain you saw nothing, no one in the forest?"

"No—no one," Milosh said. He had returned. The two men were seated at the table, speaking softly for fear of waking Cassandra. It was a small room, and voices carried—especially agitated ones. "But this does not surprise me," the Gypsy went on. "It was a show of force. Sebastian mocks you. He tells you that you have not hurt him with the piddling few servants you destroyed at the castle. He has many, many more at his disposal, from all walks of life and of every age. It was a shock, no doubt—

seeing this child—but it is a grim reality. Now you know why I told you to admit no one, Jon Hyde-White."

"Another lesson?"

"As it turns out, yes. But I did not prepare it for you; Sebastian did. The undead left the forest long before I returned. They knew I would destroy them, and Sebastian does not want that. He wants to win, to savor this—to draw it out as long as he can before he adds your life to his trophies and makes your lady wife his own."

"You said there was help to be had. I would hear of this . . . help. Soon I will not have to wait for creatures like those to bring me low; Cassandra will do it. I shall go mad if this goes on much longer, God help me. . . ."

"There is help, if you will but listen."

"Tell me, then!"

"You trust me?"

"I have no choice," Jon said through a humorless laugh.

"At least you are honest."

"I am counting upon you being honest as well, Milosh. There is too much at stake for treachery now."

The Gypsy nodded. "You have my word. I am not pleased overmuch by the little seed of doubt that still remains in you after all we have been through together in our short acquaintance but am confident that I can put those doubts to rest. I have not harmed you or your lady wife thus far, have I?"

"No, no, but neither have *they*. Yet."

The Gypsy studied him for a long moment. "Do not put me in the same company," he said at last, velvet-voiced, though the words had an edge. "I can understand why you view me with suspicion, but keep in mind that I chose you because through all the centuries I have roamed this land with this curse as a millstone 'round my neck, through all that I have suffered, I can count upon the fingers of one hand those brave souls who could not be turned. You are one. Despite the infection in you and that girl there, you still have the will to resist—the will to hunt down and destroy the very thing you have become. Most infected have become mindless servants by now. Instead, you live in a half-state, your infection halted by your will. Have you no inkling of the rarity of that, of the power? The trouble is that your will . . . that stubborn will is going to lead you to your death unless it is cultivated. My methods may seem bizarre, but I ask little when you look at your gain at the end of my tutelage. So! Think of me what you will. Soon the blood moon rises, and if all goes well, that narrow mind of yours will see the truth."

Jon stared at him. "The blood moon. Let us begin with that."

"First a few simple truths," the Gypsy said. "You will not like hearing this, but it must be said . . . regarding the thing you do not wish to speak of."

"Go on then. Say it if you must, but you waste your breath. My position is clear."

Milosh nodded. "You have wed Cassandra, but she does not belong to you. She is Sebastian's creature, needing only to be fully made to become his consort. She will remain his creature until someone else takes more of her than he has done—then she will become that vampire's. It is the way of the curse. If you were to make her your creature, you would override Sebastian's power. It would be beneficial to her. She would no longer be as much a victim. Her strength, her powers of awareness would be heightened further. It would elevate her powers to your level. You would no longer need to hover over her as you do. If you would truly be one with her, you must rethink your position. When the time comes, and it will, it would do you well to remember this if nothing else."

Jon made no reply. He would not commit to anything, but he did not like the truths the Gypsy presented. He could not countenance the thought of Cassandra being Sebastian's. It made his blood boil.

"You have seen the blood moon?" Milosh went on seamlessly, as though he hadn't expected any answer.

Jon nodded. "It was explained to me at university as being a phenomenon of a lunar eclipse."

"Yes," Milosh said, "but it is more than that, and it occurs at other times besides the eclipse, though that is what we deal with for the initial rite. It is the Vampire's Moon, called that for its blood-red color, and not without good cause, because it holds a well-kept secret—the power to arrest the 'infection.'"

"I do not understand," Jon said, his brows knit in a frown. "How can the moon—"

"The moon has phases, does it not?" Milosh interrupted him.

"Well, yes, but—"

"Does it not rule the tides? Does it not make men run mad?"

"I suppose, yes, but—"

"Ah. You want a scientific explanation? Blood is the 'tide' that rules a man's existence. It is eighty-three percent water. If you are aware—if you *let* yourself—you will feel the pull of the blood moon upon you when the ritual begins. Harness that power, Jon, and you can arrest the bloodlust and quell the feeding frenzy."

"How do I harness it?"

"Not easily," admitted the Gypsy. "But it can be done. I have done it, and I have none of the strength your calling requires. It takes great will. There are herbs that must be gathered, steeped in holy water, and that liquid must be drunk when the blood moon rises. It must be drunk in the open from a hill or a mountain peak, with naught between you and the moon but open air. The atmospheric particles in the earth's shadow that give the moon its redness create the phenomenon; this is one of the mysteries of the universe. *Your* shadow is a part of the earth's shadow, too—part of that substance that turns the blood moon red, if you will. That shadow must not be broken, and the eclipse must be viewed with nothing in between to sever the connection. You will be vulnerable to the enemy, but if you succeed, while you will not be cured, the bloodlust will no longer rule you. You will be as I am . . . so long as you repeat the rite once each year when a full moon rises. It need not be a blood moon thereafter, though there is greater power in such a moon. Now, I must warn you—the rite will not make you immune to the vampire's kiss, Jon. The undead will still be able to corrupt you and believe me they will try. This is the best that I can offer, my friend."

"What are these herbs that I must gather? Where can I find them?"

"Borage grows here in this wood. Since time out of mind it has been used to cleanse the blood of poisons and as an antidote for the bite of rabid animals. Brew a handful of the leaves. Broom grows in the rocky foothills—get enough of their tops to fill the well of your cupped palm, likewise steeped. Milk thistle—the hearts of several plants as well as the seeds are needed. You will find them in pastures. Rue you will gather in the mountains. Steep the fresh leaves and use them sparingly; it is stronger than all the rest. You will need skullcap, called mad-dog-weed by some. You will find it by the stream. Steep the whole herb. Last but not least is barsa weed, a cress that lives in the stream, the most important ingredient of all. It is the catalyst that binds the lot. Without it, the draught is useless. These all may be steeped together, then strained, and the liquid drunk. I will write the proportions down for you. They must be exact. There is no margin for error. A warning: This concoction is a poison that will counter the other poison in your blood. It's somewhat like an antidote, but more of a preventative. It would kill an ordinary man, and you will at some point believe that you are dying from the dose, but you will not, though you will have visions . . . some of them frightening. These will pass."

"I am not skilled at identifying the different species of herb," Jon said. "Skullcap and rue I know, but the others . . ."

"I am," said a quiet voice from the shadows. Both men's heads snapped toward Cassandra, who was swinging her feet to the floor. "My mother kept a kitchen garden. Her herbal cures were legendary in Cornwall. Doctors came to her for their medicines. I helped her gather the herbs."

"You're sure?" Jon said.

"I've seen broom on the rocky hillsides hereabouts," she informed them. "Its leaves are tiny, oval-shaped. It has yellow flowers shaped like peas that give off a strong, sweet fragrance. My mother used to make a distillation of perfume from them. It was much sought after by the local aristocracy, and brought a fine price. I saw milk thistles in a pasture near the inn. The leaves are gray, with silvery-white veins. The flowers have purple tops, with prickly bottoms. There are skullcap plants growing right out by the stream. One can hardly miss their brilliant blue flowers. They are soft as down and rather large, and barsa weed grows thick beneath the water. Will that do?"

"Most impressive," said Milosh, with a nod of admiration.

"How much have you heard?" Jon asked.

"I've been listening with much interest since you began," she replied.

"Why didn't you make us aware that you had awakened?"

"What? And have you sneak off and have your conversation out of my hearing? I won't be 'spared,' Jon. Like it or not, I am part of this madness. I will do my part."

"How long before the blood moon rises?" Jon asked the Gypsy.

"Less than a sennight," Milosh replied. "But you cannot pick the herbs ahead of time. They must be fresh, with the dew still upon them."

Jon nodded. "In the meanwhile?"

"You sleep by day, feed how you will, and guard against the creatures of the night once the sun sets. It will be difficult. You can be sure Sebastian also knows when the blood moon will rise."

"Will *he* not try to avail himself of the rite?" Cassandra asked.

Milosh shook his head. "He cannot, and he is fiercely jealous of that. He is undead. It is too late. Once fully made, a vampire cannot alter his fate. The Rite of the Blood Moon is only for those like yourselves, whose final transformation is incomplete. He will try to prevent you, just as he tried to prevent me—more so you, Jon, because of your calling. I cannot help you in the physical sense, but can only arm you with the means. This is a rite of passage you both must make on your own, just as I made it in the wilds of Persia where my mentor instructed me. I did not have the immunity to holy water that you both do, and I suffered nearly to the point of death. It will be likewise hard upon you, dear lady, since you do not have the protection Jon's vocation affords him—you may as well know that now."

From somewhere far off, a cock crowed, heralding the dawn. The sound raised hairs on the back of Jon's neck. Ghost-gray streamers had begun seeping through the cracks in the old wall boards, throwing thin beams of light on the dirty floor. Dust motes rode the slender shafts up and down, as if they had a purpose.

"Is it safe to go out?" Cassandra asked. "I would dearly like to refresh myself beside the stream."

Milosh threw the bolt and cracked the door ajar. Jon and Cassandra crowded close for a look at the morning. The rain had ceased, except for hollow splats as latent drops dripped from the uppermost boughs. A ground-creeping mist blanketed the forest floor, where the cool, rain-washed air met the warm ground. Entering the cottage, it groped their ankles like curious fingers.

Milosh threw the door open wider, taking a deep breath of the morning air. "It is safe," he said. "Refresh yourselves. We leave within the hour."

"Leave?" Jon said. "Why?"

"To find another shelter," the Gypsy said. "It is not wise to stay too long in one place."

Jon shrugged. "What does it matter, if Sebastian will find us anyway?"

"Why should we make it easy on him, eh? I have another place in mind. Go and refresh yourselves while I hitch Petra to the cart. We have much ground to cover before sunset, and you two must rest, too. Time always flies when one wishes it would stand still."

The water trickling over smooth, moss-covered stones in the stream was cool against Cassandra's skin. Squatting at the mossy bank, she let the ripples trickle and flow over and around her splayed fingers. How good it felt! What she wouldn't give to immerse her whole body into that sparkling clean water, to feel the swaying barsa weed between her toes. If only it wasn't so shallow.

She cupped some in her hands and drank, then drank again. She could not get her fill. Unbuttoning her spencer jacket, she splashed some water on her face, on her throat and chest and the back of her neck, but it couldn't wash Jon's words from her mind. If only she had stayed asleep, wrapped warm and safe in his greatcoat. If only she hadn't eavesdropped. But then, perhaps it was best that she had.

Rocks lined the far bank. Above, a shaft of light stabbing through the trees struck the water. It projected shimmering reflections of spangled gold on the jutting boulder overhanging the flow, as though a hundred fairy lights gleamed there. It was an enchanted moment, made more so when a spotted fawn crept close to drink. Cassandra's heart warmed to the sight, until she realized that if it were night, she would be stalking the creature to feed. Chills riddled her spine and her posture collapsed. Across the way, lit in the golden sunlight, the animal looked up. The instant their eyes met, it fled.

Cassandra dropped her head into her hands. She was too exhausted to cry, though she ached to do so, and dry sobs leaked from her throat, bringing Jon on his way back to Milosh and the cart. Before she knew what had happened, her husband had lifted her up and she was in his arms. The rich, musky scent of him filled her nostrils, dizzying her. She inhaled deeply. What was he saying? She scarcely heard. Her own nagging thoughts possessed her then, drowning out whatever words those lips were forming. It was as if she had suddenly gone deaf.

"Why did you marry me?" she asked, gazing up into his quicksilver eyes. She almost gasped. Golden reflections of dappled sunlight on the water glowing on the boulder by the stream danced in those eyes as well. He looked nonplussed. Evidently her words had naught to do with what he was saying. "Why, Jon?" she persisted. "Was it out of obligation? You didn't have to, you know. . . ."

"What are you talking about?" Jon said. "I love you, Cassandra. That is why I married you."

"You needn't pretend. I heard what you said to Milosh," she confessed. "You feel responsible for what happened to me. You are not at fault. How could you think it? You needn't have martyred yourself. I'm holding you back."

"Where is this coming from?" Jon demanded. Gripping her upper arms, he shook her none too gently. "I've held you in my arms. You have *felt* why I married you, Cassandra, and once we settle this I will make love to you. My life will live inside of you and there will no longer be room for doubt."

"You said you brought me along because your conscience wouldn't countenance leaving me behind."

"You've twisted what I said," he insisted. "Eavesdroppers never hear favorable accounts and inevitably misunderstand what they do hear. 'Tis true, my conscience would never have allowed me to leave you behind—because *I love you*. What worries me most is that in bringing you on this mad journey, I have inadvertently put you more directly in harm's way than if I'd come alone."

"Well, then, how have I 'twisted' the benefits he spoke of if you were to finish what Sebastian started in me? I should think you would jump at the chance to have my 'sense of awareness' heightened—to have a partner on equal footing instead of a bewildered, bungling ninny hammer. Am I not useless as I am?"

Jon shook her again. "Do you have any idea what you are asking of me—what such a thing entails?"

"Jon . . ."

"No! And neither do I!" Jon gritted out through clenched teeth. His glance flitted over her face, his eyes flashing wildly; she could scarcely bear to look into them. "All we have is Milosh's word that these things are so," he went on. "We also have his word that the condition affects each victim differently. With all due respect, he cannot get inside my skin. He has no idea what demons I fight to keep from ravishing you, from drinking your blood when the hunger comes upon me. I fear that once I start to drink, I may not be able to stop—and who really knows how much you can lose and still not die in my arms? What works for another might not work for you. There is no way to be certain. Even *he* says this madness affects each of us differently. You want me to take that chance?"

"I am willing to chance it," she intoned.

Jon hesitated. "Suppose I were to take too much? You would die, Cassandra, and worse still, rise up undead—damned for all eternity."

"And if you do not, the day may still, come that you will have to do to me what you did to those creatures in the castle. You heard Milosh. I am getting stronger. Are you willing to take the chance by doing nothing?"

Tears blurred her vision. She could almost feel the heat of the torch, the searing tongues of flame setting fire to her flesh, the wooden stake driven through her heart. Her mind's eye visualized a blade swishing through the air, dead aim upon her neck. Which method would he use? Which would be the most merciful . . . the most effective? Such thoughts were more than she could bear, and she broke his hold upon her with a shove that never would have budged him if it were night, and bounded back through the forest toward the cottage.

CHAPTER FIFTEEN

The lethargy that always came with the dawn somehow seemed more severe to Cassandra after her dust-up with Jon. Curled on her side in the soft hay in the wagon, like a child in its mother's womb, she shed her tears in silence. Jon, too, felt the pull of the lethargy. She could see it in his borne-down posture, which cried defeat. Had her words struck a chord; had they meant something to him? Had she driven a wedge between his reason and his stubborn resolve? She stared at his strong, broad back straining the dusty superfine fabric of his greatcoat, longing to reach out and touch him. Would he turn and give her some sign of comfort, some evidence of softening, or would the muscles in that rigid back tense beneath her fingers? She would not test it.

Though the air was cooler in the higher elevations, he hardly needed such a coat. She knew why he wore it. It held his weapons, kept them at his fingertips: the dented flask of holy water, the sacramental oil, and the pistol. Just the thought of the pistol set loose a flurry of shivers racing along her spine. Her body shifted with the motion, but Jon didn't seem to notice. Neither did Milosh. The repositioning of her slight weight was lost in the swaying of the cart as it meandered south at a leisurely pace over rough gravel that couldn't quite be called a road for the disuse that had reduced it to a ribbon of slag at the foot of the mountain that, over time, pebbles, rocks, and earth had all but obliterated.

Jon wasn't as lethargic as she. But then, he was a man, and besides, these things varied among the infected; Milosh had been right about that. He and Jon talked in hushed whispers—light banter and tentative plans for reaching a cave the Gypsy knew of, which she couldn't imagine being a suitable place to spend the night. What would keep Sebastian out? And didn't bats frequent caves? It didn't bode well.

They had nearly reached a bend in the path, a crossroads where Milosh said they must take the north road up yet another mountain peak to settle into the cave he'd spoken of, when the Gypsy reined in his horse and the cart gave a lurch as it rolled to an abrupt stop. Three men and a woman were burying something at the crossroads. They hadn't seen the cart. Motioning Jon and Cassandra to silence, Milosh jiggled the reins and urged Petra to the side of the path where they could watch unobserved from the trees.

Cassandra sat up and peered over the side of the cart. "What is it?" she asked. "What's happening there?"

"Shhh!" Milosh warned. Jon reached around and gripped her shoulder. It was the physical contact she'd so longed for since they'd had words earlier. It didn't matter that it came in the way of censure; his touch was enough. Fresh tears pooled in her eyes. She could barely see the scene taking place at the juncture of the roads. "They bury one of their dead," the Gypsy explained.

"Why here, where the roads cross, and not in a cemetery?" Cassandra queried. "Surely you have graveyards about. Are they so full that they must bury their dead along the highways?"

The Gypsy hesitated. "It could be a suicide . . . or it could be a suspected vampire. It is custom here to bury such at a crossroads, to confuse the corpse should it rise."

Cassandra shuddered under Jon's steady hand. "You mean to say they would deny a poor soul the benefit of consecrated ground on suspicion alone?" She was incredulous.

The Gypsy smiled. "Here in the Carpathians there is little room for doubt, lady," he said. "If that poor soul has been dragged from some village to such a burial, you can rest assured that there is cause. In these parts, little is needed to condemn a man, woman, or even a child. Suicides, those who have eaten the flesh of an animal killed by a wolf, those who have died violently, or a corpse which a cat has jumped over, walked over, or in any way breached its coffin—these things are only a few telltale signs. This case is one of those, you can be sure. See how the woman pleads with the men? She is no doubt begging them not to desecrate the body."

"But surely these are superstitions, not fact," Cassandra persisted.

Again the Gypsy smiled. There was no humor in the expression; it stopped as it always seemed to, at his lips, and never touching his eyes. "Dear lady, whether it be superstition or fact, vampires live in these mountains. I know, for I am one, just as you are also." He pointed. "Look . . ."

Cassandra squinted through the trees toward the chilling ritual taking place. At the crossroads the men had indeed dug a grave, while the female mourner wailed her laments and knelt on the ground beside the deep hole. The coffin was lowered, and then pelted with pebbles scooped up from the road.

After retrieving the ropes, the men began shoveling earth on top of the coffin, extracting more pitiful moans from the woman crumpled on the ground beside them. Jon's hand slipped away from Cassandra's shoulder. She felt cold with the firm pressure of those comforting fingers removed, though he did give the shoulder a gentle squeeze as he went.

One of the men began tamping down the newly made mound of dark earth—a telltale sign that a body lay beneath—and covering it over with sod, while another coiled the ropes and placed them in a wagon waiting at the side of the road. Sobbing in sorrow, the woman scrabbled up and ran off, her mournful wails living after her.

The third man took a sack from under the wagon seat and began strewing the nearby ground with its contents. Starting at the head of the grave, he strode completely around it, scattering what looked like black dust. He then walked off behind the wagon as the others drove away, strewing the dustlike particles in the manner of a farmer sowing seeds.

"What is that man scattering?" Jon asked, craning his neck for a clearer view.

"Poppy seeds," Milosh said. "There is your proof, Jon Hyde-White. The woman evidently persuaded those gravediggers to leave the body intact—it's her husband, probably. As an alternative, they have strewn poppy seeds about the grave. Vampires are compulsive beings. If that corpse does rise, it will be compelled to pick up every last one of those seeds before it can move on. They circled the grave to cause confusion. If they have spread enough of the seeds about, the sun will rise before the vampire has completed the chore, driving it back into its grave or killing it if it is of the type that cannot bear the light of day."

"Can this actually work?" Jon said.

"It is a widely practiced ritual hereabouts," Milosh replied. "Have you not seen the poppies that grow in profusion in the foothills and over the steppes? Now that you know, if you take notice, you will find nearly all those at crossroads. It has been known to work in some cases. Did you not see them pelting the coffin with pebbles?" He didn't wait for a reply. "That is another ritual."

Cassandra squinted toward the sky, where the sun had begun to sink. Where had the time gone? It seemed as if they had just set out, but now twilight wasn't far off. Together, they watched until the burial party was no longer in sight, then Milosh clicked his tongue and snapped the reins, bidding Petra to walk on. The horse pranced its feathered feet in place before bolting forward and pulling the cart back onto the path.

"Soon it will be dark," Milosh said. "There is no time to spare. We have work to do."

Cassandra swallowed as the cart lumbered again toward the crossroads. But surely he couldn't mean to . . .

The cart rolled to a stop beside the grave, and Jon and Milosh climbed down. Cassandra began to follow suit, but Jon's quick hand arrested her.

"No, stay in the cart," he said. "We shall deal with this."

Milosh snaked two shovels from under the straw in the back of the cart and thrust one toward Jon. Together, they began to dig. Overhead, the sky was blazing saffron and flame as the sun sank lower beneath purple-edged clouds. The rasp of spades slicing through earth, and the dull thud of that relocated earth crashing to ground, ran Cassandra through with chills so severe her whole body shook. She was close enough to the grave for her to see down onto the plain wooden coffin when they reached it.

The pungent smell of rich damp earth and grass oils rose in her nostrils. She could smell the blood of insects—the worms and grubs and waterbugs tunneling through the soil for the second time in the space of an hour escaping the onslaught of shovels; the blood of some was shed in the process. It was this that attracted her extraordinary sense of smell, igniting the fire of the feeding frenzy. She was gaining strength. Night was not far off. And such creatures, while sparking her craving, would not be sufficient to slake it. She would have to feed soon.

Craning her neck higher, she watched the two men pry the lid off the coffin and lift it. It was a man that had been laid to rest—a peasant, as gray as the grave—an apparent suicide. Rope was still wrapped around his neck. Plant matter surrounded him, and its scent wafted toward her, flaring her nostrils. In the pink-gold sunset she saw it clearly.

"What is that plant?" she called.

"Hawthorne," Milosh replied, rummaging through the cart. "As I said before—this is a suicide made suspect after death—a cat or some other animal venturing too close to the bier, more than likely. If it were something graver, they would never have let the woman persuade them not to desecrate the body."

"Then, why—"

"Dear lady, I am a vampire hunter," Milosh interrupted

her. "I cannot afford the luxury of doubt. It is for the good of all that we do this. If this is *vampir*, it will be one less creature we will have to combat later if we destroy it now. If it is not, the soul has already left the body." He shrugged. "So what harm do we do, eh? By destroying the body now, we prevent some other outside influence from corrupting it. These are difficult times—desperate times that call for desperate deeds. If you will follow your husband into battle—for that is what it is, this calling you take up here now—you must be prepared for such as this . . . and worse. You must steel yourself against that female part of you that finds such a thing abhorrent, harden yourself for the good of all. If you cannot look, then look away. It would be best that you did look, however, and have it behind you. Much worse awaits, believe me."

Having found a mallet, a stake, and a dreadful-looking cleaver, the Gypsy strode off hefting the weapons, climbed into the grave, and without ceremony or hesitation drove the ashwood into the chest of the corpse—one, two, three strikes with the mallet. Cassandra, who forced herself to watch, averted her head when she heard the bottom of the coffin splinter.

"The stake must pierce the coffin and pin the corpse to the earth beneath," Milosh reminded Jon. He handed him the cleaver. "Sever its head," he charged.

Cassandra held her breath, her eyes all but shut, both hands clamped over her mouth to hold back the scream building at the back of her throat. Her husband hesitated. Forcing herself to open her eyes and look again, she knelt in the straw as if frozen to stone gripping the side of the cart. Jon climbed down into the grave as well, raised the cleaver, and lowered it in one swing. The head of the corpse fell away, and Milosh reached in and grabbed it by the hair. Then, hauling the body upward, he laid the severed head facedown at the corpse's feet and tapped the lid of the coffin back in place with the mallet.

There was no blood; the body had been dead too long . . . or something had drained it. But that did not diminish Cassandra's horror at the ritual, or at the unfeeling manner in which it had been performed.

"There is no other way," Jon called from below, having read the thoughts she knew were written on her face.

"And it could have been worse," Milosh added, climbing back out of the grave. Jon followed suit, and together they began shoveling the dirt back in.

Jon thrust the cleaver blade into the ground to clean it, then handed it back to Milosh, who tucked it and the mallet underneath the straw in the cart with several other ashwood stakes. Cassandra scrunched herself up against the side of the cart to avoid contact. Would she ever be able to do such a thing? She couldn't imagine. Yet, in order to survive, she knew this was exactly what she was going to have to do.

"It is too late to reach the cave I had in mind," Milosh said. "I would attempt it, except that we are so close—so few nights until the blood moon—and I want to take no chances."

"We cannot spend tonight in the open," Jon said, as the Gypsy set the cart in motion again.

Interrupting him, Petra suddenly tossed her head and voiced a loud complaint. Prancing in place stiff-legged, the frenzied horse shied and reared sharply. It was all Milosh could do to control her until they had passed by the grave.

"More proof that we have done the right thing," the

Gypsy said, aiming the comment at Cassandra over his shoulder. "A horse will have no truck with a vampire's grave."

Cassandra didn't answer. The last rose-colored streamers of sunset glanced off the western mountains, casting an eerie red glow about the burned-out shell of Castle Valentin in the distance; it seemed still to be aflame. Cassandra could almost feel the heat of that blaze, and something more: a lust for blood. It was time to feed.

The Gypsy turned left at the crossroads. Once the grave was behind them, Petra settled down with a snort and a shudder, spreading the musky odor of horse sweat to mingle with that of some anonymous berries along the roadside. Her feathered forelegs rising high, she started down the path at a leisurely pace.

Cassandra's eyes stayed riveted to the crossroads behind, lit in the last fiery rays of the setting sun. Something moved, and she squinted for a better view. The woman had come back; Cassandra watched her bunch her apron into a pouch and stoop to pick up the poppy seeds strewn around the grave. The prickly fingers of an icy chill puckered Cassandra's scalp. Her mouth went dry. She could scarcely believe her eyes.

"*L-look!*" she murmured, tugging at Jon's coat sleeve.

Jon's head whipped around and his eyes took the direction indicated by her rigid arm and trembling finger. Milosh looked over his shoulder as well. It was he who spoke, his voice sounding in her ears like thunder, though he'd hardly spoken above a whisper.

"So, it was worse than I supposed, eh?" he said. "She, too, is *vampir.* Now do you see what I meant, about not giving the benefit of doubt?"

"Shouldn't we *do* something?" Jon intervened. "Isn't she dangerous?"

"She does not even see us," the Gypsy replied. "She is compelled. She must pick up each seed separately until all are collected before trying to claw that corpse out of its grave—and when she has done that, she will find that all her labor was for naught. Besides, dawn will break before she has gotten all the seeds. No, she is no threat to us tonight. Our paths will cross another day, and we shall deal with her then. Now we must find shelter." He nodded toward the setting sun, cracking the whip above Petra's head. The horse lurched forward. "Hold fast!" he cried to Jon and Cassandra. "I know a place, but we must reach it quickly. I smell Sebastian, and this time he is not alone."

CHAPTER SIXTEEN

The cart took another turn, and they could no longer see the peasant woman hovering over the grave, stooping and plucking poppy seeds from the ground. Though she was out of sight, it wasn't likely that Jon would ever forget his first beheading. Setting the pallets ablaze at the castle had been one thing, but this? This was something different. He tried to imagine what circumstances had brought the woman to such a pass. Was she one of Sebastian's minions—had the corpse in the grave been one as well, or had some other villain created these?

Absently he sighed, unclenching and clenching his hands into fists, an unconscious mannerism he'd adopted of late. That beheading . . . What if one day he must do the same to Cassandra? The thought had haunted him since the cottage. Could he do it? He fought the images in his imagination—that indelible stain—with all his might. She was getting worse. Stronger. More vampire. As things were going, he might have to destroy her. *Might* was the only word he would allow; the inevitability of such an end to his current course was not something he could accept.

They had come upon a little ruined church and a ramshackle graveyard that testified to gross neglect; some of the crooked stones were overturned completely, shackled to the ground with moss and fern and ivy. Ground-creeping vines and stones set too close together impeded the horse's progress, preventing Milosh from driving the cart inside the graveyard. He pulled to a halt just outside the perimeter instead, beside a narrow opening. A small gate had once been in the ornate wrought-iron fence that enclosed the churchyard, but now lay tethered to the ground like some of the gravestones, by woodbine and ivy.

All at once there came a shift in the rhythm of the cart; motion behind caused it to sway, then shudder, as a weight was lifted from it, and Jon's head snapped around in time to see a silver-black blur as a sleek panther cub twice the size of the cat Cassandra had last transformed into sprang through the air, came to ground, and disappeared among the headstones. Jon gave a lurch, set to climb down and follow her, but the Gypsy arrested him with a quick hand on his arm.

"Let her go," he said. "She needs to feed. And she will come to no harm so long as she stays on hallowed ground." He pointed toward an upright crypt a few yards off that reminded Jon of the Hyde-White crypt in the kirkyard at home. "Feed and take shelter in that vault," he said. "You will find it open. The lock was broken ages ago, and no one will hinder you for the revenants in this place are all disposed of long since. I will look after your lady wife—that she does herself no mischief in this petulant romp."

Jon flexed his arm beneath Milosh's grip. "What if there are others like us who can enter here?" he asked. Seeing the Gypsy turn to leave, he felt swamped by his fear for Cassandra. He covered by saying, "No, wait! I need to be certain. I must—"

"You *know* what you must do," Milosh said in a hiss. "The longer you put it off the worse it will be, and once she grows stronger than you . . ." Could the man read his mind, or was he reading demeanor? That was something Jon would evidently have to guard against; if an allied vampire could read him, so could an enemy. Yes, he would have to guard against that, indeed.

"I thought we decided not to broach this subject again," he responded, not quite willing to give in.

"I must broach it," the Gypsy said, "because if you are not with me in this, you are against me—and I am faced with the very thing you fear facing with your lady wife."

Slack-jawed, Jon stared. Cold chills gripped him and paralyzed his tongue. Was all this a test? Should he fail, would the Gypsy turn against him?

Milosh nodded. "I saw in you a comrade in arms," he said, "what I call a *resistor*. I told you once that they are rare, those who resist the infection. It has been so long . . ."

"It is too much," Jon finally said. "She is my wife, Milosh—my bride. I do not think I could . . . No! I *know* I could not."

The Gypsy released Jon's arm and moved behind the cart, out of his view. He sighed. "I am not so concerned over whether you can do to her what you did to that poor devil back at the crossroads; I do not expect that. What troubles me is what will become of you yourself when her strength exceeds yours—because it will. What worries me is that, as Sebastian's creature, when she reaches full potential, she will do his bidding and not yours. What will happen to you then, Jon Hyde-White? What will happen to your soul . . . ?"

The Gypsy's words trailed off, and Jon jerked around in time to see the bushy tail of a white wolf disappear in the undergrowth. He cursed under his breath; he needed to feed, but more than that, he needed to think. The image of the woman at the crossroads plagued him.

It only took a moment for him to make up his mind. Stripping off his clothes, he surged into the form of *canis dirus*. He did not fear for Cassandra's safety in the Gypsy's keeping; Milosh had come to her aid once already, and she would be fine. What he had in mind would take too long on two feet, and he was comfortable with the element of speed the four-footed dire wolf incarnation would afford. In wolf form, he would feed, slake his curiosity, and be back at the crypt before he was even missed.

Weaving among the stones, he soon exited the graveyard through another wrought-iron gate hanging half off its hinges on the only piece of fence still standing on the south side, and streaked through the wood to double back the way they had just come. Keeping well within the forest, though close enough to follow the road, he moved on feet that made no sound. How he loved the freedom of loping through the tangled snarl of woodbine and ivy, inhaling the fragrant pine, the heady scent of mulch and moss and rich, fertile soil! All around him tall ferns had furled their silver-green fronds into tight little whorls, and wildflowers had closed their buds until morning. The contrast between the beautiful and the unspeakable was jarring, but he tried not to think about that. And as the smell of blood was in the air, carrying toward him on the low-lying mist that had risen suddenly, he lifted his wet snout toward the sky and howled.

The crossroads loomed before him. He crept closer, just inside the forest curtain where he could watch unseen, but he wasn't prepared for the sight that knocked him back on his haunches. The woman was there, but she now lay on the ground; a wolf had her by the throat. Jon's instinct was to go to her aid, and he began, but a closer look halted him in his tracks again. The wolf was ripping out her throat, crushing bones, and it was no ordinary wolf; it was Milosh. Jon recognized the silver-white coat and distinct markings. *Milosh?* His heart leapt. Where was Cassandra? The Gypsy was supposed to be looking after her.

Leaking a canine whine, Jon turned and sped back through the wood. The heart beneath his broad-barrel chest was thundering in his ears, beating out a ragged rhythm. He scarcely saw the birds he frightened out of the trees, or heard the echo of the plaintive wolf cry behind; his brain was numb to all but reaching Cassandra before someone or something else did.

Parting the mist, he squeezed through the broken graveyard gate he'd exited earlier, and sped through the cemetery tombstones. He felt the need to feed, but that would have to wait. A throaty feral cry, like that of an animal in pain, drew his eyes, and through the swirling mist his night vision revealed his worst nightmare. A bat had hooked its talons into the back of a screeching black panther cub it had trapped beside Milosh's cart.

A low, guttural growl leaked from Jon's throat. He wasn't near enough to help, and he ran until his heart felt as if it would burst from his chest. Another growl became a desperate roar as he remembered the wolves on the way to Castle Valentin, and how he'd leapt over them. Adrenaline surged through his body, charging his every sinew. But he was too new at this. Could he tap that gift again? He had to try. Skittering to a halt, he crouched and, driven by another growl, sprang into the air. Soaring through the mist, he came to earth in a snarling ball of sinew, fur and muscle, his fangs finding the wing of the bat that had pinned Cassandra to the ground.

All at once, he felt himself lifted. The bat wing to which he'd attached himself expanded into the shoulder of a multi-caped greatcoat, and Sebastian surged to his full height, taking Jon with him, tipping over the cart—horse and all—with one swipe of his free arm in the process. Still in wolf form, Jon clamped his canines down hard on the superfine fabric and the emaciated skin and bone beneath that stank of death and decay.

The vampire tried to shake him free, slinging him back and forth, but Jon's lupine jaws were sunken so securely that the creature couldn't break his grip. Not even when the vampire slammed Jon's body into the trunk of an ancient pine that marked the northern boundary would he relax his grip.

Excruciating pain shot through his unprotected shoulder as Sebastian slammed him against the tree trunk again and again. Jon's advantage had suddenly become a distinct disadvantage. He no longer dominated in size; Sebastian's human height and breadth now dwarfed him, dire wolf that he was. The vampire's strength was greater than anything Jon could have imagined. He dared not let go, and he dared not hold on much longer, either; blood was trickling through the fur on his shoulder, running down his chest where the bark had cut him. Out of the corner of his eye he saw a silver surge of fractured light flash through the mist as Cassandra, now free, shape-shifted back into human form.

Petra shrieked protests, stirring the mist with her two free legs but unable to right herself, forced on her side as she was with the tack pulled up short where she'd fallen on it. The contents of the cart had spilled onto the ground when the vampire tipped it, and Jon watched through pain-crazed eyes as Cassandra rummaged through the straw, various tools, clothes, and supplies strewn over the ground. He watched her tiny white hands grab his greatcoat out of the jumble, seize the holy water flask from the pocket . . . and hurl its contents full in Sebastian's face.

A screech like that of nothing human spilled from the vampire's throat. Steam rose from his gray skin, from his clothes, from wherever the water struck, and Jon went crashing to earth as the vampire shriveled back into bat form before spiraling off to disappear into the treetops. It was then that he noticed Sebastian wasn't alone. A swarm of bats attended him. The group soared off en masse, their dark wings slicing through the air in a sawing motion.

Having fallen on his side, Jon tried to rise and fell back down again. Cassandra was beside him, her tiny hands fisted in his bloodied fur, trying to help him to his feet. Dazed, he heard her voice as if it were coming from an echo chamber. With glazed vision, he saw her tears. Marshaling all his strength he shut his eyes and struggled erect. Surging through a displaced streak of silver light, he emerged in human form in Cassandra's arms.

His chest heaved with shallow breaths, his heart thumped against her breast. They stood naked together in the drifting mist. Jon hadn't fed: bloodlust was full upon him, and he was aroused. Leaning back, he looked deep into Cassandra's eyes, into the tears swimming there, into the desperation and the passion and the ardor in that beloved face. A bestial groan escaped him as he crushed her closer still. Cold sweat beaded on his brow, and he dropped his head to her shoulder.

"Tell me he didn't . . . ," he panted, his hot breath displacing her hair. "Tell me!" He felt her shake her head. Still, he could not look her in the eye for fear.

"But if you hadn't come on when you did . . ."

Blood was pounding, thrumming, leaping in his veins. And the scent of it choked him. Then her scent possessed him—her honey sweetness mingled with that rich, metallic life force he hungered for; had hungered for since he'd first tasted her in the lower regions of White-briar Abbey what seemed a lifetime ago. His hips jerked forward in an involuntary motion as his sex leapt to life in a manner it had never done; elongating toward, touching her. The feather-light pressure of her lips against the wound on his shoulder was sheer ecstasy. His sex began to throb in rhythm with his rapid heartbeat until he could bear no more. Leaning back, he looked her in the eyes—those doelike eyes dilated black with arousal—and groaned again. All he could think was, *She is still Sebastian's creature and he has nearly claimed her. He has nearly taken her from me!*

It was no use. He was beyond stopping. His hands roamed her body frantically, memorizing every inch of her soft, willing flesh; sexual desire and the ravenous demands of unstoppable bloodlust commanded him. He dared not meet both those demands and risk killing her. The pull of the combined forces would soon be beyond his control. He had to separate them and choose while he still could.

All at once he was seeing her through a blood-red veil. His sex was on fire. A low, guttural moan bubbled up in his throat as the scent of her blood rushed up his nostrils. Her arms were holding him close, her body moving against him, the pulsating vein in her throat but an inch from his lips. Fangs descended, the pressure as they displaced his canine teeth heightening the arousal like no other he had ever experienced. He dared not take her like this, not like this.

Her voice quavered as she called out his name and he was undone. He made his choice. His head thrown back, giving a cry not unlike that of the wolf he had just left behind, he swooped down, sank the fangs into the tender flesh of her throat, and drank to the pulse of the blood-lust that drained him dry of life and strength and all resistance. Cassandra made no protest. Groaning, she held his head, forcing his lips against her arched throat, calling his name to the rhythm of the pulsebeat pounding in his ears. And he fed upon her until her head finally fell back and the breath in her lungs left her body as she lost consciousness and hung limp in his embrace.

Jon gathered his wife up in his arms. His fangs had receded, and he threw his head back and loosed a groan that chased more birds from the trees as he cradled her close, rocking her in his arms, looking through tears of dismay toward the puncture marks on her alabaster throat in the misty moonlight. His heart was aching that he had put them there after such an adamant stand against it. And why he had was chillingly plain. It wasn't because he feared one day her strength would surpass his own and leave him vulnerable. No, now she was no longer Sebastian's creature; she was his. They were forever one in all but sexual consummation, and that would come after the rite, when it could be done without the killing power of the bloodlust threatening her life. But it remained to destroy Sebastian so that the vampire could never again lay claim to her through blood.

Cassandra was so pale, so still. Had he gone too far, drained too much of her life? Snatching his greatcoat from the overturned cart, Jon wrapped it around her, yanked open the door of the vault, and carried her inside. A stone bench stood against the far wall at the foot of a coffin, and he laid her down on it, gently cocooned in the coat, and streaked back outside to the cart.

His heart hammering against his ribs, scarcely aware of the dull ache throbbing in his wounded shoulder, he snaked his buckskins and shirt out of the debris and tugged them on carelessly. Petra, still complaining, captured his attention, and he unhitched her from the cart. The minute she was free, the horse heaved erect and pranced off to graze nearby. Where was Milosh? Anger roiled inside him. If the Gypsy hadn't gone off, this might have been avoided. Jon had trusted him to look after her.

Rustling in the uppermost branches caught his eye. They weren't alone; he knew it—sensed it. Disconnected sounds all around sent him reeling in circles looking for their source, but nothing met his extraordinary vision. Still, something malefic was near. Instinct plunged his hand into the upturned cart again. As if by a will of their own, his fingers closed around the handle of the cleaver. He grabbed a stake and mallet, Cassandra's frock, and the lantern as well, which was still lit owing to the angle of the cart; had it been hanging on the other side it would have been crushed. He took one last look around and strode back inside. Not a minute too soon. The coffin lid had been pushed aside, and a creature had climbed out. He was hovering over Cassandra, who lay unconscious on the bench. The creature turned, fangs exposed, making a hissing sound that ran Jon's blood cold. Slapping the lantern down, Jon dropped the stake and mallet and lunged with the cleaver. Spinning for momentum, he lowered it with all his strength to the creature's neck, severing its head in two fatal blows. Then, heaving the body through the crypt door, he stepped outside and raised his fists to the sky—to the tops of the trees that hemmed the graveyard fence, swaying with malevolent presence.

"*Sebastian!*" he roared at the top of his voice. "Send what you will. She is yours no longer. She is mine, do you hear? Mine!" He kicked the corpse at his feet. "Have back your creature and be gone! She is mine!"

Spinning on his heel, Jon strode back inside, slammed the crypt door shut, and sank to his knees beside Cassandra, rubbing her wrists to prompt circulation. She was breathing, and her heart still beat. Why wouldn't she wake? She should have come around by now.

So much for this graveyard being safe, he thought. *So much for all the revenants having been destroyed long since.* Had Sebastian anticipated that they would occupy this crypt and secreted one of his minions here who could tread on sacred ground? Surging to his feet, Jon looked inside the coffin. There was a resident skeleton with a severed head, so that was evidently the case. Milosh had warned Sebastian wouldn't come alone.

Milosh.

Who was Milosh? Jon's hands balled into fists at the thought. The enigmatic Gypsy had a lot to answer for. Jon jerked the heavy coffin lid back in place, shutting the decapitated skeleton out of sight, and began to pace, taking long, ragged steps on legs that trembled underneath him as he viewed his handiwork—Cassandra, lying so pale and still and lifeless on the hard stone bench. Kneeling down, he gathered her against him. Her body heat gave him hope, though her hands and face were cold as ice. Was this how undeath manifested itself? Had he killed her?

All at once a noise behind captured his attention, and he sprang to his feet and spun to find Milosh on the threshold. Rage narrowed his eyes and turned his features to stone—all but the muscles that had begun to tick along his broad jaw. He hardened his countenance, stiffened his spine, and wadded his hands into white-knuckled fists at his sides.

Something snapped. "*You!*" he roared.

Rushing the Gypsy, he delivered a shattering blow to the man's jaw that sent him through the open vault door into the tangled snarl of vines and gorse, thistle and nettle, backpedaling into a listing tombstone that tripped him up. Jon went at him again as he fell backward over the headstone, with intent to haul him to his feet, but Milosh surged upright as though he hadn't fallen and, with one hand fastened to the front of Jon's shirt, lifted him and threw him through the gaping door up against the cold stone wall beside Cassandra's bench. Jon struck it hard. Stunned, he shook his head to clear his vision. Unprepared for such strength, for he'd never seen this facet of Milosh, he hesitated before lunging again.

The Gypsy's hand shot out and arrested him by the throat. "Save your fury for those we both fight," Milosh said. "You cannot win a contest with me as you are—not before the Blood Moon Rite will your strength match mine. Only then will your power be such that you might attempt it . . . if you still want to, that is. I am hoping not."

"You left her!" Jon snarled hoarsely through the Gypsy's grip. "You said you would watch after her. I trusted you!" He swept his arm wide. "Look at her!" he choked. "Look! I think she is dying!"

Milosh let him go and strode to Cassandra.

"Do not touch her!" Jon charged, stumbling after him.

The Gypsy dosed him with a scathing glance that was itself enough to halt him in his tracks, and bent over Cassandra to examine her puncture wounds. Carefully he felt for a pulse in her neck and lifted her eyelid before standing back, arms akimbo, and facing him again.

"She is neither dead nor dying," he observed. "She is in a state of shock from blood loss, which is to be expected. She will come round soon enough."

Jon raked his hair back ruthlessly. "Why did you leave her?" he demanded.

"I didn't."

"You did. I saw you at the crossroads."

"Ah. And when you saw me, what did you do?"

"I realized you had left Cassandra alone, so I came back straightaway."

The Gypsy nodded. "Very soon the sun will rise upon the hour of the blood moon. Once you embrace that rite, if all goes well you will no longer feed. It will be too late for you to take her." He shrugged. "You are a stubborn fool, Jon Hyde-White. I had to force the issue. I had no choice. You would not see reason. You say you saw me at the crossroads? That could have been *you* and *her*—and would have been—if you had not done what you did tonight and claimed this woman as your own. Sebastian Valentin must be destroyed, Jon, his disciples with him. That is paramount, and that is what I was about at the crossroads tonight—eliminating one of his minions. Cassandra was never in danger. I knew what was happening here in the graveyard, just as I knew you would save her."

"How could you?" Jon asked.

"That is not for you to question. Once you embrace the blood moon, you, too, will be endowed with such gifts. You will need those for the work that must be done. That is . . . if you are still committed to it."

Jon hesitated. He was committed to hunting and destroying vampires, but one look at his unconscious wife made him wary of the Gypsy.

"I do not trust you," he said, speaking truthfully. "I do not know you well enough, and there is something . . ." He trailed off.

The Gypsy nodded, his lips twisted in a half-smile. "I respect your honesty," he said. "And on this one point at least we are on common ground. But you stand to lose far more than I. My distrust of you can only end in one way, Jon Hyde-White—exactly as it did with the woman at the crossroads earlier. I'd think upon that carefully, see to your lady wife, and get some rest. Soon we will reach the mountain peak where the ritual must take place. Believe me, you will want to be well rested for that."

CHAPTER SEVENTEEN

Cassandra woke with a groan to total darkness. Absently she ran her fingers over the puncture marks on the side of her throat. Jon had put them there. Fiery shivers raced through her loins remembering.

It worked!

It had been a dangerous gamble—even Milosh was leery, though he had finally agreed that using herself as bait to attract Sebastian might be the only way for her to convince Jon to finish what the vampire had started.

She took a ragged breath and sat up on the bench. There was no pain. But for the light-headedness and vertigo that made her unsteady when she tried to move, nothing seemed changed. Her extraordinary night vision, like that of a cat, showed her that she wasn't alone in the crypt. Jon was asleep on the floor in the corner. He must be exhausted. He never slept at night—only during the day, when it was safer to do so. They were alone in the crypt, and she took another breath and gingerly rose from the stone bench.

Her frock lay folded neatly on the floor. Shedding Jon's greatcoat, she tugged on the frock, tiptoed to Jon's side, and gently covered him with the coat. She didn't want to wake him yet; not until she was steadier, not until she'd steeled herself against the deception. Tugging the door of the vault open a crack, she peered out into the damp pre-dawn darkness. All was still in the graveyard. There wasn't a breath of a breeze, yet the ground-creeping mist sidled in and out among the tilted headstones as if with a will and a purpose. Through the trees, she glimpsed the moon sliding low in the night sky. It was almost full; almost time. Another day, another night . . .

Cassandra nudged the door open a little wider. Milosh's cart was standing upright again, its contents replaced as though they had never been disturbed. Petra was nowhere to be seen. There was no sign of Milosh either. It was just as well. Suppose he were to betray her? Jon mustn't know what she'd done. She hated the deception, but what other option was there? He'd been adamant in his resolve not to take her blood, which had to be done before the blood moon ritual. Yes, if that mysterious rite arrested the feeding frenzy as Milosh promised, it would be too late; it had to be now, while Jon still had the urge to feed. She reasoned with herself that elsewise Sebastian's hold would be irreversible. Why hadn't Jon seen that? Nevertheless, the plain fact was that she had tricked him—something her conscience couldn't bear.

Even at that, the plan had nearly backfired. She shuddered, recalling how close she had come to feeling Sebastian's greasy fangs on her throat again. She'd known the vampire was hovering, waiting to finish what he had started. She'd meant to stay within the confines of the graveyard while waiting for Jon to discover Milosh's absence and return—and hopefully realize he must take her blood. It had been a dangerous game, and timing was vital, which was why she had nearly failed—she had misjudged the boundaries of the graveyard and strayed too close to the cart. She would never forget the terror that all but paralyzed her as Sebastian swooped down upon her with Jon nowhere in sight. She would carry forever the memory of trying to prevent the vampire from getting a grip on her with his sharp bat talons.

Reliving the nightmare, she didn't hear Jon approach from behind, and she nearly jumped out of her skin when he took her in his arms and turned her toward him. It was a frantic embrace. His trembling hands flitted over her body as if he were checking for broken bones. It was a desperate moment that attacked her conscience viciously, especially when his fingers came to rest on the punctures on her throat.

He let loose a heart-wrenching groan that brought tears to her eyes and crushed her close. "It wasn't a dream," he despaired. "My God, what have I done?"

"You have done what had to be done, Jon Hyde-White," Milosh said. Both of them turned toward him with a jerk, where he stood on the threshold behind them. Neither had heard him approach. Cassandra cast him a warning glance, to which he replied with a slow blink. At least he hadn't betrayed her . . . yet.

"The sun is rising," he remarked. "There is no time. Come, we have much ground to cover before dark, and our path takes us back into dangerous territory. Look sharp! Vampires are not our only danger now."

* * *

"I hope you're finally satisfied," Jon said to the Gypsy as the cart rolled through the forest toward the blinding streamers of blood-red dawn stabbing through the trees.

"I am," Milosh said with a brisk nod. "Though I cannot claim the credit for it, you will thank me one day, Jon Hyde-White. There really was no other way. You will see that soon enough."

Jon doubted it. He glanced back over his shoulder. Cassandra was curled on her side, wrapped in his greatcoat, sound asleep—or at least she appeared to be. How pale she was; how transparent her skin, like alabaster, marred by telltale blue veins that testified to what he had done.

"Those will fade somewhat," Milosh said, casting Jon a sideways glance as he eased Petra out onto the narrow road. "Once her body adjusts, the veins will be less noticeable. Sometimes talc is enough to hide them. If not, there are treatments that ladies know that will suffice— the sorts of things actresses use. Cassandra is very fair. She may have to resort to these. Do not look so stricken! Your wife will know what to do. Do not sell her short, Jon Hyde-White. She is a brave, intelligent soul. You are too drunk with love to to be less protective, but let her be. We have much to discuss. What is yet to come shan't be easy. We are being watched. Sebastian and his minions know what you are about, and they will try to stop you. You must be prepared for that."

"What must we do meanwhile?"

"We must collect the necessary herbs. This must be done in the morning, while the dew is still upon them. As soon as the sun rises, you must be prepared. I can put you in a position to find them. You must gather them yourselves. You must climb the mountain, build a fire, and steep the herbs to make the draught that must be drunk when the

218

blood moon emerges during the eclipse. I know just the place. The peak I have in mind is low and easily scaled."

"That is all?"

"That is much," said the Gypsy. "As I said, you must do this in the open where you will be vulnerable, and you will be in even more danger because you cannot shapeshift during the rite. Whatever your incarnation when you begin, that is how you must remain; your shadow upon the earth that drifts across the moon must not change shape. The amount of water in your blood must not alter, either, lest the balance be upset. Afterward there will be . . . consequences. The draught affects each person differently. You may hear voices or see visions. It will be difficult to separate dreams from reality. At that point you will be most vulnerable of all. You will need to protect yourself by outside means, so these must be carefully prepared before the hallucinations begin."

"Outside means? I do not understand," Jon said.

"You will be in a trancelike state, unable to protect yourself, so before you drink the draught, you two must draw a protective circle around yourselves. Straw from the cart will do; then you must sprinkle it with melted holy oil and set it afire. As long as you remain inside the circle, you will be safe. Vampires will not risk crossing the fire line. The holy oil will prevent them."

"What of those who are not put off by holy things?"

"There is still the fire, Jon. Vampires fear it, because it is one of the means mankind has to destroy them."

"You have done this?"

Milosh nodded. "With no help."

"And this rite will check the bloodlust?" It seemed so impossible, so full of hocus pocus. And yet, who would have believed any of the things Jon had lately seen?

Milosh nodded. "So long as you renew the rite as I have already told you, yes. If you do not, you will revert back to what you are now until the next blood moon. Now remember, the full moon will not save you once you let the antidote lapse. In that case, you must start over just as you are doing this first time, so I suggest you keep current."

There was a long silence. The only sound was the crunching of the cart wheels on gravel. They had reached the first crossroads, and Milosh steered Petra in a northwesterly direction, bypassing the grave, which drew Jon's eyes. There was no sign of the woman's body, and he felt chilled, imagining what had become of it. To look at the spot now, one couldn't imagine the grisly scene that had unfolded only a few hours earlier. That brought the whole nightmare trickling back across his mind, and he literally shook the thoughts loose, as a dog sheds water.

"And that will put things to rights, eh?" he repeated skeptically.

"The rite will free you from the bloodlust, Jon," Milosh said, clearly out of patience. "But it will not free your adversaries from it; never think so. What it will do is set them upon you with more of a passion to kill, and to claim your lady wife as their master's consort. In this case that would be Sebastian, since he reigns here and would not take being usurped calmly; but it is not limited to him. There are many vampires in these mountains, Jon Hyde-White. That is why you must be as I am—free of the bloodlust—in order to help me destroy them."

"And . . . if I fail?"

"Then you will become just another *vampir* in need of killing. So! You had better be sure not to fail, Jon Hyde-White. It is not a personal thing, you understand. I have grown quite fond of you and your wife. It would pain me greatly to make an end of you. I am counting upon you never to put me in such a position. Do not disappoint me."

"Where do we go now?" Jon said, changing the subject.

"There is a village close by—more a community than a village; very small, but there is an open market, and we have need of several supplies."

Jon uttered a bitter laugh. "What could we possibly need that you have not tucked away in this rickety old cart?"

The Gypsy offered a crimped smile. There was no humor in it. "Food, for one thing," he enunciated, his dark eyes flashing. "You will have need of real sustenance once the bloodlust no longer commands your appetite. A cauldron, for another thing—to brew the draught—and vessels to drink from. These implements must be new, never used, or vessels made of precious metal. We shall need rope for scaling the mountain peak; you cannot reach it by cart. Can you afford these things?"

Jon nodded.

"Good," Milosh said. "We should have no difficulty moving among the villagers here. They all know me. That you are in my company will gain you acceptance; they will take it as a good sign, since my usual company consists of those I have beheaded brought in to be burned. I told you once that there are only two kinds of people here: vampires, and those that hunt them. They do not know that I am both. These are simple folk; they could not comprehend such a thing. Needless to say, you must not let on what you both are. This means no feeding anywhere in or near the village, though you may feed once more tonight, when we arrive at our destination. Hopefully that will be your last time. Make certain you make that plain to Cassandra. Her feeding frenzy has been problematic since we met; it could be fatal now. We do not yet know how strong her lust for blood will be, now that you have made her stronger, and will not know until the sun sets."

"I will keep a close watch," Jon said.

"That is just it," the Gypsy replied. "You may not be able to. You are going to have enough of a task keeping watch of your own lusts."

"I will be able," Jon assured him.

"Good! I may not always be about to see that you do—especially when the ritual begins. It isn't only blood that you must avoid now. You will take one meal of the food we purchase before the sun sets, and then no more until after the blood moon tomorrow night. You must fast before the ritual. Afterward, you will be ravenous; at least I was, so choose your victuals carefully. You will need to keep up your strength."

Again Jon nodded. Food was the least of his worries. The look of Cassandra worried him. She seemed changed—even in her sleep something was . . . different. Again and again, he glanced over his shoulder at her honey-colored curls, feeling their silken softness with his eyes. How very beautiful she was. But for him, she would be doing the London shops, buying frocks in Bond Street, visiting the linen drapers for muslin and laces, linen and silk. She would be having refreshing ice treats at Gunter's to chase the heat, taking a pleasant ride through Hyde Park in the fine Hyde-White landau. Instead, because of him, she was clad in a torn and dirty frock. Because of him, it wasn't cool, flavorful ice that quenched her thirst and refreshed her but rather thick, warm blood—*human blood*. Instead of the elegant landau kept at the townhouse for pleasure jaunts among the fine ladies and gentlemen of the upper classes, she was riding in a dilapidated, hay-strewn cart in the company of vampires and half-vampires who hunted them.

Bitter tears stung his eyes. He blinked them back. He wished he'd never received Clive Snow's missive, wished he'd never gone to that gambling hell. Would he ever see home again? Could he ever return to Whitebriar Abbey? It wasn't likely. The worst of it was that his friend and mentor, Vicar Snow, no doubt believed he had killed that hunter in the woad field. All of it seemed so long ago and far away, it was as if it had happened to someone else. He wasn't even the same person anymore. Who or what he was remained to be seen; he was almost afraid to turn that page. Suppose the ritual didn't work? The connotations of that thought were too terrible to contemplate, and when the Gypsy broke the silence between them, Jon stiffened as if he'd been struck.

"There's something more," Milosh said, casting him a sidelong glance. "Have you looked at the sky?"

"A beautiful sunrise. Why?"

"'Red sky in the morning, sailors take warning,'" Milosh said. "An adage as old as the Bible, and as true as ever."

"I don't understand."

"Sky that is red in the morning foretells a storm on the way," Milosh explained. "If that storm lasts through tomorrow night, there will be no moon—cloud cover will hide it."

Jon stared. He could have sworn his heart stopped. He shifted positions on the seat just to prove to himself that it hadn't. Gooseflesh puckered his scalp, and his bones crackled as his spine stiffened. Such a thing had never occurred to him. Why, that would mean . . .

"We shall hope for a brief shower, no?" the Gypsy said. Jon couldn't answer. All he could do was stare at the spectacular sunrise, the glorious, blood-red sunrise warming the lane with its deceitful beauty.

"Yes, we shall hope," Milosh went on. "Meanwhile, you need to prepare your lady wife for what is to come. You need to tell her all that I have just told you about—"

"That won't be necessary," said Cassandra from behind them, her voice as gritty as gravel. "I heard every word."

CHAPTER EIGHTEEN

They reached the village just before noon. Billowing stormclouds darkened the sky, but it had not yet begun to rain, though a downpour seemed imminent. *Perhaps that is a good sign,* Cassandra thought. *If it rains now, likely the storm will pass before tomorrow night.* It was something to cling to, and she found herself anxiously monitoring the clouds' progress as they moved through the square.

It was market day, and the streets were filled with milling people. Milosh left the cart with the hostlers at the public house that served as a coaching inn. It seldom saw travelers, he pointed out; but for lost wayfarers, few ventured this deep into the Carpathians due to the grisly tales spread by the superstitious locals. Afterward he left them to visit the tinker's wagon, where he would purchase the cauldron and cups.

Choosing foodstuffs was difficult for Cassandra. It had been so long since she'd craved food, nothing seemed palatable. The smell of the various meats, bread, strong cheese, overripe fruits and vegetables permeating the square threatened to make her retch. The sickening-sweet fruit dominated, reminding her of the overripe blackberries she'd eaten while fleeing another village. She gagged, remembering, and covered her nose and mouth with her hand.

Jon wasn't much help in that regard either, though together they managed to choose several loaves of bread—one barley loaf, one large flat loaf of wheat, and one made with dark rye flour and studded with whole grains. They also purchased a generous slab of cheese made from goat's milk, some fresh and dried fruit, honey, and a small cask of rich brown ale, none of which tempted Cassandra. Milosh added some dried spiced sausage meat and several crocks of wine, then moved on to fetch rope.

Cassandra accompanied Jon as he bargained with the hostlers for two horses—a fleet-footed black gelding for himself and a sorrel mare for her—complete with saddles and tack. Leaving them to be readied for travel, they moved through the market, examining the wares of some of the other vendors before they were packed up for the day, which seemed imminent as a fugitive wind rose and suddenly brought the clouds closer.

They were just about to go back to the inn to collect the cart and horses when a table spread with women's clothing caught Cassandra's eye. Unthreading her arm through the crook of Jon's elbow, she moved toward it, a close eye upon the wares. One woman had snaked a sprigged muslin frock from the pile and was holding it up against her plump body, while another woman jeered, looking on. Cassandra sucked in her breath and ventured closer still. Reaching out, she ran her fingers over a blue voile morning frock the color of robin's eggs.

"Do you fancy something?" Jon said, leaning close.

"Well, of course you must. Your own frock is quite ruined. Forgive me. Here, let me buy it for you." He reached to take the blue voile from her, but she arrested his hand and rummaged deeper into the pile to produce a yellow muslin round gown, a white muslin frock, and a bottle-green spencer. Putting them down again, she grabbed his arm and led him away, out of earshot of the vendor tending the table, who was trying to convince the woman with the sprigged muslin that the gown would fit her.

"I don't understand," Jon said. "Don't you want one? You seemed so taken with them—"

"Shhh!" she warned him. "They are mine, Jon!" she said in a whisper. "See there . . . beneath the table? My trunk! The coachman made off with our things when they found me out at that inn. I saw him ride off with the trunks still strapped up top. How has it come here?"

"I don't know," Jon said, clearly nonplussed.

"Suppose some of those villagers are here—the ones who meant to beat me to death and burn me in that bonfire. Oh, Jon! Suppose someone recognizes us!"

"Be still. If that were so, someone would have come forward and accused us by now, I should think. But all the more reason for us to buy something from that table. I shall do so, then we shall find Milosh and be on our way."

"What? Buy my own things? You can't be serious."

"Just so. What better way to take suspicion off ourselves, should someone be watching. Besides, you cannot go about as you are. That alone is cause for suspicion. You look like a Liverpool street urchin. Come, follow my lead. Pretend you've never seen those frocks before. Trust me."

Cassandra stayed close beside Jon as he strolled back to the table. Giving her arm a reassuring little squeeze, he began rummaging through the garments.

"Which one has struck your fancy, my dear?" he said, lifting up the blue frock. "This one, I think, wasn't it?"

Cassandra nodded. She didn't trust herself to speak. The vendor had left the fat woman's side and come at once to theirs, fussing over the wares on the table.

Jon continued to look over the selection. "Here's a nice one," he drawled, snaking out the yellow muslin round gown. "On second thought, no," he said, holding it up to her. "A bit outdated, I think, and a bit too large for you as well."

As he moved to return it to the table, Cassandra's hand took his. "I don't mind that it is outdated," she said. "I love the color, and it should fit well enough. It looks large, but that is the style of it."

"These are the latest London fashions," the vendor said, bristling as she straightened the frocks they had mussed. "Straight off the ship from Gdansk, the peddler assured me."

Jon draped the yellow over his arm along with the blue, then reached into the pile again. "I shall take these as well," he said in his best Romanian, complete with sign language, taking hold of the sprigged muslin the fat woman had discarded as well as a white muslin morning frock and an indigo cloak with a hood. "By the look of that sky, this might come in handy," he observed of the cloak.

Cassandra voiced a mock objection.

"No, no, I insist," Jon said, then to the woman: "It is our honeymoon, you see," he claimed, "and there wasn't time to choose a proper trousseau before we sailed. Not if we would take advantage of fine sailing weather."

The vendor's eyes brightened. "My lady is fortunate indeed to have such a generous bridegroom," she said.

Wadding the frocks in a bundle—all but the cloak, which Cassandra slipped over her shoulders—the woman chattered on while Jon paid. Still chattering, she wrapped the rest in brown paper and tied the bundle with string just as the first fat raindrops began to splatter down.

Cassandra scarcely heard much less understood what the woman was saying. She stared down at the dark pattern the drops were making on the wrinkled paper—one, two, and then a flurry that made a hollow sound.

"There, then!" Jon said, tucking the bundle under his free arm. He gestured toward the clouds boiling and thickening overhead. "We had best be on our way before we take a drenching." And he steered Cassandra away from the table as the vendor swept the rest of her wares into the open trunk at her feet.

The rain worked to their advantage. Everyone was running helter-skelter, protecting their wares from ruin in the downpour and seeking shelter from the storm. Few took notice of them as they made their way to the stables behind the public house in search of Milosh. Thunder rumbled through the foothills, amplified beyond by the mountain peaks—Cassandra felt the vibration through the soles of her Morocco leather slippers. Lightning speared down in snakes and flashes, streaking across the fields, while the rain sluicing down in slanted sheets broke the wildflowers' backs and sheared off their colorful heads.

Milosh had stretched a tarpaulin over the bed of the cart. He was tying it down underneath the stable overhang out of the rain when they reached him.

"To keep the straw dry," he said. "We need it for the fire. The horses are ready. As soon as the storm slackens some we'll be on our way."

"We need to go *now*," Jon whispered. "One of the vendors has Cassandra's trunk. She was selling her things in the open market. That trunk didn't get here by itself. The coachman who brought us from Gdansk drove off with it the night those villagers nearly killed her. I bought a few of the dresses so we wouldn't look suspicious, but we should go. We aren't safe here now."

"That was a wise move," Milosh said, "but we can't ride off in *that*." He gestured toward the horizontal rain and white lightning flashes dancing all around. "We will arouse suspicion. We shall go into the public house and have a meal while we wait. I told you, they know me here. They make a fine goulash. Then, when the storm breaks, we will be on our way with no one the wiser."

Cassandra wasn't convinced, but there was nothing for it except to comply. They were drenched before they reached the pub, and Milosh was right; it would have seemed suspicious had they driven off in such a tempest.

They weren't the only ones who took shelter there. The pub was crowded and noisy, reeking of the stale brew that had ripened in the floorboards over time and dirty wet clothes on unwashed bodies. The only saving grace was the goulash. Milosh had been right about that as well. She welcomed the hot, salty gravy trickling down her throat, and since lamb was plentiful, it was overflowing with meat. They had nearly finished when the publican caught Milosh's eye and jerked his head toward the ale barrels, signaling the Gypsy to join him there. He wasn't gone long. Cassandra watched him glance in their direction several times while the man whispered in his ear. The look in his eyes bespoke caution, and though cold chills walked the length of her spine and the fine hairs on the back of her neck flagged danger, Cassandra concentrated on the goulash as if she hadn't noticed.

Jon was watching the conversation also, though he didn't let on when Milosh swaggered back to their table. He didn't bat an eye when the Gypsy took all three tankards in one hammish hand and started back toward the ale barrels.

"Steady," Milosh warned, "while I fetch us more ale."

"Something is wrong," Cassandra murmured, her eyes fixed on the goulash. Her stomach turned suddenly, and bile rose in her throat. She could no longer abide it.

"Whatever it is, we must trust Milosh to handle things," Jon said. "The storm will soon be over and we will be on our way."

As if in contradiction, lightning lit their table, glaring through the dingy window above them as it struck a small fruit tree outside. A deafening thunderclap followed that shook the whole public house, rattling plates and tankards on the tables and in their niches on the wall. Cassandra reacted to that. It would have seemed odd if she hadn't. A frightened response from all the patrons twittered through the common room as Milosh returned with the tankards.

"As soon as the rain gives, we will away," he hissed. "And we must be off soon if we are to reach our destination before nightfall."

"What did the publican want?" Jon queried.

The Gypsy hesitated. "Do not be alarmed," he replied. "He wanted to warn me. Word has spread of what occurred at that inn the night we met. The townsfolk haven't given up. You are still being hunted. I expected as much. I know these people and they are relentless. You two fit the description, of course, and he wanted to know how well I know you. I put his mind at ease, so you must do naught to spoil that or we are all in danger. I told him that I am your travel guide, that you are devout Christians making a wedding trip visiting the Orthodox priories in the mountains."

"And he believed you?" Jon asked.

Milosh nodded. "He knows I would hardly be in the company of those I am committed to destroy."

"Did someone point us out to him?" Cassandra asked over the rim of her tankard. It was all she could do to keep her hand from shaking, especially when another thunderclap rattled the windowpanes.

"Yes," Milosh said, "but they are gone now and I have put his fears to rest. I told him I was at the inn the night it happened, that I saw the fugitives, that the girl in question was older, and that her companion was dressed in the office of a clergyman. Now finish that. The thunder grows distant. Soon we will be on our way."

The gelding and the sorrel mare were no less skittish in their company than those in Jon's stable at Whitebriar Abbey. The trio excused the phenomenon to the hostlers, however, as fright due to the storm, and made their departure from the public house as soon as the rain lessened to a misty drizzle. There was no hope of it stopping altogether. Sinister, black-rimmed clouds stretched from horizon to zenith, bold testimony that the foul weather had just begun. It seemed more like twilight than mid-afternoon.

Steam rose from the path they took into the forest at the foot of the mountain, where the cool sluicing rain had met the hot ground. The music of a gurgling stream, swollen and overflowing its banks since the rain, echoed

from within the forest, and farther in, the roar of a waterfall that fed it rumbled in the distance. Cassandra closed
her eyes and imagined that cool flow washing over her,
soothing her tired body, reviving her spirit. All around
them the pungent forest smells rode the rain-washed air.
Pine and fern mingled with the scent of ripe berries and
wild mushrooms. The camphoric aroma of purple myrtle
growing wild on the forest floor and the woodsy essence
of rosemary and bark blended with the heady scents of
moss and mold. They all came together in an evocative
explosion that took her breath away.

All at once, Milosh reined Petra in and raised his nose,
sniffing the multifragranced air. At first Cassandra
thought he was singling out all the layers of nature's
scents just as she was, then he began sweeping the forest
with his eyes.

"What is it?" she said.

Milosh laid a finger over his lips. "I hear . . . something," he whispered. "I have since we left the village.
We aren't alone in the woods."

"Vampires?" Cassandra murmured.

"I am not certain," the Gypsy replied.

Jon raised himself in his saddle, his eyes snapping in all
directions. "Should we turn back and see if they follow?"

Milosh replied, "We need to cover ground to reach our
destination in time. As it is, we are behindhand because
of the storm, and another downpour is on the way. It often happens at this time of year. One storm will follow
another . . . sometimes for days." He climbed down from
the cart. "Give me your horse," he said. "Guard the cart
well. Everything you need is in it. Follow this path. It will
lead you to a cave in the hills behind the waterfall. It is a
small cave, fed by a mineral spring at an upper level, but

it will suffice. There is a narrow approach that will accommodate the cart. I have used it many times; this fits nicely inside. You will be safe there. The vampires will not cross the water."

Jon gave a skeptical laugh. "Sebastian had no difficulty crossing a stream when he stalked us in Scotland."

"How deep was that stream?"

"It wasn't deep. He stepped right in it."

"He will not step in the falls, believe me. Now go! Do as I've said. If all goes well, I will join you shortly. If not, you still know what you must do."

"I know what you're thinking," Cassandra said, watching Jon glance over his shoulder as Milosh walked the gelding into the thick of the wood and disappeared. "If you didn't have me to contend with, you might be able to help him."

"That isn't fair," he argued.

"Maybe not, but it's true."

"Something has been troubling him since we left the public house," hedged Jon. "Milosh is a vampire hunter. His instincts are excellent, his senses extraordinary. If he feels a presence, believe me, there is one. If it is a vampire, it is of the sort that can go about in daylight. But I do not think it is. More than likely, it is those who have been searching for us. They have picked up our trail."

Cassandra gasped. "Jon, we cannot stand against a mob!"

"No, we cannot. That is why Milosh stayed behind; I would stake my life on it. We must do as he says. We must find the cave and wait."

Cassandra said no more, though her mind was reeling with questions that unfortunately only Milosh could answer. She and Jon were both too new at the condition to puzzle things out, and conjecture only led to anxiety. It was bad enough agonizing over whether after all their preparations rain clouds might obscure the blood moon; now one of their number might well be facing mortal danger. Making matters worse, they were very visible in the cart, but they needed the conveyance nonetheless.

They spotted the waterfall just before dark. Just as Milosh said, there was a cave behind it, and a narrow path gouged in the rock barely wide enough for the cart. The rain had held off, though the stormclouds had summoned an early twilight. The rocky approach was slick with algae, and Petra complained when she nearly lost her footing on the slippery path. Cassandra went first. She had nearly reached the falls when the heart-stopping howl of a wolf turned her. Frozen on the brink of the cave, both she and Jon stared. Behind, the eerie green darkness of the forest was dotted with the flickering light of moving torches—dozens of them—moving straight toward them.

CHAPTER NINETEEN

"Have they seen us, do you think?" Cassandra asked.

Jon stared toward the torches bobbing through the forest. The sight chilled him to the bone. They would be trapped in the cave, walled up in the mountain that was supposed to be their salvation. On the other hand, there was no way they could outrun the vigilantes in the cart; even riding double astride the sorrel mare, progress would be slow, and they would be at a disadvantage traveling through unfamiliar territory without Milosh to guide them. Judging from the position of the torches, they hadn't yet been seen, no doubt thanks to the Gypsy. Then the wolf call came again, piercing and shrill, and he knew.

"Into the cave. Quickly!" he said.

Cassandra coaxed her mount behind the waterfall into a large, deep cavern, and slid from its back while Jon drove the cart into the niche. The cascade of water, spindrift, and rising mist created a blind that literally hid the cave entrance. It was pitch dark inside, the only light reflecting off the curtain of water sluicing down.

Jon reached Cassandra in two strides and took her in his arms. "That wolf howling was Milosh," he said. "I'd stake my life on it. He is trying to tell us something." She was trembling, and he folded her closer against his thumping heart, aroused by her softness, by that exquisite body so malleable in his arms.

"Are we going to die here, Jon?" she murmured.

Her misty eyes, dilated in the darkness, sparkled with a phosphorescent shimmer in the defused light seeping through the waterfall. How lovely she was. How fragrant and fine. His loins were drenched in fire for want of her; his fangs had begun to descend for need of her. How would animal blood satisfy after her sweet nectar? It would have to. Just once more. He would not take her blood again. If everything went according to plan, neither of them would be ruled by bloodlust after tomorrow night. Everything hinged upon staying alive to reach that hour. There was only one way.

"As we are, we do not stand a chance, Cassandra. I believe Milosh is trying to tell us that our only hope is to change into our animal incarnations, just as he has done, if we would escape that mob. That is what must be, and we must do so before they are close enough to see us leave this cave."

"I'm frightened, Jon," she murmured.

"You will be far more frightened if that mob lays hold of you. Become your animal. I will follow. Once we enter the wood stay close to me—at least within my sight."

His kiss was hard, passionate, and swift before he put her from him. Cassandra slipped off her frock, while Jon tugged off his boots and peeled off his shirt and buckskins.

"Go!" he said through clenched teeth. "And remember to stay close to me. We do not know what we are facing. They likely aren't expecting us in our animal forms, but take no comfort in that. Wolves and panther cubs are also hunted here."

It was no mere panther cub that spiraled to the ground in a silver shaft of displaced motion but a full-grown black panther, its iridescent green eyes blazing. In a blink, Jon took his wolf form, and they exited the cave together, blending into the misty darkness.

Keeping to the dense undergrowth, Jon led Cassandra toward the torches haloed eerily in the mist that soon would give way to rain and douse them altogether by the look of the sky. That was his greatest fear. Jon needed to see his enemies, not blunder into them in the dark. Relying upon his extraordinary night vision, that byproduct of the condition, to help prevent that, he charged boldly forward, a sharp eye peeled for Milosh's white wolf somewhere in the midst of the advancing mob. It did not bode well that they hadn't heard his howl again. Should he give his own howl in hopes Milosh would answer? He opted against it. As it was now, he and Cassandra were next to invisible. It would not do to call any attention to themselves.

The advancing torchbearers were far more in number than Jon had anticipated. They were spread out wide in a semicircular arc through the forest. Some were on horseback, but most were on foot, and they were not unlike a veritable army. So much blood waiting to be taken—*begging* to be taken—he could smell it. He could taste it—could feel the vibrations thundering in the collective veins of that mob, whose anger had risen to fever pitch. It would be a small matter to select one victim from their flanks to satisfy his feeding frenzy. He couldn't be sure of himself with Cassandra unless he did, and even at that, he would not trust himself alone in her presence again until after the ritual.

It was a silent attack; one of the last stragglers decided the issue for him when the man sighted him prowling through the undergrowth and raised his pistol. It was more self-defense than anything, which salved Jon's conscience somewhat as he fed, and soon the villager was rendered unconscious. Such was not the case with Cassandra, who'd evidently followed his example; he saw her dragging something into the underbrush. He wasn't near enough to tell if it was animal or human. How sleek and beautiful she was—even in her panther incarnation. Especially then. Did she enjoy the transformation as much as he? He must remember to ask. A twinge of shame shook him—of remorse—but only the tiniest twinge; there was nothing for it, no use denying that, though he despised the condition, loathed what he'd become through no fault of his own, he loved the speed, the fleet-footed freedom of his wolf form, and he couldn't help but be glad that aspect of the nightmare would carry over after the ritual.

He watched Cassandra until she disappeared into shadow. How lithe and swift her gait was while moving through the heart of darkness in that ink-black forest. The torch bearers had moved past them and split in two divisions, one flank following the road northward while the other was halfway up the mountain. Had they found the cave, discovered the cart and their belongings? Jon was too far away to tell. His mission then was finding Milosh. There was no sign of the gelding, either. He must wait for Cassandra, and remain concealed in the search. He took no comfort in the villagers' distance. They would return. He must look sharp for that. The danger was far from over. His raised hackles were testiment to that.

"This way! Follow the road," Milosh barked at the swarming mob combing the forest. They were coming too close to the waterfall and the cave behind where his wagon waited—close enough to hear the animals concealed inside. He heard Petra's frenzied whinnies clearly, but that he hoped was due to his extraordinary hearing. The gelding underneath him heard, too. He was afraid of that.

Only half of the men were following him; the rest were scaling the mountain. He cursed under his breath. If only the rain would begin it might drive them back, at least until morning, giving him time to find Jon and Cassandra and choose a new hiding place—a new peak to climb for the ritual. One thing was certain; as perfect as this location was, it wasn't safe any longer . . . unless somehow he could persuade the mob to leave. He'd seen many mobs. Looking at this one, swarming like ants, their voices raised in ugly indignation, he was not encouraged.

Jon and Cassandra still didn't trust him. They were still wary. That was just as well. If they were leery of him after all he'd done to prove himself, they would be leery of everyone else, and that might just help them, might just spare them some of what he had suffered over time. He rubbed his neck where the rope burn still puckered his flesh and pained him in damp weather. It was almost an unconscious gesture now. Those scars were centuries old, but they still annoyed him; a cryptic reminder of his fallibility.

Had Jon and Cassandra heard his howl? Had they

shapeshifted? It was the only warning he could give before changing back to human form. Since then, he had been too busy trying to lure the villagers away from the waterfall. If they had heard, there was a chance. If not . . . No, he wouldn't think about that. He needed allies. He had singled out Jon and Cassandra, had prepared them for the blood moon ritual. He'd spoken honestly to Jon earlier; he could count on one hand the times he'd done that for anyone in the last 300 years. He knew what they were suffering. And they were so much in love, just as he had been with his wife. Cassandra was growing stronger. In her innocence, the infection affected her differently. Milosh shuddered at the thought of Jon facing what he himself had faced, of having to do to her what he'd had to do to his own wife in order to give her peace. But he shook off those thoughts as a dog sheds water. He had to keep the villagers away from that waterfall. That and that alone drove him now.

"Not that way!" he called. They shouldn't want to attempt the peak in the dark—too many pitfalls. "This way, I tell you!" But they swarmed up the mountainside.

Cursing under his breath, Milosh turned his gelding toward the waterfall, only to rein the animal in again at sight of one of the villagers leading Petra out of the cave. He was waving Jon's clerical clothes in the air. Another had hold of the mare. Chills traveled the length of Milosh's spine, and his hackles raised. He dug in his heels and the gelding lurched forward.

"Leave that! It is my wagon, you fools!" he called at the top of his voice.

"How many horses can one man ride?" the second villager jeered, snapping the mare's reins. "This and that cob beneath you are *their* animals!"

"Are you a priest then, too?" the leader of the mob barked at Milosh, brandishing the black clothing gripped in his fist. "You lied! You're helping them. You're one of them! I was there when they got away. I saw them! I recognized them! *Vampires*—all of you!"

"You know who I am," Milosh shouted over the men's words. He was keeping his distance. This was going to turn ugly. He knew it; he could feel the noose tightening around his neck. He could hear the sinister rumble of the angry crowd's voices rise to fever pitch, feel the heat of the bonfire, feel the scorching flames—but it wasn't old memories come back to haunt him; this was real! Too many torches in careless hands had set the forest afire. Flames now shot along the ground, igniting the dead leaves and pine needles on the forest floor that the rain hadn't penetrated deeply enough to reach. Fire shot up the tree trunks in a flash. In seconds, an inferno separated Milosh from the mob. They had been driven back from the heat of a virtual wall of flames. Crazed with fear, Petra reared and bolted, knocking down the man who'd held her. The fallen man's screams ringing in his ears, Milosh tried to reach him, but the fire was spreading so swiftly, literally jumping from tree to tree, it was impossible.

With all the breath in his lungs, he whistled for Petra. The horse charged forward, answering the call with little regard for the man screaming and writhing at her feet, and the cart wheels rolled over him as she streaked off at a gallop, those wheels shooting out flames fanned by the cart's momentum. The mare bolted as well. Milosh couldn't see her now; she had gone the other way and disappeared into the pandemonium unfolding all around.

Thick, black smoke was rising, blacker than the blackest night. The men scaling the mountain had scrambled back down and now were being driven toward the village by the fire. All, that was, but a few stragglers along the fringes that Milosh saw only in glimpses through the mushrooms of smoke in the way. Pulling back on his reins, he turned the gelding in the direction the cart was taking. The animal spun and reared back on its haunches, nearly unseating him before bolting after it. But the horse's crazed motion wasn't what nearly evicted him from the saddle; it was the impact of a pistol ball ripping through his back—or was it his shoulder? He couldn't be sure. He had to shapeshift. He needed to become the wolf to escape. He couldn't let them find him like this. But how could he shift, and where could he go if he did? What would happen if he died? Would he rise, undead? Would the evil that had infected him so long ago win a posthumous victory at last? There was no way to know except to put it to the test, and he wasn't ready to succumb.

At first there was no pain. Then feeling came trickling back, slowly, like the petals of a flower unfolding—a blood-red flower opening to the rhythm of his thundering heart, the pain more agonizing with every shuddering beat until he could barely stand it. *Blood.* His shirt was soaked. He stripped it off, tossed it down, and lay low over his horse's neck, his hands fisted in the animal's mane until he could hold on no longer. The pain was excruciating. Vertigo smeared from view the flaming cart hurtling toward the river. Another shot rang out behind. Falling was Milosh's last conscious sensation.

CHAPTER TWENTY

Jon couldn't wait for Cassandra any longer. The fire was spreading, and the mob was streaming back in their direction. He raised his snout, sniffing the air for her scent, but all that met his flared nostrils was the stink of burnt wood and the scorched fur, flesh, and sinew of woodland creatures trapped in the holocaust. Throwing back his head farther still, he loosed a howl like nothing that had ever before left his throat. It reverberated through his barrel-chested body from his head to the tip of his bushy tail, which was now tucked between his legs to avoid being singed.

Picking his way over the forest floor, avoiding the patches of spreading flames, he made it to the place where he'd last seen Cassandra dragging her prey. The deer she'd drained lay dead in the underbrush, but there was no sign of her. She hadn't come back out of the dense brush; he was certain, as he hadn't taken his eyes off the spot where her sleek, black panther incarnation had disappeared from view.

He howled again, but still there was no answer from Cassandra—or from Milosh either, who was conspicuous in his absence. Jon's heart felt as if it were about to burst from his chest, as if he had run himself nearly to death; but there was no exertion, he was standing still. Snapping back and forth, his eyes viewed all directions, but he saw nothing. He dared not shapeshift to continue his search, either. He could cover more territory in wolf form. But which way?

Sniffing the ground, he called upon his extraordinary senses to help him pick up Cassandra's scent. It was no mean task, what with the overpowering smell of blood and char, and with the thick smoke clogging his nostrils. Yet there was a way out, one where she could have escaped without him seeing her. His nose pressed so close to the ground that he tasted the soil he padded upon; he sniffed and sniffed, inhaling the scent of bark and fern and moss and mulch until her sweet scent finally came through.

Head bent low, where the smoke wasn't so thick, he ran along, picking up speed as he moved deeper. Yes, she had come this way. Was she lost? Disoriented? Why didn't she come back out the way she'd gone in? It didn't matter; nothing did but that he find her. The fire was all around him now. He couldn't go back the way he'd come; it was blocked by a wall of fire that spread from behind to the ground he was covering. Again and again he howled, but there was no response. *Why doesn't she answer?*

There was so much fire, it was ludicrous to look for torches. There was no alternative but to take the only way out the situation presented. It took Jon in a north-easterly direction. Nose still to the ground, he padded swiftly through the forest, clinging to her scent. All the while, the fire crept behind him. He felt helpless in this wolf's body; he needed to be himself. And yet, he also needed the fleet-footed aspect of the dire wolf. Head down—he feared to raise it even for a moment—he might lose Cassandra's precious scent—he ran on, weaving in and out among the trees, through the belching puffs of thick, black smoke. He ran on instinct alone. The uncanny phenomenon of his powers when he took the form of *canis dirus* never ceased to amaze him—like now, when his furry feet seemed to find the way through that tangled snarl of moss and vine, nettle and briar, all on their own.

The form did, however, have its drawbacks. He relaxed his guard. He became careless. So absorbed, he failed to see one of the villagers approaching, parting the bilious clouds of smoke as if they had spat him out, until the man was nearly upon him. Up until then, Jon had been careful to remain hidden. When he looked up, it was to stare down the barrel of a well-seasoned flintlock pistol in the hand of a man who, judging from his posture, knew how to use it. He had taken aim. The blood-chilling click as the man cocked his weapon blasted Jon as if the ball had already left the chamber. His heart took a tumble in his breast. He was too near; the man was at close range. Their eyes met. Jon tasted death, his hackles raised. The black, silver-tipped fur standing up along the length of his spine lifted the ruff that wreathed his thick neck, grieving the bruised skin and muscle still tender from his battle with Sebastian by the graveyard. His jaws parted, and he emitted a deep, guttural growl from deep in his throat. Facing death, his last thought was of Cassandra. But then there was another sound, the spitting, hissing, rich rasping growl of a cat—an angry cat.

Cassandra!

Was she a figment of his imagination? Had he summoned her with his will alone?

In a blur of black fur silvered with speed, the panther slammed against the villager's left side, spoiling his aim. The pistol discharged. Flames spurted from the barrel. Traces of white smoke mingled with black. The acrid stench of gunpowder shot up Jon's nose. He felt himself twisting as the pistol ball whizzed past him. He crashed to earth with a thud, on his side, a searing pain ripping through the side of his neck.

Cassandra! Sleek, beautiful, beloved Cassandra. A canine whine leaking from him, Jon shook his head, scattering blood from a graze wound on his neck. His fur was covered with it.

The smoke was so thick now it narrowed his eyes. The villager had stopped screaming, but the panther still growled. Jon was glad of the black-edged curtain that spared him the sight of the price the man was paying for that pistol shot.

He attempted to rise, failed, and tried again more successfully. Feet apart to steady himself, he shook his whole aching body as if to shed the incident altogether, and let loose a howl that rose above the roar of the holocaust closing in all around them. It brought Cassandra leaping through the smoke—black against black, her magnificent green panther eyes iridized with battle madness. At once she was by his side, swatting him with her great paw. It was a playful swat, a feminine swat, a joyful, loving, triumphant swat. It was obvious that she was as glad to see him as he was to see her. He showed his understanding with a high-pitched whine while nuzzling her shoulder, extracting a throaty purr from her as she licked the blood from the wound on his neck.

Her doctoring was, however, short-lived. The man she had taken down was not alone. Others were hidden behind the smoke blanket; Jon could sense them. He could feel the clamor of their hasty feet through the ground in his sensitive paw pads. Cassandra must have felt it, too, for she turned and bounded seamlessly northward, away from the smoke, and dove into a convenient thicket. Following close behind, Jon kept up with her pace. How he wished they could shapeshift and he could hold her in his arms. Only hours until the blood moon—*the blood moon!* Tomorrow. He had almost forgotten.

Overhead, lightning speared the sky and fat raindrops began pelting them. His heart sank. Was this a good sign, or bad? The sky needed to be clear to view the eclipse and the strange blood-colored moon it caused. It wouldn't be visible in the rain. Another thought struck: *The fire will have burned nearly all of the herbs.* Where would they gather more here? And without Milosh, how would they know where to find them? Jon had to find the enigmatic Gypsy! And with that thought to drive him, he followed the thicket eastward, a close eye upon the sleek, black panther streaking through the underbrush ahead.

This was much better than blundering about as a helpless kitten, Cassandra thought, and this new incarnation was much more efficient than the clumsy cub of the species had been. If the situation weren't so grave, she would actually enjoy it. Streaking through the thicket, only one thought drove her—somehow, she had to get back to the waterfall and Milosh's cart; she couldn't resume human form without her clothes, and there was only so much she could do as a panther.

Glancing back over her shoulder, she monitored Jon's progress. He was right behind her. He wasn't badly hurt, just grazed, but he must be in great pain nonetheless. Her heart was still hammering against her ribs from the horror of seeing him staring down the barrel of that villager's pistol. She hadn't killed the man, but he wouldn't use the hand that aimed that gun again. He was the least of their worries. They had to avoid the others, find Milosh, collect the cart, and move on while the fire covered their escape. It had to be now, before the heavens opened up and the random raindrops that had begun to fall came pelting down in earnest.

She had no idea where she was going. Sniffing the smoky air, she tried to pick up the scent of water, but all that filled her nostrils was the stench of fire. As if Jon read her mind, he surged past her, speeding eastward. Time was slipping by. Trusting his heightened sense of smell, she followed as he led her along the fringes where the fire had not yet spread toward where the waterfall should be behind the smoke screen. Amazed at how the flames had changed the look of the land, Cassandra stayed close behind him, a close eye peeled for any stragglers fleeing the blaze.

It seemed an eternity before the waterfall came into view in brief glimpses through the billowing smoke. It could be reached by running past, then doubling back through some ground cover that had been spared by a wind Cassandra hadn't even noticed until that moment. The rain was coming more heavily now, though it didn't seem to be doing much to douse the fire. They had passed the waterfall by and were continuing eastward when all at once another scent threaded through her nostrils. *Blood.* Fresh blood. Jon must have smelled it, too, because there was a hitch in his stride, and he turned south, his nose bent to the ground.

Whose could it be? she wondered, bounding after him.

Milosh! a voice said in her mind.

What was this? Did Jon answer her thoughts? Could they communicate without speaking?

Yes. The answer came ghosting across her mind. *But evidently only at close range, or you would have heard me earlier when I was so desperate to find you.*

And spared you your wound. Oh, Jon! Is it bad?

No, but this is, he replied, routing a bloodied shirt out of the brush. *It is Milosh's.*

Cassandra raised her nose and sniffed the air. *Leave it,* she said. *Come!*

Aiming farther eastward, Cassandra bounded on swift legs into the brake at the foot of the mountain, with Jon following. They hadn't gone far when she slowed her pace. Some anonymous bulk lay facedown in the grass and nettles, close by a little stream.

Jon howled into the wind. *Milosh!* he cried. *Is he . . . ?*

She inspected the body. *Not yet, but he has lost much blood, Jon. He has been shot. And there are two wounds.*

Stay with him while I fetch the cart.

Cassandra raised her head. *No, wait!* She glanced about. *It isn't at the waterfall. Look there!* He followed the direction of her eyes. *That mob must have found it. See? It's there—or what is left of it is. Downstream, in the water!*

Before Jon could respond, Cassandra clamped her jaws around the waistband of Milosh's breeches and lifted him up, half carried him the way a mother cat transports its kittens. Half dragging his inert body through the undergrowth to the damaged cart, she let him down on some soft grass.

A *dose of his own medicine*, she thought ruefully, wondering if Jon would hear. *I have carried the Gypsy as he once carried me. A pity he isn't conscious to appreciate it.*

If a wolf could smile, she had the distinct impression that her beloved husband was doing so. He did not oppose her. They turned and surged into their human forms and each other's arms. It was a powerful embrace, during which Cassandra satisfied herself that his neck wound wasn't serious. Both naked and aroused, their bodies trembling with desire, they clung to each other in mindless abandon, oblivious of the rain sluicing down over them. But the respite was brief; there was no time to satisfy those urges. Snatching their clothes from underneath the tarpaulin, they tugged them on; then together they lifted Milosh into the cart, and Cassandra covered him tent fashion, while Jon assessed the damage to the wheels. Everything else on the cart seemed intact.

"Is it badly burned?" Cassandra asked. Climbing up beside Jon, she tugged the hood of her cloak close around her. The rain had become a downpour.

"The back wheels are badly charred and some of the spokes are gone," he said.

"Will they bear our weight?"

"Not for long. But we need to address Milosh's wounds. We cannot do that in the open in the teeming rain. We have to find shelter."

"Back to the cave?"

Jon shook his head. "We cannot go through the fire. Even if we could, the villagers will return once the rain puts it out. There may even be some stragglers wandering about, like the one who shot me. We must away." To Petra, snapping the reins, he commanded: *"Walk on!"* The horse bolted forward, her complaints amplified by the downpour.

"But where . . . ?" Cassandra persisted.

"There is only one safe place I know of," Jon said. "The cottage."

"But the vampires!"

"We have little choice. We will be fortunate to make it that far; it must be well past midnight. Yet there is another reason. Tomorrow we must gather the herbs for the ritual. They were plentiful there—you said you saw some by the stream? You know where to find them there. God alone knows where we'd find them anywhere else without Milosh to show us. We shall just have to chance it. Now, look sharp. Do not delude yourself that Sebastian lacks our whereabouts. I feel his presence in the very marrow of my bones, Cassandra. The smell of blood surrounds us—mine and Milosh's—and that will bring him. I do not mean to frighten you, but we will not be safe until we reach that cottage and lock ourselves inside."

Cassandra said no more as the cart lumbered forward. She did as Jon bade her, keeping watch, though her eyes strayed longingly to the blood still seeping from his neck wound. No matter how she fought the magnetism of the feeding frenzy, it remained there, lurking, potent.

How handsome Jon was, all mussed by the ordeal and the storm. He had raked his dark hair back from his brow, but a stubborn lock had fallen forward and cast his quicksilver eyes in shadow. The muscles had begun to tick along his broad jaw, and his sensuous mouth had formed a white, lipless line. He didn't look at her, but she knew why. He was aroused, just as she was. He was clenching his teeth in an attempt to hold back the fangs. She had seen him do it many times, but it never worked; she could even now see the bulge of those fangs outlined clearly beneath his upper lip. The sight thrilled her, for her own had begun to descend.

Cassandra took a ragged breath. A crawling chill riddled her body with gooseflesh, one that had nothing to do with being soaked through. Jon was wrong. They wouldn't be safe once they'd locked themselves inside the cottage—then, least of all.

CHAPTER TWENTY-ONE

It was well into the wee hours when they reached the cottage. Jon burst through the door, carried Milosh inside, and laid him on the pallet. The door hadn't been locked; it wasn't even closed. Open a crack, it gave as he hefted his weight against it and almost undermined his balance.

Cassandra went at once and filled Milosh's cauldron with water from the stream, then carried it back to the cottage. She lit the cart lantern, sparking a flame with flint and the dry, combustible bits in the Gypsy's tinderbox. Meanwhile, Jon unhitched Petra for the night, and rummaged through Milosh's tools for some suitable knife to remove the pistol balls from the Gypsy's back and shoulder. There were a number of suitable blades to choose from, and he carried the lot inside, bolted the door, and lit a fire in the hearth.

"It's hardly cold enough for a fire," Cassandra said, looking on as he fanned the flames with a nearby bellows.

"You will likely burn the cottage down. From the look of it, that hearth hasn't been lit in ages."

"We need it nonetheless," Jon said, tossing in more wood from a pile in the corner. The logs were moldy, and he grimaced and coughed as green spores drifted up his nose. He thrust a rusty poker in between the logs to heat it, then hung the cauldron on a hook suspended above the flames. "Milosh's wounds must be cauterized once I remove the pistol balls," he said, adding a blessing over the water. "It will soon be light, and we also will need holy water for steeping the herbs we collect. Readying hot water now will serve two purposes: I will use some to cleanse the knives I must use on Milosh"—he gestured toward a bucket in the corner—"and the rest will be ready to receive the herbs for the draught."

He took up their lantern, knelt down beside the pallet, and examined Milosh's wounds. "This one is little more than a graze," he observed. "The bone stopped the bullet; I can see it." Probing the other, Jon frowned. "This one wants more surgeon's skill than I possess, I fear," he said. "It is much deeper. I shall try, but he has lost much blood." He shook his head and staggered to his feet, taking Cassandra in his arms. "As soon as the water boils, we shall begin. I will need you to help me. You aren't going to swoon, are you? If you are, tell me now so that I will be prepared. I haven't much experience at this. I dug a pistol ball from the shoulder of an unfortunate horse my brother accidentally shot once, but I was little more than a lad."

Cassandra shook her head that she would not swoon. "What if—"

"Shhh!" he cautioned, interrupting. "I hear something."

Scarcely breathing, Jon waited. The sound came again from the rafters: a rustling noise, like paper being shuffled. His feeble lantern light showed nothing, but the tongues of flame leaping in the hearth cast tall shadows on the ceiling and at last exposed the author of the noise. A great black bat hung upside down from the corner beam, unfurling its wings. Cassandra screamed.

Before their eyes the bat surged, expanded, and transformed into a tall black figure draped in an ill-fitting, multicaped greatcoat. *Sebastian.*

"But we didn't let him in!" Cassandra whispered.

"He was already here when we arrived," Jon murmured. "Damn and blast! I should have known. I should have searched! The door was ajar, remember? He needs no leave to enter where no one waits to grant or deny him access. He knew we would come here. What other choice did we have? He was waiting for us, choosing his moment to make his presence known. Stay behind me, and do not look into his eyes!"

Glancing about, Jon searched for some weapon to use against the advancing vampire. How hideous he was, as gaunt as the grave, moving eerily upon feet that made no sound—he almost seemed to be floating. And it was still hours before dawn, much too long to hope that the rising sun would spare them.

Jon cast a furtive glance toward Milosh. The Gypsy hadn't moved, and Jon prayed he would not now, else he draw the vampire's attention. Sebastian had been hungering for the Gypsy's blood for centuries, he knew. Right now, the vampire was salivating over his, which was preferable, since at least he had the means to defend himself, consciousness, and a righteous spirit, even if he was infected. Milosh was helpless, and Jon felt himself too inept to come to the man's aid, especially with Cassandra to protect as well.

Taking his wife with him, Jon inched toward the door and unlatched it, opening it a crack.

"What are you doing?" Cassandra hissed. "What if there are others?"

"If there are, they cannot enter without an invitation," Jon said. "And there must be a means for Sebastian to exit."

"What? You imagine you can just say 'shoo,' and he will leave us? You dream! I must change, and my panther will rip his throat out!"

"*No!*" Jon said through clenched teeth—a little too loudly, for it prompted a sardonic smile to crease their foe's lips. "Stay as you are!"

"But why?"

"I do not know, only sense that you must. My instincts dictate it, and I must trust them now if I trust naught else."

"I am amused by this little farce but out of patience," Sebastian said. He had begun circling before the hearth. Jon kept his distance, his gaze fixed upon the vampire's chin rather than his rheumy, red-rimmed eyes. Those eyes glowed with an iridescent glaze and the pupils narrowed to the shape of a snake's. Their pull was irresistible—even indirectly, Jon was finding out.

"*Do* not *look into his eyes!*" he warned Cassandra again, this time with unequivocal emphasis, keeping her well behind him while still searching for some weapon to use against the vampire, who had begun to move closer.

"You cannot escape me," Sebastian gloated. "You exist to play the game only because I allow it. The contest stimulates me. But take no comfort in that. I tire of such amusements. It can only end in one way, Jon Hyde-White. And it is only a matter of when."

"You were a bishop of the Church. Why did you not resist the vampire who made you, as I resisted you?" Jon queried. It wasn't wise to provoke the creature, but he was curious—and he needed to stall for time.

"Silence!" Sebastian roared, his breath a mighty, foul-smelling wind that ruffled Jon's hair, billowed Cassandra's frock, and stirred the flames in the hearth until they writhed and danced and shrank as if in terror. Cassandra's grip upon Jon's arm was bruising despite the superfine coatsleeve. His muscles flexed beneath her fingers, and no words were needed. "I think it ends here now," the vampire went on. "We shall see how well your God serves you when you wake in Hell, and *she* wakes as my consort for all eternity."

Sebastian lunged then and lifted Jon off the floor by his throat, his clawlike talons fast in Jon's shirt, coat collar, and the flesh still smarting from the open wound Jon had taken in the forest. Jon clawed at the bony hand that suspended him off the floor, kicking wildly. His air supply all but choked off by the vampire's grip, he bared his fangs as Sebastian did, extracting a bloodcurdling laugh from the vampire.

"Ohhhhh, so you mean to fight me?" Sebastian asked. "*You*—my creature, mind—mean to pit your powers against mine? Against me?" He thumped his chest with his free hand, balling it into a white-knuckled fist while shaking Jon with the other. It all but rendered him senseless.

Jon's breath was coming short as he tore at the hand strangling him. Blood was seeping from the wound on his neck again, the torn flesh breaking open at the rough handling. Vertigo had begun to star his vision with dancing white pinpoints of light when Cassandra's scream brought him back from the edge of unconsciousness. *Cassandra!* What would become of her if he succumbed?

"N-no, Cassandra! Stay back . . ." he choked out, knowing full well that she would not obey—and he was helpless to prevent her from getting involved. Screaming again, she skirted him and flew at Sebastian's back, climbing the monster as if he were a tree, her fists buffeting his spine, battering his shoulders, pummeling his bald head.

The vampire reached behind with his free hand, plucked her off his back as easily as if she were a broom straw, and flung her across the room. She fell hard to the floor, and slid into the wall beside the pallet where Milosh was groaning awake.

Stay down. My God, stay down! Jon's mind was screaming. If she heard, she paid him no heed. Scrambling to her feet, she ran to the cauldron where the water Jon had blessed was coming to a boil, and searched among the hearth tools for something to tip it.

Holy water. And the oil! As though a light had suddenly blazed alive in his brain, Jon let go of the vampire's fist at his throat and plunged one hand into his pocket, rummaging for the silver container of holy oil he'd nearly forgotten. After a moment, his fingers closed around it. Keeping an eye upon Cassandra struggling with the cauldron, he tugged at the lid with all his one-handed strength, his heart hammering so fiercely he feared it would burst in his breast as the vampire sniffed the blood leaking down his neck.

Reaching out with a free hand, Sebastian wiped that blood onto his fingers and licked them clean one by one. "You will be delicious, though it is a pity to drain you and end this," the vampire said, "but you know I must. I always finish what I start . . . however long it takes me."

Jon's eyes were snapping in all directions. He could barely breathe. Sebastian's fangs were inches from his throat. Over his shoulder, he saw Milosh attempting to rise, while to his right Cassandra had unearthed a pair of tongs and was trying to get a grip with them on the hot cauldron. One last tug of his fingers on the lid of the sacramental oil container removed it, and he plunged his thumb into the unction inside. Yanking his hand out of his pocket, he slammed his thumb squarely in the center of the vampire's forehead, making the sign of the cross on Sebastian's cold gray skin.

"*Now*, Cassandra!" Jon choked out, for the vampire's grip had tightened. The monster had swooped down toward his throat, his fangs fully extended. "Tip it now!"

Sebastian screamed at the touch of the oil. Smoke was rising from the burn it had left in his ashen, blue-veined skin. Out of the corner of his eye, Jon saw the cauldron tip, spilling scalding holy water over the floor, over Sebastian's feet. It splashed higher, and the vampire loosed a guttural shriek and threw Jon down. Clutching his head, the creature spun and surged to a grander height, challenging the ceiling in the little cottage, taking the same form Jon had seen him morph into at the castle. Great wings strong enough to break a man's back flailed the air. Jon scrambled out of the way, jumped up, and took Cassandra in his arms. Smoke rose from the vampire's feet, where the holy water singed.

This was the true creature—half human, half bat, an abhorrent corruption of a holy man. Angry tears stung Jon's eyes at the terrible waste. This creature had once been a bishop of the Church, he reminded himself. It stood before him now, convulsed by wracking, unnatural spasms. Something stabbed at Jon's innards, as if a giant fist gripped his guts. He longed in that split second to move forward, to put the creature that was writhing and spinning before him in a smoky swirl out of its misery. His fangs descended.

"No, Jon!" Cassandra shrilled, holding him back. "Don't go near it! Let it go!"

"*Jon.*" Milosh's feeble voice echoed from behind. "Not that way. You mustn't. Not . . . that . . . way . . ."

Sebastian hissed at Milosh like a snake. "Gypsy! Your hour comes soon enough." He spat at them all: "Take no comfort in this little victory. You are dead—the lot of you!" Then, shrieking like a banshee, he folded his gigantic wings over his head and spun like a cyclone, taking the cottage door off its hinges as he crashed through and disappeared out into the rain.

Jon crushed Cassandra against him, his fingers threaded through her honeyed curls, holding her face against his thundering heart. Then he pushed her away, his hands racing desperately over her body.

"Are you hurt?" he murmured. Gripping her chin, he turned her face to and fro in the hearthlight. "You took a nasty fall, Cassandra."

She shook her head. "No, just had the wind knocked out of me," she murmured.

Spinning toward the pallet, Jon stared toward Milosh, who had lost consciousness again. "He is badly hurt, Cassandra," he said. "He has lost much blood. I must try to do what I set out to do. You must keep watch. There is still at least an hour before dawn. Sebastian will not return—for all his bluster and bravado, he must regain his strength before he comes at us again—but he has minions aplenty. We dare not relax our guard, not for a moment."

"The door!" she reminded him.

It was hanging by one hinge, and Jon strode to it, dragged it upright, and began tugging it back into place. Behind, the sound of Cassandra's gasp turned him toward her.

"Look!" she cried, pointing through the open doorway.

Jon's head snapped up, and he took a chill that wracked his body. There in the teeming rain stood three mute urchins—two girls and a boy—trailing what looked like grave clothes.

Jon let the door fall from his hands. "Remove the knives," he said, "and fetch me what's left of the water in that cauldron." He stared out at the three undead children.

Cassandra did as he bade her, but she hesitated before handing over the cauldron, her eyes brimming with tears. The three pitiful waifs were moving nearer, their desperate wails begging admittance, their pleading, outstretched arms cunningly irresistible.

Jon tugged the cauldron out of her hands. "Have you forgotten the child when we last stayed here?" he asked. "If they are vampires, this will repel them. If they are not, no harm will be done." But when he tossed the contents of the cauldron full in the waifs' faces, fangs extending, all three hissed and shrieked. Then they spun off in the form of bats, their sawing wings unfurled, to disappear into the treetops.

Cassandra turned away, clearly ill. Jon would not admonish her. Had he not just felt remorse over Sebastian, of all things—over the tragedy of one of God's anointed having fallen? He was committed to his mission, to destroying the undead, to bringing the peace of the grave to these victims, to becoming a ruthless hunter of creatures like himself and to either send them to hell or to save them from it according to the severity of their infection.

But was Cassandra similarly driven? Could he expect her to be?

He snatched a hinge bolt from the floor where it had fallen, tugged the door upright again, and slid the bolt through the twisted top hinge. The door hung awry and would not close tightly enough. Still, it would have to do. Dragging the table across the room, he wedged it against the gaping door and turned back to the chore at hand, that of attending to Milosh.

CHAPTER TWENTY-TWO

Jon staggered back from the pallet. It was covered with blood—so much blood, it was torture. It affected Cassandra as well; he could see it in her eyes. And how could it not? Once one was infected, the craving for blood was unstoppable, insatiable. It was always present. The metallic aroma could be detected at great distances. It made a person mad.

He reflected on his own control. Milosh had remarked upon its rarity. Was it his vocation that gave him the power to resist? Was it his faith? Had it been Sebastian's lack of faith that made him succumb and become the creature he now was? Clive Snow had touched upon that topic, too, though it seemed like a lifetime ago. Did he truly have a greater will? Or was it simply that Sebastian hadn't fully infected him?

Staring down at Milosh's inert body, Jon heaved a mammoth sigh. How long could he continue to fight the urges? They were getting stronger. How long could he keep himself from doing great wrong, from becoming a full-fledged vampire ineligible for the saving grace of the blood moon ritual? If all went well, he would only have to fight for several more hours, but the opposition was swiftly mounting against him: the rain, for one thing; having been driven back to a veritable nest of vampires for another; and now Milosh. The blood moon ritual was to take place during the eclipse. Even if the rain stopped, the vampires roaming the forest would rise then. It would not be safe to leave Milosh alone, and yet Jon could not be in two places at once.

An eerie, hollow knocking at the door had begun, jarring him back to the present. The sound sent waves of paralyzing shivers up and down his spine. *Thump . . . thump . . . thump*. Over and over the sound came, in an impossibly steady rhythm. The table Jon had leaned against the broken door secured the bottom, but the door shuddered with every knock.

Cassandra rushed into his arms.

"Shhh," Jon soothed. "They smell the blood, but they cannot enter unless we let them."

She gasped. "Jon! The poker—quickly, before he wakes!"

Jon cursed under his breath, striding to the hearth where the poker had been heating. He carried it back to the pallet. He'd left it in the fire too long; now he would have to wait until it cooled a bit.

"Damn and blast!" he muttered, waving the poker impatiently.

Thump . . . thump . . . thump. "I am so cold. Let . . . me . . . in . . ." a small voice said from the other side of the door.

Cassandra lurched as if struck. Her hands flew to her ears. "Is there nothing we can do? Is there no way to make them stop?" she cried.

"Morning comes soon," Jon said. "Ignore it. It is naught but vampire glamour—the way they seduce their prey. It isn't real, Cassandra. They are vampires, and deserve no pity."

"Is that what I will get?" she sobbed. "What *you* will get? No pity? That could be us on the other side of that door, us luring some unsuspecting soul to its damnation."

Thump . . . thump . . . thump.

"Pay no attention," Jon said. "The poker is ready. Here, hold the lantern. I must do this now or we shall have to wait while I heat it all over again."

Cassandra held the lantern while Jon cauterized the wounds. He stiffened during the knocking, but still he lowered the hot poker to the Gypsy's back and shoulder. The stench of burnt flesh rose in his nostrils, and he coughed back nausea that threatened to make him retch. The pistol balls had come out whole, and the bleeding was stopped.

"You haven't answered me," Cassandra said as he discarded the poker.

Stripping off his greatcoat, Jon removed his empty holy water flask, his holy oil, and his pocket pistol, then laid the coat over Milosh. He straightened and faced her.

"Will we be like . . . like *that?*" she moaned, flinging her arm toward the door.

He'd been hoping she wouldn't pursue it, but that was clearly not to be. He took her hands in his, ignoring the fact that the touch of her soft skin set his heart to racing and the scent of her ignited a firestorm in his loins. Would dawn never come and bring the lethargy that killed desire? It was becoming harder and harder to resist her. How long before he no longer could? He viewed her now through an iridescent haze, just as he always did when he was aroused. He had seen the same veil glaze her eyes many times, but never like now, with their mutual needs both at their peak.

He led her to the chairs that had rested by the table before he moved it and sat her down in one beside the hearth. Dragging the other chair to the opposite side of the hearth—as far as he could range himself from her and still be heard speaking softly—he set the pistol, oil, and flask on the mantel, and sat also.

Sweat was beading on his brow. He raked back his hair ruthlessly. How forlorn she looked! He longed to reach out and take her in his arms. Braced upon his knees, his hands were clenching in and out of white-knuckled fists, literally itching to seize her, to walk his fingers through her honey-colored ringlets, to kiss her misty eyes, to breathe in her sweet essence and never let her go—but he could not, must not. Were he to touch her . . . He drove back those provocative thoughts once more.

Thump . . . thump . . . thump. "Let . . . me . . . in . . ." the child's voice moaned again, bringing an end to his hesitation. Cassandra had nearly jumped out of her chair at the sound, as he had also, even though he expected it; even though he knew the undead hand that rapped on the door would continue to do so until first light.

"That is what we are trying to prevent," he said steadily, "and why we must perform the ritual Milosh described. I only wish he were conscious. There is much I need to know before . . ." He hesitated. He was thinking aloud now. No, it wouldn't do to give her more cause for alarm. They had enough to worry about. Praying that Milosh would come around before it was time for the ritual, he went on speaking in as positive a tone as he could muster with that incessant thumping—banging, pounding—breaking his concentration each time he drew breath. "No matter," he said buoyantly. "I shan't lie to you. I do not know what is to come. My first goal in all of this is to find a means of arresting the bloodlust. We will still be vampires, Cassandra; there is nothing to be done about that. There is no cure. We are what we are. But if the blood moon ritual works, we can control ourselves, and together we can save many like us. And we can . . . commit ourselves to destroying those who are beyond our help for as long as we live."

"And how long might that be?" Cassandra asked. Her voice was harder—more scornful—than he had ever heard it.

He cocked his head sadly. "I do not know. Milosh has lived for centuries and has traveled all over the world. He learned of the blood moon ritual in Persia. He has been lucky in his travel, I suppose. It must be a lonely existence, otherwise. Such a life demands many sacrifices, because while those around us will change with age, we shall not, so long-time attachments won't be possible. We will travel, too. We will be as Gypsies, and our journeys will take us to the far reaches of the world."

"If when all is said and done we are still to be . . . what we have become, why do we need the ritual?" she asked. "Why can we not continue as we are? We have the power to resist the condition . . ."

"But for how long?" Jon said. Opening his mouth, he bared his fangs. She gasped. "Have you any idea what I am suffering right now just to keep from seizing and ravishing you—to keep from draining the rest of your very life force? You are still part human, and the . . . corruption in me wants to drain that humanity away. And I see the same bloodlust in your eyes—it gleams like green fire. Look, and you will see it. It is only a matter of time before we destroy each other if we do not act. Milosh is living proof that this ritual works. Have you ever seen him feed?

Have you ever even seen his fangs? No. This worked for him. Please God, it will work for us as well."

"You still haven't answered my question. How long will we live?" Cassandra asked. "I love you, Jon. All I want is an honest answer."

Jon's posture collapsed. "I cannot give you one," he said. "I do not know the answer. If the blood moon ritual works, we will be spared . . . *that*." He made a wild gesture toward the wounded door, which was vibrating under the assault of the fists of creatures caught between life and death on the brink of Hell itself. Cassandra covered her ears. The pounding came more desperately now, as if the creatures at the door had heard every word and were responding. The steady drone of the rain didn't help matters; it made the knocking all the more melancholy.

Thump . . . thump . . . thump. Thump . . . thump . . . thump. Thump . . . thump . . . thump.

Would it never stop? Still, Jon gave a pretense of ignoring it. "I need you to listen to me now," he said. "Listen, and pay attention. This may well mean your life."

She looked up at him with those haunting, doelike eyes. How could he earn her trust—and live up to it once he had earned it? Would she listen to what he was about to say? He almost laughed. Never had he met a woman possessed of such an unshakable mind of her own. Not once since this odyssey began had she done as he bade her. He had told her to stay in her rooms at Whitebriar Abbey, and she had promptly left them. He had told her to stay in her room at the inn, where she was safe, while he fed, and she had left that also, and started the chain of events that brought them to this hour. Even Milosh had remarked she must be "taken in hand" for her impetuous behavior, albeit bloodlust-driven. With all that had gone before, dared he expect she would heed him now?

She didn't reply, and he went on quickly. "You think Sebastian and his minions are your only danger," he said scornfully. "Well, they are not. *I* am. And that I love you will not spare you. It only makes matters worse, because my craving for you is twofold, and I am fast losing my control." He surged to his feet and snatched the pistol off the mantel, thrusting it toward her. "Take it," he said. "We still have a day and part of another long night before the ritual is complete. You should be safe enough during the daylight hours, because of the nature of our condition, but just the same, I beg you, keep your distance from me. And this is the most difficult bit, because you've never once heeded me in the past and you *must* heed me now; but if I cannot control myself . . . I want you to use that. No! Do not speak. You must use it, Cassandra. You can go on without me if needs must—I know it; I have seen it. I saw your strength in that burning forest." He closed her hand around the pistol and backed away as if he'd touched live coals. "Keep it on your person. It will not kill me—the bullet is not silver—but it will stop me, at least for a time. There will be much blood afterward. That will bring vampires and I will be vulnerable. If I am set upon, or if you . . . well, you know what you must do. You will find everything you need in Milosh's cart."

"Have you gone mad?" she shrilled.

"Believe me, I have never been more sane, my love," he murmured. "Because if I feed upon you again the way I did the last time, I will bleed you to death. I will not be able to help myself—to stop myself—and you will become like the entities in Sebastian's dungeon—a mindless, soulless creature of the night, of the outer darkness, lost and damned forever. Now, promise me."

Staring down, Jon watched her finger the cold pistol barrel. How fine her tender skin was. He could see the tracery of tiny blue veins on the back of those hands. They seemed to dance when she moved her fingers, drawing him like magnets.

He backed away.

Thump . . . thump . . . thump, the knocking continued.

"Do you hear that?" he thundered, causing her to lurch in the chair. "Promise me," he demanded.

She looked up. There were tears shimmering in her eyes. "I . . . p-promise," she murmured, the words barely audible. She slipped her hand into the slit on the side of her skirt and pulled out the little pocket she wore on a cord beneath. Hesitating, she slid the little pistol inside and tucked it away again. Only then did Jon draw an easy breath.

"You have given your word. You must keep it," he said, then said no more.

The blood-chilling knocks ceased at dawn. So did the rain, but a huge, fiery red sun peeking through the trees along the eastern slopes had turned the sky to flame, a harbinger of more rain on the way.

Cassandra kept her distance from her husband, who was clearly addled—if he thought for a minute she would shoot him, he had to be. She looked after Milosh, who seemed to be sleeping peacefully, tended his wound and moistened his lips with the few drops of water remaining in the cauldron, while Jon took the bucket to fetch more from the stream.

The fire had nearly died to embers, and Cassandra added more wood and stirred it to life again. They would need boiling water to steep the herbs they would gather. They would collect those together. As vehemently as Jon insisted they keep their distance, he would not brook a far separation. Too much was at stake, and too much had gone wrong already.

"How is he?" he asked, striding in with a brimming bucket.

"I do not feel fever," she said, brushing Milosh's brow with the back of her hand. "He's clammy-cold."

Jon filled the cauldron, hung it over the flames, and blessed the water. "I must try to rouse him," he said, striding to the pallet. "We cannot leave him alone without telling him what we are about. He will be disoriented when he wakes. If we are not here, he may think we've abandoned him."

Cassandra stepped back, and Jon crouched down beside the Gypsy. "Milosh!" he said, nudging him. "*Milosh! Can you hear me?*"

A feeble groan replied.

"That's right, open your eyes," Jon urged, giving another nudge.

The Gypsy's eyes opened. Shuttered and glazed, they slowly focused. "Am I dead . . . finally?" he murmured. "I feel so . . . strange."

"No," Jon replied. "You've been shot. We've doctored you. You'll mend, but we must leave you to collect the herbs. Will you be all right until we return?"

"W-where . . . are we?"

"At the cottage."

"Ah! Well done. Go." He gave a bitter laugh. "I will be here when you return." Jon gave a nod and turned to go, but Milosh called him back. "Jon . . ." he began. "Thank you."

"Do not thank me yet," Jon replied. "It's far from over. I am not comfortable leaving you alone here, even now that the sun has risen. I have in mind to nail a swivel board to the door, and to bar it from the outside when we leave. Will that keep any stragglers out, or do I waste my time?"

The Gypsy nodded. "Do what needs must," he said. "I-is there more water?"

Cassandra took up the dipper hanging by the hearth. The water was still cool, having just been retrieved, and she scooped some from the cauldron while Jon worked on the door. Milosh had lost consciousness when she reached him. His mouth had fallen open, and she knelt to moisten his lips anyway, only to drop the dipper as she stared down at him in his slack-jawed oblivion.

"Jon!" she called in a hushed whisper, fearful of waking the Gypsy. "Quickly!"

Jon set the tools aside and approached the pallet, his frown evidence of his confusion. Milosh stirred but did not wake, and Cassandra fell back from her kneeling position on the floor. She crawled backward like a crab, away from the unconscious Gypsy, her finger wagging toward him.

"What is it?" Jon asked, squatting down.

"L-look!" she got out around a dry lump that had constricted her throat. "What does it mean?"

Jon stared down at Milosh's gaping mouth, and at the deadly fangs that had descended, distorting the shape of his lips. The Gypsy muttered something unintelligible in a foreign tongue. Was it Latin?

"*Kyrie eleison*," Milosh said again.

Raising her to her feet, Jon put Cassandra from him just as swiftly. "Stay back!" he gritted through clenched teeth.

"But what does this mean?" she persisted.

"I do not know," he returned, "Except that we cannot trust anyone or anything."

CHAPTER TWENTY-THREE

The sun that turned the sky to flame had disappeared behind a dense cloud blanket by the time Jon and Cassandra set out to collect herbs; no trace of the glorious crimson glow remained. Was that an omen of ill boding? Jon heaved a ragged sigh. Everything seemed to fall into that category now.

It took them until midafternoon to gather most of the specimens. Borage grew next to the cottage. They found milk thistle in the pasture that girded the foothills, where they also found plenty of broom. Rue was the hardest to find, for it grew on the mountain slopes. There wasn't time to collect it on foot, so they hitched up the cart and found it growing in great profusion on the mountainside just off the path, the very same path that they would take tonight to perform the ritual. It was farther from the cottage than Jon had wanted to travel—especially now, with Milosh as he was. That phenomenon was nagging at his beleaguered brain, as if he needed more worries.

He had scarcely reined in when Cassandra hopped

down with the bucket and began collecting the tongue-like leaved herb. How lovely she was, with her honeyed hair blowing in the wind and her muslin frock billowing about her; how wraithlike and delicate. It was impossible to believe that this exquisite creature—the very same that had captured his attention and his heart on the crowded dance floor at Almack's—was an infected vampire who could shapeshift into a sleek black panther or succumb to ravaging feeding frenzies. Those conjured images aroused him, so he shook himself like a dog—a mannerism he'd found himself adopting more and more of late, in a vain attempt to shake such visions loose before they triggered his own feeding frenzy. He shifted on the seat of the cart. His arousal was challenging the seam in his buckskins. He almost laughed aloud: That lethargy supposed to curtail lust during daylight hours was a myth!

Cassandra turned, and he thrilled at the sight of her laden with rue. How pale she was, how opalescent her skin, though the apples of her cheeks were lightly flushed; no doubt from holding her head down while picking the herbs. It was the first color he'd seen in her since the nightmare began. The sight of her thus took his breath away.

"I have it!" she chirped, waving a branch for him to view. "I am so glad we found it. Rue and barsa weed are the most important herbs in Milosh's brew—and, he said, the most dangerous if the proportions aren't right. I know where to find barsa weed. It is this I feared we wouldn't find." She bounded through the rue, which was swaying in a gentle wind; her frock spread wide, oyster white against a matching sky.

"Yes, well, time grows short. We must get back," he said tersely. It was his only defense. It was that or seize her then and there, and ravish her in the fragrant bed of rue. He couldn't take the risk.

Cassandra tucked the herbs she'd gathered into the bucket, which contained a little water to keep them fresh. There were only two more herbs they must gather: skullcap, by the stream sidling like a lazy snake through the forest near the cottage; and the cresslike weed that grew in the water. The skullcap had been saved for last, to preserve its delicate, downy blue flowers that mustn't be bruised else they fade and quickly lose their potency. They found it readily enough, and refreshed themselves beside the stream as well.

Returning to the cottage, Jon saw immediately that something was amiss. The door he'd taken such pains to fasten with a pivotal bar from the outside was gaping open on its wounded hinges, the bar in splinters on the ground. Letting loose a string of expletives, he snapped the whip over Petra's head and the horse bolted forward. Praying that his eyes were deceiving him, Jon drove the animal relentlessly the last short distance, jumped down, and burst into the cottage, his eyes snapping in all directions. It was empty. Milosh was gone.

Cassandra rushed in after him, carrying their brimming bucket of herbs. She gasped as Jon straightened from the empty pallet with Milosh's clothes in his hands.

"He has become a wolf," he guessed dismally. "By the look of that door, he must have been desperate to leave here. He must be possessed of uncanny strength. I have never seen the like. All the other times he was quite docile . . . except for that one time at the crossroads, and even that was methodical unlike *this*."

"What does it mean?" Cassandra asked. "He is hardly fit for such exertion. What do you suppose possessed him?"

"I do not know, and we cannot waste time wondering. He hasn't disturbed anything else. The water is boiling. The herbs must be prepared and steeped, then cooled. The draught must be strained after, and I see no sieve. I shall look in the wagon. Perhaps—"

"There is no need," Cassandra interrupted. "My mother used gauze to strain her simples. My petticoat is made of such; a piece of it will suffice."

Jon nodded and stalked toward the door.

"Wait!" she called after him. "Where are you going?"

"Outside," he flung over his shoulder. He had already reached the threshold. "You mustn't worry, I shan't go far."

"What if he should return?" Cassandra said. "Do not leave me, Jon."

"If he does, I will get to him before he comes anywhere near this door. I will be right outside . . . at a safe distance. But trust me on this, Milosh is not the only danger facing you right now, Cassandra—nor is he the gravest."

In a blink Jon was gone; only the sound of the heavy crunching of his boots on the soggy forest floor remained, and finally that grew distant. Cassandra shook visibly with chills. The last words he'd said had raised her hackles. He was speaking of himself, she knew.

Absently she reached to touch the pistol in her pocket. No! How could he expect such a thing of her? She wished she'd never touched the weapon, much less taken it. Did he think she could so easily put aside her feelings and do that? How could she, when all she wanted was to live in his strong arms? She hungered for his touch, for his kiss, for his sex moving deep inside her, something she had thus far only imagined. Of course he knew; she could see it in his eyes. She could hear it in his deep, throaty voice through gritted teeth, whenever he struggled to keep his fangs from descending. It was the same for him, had been from the very start; she had seen it on the night when, to her horror, he'd plunged those deadly fangs into his own flesh rather than put her to the hazard. He knew the pull of the feeding frenzy. He didn't trust either of them to resist it. And it would be worse now, when the sun set, because they could not feed. Milosh had said they must fast before the ritual.

Cassandra beat back her thoughts with the demands of the present. The sun had passed its zenith long ago and was already sliding low behind dense cloud cover. Soon they must begin their ascent, and the herbs had yet to be brewed; the water was carefully measured and ready to receive them. First the bristly textured borage leaves, then the sweetly fragranced broom tops, following the exact recipe Milosh had given her. With great care, for they were sharp, she peeled away the prickly milk thistle bottoms and added the hearts and seeds to the cauldron. Next came the skullcap—the whole herb. The delicate blue flowers blended with the yellow blossoms of the broom, turning the draught a brilliant shade of green. Last but not least she added the fresh rue and barsa weed leaves, counting carefully.

Tart sweetness and earthy scents rode the steam rising from the cauldron as she stirred. Inhaling alone was intoxicating, and she stood back from the hearth and let the brew simmer. Her head was throbbing. Nausea overtook her. The room began to spin, and she dropped into the chair beside the hearthstone, bent forward with her elbows propped upon her knees, and lowered her head into her hands. She felt weightless, as if she could float up to the rafters if she didn't find something to hold on to.

Why wouldn't the room stay still? Why was everything all wavy, like the fabric of her best moiré evening frock? It was as if the cottage were alive, had a pulse. She shut her eyes and it echoed in her ears—*thump . . . thump . . . thump*—like the blood-chilling knocking at the cottage door that came in the night, riddling her with gooseflesh. If breathing the steam could have this effect, what on earth would drinking the stuff do? She gagged at the smell. What if she couldn't keep it down? Milosh hadn't prepared her for *this*.

She tried to rise but couldn't. Her legs wouldn't support her. She wanted to call out to Jon, but she couldn't do that either. Forcing her eyes open, she tried to see, but all that met her gaze was the thick, corpse-white mist drifting toward her from the cauldron. Then all at once her vision narrowed and a shape took form; a large white wolf with a silver-gray streak down its back, its red-rimmed eyes staring through the steam and glowing.

The animal was so close. It looked so real, but it wasn't; it was only a vision—or so Cassandra thought until its lips curled back, exposing long, curved fangs. They were dripping with blood. The wolf raised its head and howled toward the ceiling. It was a silent howl. No sound came from the beast as it howled again, then stood upon its hind legs and drank from the boiling cauldron.

Why didn't it burn its paws, its tongue? The cauldron was scalding hot. Stark terror found her voice and Cassandra screamed, vaulting out of her chair, but her trembling legs wouldn't work as she started to run. Looking back toward the cauldron, she fell to the floor and screamed again. The wolf specter evaporated, drifting upward with the steam before her very eyes . . . and disappeared.

Jon was at her side in seconds. Raising her up, he wrapped

a firm arm around her waist and led her out into the damp, sweet air. Gasping for breath, Cassandra shook her head, as if to disperse the visions that would not leave her mind.

"What the deuce happened?" he wheezed. "That ghastly smell—no wonder you swooned."

"I didn't swoon," she snapped at him. "I saw . . . I mean . . . that is to say . . . I do not know what I saw, or *thought* I saw. A wolf, I think. At first I thought—but no . . . it couldn't have been. I blinked and it was gone. Milosh said there would be visions when we drank the draught. He never said they would occur from breathing the steam."

Coughing, Jon sat her down on a tree stump close by. "Do not move from there," he said. "I'll take the pot off the fire. It's boiled enough. We shall let it steep and cool. We must set out before the sun sinks behind the mountains, anyway; the less time traveling after dark the better. In the open we will be vulnerable to attack. We must minimize the risk by covering as much ground in daylight as possible. Neither of us has slept, and our wits must be sharp for this."

He strode off into the cottage then, and Cassandra's posture sagged as she stared after him. Should she tell him about her vision in detail? No. There was no need. It was only a figment of her imagination induced by the potent steam; nothing more. Surely she was subconsciously worried about Milosh—about the fangs she'd seen protruding from his mouth. Had he reverted to a bloodlusting vampire? Were they in real danger from him now, too? Those thoughts were what had conjured the vision . . . weren't they? Or had she just discovered another of her gifts—the power of premonition? If that were so, what did this vision mean?

No! She would think on it no more. It was pointless. Instead she gulped the sweet, pine-scented air and listened to the bird music coming from the trees. Slowly her head cleared. Though the nausea remained, the world around her no longer resembled moiré silk, and the sickening tart-sweetness that had overwhelmed her was purged from her nostrils by the heady scent of honeysuckle, rosemary, and wet pine. Removed from the fire, the contents of the cauldron ceased producing steam. Only the faintest tufts escaped now, and once the cottage was aired, she went back inside. Jon went with her.

He hefted the cauldron on top of the table, while Cassandra tore a length of her petticoat away and stretched it over the bucket. It took some time for the draught to cool. While they waited, Jon kept vigil just outside the open cottage door. All the while the sun was sliding closer to the horizon. Cassandra was thinking, What if after all this the ritual should fail? What if the clouds that had hovered all day refused to let the moon shine through? What if Milosh . . . No, she wouldn't think of that. It was only an air dream brought on by lack of sleep and that deuced steam.

"Hold the gauze while I pour," Jon said, snapping her out of her reverie. He was standing with the cauldron poised at the ready over the wooden bucket.

Cassandra shot out her hands and held the gauze, while Jon poured the pot's contents at a trickle through the fabric, allowing time for the strange-smelling greenish brew to penetrate the cloth. Not a drop was lost, and once he'd poured it all, Cassandra took the flask that had once held holy water from the mantel where Jon had put it when he emptied his greatcoat pocket and, with the ladle, filled it to the brim with the brew.

A blustery wind was stirring, the sky's slate-gray clouds racing before it. That could either mean that the predicted storm was imminent, or that the wind would chase the clouds away altogether. There was no time to waste worrying, however. It was time to go.

They didn't bother to lock the cottage door. What was the use? If Milosh in wolf form could crash through a door barred on the outside, who knew what Sebastian and his minions could do when there was no one inside to keep them out? Taking the holy oil from the mantel, the tinderbox, and a handful of dry firewood and twigs from the chimney corner, Jon shrugged on his greatcoat and they set out in the cart to climb the mountain, which thankfully was no more than a glorified hill compared to others in the range.

It was a gradual incline, winding lazily toward the summit. They soon passed the patches of rue among the rocks that edged the grade where Cassandra had gathered the herbs earlier. From that point the path steadily narrowed until it was barely wide enough for the cart to pass. Several yards farther on, it ceased altogether. From there, they must continue on foot. It wasn't far, but the sky was darkening, bringing the twilight early, and a stiff wind whistled through the crags. Jon climbed down just as the heavens opened and the rain came sluicing over them.

Cassandra climbed down also, raising the hood of her indigo cloak, while Jon untied the tarpaulin that had protected everything during the last storm, and began rummaging beneath it.

"What are you looking for?" she queried.

He lifted out the small bundle of kindling and handed it to her. "Here," he said, "keep this dry. We need it to light a fire to melt the sacramental oil."

She had nearly forgotten. Tucking it beneath her cloak, she watched while he raked some straw into a similar bundle and handed that to her also.

"We shan't need the beakers Milosh bought from the tinkers," he said. "We have enough to carry. We can drink from the flask. We shan't need the rope, either, to scale this peak. It's no steeper than the tor at home, and there's plenty of gorse and bracken."

All at once Cassandra staggered. The eerie vision of the white wolf drinking from the cauldron flashed before her eyes, and she gripped the side of the cart for support. Jon didn't seem to notice. Still rummaging, he collected several other tools, including the deadly cleaver, and was just about to tie the tarpaulin down again when something caught her eye: a curved-sided wooden trencher.

The cryptic vision came again. This time, she was prepared and paid closer attention. Though the vision's rampant flashes were debilitating, she tried to extract whatever message lurked beneath the surface. The wolf's red-rimmed, yellow-green eyes blazing through an iridescent veil were haunting. The bared fangs dripping blood were terrifying. The bone-chilling flashes had begun when she first glimpsed the trencher. As she reached for it, Jon arrested her hand with a quick grip on her wrist.

"Leave that," he said. "It's still a good distance to the summit, and we shan't need it."

She wriggled her arm free. "We need it," she said. Claiming the trencher, she tucked it under her cloak with the rest.

"What for?" he asked. "We shan't be eating up there, Cass. It's just one more thing to carry."

"We just do," she said, moving out of his reach. She sighed. "By the look of this rain, we shan't need any of it.

What will we do if all this hides the eclipse?" The conversation needed changing. She could tell him about the visions, but he would think her a complete ninnyhammer. Besides, how could she convince him it was anything but her imagination if she wasn't convinced herself? Still . . . it was passing strange.

"Have you ever seen an eclipse of the moon?" he asked. Cassandra shook her head.

"There was one when I was at university," he said. "'Twas a beautiful sight—it lasted for three hours. The moon was ghost-white when it began, but when it sank into the earth's shadow, it turned orange. Then, when the eclipse was total, it became blood-red. 'Tis an eerie sight. It is at that stage we must drink the draught. It is also then that we will be most vulnerable to other vampires . . . and to each other."

Cassandra ignored the last. "But how will we know when the eclipse is total if we cannot see the moon?"

Jon gazed at the heavens. The rain was slackening, and the clouds were zipping along at a steady pace. "Unless I miss my guess, the storm will pass over," he said. "I only hope it is in time."

They said no more during the climb, and Cassandra was thankful for that. It was full dark when they reached the summit, a flat plateau, an under-cliff with a shallow jutting crag that made a perfect shelter from the rain. The natural rock formation afforded a perfect seatlike ledge upon which to rest, and Jon saw her to it, and busied himself preparing for the ritual.

None of this was visible from the land below. From there, it had appeared just as all the other mountains. Now they were on the far side of the peak: the side that showed the vastness of the mountain range like jagged teeth stretching as far as the eye could see, with what appeared to be a deep, bottomless gorge between.

Jon was keeping his distance, pacing the flat table of rock tufted with patches of green. She knew why. She felt the feeding frenzy beginning; he must as well. It was stronger tonight—stronger than it had ever been. Was that because they had fasted, or was it the pull of this blood moon they couldn't even see? Gradually, the rain slowed, then stopped altogether but for a stubborn drizzle. Nearly an hour passed before that faded, too, the only noise an occasional hollow splat as rain that collected in puddles on the rocky overhang above dripped down.

Jon had been watching Cassandra from the edge for some time now. She tried not to make eye contact with him, but she couldn't help it. That quicksilver gaze of his drew her own like a magnet. The condition had progressed in them both. Would they be able to resist the bloodlust coupled with a desire that was palpable even at this distance? Was he thinking the same? A tremor passed over his hooded eyes as if he'd read her thoughts, and he prowled closer, until she could inhale his evocative woodsy scent stirred by the wind, until she could smell his blood. She tried to steel herself digging her fingertips into the rocky bench she sat upon, her body gone rigid. Instinct told her not to look him in the eyes.

"Do you have the pistol?" he gritted through clenched teeth.

She had seen him fight like that dozens of times, mostly when he tried to hold back the fangs. It never worked; they always descended nonetheless. She swallowed. Yet the frightening thing was, she wasn't afraid.

She nodded.

"Remember what I told you, Cassandra."

How could she ever forget?

He pointed skyward. "Look . . ." he said.

Cassandra followed his outstretched arm with her eyes. Stars were peeking through the clouds in random clusters. Was that the upper curve of the moon? She blinked, continuing to stare. *Yes!* The clouds were racing before it, giving brief, teasing glimpses. The eclipse had not yet begun.

"Give me the wood and the straw," he said, his hand extended.

Cassandra had forgotten all about the bundles beneath her cloak. She handed them over, being careful not to touch Jon in the process. Their hearts were beating in a similar rhythm. She could hear it—she could *feel* it. She had forgotten about the trencher, and in her haste it fell, making a hollow sound by glancing off several rocks.

Jon kicked it out of the way and raised her to her feet. "I cannot bear that look in your eyes," he murmured, "but you are right to fear me. The bloodlust is so much stronger now. It could be the pull of the moon, or our progression . . ." He ran the back of his hand lightly across her cheek.

"I don't fear you, Jon," she murmured, instinctively kissing his hand. "I fear what will be if this doesn't work. We cannot go on like this—loving each other, wanting each other, in terror of each other, afraid that our love will damn us."

He put her from him, raking back his hair ruthlessly. "Help me with the fire," he said. "We must both prepare this, Cassandra—and no matter what occurs, you must finish the ritual."

"You are scaring me now, Jon," she murmured.

He spun toward her, his eyes glowing in the reflected light of the moon, partly visible now. "And well you ought to be scared," he snapped, flinging his arm toward the heavens again. "It has begun. Do you feel it, the pull? Milosh never said it would be like this. I do not know if I can withstand it. And we are not alone on this mountain. I can sense . . . Perhaps once we build the fire."

Cassandra felt it, too—a discernible presence. She thought of the creatures of the night that had pounded upon the cottage door, of Sebastian in his natural form, that hideous half-bat, half man, so huge his head challenged the cottage ceiling; and of her husband, ready to die to keep her safe from harm at his own hands. The moon, ghostly white, was nearly free of the clouds now, though a different sort of shadow had begun to cross its face. The eclipse had begun.

Cassandra was suddenly struggling with her demons, with her longings, with the carnal demands of a body over which she had precious little control. She pretended she didn't see the flock of what appeared to be birds but which she knew were bats streaking in silhouette across the alabaster moon. She pretended she didn't hear the plaintive howling of wolves. Did Jon see or hear? Did he suffer visions? Was that why he was so adamant about the gun? His demeanor while struggling with the fire was proof enough that at least some of her suspicions were correct.

She laid out wide a ring of straw at Jon's direction. Meanwhile he stripped off his coat and cast it aside, then took up the tinderbox and the dry wood and started a fire in the center of the circle. He next propped the sacramental oil container near enough to the flames to melt the solidified oil, but not so near that it was in danger of catching fire; then he paced the flat plateau like a caged lion waiting for it to render. Once it had, Cassandra sacrificed another piece of her petticoat for Jon to hold the

tin so he wouldn't burn himself, and he walked around
the circle sprinkling the holy oil on the straw.

"It doesn't matter if it hardens now," he said, closing
the circle. "This oil is flammable in any form." The gauze
scrap of Cassandra's petticoat had become saturated with
the unction, and he wrapped it around the end of a stick
he'd set aside when he built the fire, then brandished it.
"To ignite the circle," he explained. "You do not want to
get too near."

"Should we ignite it now?" Cassandra asked.

Jon studied the sky. The moon was clearly visible, but
only darkened by half. It had taken on a peculiar orange
tinge. It was happening! But their mission would not be
quickly resolved. It would be awhile before the eclipse
was total.

"No," he said. "If we light it too soon, it will burn out
before it's needed. Besides, it must be lit from inside the
circle, and we must stay inside the circle once it is."

Cassandra nodded. "Where is the draught?" she asked.

"In my coat pocket," he replied. Striding toward the
ledge, he stooped to pick up his greatcoat. A rush of wind
suddenly made the flames dance in the central fire. There
was no time to give warning, though a scream spilled
from Cassandra's throat, and a black blur of motion
slammed into Jon just as he straightened. The attack sent
the greatcoat—draught and all—sailing over the edge of
the mountaintop.

Sebastian!

Rooted to the spot, Cassandra screamed again. The
sound reverberated in her ears as if it were coming from
an echo chamber. Before her eyes, her husband and the
vampire wrestled, teetering on the ledge, while overhead,
the earth's shadow crawled ever closer to eclipse the

moon. The sphere's orange hue was slowly turning red. It was nearly time. Had this all been for naught? Cassandra screamed again.

"Get inside the ring and set it afire, Cass!" Jon charged. He had a grip upon Sebastian's throat, but the vampire's clawlike fingernails had shredded his shirt and gouged the flesh beneath, drawing blood. "Now, Cassandra! You'll be safe inside the ring. He will not cross over fire and holy oil—"

"The draught!" she sobbed. "It's gone!"

"*Light . . . the . . . fire,*" he repeated, gravel-voiced.

That command brooked no opposition, and so Cassandra took up the gauze-wrapped stick and stepped inside the circle. She was just about to touch the gauze to the flames when a bloodcurdling howl froze her. It ended in a vicious snarl, and Cassandra watched, mouth agape, as a great white wolf with a silver-ridged back streaked through the air and impacted Jon and Sebastian, still struggling on the brink.

For a moment Cassandra couldn't believe her eyes. *Milosh?* It was; his wounds were clearly visible. Her heart skipped a beat. The conflict was so close that she couldn't tell which figure the wolf was attacking, but then Sebastian roared and cried out in pain. Milosh had nearly bitten off his ear. Enraged, Sebastian grabbed the wolf by the throat and hurled him to the rocky ground. Milosh fell hard on his side with a pained yelp and could not rise.

Cassandra felt her fangs descending. The scent of fresh blood filled her nostrils from all quarters—that of all three combatants. The pull was unbearable. But so was the pull of the blood moon, nearly eclipsed; another thing Milosh had neglected to mention. It was as if an unseen tether were reining her in, drawing her ever closer with each breath she drew, so great was the magnetism.

She plunged the oily, gauze-wrapped stick into the fire, but she did not ignite the circle. Instead, she sprang forward and set Sebastian's greatcoat afire. The flames quickly spread to the clothes beneath, and the creature let Jon go, shrieking and peeling off the flaming layers as he shriveled to a silvery streak. A moment later he disappeared, roaring, into the night.

Cassandra knew but a brief moment of relief before her blood ran cold again, and she gave another scream. Jon had leaned over the brink, surged to his feet, and jumped! Scarcely able to put one foot before the other, she staggered to the edge and looked down, expecting to see her husband lying sprawled out dead somewhere below.

A string of involuntary shrieks poured from her, and her eyes flew in all directions, sifting through the darkness. The mysterious moon spared just enough light to show her Jon's greatcoat. It had snagged on a petrified root cluster protruding from a narrow ledge jutting out from the sheer face of the mountain. Jon was standing upon that rocky shelf, stretching toward the coat, which was flapping in the wind just out of reach. Cassandra held her breath as he straddled the branch and shinnied out upon it until the coat was within reach. Her hand clamped over her lips, she watched him snatch the coat and shinny back to the shelf.

Staggering away from the edge, Cassandra looked up at the moon. Indeed, it was blood-red, nearly eclipsed. It was almost time—only minutes remained. She must light the ring of fire. But first she ran to Milosh, who lay panting helplessly, blood dripping from fangs he would not or could not retract. There was no menace in that for her. And his yellow-green, red-rimmed wolf's eyes were pleading.

The trencher! My God, is this the meaning of that cryptic vision?

She tossed the flaming stick down on the rocky ground and ran to the natural shelter where the trencher had fallen. Snatching it up from among the random tufts of grass, she spun around to find herself seized and swept into Jon's arms.

He had tossed his coat inside the unlit circle and now pulled her into a smothering embrace. At first it was pure passion and relief as he cleaved to her, but then that changed; his sensuous lips clamped tight over clenched teeth told her all too well he fought the fangs, even as she herself did.

Frantic hands roamed her body, pulling her closer against the bruising force of his arousal. The bloodlust was unbearable. Palpitating spurts like liquid fire surged through her moist sex, and her arched body reached for him as her fingers threaded through his dark hair, wet with the evening dew. Their thundering hearts beat against each other as one, their loins responding with a jerking reflex. She looked him in the eye—those quicksilver eyes, red-rimmed now and hooded with bloodlust and desire. This was what he had warned her of, why he'd insisted that she carry the pistol. He could not stop, and she could not resist him. He was her husband. But this was beyond conjugal bliss; it was that combined with a ravenous urge to devour—to possess. It was an urge so powerful it usurped the instinct of self-preservation inherent in all creatures and bound them together in mindless oblivion.

Foxed by his ardor, by the fangs inches from her flesh that could destroy her, Cassandra only heard the white wolf's growl from the distant periphery of her consciousness. It wasn't until the great wolf slammed into them, separating them, driving them into the circle, then collapsing itself just outside the ring, that sanity came trickling back.

"Cassandra," Jon moaned, his eyes a study in shame and grief as he fought his way back from blood madness.

"Help me get him . . . inside the circle," she grunted, tugging the wolf's inert body. "I cannot lift him on my own."

Jon staggered to her side and, reaching down, lifted the wolf into his arms. He carried it inside the ring of straw. The motion stirred Milosh to consciousness, but the most that the Gypsy could manage was a half-upright position resting upon his front legs, his eyes glazed with pain.

The moon shone down in full eclipse, its blood-red halo glowing eerily. Jon's hands were trembling as he ignited the straw circle with the gauze-wrapped stick. They were still trembling when he opened the flask and handed it to Cassandra.

"Three swallows," he said. "Hurry. It must be now, Cass."

She tilted the flask and swallowed once, twice, three times, all around a grimace. It was foul-tasting, bitter. She was hoarse from screaming, and she coughed once the last of it had trickled down her parched throat. *Please, God, don't let me retch*, she prayed, handing the flask back.

Jon downed three swallows himself and was about to close the flask when her quick hand caught his. "Give it here," she said.

Clearly nonplussed, he handed it back, and she dropped to her knees on the cold stone plateau and poured some of the draught into the trencher she'd brought. Vertigo was robbing her of her vision. The blazing circle of fire seemed to spin around her; the surrounding darkness was sprinkled with glaring white pinpoints of light. Or, were they the stars? She couldn't be sure. She was as good as castaway, but she slid the trencher toward the wolf and watched him lap from it greedily.

"I don't understand," Jon murmured. "Is this why you insisted upon bringing that deuced trencher? How could you possibly have known?"

"I had a vision," she said, but said no more, for she spiraled down into blood-red darkness.

CHAPTER TWENTY-FOUR

The orchestra had struck up a country dance—nothing scandalous, like the new waltz everyone was twittering about. Wrapped in a cloud of another scent, Jon scarcely noticed the aroma of stale cake, or the sickening tart-sweetness of fruity ratafia and almond-flavored orgeat assembled on the refreshments table along with the stronger libations for the men in attendance.

Miss Cassandra Thorpe. How fetching she was, wrapped in a cloud of apricot-colored tissue silk that made her skin glow. How gracefully she tripped across the labyrinth of his memory. Her provocative scent threading through his nostrils rose above the stench of blood and charred wood, and he was there, really there—at least it seemed so. Milosh had said there would be hallucinations.

From the moment he had taken her gloved hand and led her out on the dance floor he had sealed their fate. The first time he turned her lithe body to the strains of the country music, he knew he must make her his—knew it despite the chastisement that followed, the angry indignation of Lady Estella Revere and her harridan mother, who had earmarked him for her daughter, and the righteous indignation of Lady Jersey, who'd taken him to task over wasting the occasion upon a totally ineligible lady's companion. He still bled inside for the embarrassment—not for himself, but for Cassandra, though she didn't seem to mind. All in all, it was a pleasant hallucination featuring that which he'd loved most before exchanging orgeat and ratafia for herbal poison and blood. . . . But that comparison quickly plunged his thoughts toward something he hated with every fiber of his being—*Sebastian*.

Jon moaned as his dream took a darker turn. All at once, he was back in that dingy gambling hell, his nostrils filled with cheroot smoke, with the odor of unwashed men, the sickening-sweet ghost of Blue Ruin and other anonymous spirits long-ripened in the scarred wood floorboards. He saw again the tall dark shadow, the strange-looking man impeccably dressed in the latest London fashions who introduced himself and offered to point out an alternate method of finding the parishioner he was seeking. Jon relived, as if outside himself looking on, how eye contact with the monster had clouded his mind. All at once he was back in that wharfside alley reeking of fish, raw sewage, and rotting produce, sprawled on the slimy, filth-encrusted cobblestones peppered with spent cheroot butts and broken glass. He felt again the sharp fangs piercing his flesh, struggled again through his dazed disorientation and the aftereffects, the cruel realization that he had been infected.

Dark, swirling fog drifted over him in the hallucination. He didn't want to see more, but it visited him nonetheless: the heart-stopping moment when he saw

Cassandra lying on the ground in Vauxhall Gardens, the creature feeding upon her, infecting her. *No!* His mind screamed, but the relentless visions would not fade. Jon fought with all his might to open his eyes, but he could not. He lay helpless, while the whole nightmare played out before him, until a voice like thunder at last bled into the rest.

"You cannot escape me," it said, then burst into a spate of mocking laughter.

Did he dream that voice? Had it simply ghosted across his mind, a byproduct of the draught like all the rest? Was it a direct communication through thought, the way he communicated with Cassandra when they were in their animal incarnations; or was the voice real? His eyes snapped open. Sebastian was nowhere in sight.

Jon shook himself like a dog and tried to rise. His head was spinning. The mountain seemed to be whipping around, out of control, and he staggered like a drunken lord when he finally struggled upright on the third try. It was still dark. The moon had disappeared, but the stars blinked down innocently upon what had been a life-and-death struggle between the living and the undead. He held his head as if his hands would keep his brain from bursting; it felt about ready to explode. If only his eyes would focus. If only he could remember . . .

Cassandra! She was unconscious on the other side of the circle. Calling her name, he reeled past the fire that had dwindled to glowing embers, stumbled over his great-coat, and dropped down beside her. Was she breathing? He gathered her into his arms and shook her gently— how soft, how sweet and fragrant she was . . . and how still. How deathly still.

"Cassandra!" he gritted out. His teeth were clenched

to hold back the fangs, just as always when he was aroused. But there were no fangs. He ran his fingers along the edge of his teeth, scarcely able to believe it. He was on fire for her, but there was no bloodlust, only the raging heat of desire. "Cassandra," he murmured, "it worked. The draught . . . it worked!"

Murmuring her name again, he smothered her with kisses. After a moment, she stirred and her eyes came open halfway. Her fingers were warm as they flitted over his face. It was as if she didn't trust her eyes. All at once she was clinging to him, sobbing his name, fisting her tiny hand in his hair as she returned his kisses. He folded her closer, and her body arched against him—reached for him—and he was undone. They were alone on top of the mountain. In that moment, they were the only two people on earth.

Still gritting his teeth, for he could scarcely believe it, he dropped his head down to her shoulder, his lips a hair's breadth from the vein at the base of her throat and the blood pumping through it, but there was no feeding frenzy. Yes, the flow of her blood—her life force—aroused him. Yes, his heart beat to that same rhythm. Yes, it sent shock waves coursing through his body, through his sex. But this was carnal desire not bloodlust that drove him, and he was experiencing it as if for the first glorious time in her arms.

His hand was shaking as he traced the blue veins visible through her opalescent skin. It wasn't safe to make love to her here, but she gently kissed the fingers caressing her cheek and he melted.

"Milosh . . . ?" she murmured.

"He's not here," he replied, his eyes searching hers, which were dilated with desire in the last of the fire's dying embers. Judging from the absent moon and the position of the stars, dawn was not far off. The fiery ring that enclosed them had long since burned out, and a cool mist was rising over the mountain from the gorge below. It cast a ghostly aura over the scene of what had been a horrific battle.

If it weren't for Cassandra's quick thinking, setting Sebastian's clothing afire, Jon would have lost that battle. At last he knew why Milosh had never been able to vanquish the vampire. Sebastian was possessed of an incredible physical strength that neither of them could match. If one thing was learned from the confrontation, it was that brute strength was not the way to kill the creature. It was only by wits, by cunning, that they would be able to conquer the centuries-old vampire.

Milosh. The Gypsy had proved his mettle, his loyalty, but still he remained an enigma. Nonetheless he had played a noble part in their protection, even to the point of attacking Jon when his bloodlust threatened Cassandra. Where was he now? His wounds had been serious to begin with, not to mention whatever other injuries he had sustained in the last confrontation. Had he crawled off somewhere to die? What sort of premonition had Cassandra had that made her insist upon bringing that trencher? How could she know that Milosh might need the draught as well and, more pointedly, how could she possibly know he would be in wolf form when he appeared?

All these questions cried out for answers, but not now—not when Cassandra's soft flesh was calling to him. Not when her delicate, blue-veined hand had grasped his and was guiding it to the skirt of her frock and what remained of her petticoat, pushing it up, exposing her sex to his gaze—and to his plunder.

Hungry eyes devoured the sight of her. The soft moans leaking from her arched throat compelled him. One by one, all restraints were discarded until they both lay naked under a blanket of mist. Free of the bloodlust, it was as if each place he touched was being touched for the first time. Every nuance of their coupling was an awakening, bursting to life and awareness in a way he'd never dreamed possible.

He wasn't prepared for the power of this passion that consumed him as the flames had consumed the straw. He wasn't ready to make love to his exquisite bride without restraint, without fear—without having to plunge his deadly fangs into his own flesh to keep himself from destroying her tender body. This was all new to him, and he embraced it greedily.

Long, languid kisses deepened with desire, the taste of her honey-sweet skin, the thrill of her innocent abandon—all these things were happening for the first time. Yes, his heightened sense of smell detected her blood, but it no longer commanded him to drink from those delicate veins. Gone was the dark rapture of their embrace. What remained was rapturous, yes, and all-consuming, but gone was the peril. The blood moon ritual had allowed them to take their union into the light.

He groaned as his tongue found first one hardened nipple and then the other—something he'd dared not savor before, his fangs always at the ready. She was malleable beneath him, her arched body begging for penetration. Groaning again, he held back—not from fear of draining her blood this time, but to give her the most pleasure his body could provide.

Spreading her thighs, he entered her slowly, stretching her virgin flesh until it gave admittance to his anxious member. All the while, her haunting, dilated eyes trans-fixed him. No more than a brief flash disturbed their shimmer as he entered her, gliding on her moist heat. She felt like hot silk against his hardness. Her sweet breath caught in her throat and he moved in her, riding her rhythm. Her hands raced over his back, over the indenta-tion of his narrow waist, and cupped his taut buttocks. Jon groaned. She was touching him in ways they'd never dared touch before.

Deep, guttural murmurs seemed to echo from her very core as she clung to him, moving against him, whispering his name as she arched her spine, reaching to take him deeper. It was more than he could bear; more than he'd dared hope for. His sex was on fire, his body undulated against her.

Only when he felt her contractions sheath his sex—only when he felt her climax seize his member, felt the friction of her moist fire—did he plunge himself deeper . . . and deeper still until he'd filled her. Mindless oblivion took him then, just as it did her. He could see it in the dilated luminescence of her eyes. He could feel it in the hammering of her heartbeat against his, in the rhythm of her hot breath puffing against his skin, slick with sweat. She was his as he had never had her. She was totally his at last.

A bestial howl escaped him as her sex tightened around his engorged member again, and the seed of his life rushed from him in a steady pulsating stream. The breath left his body in the shape of her name, and he gathered her to him voraciously. The mist embraced them then, caressing their bodies, drifting over their moist skin. Neither spoke. There was no need. Below, the first signs of the lightening sky crept over the distant hills. All was still until a deep-throated roar of laughter rumbled through the mountains like thunder.

"You cannot escape me," a disembodied voice boomed through the utter stillness. Cassandra heard it, too, and shuddered at the sound. She clung to Jon, crowding closer in his arms. The vampire's message was chillingly plain; though they'd had their little victory, the race was not yet run.

The sun had risen over the mountains by the time they reached Milosh's cart. Jon was hoping to find the Gypsy there, but the cart was empty, just as they'd left it.

"Where do you suppose he's gone?" Jon asked, his narrowed gaze sweeping the mountainside. "He was barely conscious to lap up the draught—in no shape to put himself through what he did up there. I wonder if he even has the strength to change back."

"I do not know," Cassandra said. "If he hadn't come when he did—Jon, it took the both of you, and still . . ."

"How did you know to bring that trencher? You said you had a vision . . . What exactly did you see?"

Cassandra drew a ragged breath. She had changed her soiled frock and torn petticoat, choosing a white sprigged muslin morning dress sprinkled with dainty roses from among her frocks he had repurchased at the open market, and was tugging it into place. How lovely she was in that frock. How he wished he could have bought back all of her things.

"I didn't understand what I saw at the time," she said, "only thought that it might be important I see it. The rest came to me when Milosh crashed into you and Sebastian on the mountain. If you remember, he said that we could not shapeshift during the ritual—that whatever incarnation we were in when we began the rite, we must stay in. Breathing the steam from the herbs brought on the vision, and I saw the wolf standing on its hind legs, drinking from the cauldron. When I saw the trencher, I just knew I must take it."

"Did you have any visions after you drank the draught?"

She hesitated, then shook her head. "No . . . none."

"I had no visions from the steam, but I did from the draught. It evidently has affected us differently. It might be wise to keep a supply of the herbs on hand. Your . . . 'powers,' if you will, must be different from mine."

"What did you do up there?" she said. "My heart nearly stopped when you jumped off the mountain to get that coat. What were you thinking?"

He took her in his arms, soothing her. "That's right," he realized. "You don't know. I didn't, either, until Milosh showed me. Watch."

Crouching, he sprang into the air and drifted slowly to earth some yards distant. Cassandra watched, mouth agape.

"I was never in any danger," he said. "It works both ways. I am able to jump down or leap up. The ledge below was wide enough to accommodate me, and I'm better at it than I was the first time."

"Can I do that?" she murmured. "As a panther I can, but I never dreamed . . ."

Jon smiled. "We won't know unless you try," he said, holding out his arms.

Following his example, she crouched and sprang, landing on her feet close beside him, and went into his embrace.

"I'm sorry I frightened you," he murmured, grazing her cheek with the back of his hand. "There wasn't time to explain."

Cassandra nodded. "What do we do now?" she asked as he helped her onto the seat of the cart.

"First, we go back to the cottage and see if Milosh has returned there. We need to know what caused him to revert back to what he was before his first blood moon ritual. We need to know when and if it will happen to us, Cass—our lives could depend upon it. He said that as long as we repeated the ritual regularly we would stay as we are now. That seems untrue. We need to know why."

Cassandra's expression clouded. "I don't think I could bear to go back and become as we were," she murmured. Her misty eyes brought a lump to his throat.

"We are what we are, Cassandra," he said. "There is no way 'round it. We must take what boons Providence allows. Now, we have work to do—vampires to run to ground and destroy, beginning with Sebastian. We must seek his resting place during the day and destroy him, and we risk dealing with his creatures of the night until we do."

"A-and then what?"

"And then we do what needs must for as long as needs must. Just because we no longer suffer from the bloodlust doesn't mean that we are cured. We will be hunted more relentlessly than we were before by the undead who cannot bear our privilege. No matter what occurs, we are what we will always be—vampires."

CHAPTER TWENTY-FIVE

The cottage was empty when they reached it, but there was nothing to be done, no time to hunt for man or wolf; they dared not waste the daylight while they were safe from Sebastian. Jon filled the empty flask with water from the stream and blessed it. Then, collecting wooden stakes, the mallet, a second flask of holy water so they could each arm themselves with one, and Milosh's deadly cleaver, he put them in a sack and they set out straightaway.

Cassandra didn't court conversation. She was afraid Jon would read her thoughts. She had lied when he asked if she'd had any more visions; she'd had one under the influence of the draught, but she couldn't tell him now. She had the power of premonition, there was no question. That she'd had this one during the rite only magnified the urgency of the message. The moment Jon's seed filled her, she knew she had conceived, and she knew it was a son. She also knew that for some reason it was vital that she know it now, when it would ordinarily be too soon to know, too soon to guess. She didn't question why.

Through some mystical phenomenon, she'd felt the child take root in her womb when they'd made love, and in her vision she'd seen its birth. How would Jon take such news? Would he welcome or abhor a child of their union? It was too soon to know. She couldn't tell him—not yet. Not until they were safely on their way back home to England, for that was where the child would be born. No, this she would keep to herself awhile. He was not ready to hear it now, and she was not ready to hear what he would say.

Cassandra didn't ask any questions, not even when they neared Sebastian's burned-out shell of a castle at the top of the first mountain they had climbed. It was daylight, after all; they would be safe until dusk. That there still was no sign of Milosh wasn't encouraging. She had seen Sebastian in action. Even with Milosh to help them, she couldn't imagine how they would defeat the vampire.

The thought of descending into the bowels of that castle again turned Cassandra's blood cold. Sebastian had brought her there the last time, as bait for Jon. So much had happened since, all of which seemed as if it had happened to someone else. It was midmorning when they left the cart where it had been left before. Cassandra remembered the place well, remembered the indignity of being carried in Milosh's great wolfish jaws and stuffed without ceremony into a foul-smelling rope mesh sack, albeit for her own good. Somehow, everything looked different now.

They hadn't met a soul along the way. That had been a worry, since they would still be hunted. Jon was careful to stay far afield of settlements. The villagers were unlikely to be hunting vampires in broad daylight, but they would surely recognize them, as well as Milosh's cart, to say nothing of Petra, who had for a time exchanged places with one of the townsfolk's animals. Caution was the watchword, and they'd kept well to the fringes of the narrow path that sidled upward, where tangled snarls of nettle, thorn, and young saplings hemmed the approach to Castle Valentin.

They hadn't gone far when Jon's hand on her arm slowed her pace. "Look sharp from here on," he said. "When I came this way with Milosh searching for you, a band of wolf shadows blocked our way. It was then that Milosh pointed out my ability to jump great distances."

"But that was after dark," she said.

"Yes, but we do not know that all Sebastian's minions are nocturnal. He is a ruthlessly cunning entity. He has had centuries to perfect his defenses. It would only stand to reason that he has servants of all sorts to see to his needs. The only hope we have of besting him lies in his overconfidence. That breeds mistakes. This will be more a battle of wits than physical warfare. We are novices, inept by comparison. Do not delude yourself: It shan't be easy."

Cassandra said no more. Castle Valentin loomed before them, demanding all their attention. They hadn't seen up close the ravages inflicted upon the ancient keep by the fire. The damage was staggering. The great, iron-spiked doors were no more; their ironwork littered the ground. Entering in, they stepped with caution. All around, the floor was heaped with slag, cinder, and ash. The malodorous stench of burnt wood soaked with rain and the permeating stink of foul, decaying flesh rose up in Cassandra's nostrils and threatened to make her retch.

"I think it best that we stay together," Jon said, "but if you would rather remain here . . ."

He was studying her closely, and she could only imagine what was written on her face. She did not want to be there at all. The sight and smell of the place—even in daylight—recalled memories unpleasant enough to drain the blood from her scalp and cause her knees to wobble. Which would not do. If she was to assist her husband in his new calling, as she'd resolved, she would have to steel herself against unpleasantness and fear. But it was all so new.

"I am not fond of viewing burnt corpses," she said, "but I expect I shall have to get used to it, shan't I."

"And worse, I have no doubt," he agreed. "As long as there are *vampir*, it will be thus. I'm sorry, Cassandra, it is that or lose our souls. Hunting down and destroying these creatures is our salvation—our redemption, if you will; I do not know a better way to put it. We must help others like ourselves, those caught in between, and rid the world of those beyond our help. It is hardly what I had planned as a life for us, but 'tis a noble enough calling."

"Agreed," she said. "But I do not agree that we should stay together now. Since time is short, it would be best, I think, if we search separately. We can cover more territory apart."

He gave the matter thought. She read opposition in his eyes, but at last he nodded. "Very well," he said. Reaching into his greatcoat pocket he drew out his flask of holy water and handed it over. "Take this," he said. "Use it if needs must, but stay within shouting distance. The holy water will repel but not kill vampires, Cassandra. Likely you will need me for that. Besides, from the look of the place, it isn't only vampires we need worry about. The fire has undermined some of the castle's structure—the important parts, like the beam supports. There are bound to be pitfalls. You could misstep and do yourself a mischief. Test your steps before you take them."

"I'll be careful," she assured him, climbing over the slag on the threshold that had spilled across the Great Hall. They both agreed that unless they came upon a passageway or chamber that had been overlooked when they first visited the castle, it wasn't likely that they would find anything. The purpose of the visit was to make certain they could rule out the castle as Sebastian's resting place. Then they would move on and search elsewhere.

Some rooms were impassable, and one staircase was hopelessly blocked where wooden beams had fallen across the span. Jon went below alone; since he had burned Sebastian's resting place and set the other pallets ablaze, he would know if anything had been disturbed there since. Cassandra made no objection—she had no desire to revisit Sebastian's dungeon. She stopped on the landing at the top of the staircase where a tapestry on the wall in the recessed alcove had been half consumed by fire. She tore it down . . . and revealed another door.

"Jon!" she called. "I've found something!"

Bounding up the narrow staircase, he was at her side in seconds.

"Here," she said, pointing. "Did you enter here when you burned the castle?"

"No," he said, fingering the large iron ring that served as a latch. He gave it a tug, and the door creaked open to a narrow, tunnel-like corridor sparsely lit by torches in wall sconces that reeked of some anonymous rendered fat. "Stay behind me," he said, nudging her back with his arm spread wide.

There was no alternative; the tunnel was so narrow that two couldn't walk abreast. The stench was unidentifiable, and unbearable. Cassandra grimaced, covering her nose and mouth. The smell worsened the farther they went, and she gagged and gagged again while attempting to keep back the bile that kept rising in her throat.

"Someone or something must tend these torches," Jon observed. "Look sharp!"

No sooner had he spoken than the corridor underfoot changed from solid rock to a wide metal mesh that was hard on the soles of Cassandra's leather slippers.

She stumbled. "What is this?" she murmured.

"Some sort of grate," Jon replied.

Slipping a firm arm around her, he took a torch from its bracket and lowered it to the floor for a better look. A rumble of discordant sound drifted upward. It grew louder. *Voices!* All at once, hands shot through the open grille-work; grasping, clutching. Cassandra screamed in spite of herself as pinching fingers closed around her ankle.

"The holy water," Jon cried. "Use the holy water."

Fumbling with the flask, she fought to keep her balance as Jon tried to loosen the fingers from her ankle. Opening the container at last, she sprinkled the holy water through the grate, and a heart-stopping chorus of shrieks rose from the creatures below. The hand fell away from her ankle trailing smoke.

Unfortunately, so many other hands were gripping the grating from below, a section gave way and fell in. Screaming, Cassandra slid down the length of it, grabbing fast, just short of falling into the sudden pit below where creatures were milling and moaning and shrieking their complaints. Needing both hands, she dropped the holy water flask. It struck the stone floor below, making a hollow clang that rang in her ears like that of a bell, and she loosed another troop of screams as the creatures—untouched by the splashed holy water—groped her feet, her legs, and her waist familiarly, meanwhile tugging upon her with the intent to pull her all the way down.

To her horror, her fangs began to descend. There was no arousal, no feeding frenzy, but the fact that they appeared at all was devastating after the blood moon ritual—and in daytime, too! Hadn't the rite worked after all?

"Cassandra! Take my hand!" Jon thundered. His section of the grating was still intact. He threw down his sack, flattened himself prostrate on the grillework, and reached for her. "Quickly," he commanded. "Before my side gives way as well."

"I cannot let go!" she sobbed. "If I do, they will pull me in."

"You must! Now, Cassandra!"

She tried, then quickly grabbed fast to the grating again. "Nooooo!" she wailed, shaking her head. "I cannot, Jon. They are too strong!"

"Trust me! You must or you are lost. I have the strength to pull you up!"

Cassandra shut her eyes and let go with her left hand, reaching for Jon above. She cried out as she felt his strong hand close around her wrist, then cried out again as he started to pull her up—the monsters below were pulling, too.

"Now the other hand. Now . . . I've got you. Kick your feet. We are stronger than these. They are sluggish, lethargic yet, because of the daylight. Their only advantage is in their number."

"But there are so many," she realized. "Too many for our weapons, and I've lost the holy water."

"Never mind. Just concentrate on getting out of there."

Cassandra did as he bade her, fisting her fingers in the sleeve of his greatcoat, and kicked wildly as he pulled her free of the grating. But one of the creatures came with her—a woman, clinging to her skirt. Jon had scarcely set Cassandra on her feet and shoved the creature back through the grating when three more climbed out of the chamber below, using the section that had fallen in as a ladder.

"You are right," Jon agreed. Snatching his sack, he tossed it over his broad shoulder and grabbed Cassandra's arm, pulling her along in the tunnel. "There are too many. Quickly!"

Running back the way they'd come, they plucked torches from their brackets one by one as they went and tossed them behind to slow their pursuers' progress. Still the vampires came, moving like automatons, as if to the beat of a galley drum. They showed no fangs, but Cassandra took no comfort in that—neither had Jon in daylight hours before the blood moon, or she, either . . . until now.

They reached the door to the tunnel, which they had left open when they entered, and tried to close it on the advancing creatures, but the combined weight of the vampires was too great.

"It's no use," Jon gasped. "Leave it. Run."

Together they raced through the alcove and up the stairs with the creatures close behind. They had nearly reached the Great Hall when another clamor met their ears. A mob of angry villagers was swarming through the open castle doorway, waving clubs and wattles, pistols, knives, and axes, their surly voices raised in righteous indignation. Cassandra screamed. They were caught.

"*There they are!*" the leader of the villagers shouted, pointing. "She's the one! Look! There are more . . . !"

"Where can we go? What can we do?" Cassandra cried. "We're trapped here."

Indeed they were, between the steady stream of vampires coming from one direction and the villagers advancing from the other.

Jon pointed at the blocked, free-standing staircase. "Jump," he said. "The way I showed you before. *Now,* Cassandra."

Cassandra let go of his arm, focused on the all-but-invisible landing above the slag and fallen timbers, bent her knees, and leapt into the air. Jon followed after and grabbed her in his arms as she teetered on the edge of the landing. The far side of the balustrade was missing, and it was a long drop into darkness below.

"We need to jump again," Jon said.

Cassandra stared over the edge. "You can't mean down *there.*"

"We must," he said. "Eventually they can scale that mess on the stairs. They'll get up here. I searched this castle. I do not know what shape it's in, but there is a corridor below."

"But we don't know what's down there, Jon. Not after the fire."

"No, but we do know what'll be up here. On the count of three. Hold on to me this time, and scream. I want them to think . . . Never mind, just scream!"

Cassandra loosed a spate of mad laughter. She would need no coaxing to scream.

"One . . . two . . . threeeeeeee!"

CHAPTER TWENTY-SIX

"They could not have survived such a fall," one of the villagers barked, his coarse voice echoing from above. "Get the others! Hurry! They're getting away!"

They dared not make a sound, and Jon clamped his hand over Cassandra's mouth and moved her deeper into the shadows as debris drifted down, loosened by the villager's feet above. He'd been right. They were in a corridor—a narrow one; his night vision picked it out clearly.

"Shhhhh. Not a word," he whispered, removing his hand from her mouth. "They think we're incapacitated. The others will distract them, which is only fitting. Let that mob up there destroy what the two of us alone could not. We will have fewer to contend with after . . ."

"What?" she whispered.

Jon hesitated. "The villagers will leave soon—the minute the sun sets. None will stay in this place after dark. That won't be long, judging by the glimpse of sky I had when we were in the Great Hall. We cannot very well go along with them, and they will surely post watchers outside. I wanted to have had done here and been away before dark, but that isn't possible now. We shall have to spend the night." As his wife shuddered in his arms, he pulled her closer. "If Sebastian's resting place is here and we can find and destroy it before dawn, as I did the one in the dungeon, the sun might destroy him for us. That is the most we can hope for."

"And the least?" Cassandra asked.

"That we elude him until dawn, find his resting place, and use the implements in this sack to destroy him there."

"No doubt they have found the cart," she said.

"Unfortunately, I believe you are right—unless Milosh came upon it. I wish I knew how he fares. I am not liking that he has not returned in either form."

The screams of dying vampires and the raucous shouts of the mob funneled down the wounded staircase and were amplified by the acoustics from the castle's construction. It was a bloodcurdling racket, and Jon pulled Cassandra closer, soothing her. The most horrible thing was that he could read her thoughts—technically they were like those unfortunate creatures being slaughtered by the mob, and had come frighteningly close to sharing their fate.

Flickering light blazed from above, throwing grotesque shadows on the walls along the corridor. Plumes of smoke and the stench of burning flesh filled Jon's nostrils. It wasn't safe to stay any longer; they could be seen now if someone looked below. He led her farther on to what had once served as servants' chambers and whisked her inside one. It was small, the only furniture a Glastonbury chair and a straw pallet. One high-set window was shuttered on the inside, like so many others he'd seen since they arrived in Moldovia. Standing on the chair, he cracked the shutter and squinted toward the setting sun.

"Just as I thought," he said, latching the shutter again. "It will soon be dark."

The terrible racket grew. Despite the closed door, shrieks and screams and angry voices filled the musty air. They had no means to make a light, and wouldn't even if they could. Instead, Jon counted upon his night vision. He saw Cassandra's wasn't as advanced, and his heart went out to her, watched as she felt her way around the chamber, groping in the dark.

"What is happening up there?" she murmured, clapping her hands over her ears.

"They are burning bodies in the Great Hall."

Cassandra blanched.

"You must remember, these creatures are not human any longer, Cass. They are undead—*his* creatures. Destroying them frees their souls and brings them peace. Fire is a way of doing this. It shan't affect us here below. All that would burn already went up in flames when I set fire to the place. It will not spread; it will burn itself out. You will see."

"It could be *us* up there," she sobbed. "We are no different."

"But we are, Cassandra," he returned, shaking her gently. "Yes, we are infected, but we are not wholly undead like those unfortunates up there—not mindless minions of the one that made them. If we were, the blood moon ritual would not have worked. But it *did*, so no one ever need know. It is too late for that among these villagers, of course, but wherever else we go in the world, people will know us as vampire *hunters*, because that is what we have become—and we have Milosh and the blood moon to thank for it."

Cassandra dissolved into tears, and so he took her in his arms. "My God, what is it?" he asked.

"T-the blood moon," she moaned. "It may have worked for you, but it hasn't for me."

He felt the blood drain from him. "What do you mean? Of course it worked for you. We made love without fighting back the feeding frenzy. How could you doubt?"

"It may have worked then, but no longer. It didn't last, Jon."

"That is absurd! How can you say that? What makes you think it?"

She hesitated. "Before, when I was trying to escape the creatures in that pit, my fangs . . . they came back."

"Was there hunger, bloodlust?"

"N-no. They just . . . descended. I nearly lost my grip on the grating when it happened. They didn't recede until we jumped down to the corridor outside. It happened to Milosh, too, don't you remember? Could the effects of the blood moon have worn off in us both?"

"I have no idea," Jon said, his brows beetled in a frown. "If only Milosh were here. There is so much we do not know that only he can tell us."

"Has it happened to you?" she murmured.

"No," he said. "The condition affects each of us differently, however. And that there was no feeding frenzy puzzles me. Are you certain?"

She nodded against his chest.

"Did it happen when we made love, Cassandra?"

"No," she sobbed. "And I was so happy . . ."

"Shhhh. We will sort it out," he soothed. "Milosh said that once the blood moon ritual was performed, we would no longer be slaves to our infection—that it would curtail the bloodlust, the feeding frenzy." He shook his head. "We need to finish what we've come to do here and then find Milosh." He led her to the pallet. "Lie down and rest. I will keep watch. As soon as it is safe to go abroad, we will go and search together."

It was some time before Cassandra fell asleep. Finally there were no more screams and shouts from above, and Jon drew a ragged breath. Night had fallen. The villagers had fled back to the foothills and all was still. Jon brushed back his hair. Cassandra was sleeping soundly. He hated to wake her. Still, he was anxious to finish what they'd come to do. Then they could concentrate on finding Milosh.

Twice, he opened the door a crack and closed it. There wasn't a sound. The glow of the flames had disappeared, and once more the corridor had been plunged into darkness. No noises met his enhanced hearing, and yet he sensed a presence. He opened the door a third time, straining his eyes and ears. No, it wasn't his imagination; though he could neither see, nor hear, nor smell the presence, something *was* there. Was it Sebastian?

He took up his sack and glanced behind toward Cassandra, who was sleeping soundly. Exhaustion—total, strength-draining exhaustion had overcome her. What she had told him was troubling, but he dared not let on that it was. And if he were to wake her, that fear would undermine his concentration. There was no room for distractions now. He stepped into the corridor and closed the door; he would stay in sight of it.

As he approached the hole from the staircase on the second floor, something fell—bits of debris sifting down drew his attention. Someone or something was standing on the fallen timbers blocking the staircase. Jon's heart skipped its rhythm. Gooseflesh puckered his scalp and raced down his spine. Stepping back into the shadows, he focused narrowed eyes on the timbers above. Something moved—something white. Backlit by a shaft of moonlight stabbing through the open doorway, a four-legged image took shape.

"Milosh?" Jon murmured.

A low, mournful howl broke the silence, and Jon leapt to the ground floor in a seamless bound; he was getting better at that. He'd scarcely landed when the wolf padded down the blocked staircase to the Great Hall below, and surged to his full height. Dropping the sack, Jon stripped off his greatcoat and gave it to Milosh, who stood naked before him. The Gypsy shrugged it on gingerly over his wounds.

"Where the devil have you been?" Jon spat through clenched teeth. "We feared you were dead."

"You were nearly correct," the Gypsy said. "I needed time to heal. You did a fine job, but that fall I took on the mountain weakened me. I needed time to regain my strength before I could change back. I probably should have waited a little longer as it is. I am still not at my most powerful."

"What are you doing here? Don't you know what just occurred?"

The Gypsy nodded. "I saw the light the fires gave off from below, and I came straightaway. I knew I would find you in the midst of it."

"The cart? Have they burned it?"

Milosh shook his head. "No, I'd hidden it deep in the forest while they were at their carnage. Where is your lady wife? I owe her a great debt."

Jon gave a start. "*Cassandra!*" he cried, striding back toward the staircase. "Good God, I left her sleeping below."

The Gypsy followed. "My wounds made it necessary for me to take part in the blood moon ritual," he said. "She has the gift of premonition—I doubt she understands it yet—and I was able to reach her with the help of the steam from the draught. It brings visions to some. It is a very potent elixir. I was too far gone to shapeshift. Technically, by human standards, I died from blood loss. Death cancels all things, Jon Hyde-White."

They had reached the edge of the slag heap that once was a staircase, and Jon hesitated. "Is that why your fangs descended? We saw them."

Milosh nodded. "Yes," he said. "There is much I have yet to tell you. I believe that is why I fought so valiantly to live. I am so tired, my friend, and so lonely. It is different for you. You have your Cassandra. I have no one. But for you and your lady wife, I would have welcomed death at last."

"Forgive me for ever doubting you," Jon said, shamefaced. "If you hadn't come up on that mountain when you did . . ."

Milosh dismissed the apology with a gesture. "Now you see why I could not destroy Sebastian on my own," he said. "He is a fearsome adversary. But enough of that. The ritual—were you able to complete it?"

Jon nodded. "Your fangs . . . when you were so low . . . did the desire to feed return as well?"

"No," the Gypsy replied. "The blood moon does not eliminate our fangs, Jon. You still have them, as does your lady wife, and you may use them to defend yourself if needs must—they will descend, built-in weapons, when they are needed. Your emotions will govern them. Still, you will not feed through them, nor will you infect another as long as the Blood Moon Rite protects you. This is one of the mysteries I have yet to explain . . . why I fought my way back. Why do you ask?"

"It happened to Cassandra earlier," Jon said. "We found those creatures that the villagers have now burned in a cell. The grate in the floor we traveled gave way, and Cassandra nearly fell in. When it happened, her fangs descended. She fears the blood moon ritual didn't work because of that. Come! I must get back to her. I shouldn't have left her alone this long, but she was so distraught, and she was sleeping so soundly, I was loath to wake her."

Together they leapt below and started along the corridor. Jon felt as if a heavy weight had been lifted. Things were going to be all right after all. There was new spring to his step and, once again, hope.

"She has naught to fear," Milosh said, struggling to keep up. "Her emotions triggered the fangs—as long as there was no feeding frenzy."

"You do not know how welcome this news will be, Milosh, but I will let you tell it. Cass is more likely to believe it coming from you than it would from me."

"Have you found Sebastian's resting place?" the Gypsy asked.

They had reached the chamber where Jon had left Cassandra sleeping and he hesitated, his hand on the door latch. He said, "I was about to ask you the same question."

The Gypsy shook his head. "No. I have only just arrived," he replied, "but we will. I have suspected all along that he never left this castle; that he has another coffin hidden in some secret place here. Together we will flush him out, or find that bed and kill him in it. You must show me the place you spoke of . . . the cell. The night is young. We shall begin there."

Jon lifted the latch and ushered Milosh inside. At first he thought his eyes were playing tricks on him. Goose-flesh crippled his spine and rooted him to the spot. His eyes, leaping in all directions, begged the darkness to give birth to that beloved form—begged his preternatural vision to show him that exquisite body, those soulful eyes so like a doe's, and those silken curls he loved to stroke with his fingers. But the chamber was empty. Cassandra was gone.

Cassandra cursed the darkness and her ineptitude at seeing through it as Jon could. Why had he left her alone? What could have been so vital that he'd left her vulnerable to Sebastian for even a second? And what magic had the vampire called upon to silence her while he carried her out of that chamber without a sound?

She blamed herself for the latter. If she hadn't strained through the darkness to see, meeting those hideous red-rimmed green-fire eyes just long enough for him to cloud her mind, she would have screamed the castle down. She was a novice at this. How could she hope to outsmart this centuries-old creature? That she had come this far without being made to face his deadly fangs again—cruel, awful things caked with old blood—she knew was no great feat on her part. Finishing her was evidently not paramount to him, otherwise he would have done so already. Mesmerized as she was, she had been in no position to prevent him. It was Jon he wanted more. What delectable part she was to play in her husband's demise had not been made known to her. She expected it to be creative—but unsuccessful, if she could help it.

She had to break free. Her first thought was to shapeshift into a panther as she'd shapeshifted into a kitten at Whitebriar Abbey, or a cat in this very castle. But it would not be as easy this time. She was neck-shackled to a wall slimed with mildew and rising damp, alone in some malodorous chamber. Groping for her throat, all but blind in the dark, she discovered a spiked iron collar. It had begun to chafe her neck. There was scarcely enough room for her to slip her finger underneath. Even if she shapeshifted into a panther, her head would be too large to slip through. Sebastian was a cunning adversary. He wasn't going to make the same mistake again.

She walked her fingers the length of the chain attached to the collar to where it was fastened to a large iron ring in the wall. Each heavy link was as large as her fist. She could scarcely bear the weight. Her heart sank. Even if Jon were to find her here, he could never free her without the key.

The door opened, but her hopes were raised only to be dashed, for the dark-clad, cadaverlike form of Sebastian Valentin swept over the threshold and stood above her, staring down, bony fists braced on his hips spreading his greatcoat wide. This one wasn't burned. Had he restored it through magic, or simply donned a fresh one? He seemed to be floating. Was he levitating? She took a chill: His feet weren't touching the floor.

He was backlit by torchlight from the corridor outside, and Cassandra fixed her gaze at a point in the middle of his chest. She would not look him in the eye again. Nonetheless, those rheumy, red-rimmed, iridescent eyes burned toward her, and though she could not—dared not—make out the rest of his features, she got the distinct impression from his demeanor that he was gloating.

"Little fool," he said, his voice cracking like a whip. "Did you think you could escape me—*me?*" He thumped his chest. "Your powers are too weak to take on that challenge. But that is my fault, isn't it? I should have drunk more of you—drunk my fill. And so I shall . . . but not yet. No, I desire an audience for that. I do not need to name the spectators, do I? Soon they will receive their invitation."

Cassandra shuddered visibly; she couldn't help it. Of course Sebastian saw, and heard the chains rattling. It wrenched a chorus of hearty guffaws from him. How such a sound could come from such an emaciated body eluded Cassandra. He bent closer, and she shrank from him, from this oppressive shape that exuded malice, from the foul stench of him like something wasting in the grave, sickening sweet and ripe with decay. Her nostrils flared and bile rose in her parched throat. When he reached for the iron collar, she lurched as though she'd been struck.

He clucked his tongue. "The day will come, Cassandra, when you will beg for my touch," he said. "Then there will be nothing unique about you. You will be as all the others—mindless, obedient pawns. So dull, so ordinary . . . not like now, when you command my full attention. It's the thrill of the chase, you see." He shrugged. "Once there is conquest, it all becomes so . . . plebian."

"If you have so many others, what do you want with me?" she snapped, knowing all too well such a comment was provocative. She could not bear his closeness. Her hands were balled into fists, her fingernails digging trenches in her palms. She longed to spit in his ugly face but curtailed the urge, her lips clamped shut on the impulse. But her tongue she could not control.

He must have seen better in the dark than she—well, of course he did—because he gave a giddy, lighthearted laugh. "Take care," he said. "Defiance only stimulates me, and believe me, you do not want that. But you will learn why. All in due time, my dear . . . all in due time."

To her surprise, out of the corner of her eye Cassandra saw a glint of metal—a strangely shaped key that fitted the octagon-shaped lock on her collar. The click of the latch resonated through her body, and in a split second she knew what she must do. As the collar fell away, she leapt into the air in a silver-black surge of light that knocked the vampire back on his haunches, and hit the cold stone floor running on all four panther feet. There hadn't been time to remove her petticoat and frock. Running crazily, her great paws tangled in the sprigged muslin twisted around her body, she covered some distance before shedding the frock. Behind, Sebastian's blood-chilling roar resounded along the corridor, accompanied by a foul, flesh-scourging wind.

"Yes. Run, little fool!" he bellowed. "You cannot escape me. You only make the game sweeter. Go ahead—run! There is nowhere to go but back into my arms!"

Another chorus of vile laughter followed, and a bat soared overhead close enough to graze her raised hackles, then soared off into the darkness beyond. Throwing her head back, Cassandra opened her mouth to let out the roar begging to escape, but something else came with it: fangs—long, needle-sharp vampire fangs. She roared again. She had almost forgotten the recurrence of her fangs, and their appearance now nearly broke her stride.

Sebastian had disappeared. Despite his bluster, was he scared? He was no match for her panther in bat form and evidently did not wish to test his mettle against the great cat in his human incarnation, either. She had won this round, not really knowing how or why, but there would be more before all was done; of that, if nothing else, she was certain.

Amazed at how well she could still reason in her cat body, she spun and streaked back the way she had come. Lost in an unfamiliar part of the castle, she needed to get her bearings. She also needed to find Jon . . . but that could wait. He deserved to suffer for leaving her vulnerable. If she could find the vampire's resting place, if she couldn't destroy him, she would lead Jon to it after dawn.

Bounding back over the musty stone floor, she reached her frock where she'd shed it, then paused. No, she should stay as she was. Hadn't Sebastian just proved her strength in panther form by fleeing? Her confidence bolstered, she continued on but slowed her pace to a voluptuous slink. The fangs had receded; her mouth would close again. Keeping to the shadows, she began her exploration.

CHAPTER TWENTY-SEVEN

"It's this way," Jon said, rushing Milosh along the dank corridor off the Great Hall. "Be careful. There may be minions left."

When they reached the grating that had fallen in, Jon pulled up short. "It was here that I nearly lost her," he said. "There were so many below."

"I don't smell anything down there now," remarked Milosh, "but we can leave no space unsearched. I have been in this castle many times, though never below this grate. There is much here that I have never seen. It was carved out of the mountain centuries ago, this fortress, this house of the undead, and it has struck fear into the hearts of the simple folk hereabout since the first stone was stacked. You saw how even the priests of the priory fear it. Fire has taken it to the bare bones many times, my friend. The torch you set to it was but one of many that have touched it over the years." Jon started to leap down, but he was stopped by Milosh's hand on his arm. "That pit will be there when we return," he said. "Let us first follow this grating to the end."

Together they leapt over the hole in the grate and continued. Milosh grabbed a torch from its bracket on the other side, for the corridor beyond was as black as tar. Jon's night vision was primed, as were all his other senses, but his inner panic over Cassandra's fate canceled common sense. He staved ahead with all the stealth of a juggernaut, and more than once Milosh had to hold him back, for he was struggling to keep up.

Past the grating there were no chambers. After a time, the corridor ended in a wall and a door. Jon tugged that open and started to walk through, only to teeter on the threshold. Empty air stretched before him. The door was carved in a sheer-faced mountain wall and opened onto an unfathomable drop into the night mist swirling up from the foothills below.

A quick fist in his shirt yanked him back from the edge just in time. "You cannot breach *that* span," Milosh said wryly, pulling him to safety. "An exit for Sebastian as a bat, I suppose, or a trap for unsuspecting vampire hunters like ourselves. This place is full of traps. Come! I want to see that cell below."

Retracing their steps, they leapt down into what was no more than a pit. The echo of the vampires' mournful moans and wails whispered across Jon's memory. His mind's eye saw Cassandra dangling from the caved-in grating, and he groaned aloud.

"I have to find her," he despaired.

"Panic will not help you do that," Milosh said. "You play right into Sebastian's hands. It is a battle of wits now, and yours are frayed."

"I have her scent, Milosh. She is either here somewhere or she has passed through recently.

Milosh held the torch aloft. "There is no exit from this

pen," he said. Pacing off the perimeter, he felt no hidden openings; the walls were solid granite, at least a foot thick. Then he raised the torch higher, revealing a gallery above, off in another direction. He did not leap this time, but walked right up the wall. Halfway up, he turned. "Well? Are you coming or not?" he asked.

"Me?" Jon said. "Are you suggesting I can walk up that wall?"

"We shan't know unless you try," Milosh returned, continuing on to the balustrade at the top.

Jon took a cautious step and, to his surprise, defied gravity to follow the Gypsy.

Milosh laughed. "You are not the most graceful vampire I have ever mentored," he said, "but you are learning. You need to become familiar with all your powers, Jon, your unique gifts. You never know when you will need them."

"I do not want my 'powers,'" Jon growled. "I want my life back—the life Sebastian stole from me, and from Cassandra because of me. I had a calling, a direction. My life was ordered, my future ordained. It was a good life, and it would have been a good life for Cassandra as well. I would have made it so. As it is now—"

Milosh spun him around. "That life is *over*," he snapped. "You can never have it back. You must face that here and now, before we take another step. I did not go through everything I have done since I met you, nearly losing my life in the bargain, only to have you fail at the end. You have a new calling. You are a vampire hunter. You are still doing God's work, never doubt that. You will free the ransomed souls held captive by Sebastian and his ilk and give them back to God. Accept your fate. Embrace your gifts, Jon Hyde-White. Learn to use them, and teach your lady wife to do likewise. It could be far worse.

You could be undead, damned to slaughter and corrupt with no memory that you ever had a calling."

Jon hung his head and nodded. Of course Milosh was right. What other choice was there but to accept his lot and make the best of it? That meant accepting the truth: He and Cassandra were vampires for the rest of their lives. He'd known it, but he hadn't accepted it until now.

Chambers lined the north side of the corridor, and he and Milosh assessed the distance. A few torches were lit in this quarter, and a hazy veil of golden light flickered amongst the distant shadows. Jon hesitated, deciding. "There's little time. We'd best split up to search," he said, flinging his arm eastward. "I'll take this side, you take the other. We'll meet back here."

The Gypsy nodded.

"You have the residue of the sacramental oil in the pocket of that coat." Jon said. He dropped his sack and opened it. "Take whatever else you need."

Milosh pored through the sack and snaked out a stake and the mallet. "You keep the cleaver," he said. "Let us do this quickly. I do not have a good feeling about it."

Jon didn't have a good feeling about anything in the vampire's castle. Opening every door along the way, he thrust his torch inside, searching each room with anxious eyes for some sign of Cassandra or Sebastian's resting place; but there was none. The rooms were sparsely furnished, cold and austere. It was plain that they were never used for anything but storage. Everything was frosted with cobwebs and dust; pallets were shackled to the walls with webs, and the mildewed dust that collected everywhere bore no trace of either fingers or footprints. Like everything else in the castle, these chambers cried of death and of the dead.

Jon had nearly traveled halfway along the corridor when something on the floor caught his eye. He snatched it up and held it to his nose—Cassandra's frock! Had she shapeshifted? He prayed so. The alternatives tripping across his mind were unthinkable. The frock was heavy in his hands. Turning it inside out, he uncovered the pocket suspended on a cord beneath the skirt and unearthed the pistol he had given her; it was still loaded. Stuffing the gun under the waistband of his breeches, he added the frock to the sack and rushed along the corridor to continue his search.

He was suddenly frantic. She had been here! This was his first tangible lead, and it gave him hope that he was close. He dared not call out for fear of attracting the wrong kind of attention. His heart was thudding against his ribs as he flung open first one and then another of the heavy old doors. Nothing met his eyes but gobs of malodorous dust, and spiderwebs strong enough to ensnare the bats that he now and then glimpsed hanging from the rafters. Were these creatures of the night, Sebastian's minions, or were they harmless animals that had taken shelter here? Whichever, they made no move to assail him; but for the occasional gleam of a shuttered eye, or a warning squeak, they paid him no mind at all.

He soon reached the end of the corridor. It terminated in another staircase leading upward. He hesitated. Cassandra had not been in any of the chambers he'd checked. The staircase was the next logical place to explore, but not without Milosh. Spinning around, he sprinted back along the corridor to the place where they were to meet, just in time to see the Gypsy striding out of the shadows to join him.

"Nothing?" Jon asked.

"No, no trace. These chambers have not been in use for some time."

Jon dragged Cassandra's frock from the sack. "She shed this back there," he said, pointing. "There is a staircase. I thought we'd best search that together."

Milosh smiled, clearly pleased. "You never give her enough credit, my friend," he said through a lopsided smile. "I knew that from the moment I carried her, a mere cat, in my teeth from this accursed castle to my cart. She fought me to a fare-thee-well. She has evidently outsmarted our host. Hah! That is more than we have been able to accomplish between the pair of us. I can almost feel sorry for Sebastian at her mercy."

Jon scowled. He wasn't about to go that far, but he got the point, recalling the most recent of Cassandra's feats. It was she, after all, who had set Sebastian's clothes afire on the mountain—and not a minute too soon. Taking her blood had advanced her to his level. She was no more the helpless kitten; she was a sleek black panther. How could he keep forgetting how she had evolved? And why? The answer was easy: He worshiped her, could not help wanting to protect her. He would do so with his dying breath, with the last beat of his heart that lived only for her. Would he ever get the chance to tell her this, to take her in his arms, to live inside her exquisite body again? These thoughts banged around in his brain as he and Milosh ascended the narrow staircase into darkness.

Cassandra was in her element in panther form. As black as the shadows, she prowled the hall, bounded up and down staircases as wild as the wind. How she loved roaming free as a panther. She must remember to ask Jon if he enjoyed prowling as a wolf. It was the only aspect of the condition that she did love, though she'd come to terms with the rest. She could bear anything as long as she could be with Jon. He was her very heart.

The halls were deathly still around her, but she took no comfort in it. Sebastian was lurking somewhere in the castle, waiting. Her objective now was finding his resting place. He was too intelligent to face her down. No, he was too cunning for that. Her panther could rip his throat out and annihilate him altogether if he were in bat form. One chomp of her great teeth would crush his bones. There were ways, of course, that he could vanquish her; there were always ways. But those were fewer than if she was in human form. It was then that she was truly vulnerable.

The whole castle seemed deserted. It was unnatural, as if she were the only living creature in it, and yet she felt as if a hundred eyes were watching her every movement. Nothing hindered her, however, and she soon abandoned the upper regions in her search. It didn't seem likely that Sebastian would rest in daylight hours in the castle proper, where anyone might find him, and she soon began searching for other staircases leading below. At last she found one, a very narrow spiral leading down from the back of one of the third-floor chambers. It led to a tunnel carved in the rock. She padded along cautiously. Her extraordinary sense of smell was active now, and, nostrils flaring, she loped along, eyes snapping back and forth across the span, where what appeared to be crypts had been gouged out of the granite. The castle was carved literally out of the mountainside.

Cassandra noticed at once that, though cobwebs lived in the far corners, no dust existed here. As far removed from the house proper as this tunnel was, it was well traveled, unlike the rooms above, where thick layers of dust coated everything like snow. Torches in wall brackets at intervals lit this passage as well, though they were few and far between, throwing just enough light for her to see the coffins in the cryptlike cubicles. There were six, three on either side of the tunnel, and all were empty. She raised her head and sniffed the air. Sebastian's scent filled her nostrils, the sickening sweetness of corrupted flesh—of death, and stale blood. It was much stronger to her panther nose than to her human one. Had she found him? Yes; her raised hackles were testimony enough of that. But who were the other coffins for? There was no way to tell.

She had found them, but she could not in her present shape destroy them. She needed Jon for that, and she spun around and raced back the way she'd come, past the cubicles, through the narrow tunnel to the landing, and to the staircase winding upward from an empty room no bigger than a closet. But she wasn't alone. Out of the shadows a dark figure emerged, blocking her path, his red-rimmed eyes glowing in the bleak semidarkness. His cold laughter filled the span, bouncing off the crudely hewn walls, echoing down the tunnel on a fugitive wind that had risen out of nowhere.

Sebastian.

CHAPTER TWENTY-EIGHT

"She has come this way," Jon said, sniffing the musty air. This time it wasn't wishful thinking. He wasn't imagining it; her scent was so strong here, it seemed a living, breathing presence with a pulsebeat of its own.

They had been searching for hours and found nothing in the upper regions, though Jon didn't expect to locate Sebastian's resting place where anyone might easily come upon it. Sebastian was too clever. Wherever it was, it was well hidden—and there was probably more than one. For centuries, the creature had evaded those who hunted his kind. He knew well how to play the game; he had practically written the rules.

Jon wasn't overly concerned about finding Sebastian; sooner or later the creature would appear. It was Cassandra he was worried about. They should have found her by now. They had checked every recess, every chamber and staircase in the upper regions, from the Great Hall to the battlements, and found no sign of her. Sebastian roamed the halls of Castle Valentin and she was at his mercy, and despite Milosh's insistence that she was not to be sold short, Jon couldn't imagine her holding her own in such a confrontation.

"That is not all I smell," Milosh said in a low murmur. "*He* is near. I smell his excitement. I have hunted this vampire for centuries, Jon Hyde-White. I know him. When his feeding frenzy is at its height, he gives off an odor unlike any other. My ability to detect that odor in advance has saved me on more than one occasion. It is one of my most useful gifts."

They were on the brink of a steep, narrow staircase roughly hewn of stone. It wound down into dusky semi-darkness. Something occupied that space hidden from view, something darker than death and colder than the grave. Jon could taste it collecting at the back of his palate, metallic and cold, like blood—like death itself, for, indeed, death had a flavor, salty and strong.

The thunder of Sebastian's laughter drifted up the staircase from below, drowning out the shuffling noise of their hasty approach. The staircase was carved three stories deep into the castle's very bowels. When they reached the second-to-last landing, the room at the bottom came into view. For a moment, Jon froze. He heard a great cat's guttural, rattling growls before he saw it; Sebastian's greatcoat was spread wide from his outstretched arms and in the way, but Cassandra as a panther was backed into a corner. Her long fangs were bared, catching glints of reflected light from the torches. The animal's hackles were raised. It was poised to spring. He could see the cords in its long, sleek legs standing out in bold relief. The sight took his breath away. She was magnificent!

Milosh pushed against him from behind, trying to pass on the narrow stairs, but Jon's arm shot out, preventing him.

"No. Wait," he whispered. "Do not distract her. Do not give him the advantage. We are close enough to come to her aid if needs must."

The Gypsy gave a throaty chuckle. "Now who is singing the praises of your lady wife's prowess, eh?" Jon scowled at him. It was but a sidelong glance; Cassandra had his full and fierce attention now, and thus far Sebastian hadn't seen them lurking on the landing above.

It was only seconds, but it seemed an eternity before the panther sprang; then everything happened so quickly there was no time to react. All Jon saw was a silvery streak as the animal sailed through the air and impacted the vampire, then sank its fangs deep into the monster's throat. Jon heard flesh tear and bones crunch. Sebastian shrieked. It was a sound so vile Jon almost lost his footing on the step. Enraged, the vampire seized the panther around its throat, tearing it from the bleeding wound, its long talons attempting to snap the great cat's neck. The animal went limp in the vampire's grip. Garbled sounds came from its open mouth around its protruding tongue. Its eyes were glazed and bulging, its front feet twitching in a spastic rhythm.

In the blink of an eye, Jon was in motion. "*No!*" he cried with a bestial howl. He sailed through the air, his fangs fully extended, and slammed into Sebastian feet first. The impact loosened Sebastian's grip on Cassandra, whom he flung against the wall. She struck it hard, and slid to the floor in a limp heap of fur.

Enraged, Jon spun in midair and careened into the vampire again, sinking his fangs into the gray, foul-tasting flesh of the vampire's throat with the full intention of finishing what Cassandra had started. There was no danger of bloodlust, though the vampire's gore covered him;

he would drink no blood with his needle-sharp fangs. Just as Milosh had said, they had become weapons, stabbing like knives deep into that corrupt flesh, the evidence of their effectiveness the creature's pain-wracked shrieks.

Milosh had gone to the panther's side. Cassandra tried twice to stand but fell back both times. A third attempt failed also, but this time she retched before sinking back down to pant on the cold granite floor.

Stay! Milosh charged, speaking with his mind. Struggling with the vampire, Jon was out of range of reading his thoughts. The Gypsy squatted on his haunches, looking deep into Cassandra's dazed eyes, deeper than any mortal man could. Stunned by what he saw there, his breath escaped in a strangled gasp. Still, he needed to be certain, and he leaned closer, sniffing her aura, sniffing in the way of a dog or wolf. No, he hadn't been mistaken. There was no question. She was with child! *Have you told him? Does he know?* he asked.

No, please. I beg you . . . , her mind responded. *Do not speak it! Say nothing! It is mine to tell . . . when the time is right.*

Can you change back? he queried.

I . . . I don't think so. Not yet.

Milosh frowned, stroking her head. *Fine. Lie still then,* he commanded her. *Stay down. Protect your litter.*

He staggered to his feet. He could not afford to be rattled now. Across the way, Jon was holding his own against Sebastian, but he knew well the cunning monster's taste for deluding his victims into believing they had the upper hand. Self-confidence bred mistakes; Milosh had learned that lesson the hard way. Casting a quick glance over his shoulder to be certain Cassandra had obeyed, he joined the fight just as the vampire flung Jon against the wall in much the same manner that he had Cassandra. Jon twisted in flight and hit feet first. Calling upon his new-found gift, he loosed a battle cry, ran up the wall, across the ceiling, and dove on Sebastian below, impacting him with force enough to bring the monster to his knees. Meanwhile, Milosh—fangs extended—groped the great-coat pocket for what remained of the sacramental oil. There wasn't much, no more than a thin coating; but a fingertip full was all he needed. Scooping it out, he smeared it on Sebastian's forehead, making the sign of the cross as Jon attacked the creature again.

Sebastian screeched as smoke rose from his anointed brow, his nostrils, and his bulging rheumy eyes, which rolled back in his head so that only blue-veined white was visible. All at once his body began to spin as if caught in a whirlwind. The force threw both Jon and Milosh against the wall, and the vampire dissolved into a whirring, squeaking, flapping swarm of bats—dozens of them; *hundreds* of them—soaring up the staircase helter-skelter to disappear into the darkness of the upper floors.

"You cannot escape me," echoed through the chamber. But there was no laughter. Their foe was weakened, in pain, but this was not over; it was far from finished. There was still a little time before dawn. They had to find Sebastian's resting place and destroy it before the sun rose.

Milosh attempted to right himself. Jon was beside him in seconds, lending his arm in support. "Are you bitten?" he asked.

"No," Milosh replied, shaking his head. He knew well how to protect himself from bites; he'd had centuries of practice. "My wounds," he explained, "they are not yet healed enough for doing battle."

Jon stood him up and dusted him off. Behind, the panther, too, was on its feet. A loud roar turned them both toward the great cat. *Follow me*, Cassandra's mind spoke, evidently to them both.

The panther padded past them into the tunnel. Nonplussed, the men stared at each other, then followed her into the narrow space.

"Good God!" Jon cried at sight of the crypts. "You found these? We have searched the castle top to bottom looking for Sebastian's resting place, and you . . ."

Not quite "bottom," Cassandra corrected him. *I found these before he found me.*

Jon went to the sack he'd left by the stairs and fished out her frock. *Do you want to change back?* he asked her. *I will stand guard while you do. There's no need for mind speech now. We've much work to do.*

In a little while, Cassandra replied.

Why? You haven't been bitten . . . ?

No, I think I might be . . . of more use as I am. For now.

Milosh gripped Jon's arm. "Let her stay as she is for awhile," he said. "She will change when she's ready. Come! We have much to do, and so little time to do it."

He studied Cassandra's eyes. He dared not use mind speech now to voice his questions, as Jon was close enough to hear also. What if she couldn't change back? No! He wouldn't even entertain that thought. He hated secrets, though he was good at keeping them. But there was no time for that muddle now. There were more coffins to burn.

Jon stared down into the coffin, at the soil spread over the bottom, and took a chill, remembering how he had collected earth from Whitebriar Abbey for himself before he and Cassandra embarked upon their journey. That was before he knew he wouldn't need it. He had taken some with him on the *North Star*, and kept it close just in case. What had become of it? Had it ended on the bonfire with the rest of his belongings? It didn't matter. All that seemed a lifetime ago. He plunged his torch into the coffin, then shrank back from the stench of the subsequent blaze. The flames smelled foul, of Sebastian, and bile bubbled up in Jon's throat. It must have affected Cassandra as well; still in panther form, she had crept back under the staircase, and was quietly retching.

Milosh was torching the coffins on the other side of the tunnel, while Jon set fire to the two remaining on his side, and the Gypsy flung the remains of his flask of holy water into the midst of the fire. The moment the flask hit, a crack formed in the floor and the alcoves began to shake.

Crumbling rock and the heat of the flames drove both men dancing around the fissure in the center of the tunnel. Great clouds of sooty smoke belched toward them, filling that narrow space, spilling into the little chamber that housed the staircase where Cassandra waited. There was a door at the far end of the tunnel. Coughing, Jon staggered toward it and flung it open to the night air. It, too, opened on the sheer-faced drop, but he was more careful this time, before Milosh called out to warn him. The floor beneath his feet began to shake, and loose rocks rumbled down the mountain.

Slowly, from where the coffins blazed in their crypts, the smoke began drifting out through the opening. Once it had dissipated enough so they could see what they were doing, Jon and the Gypsy, with the help of the tools in their sack, broke the hinges on the door: They were rusted through, and it wasn't long before it went tumbling down the side of the mountain.

"Now when Sebastian or his minions come here for sanctuary from the sun, it will flood this tunnel to greet them," Jon said, clapping the dust from his hands. "Do you think there are more coffins stashed away somewhere?"

Milosh shrugged. "We must hope not," he said. "Feel the floor shake beneath us? This whole section has been undermined by the first fire. It is not safe. And soon it will be light. We have done all that can be done here."

They had just begun to part the last tufts of smoke belching along the tunnel when Cassandra met them halfway. She had shifted back, and she floated toward them in a cloud of white sprigged muslin—soiled and somewhat the worse for wear, thought Jon, looking at her in dismay. Her confrontation with the vampire had altered her. She was as white as milk. There was no color whatsoever in her cheeks, and her gently bowed lips were as chalk.

"No! Don't come!" Jon called. Rushing her into his arms, he led her back along the corridor to the safety of the little room at the end of it, but she pulled back when he attempted to kiss her.

"What is it?" he asked, searching her face. "What's wrong?"

She gestured. "Your fangs," she said. "I saw them—on both of you. It didn't work . . . the blood moon ritual . . . It didn't work for any of us."

Jon burst into laughter, his head thrown back. "Silly goose, is that all?" he said.

"That is much, considering," Cassandra snapped.

"You had best tell her," Jon said to Milosh. "She'll never believe it coming from me."

Milosh cleared his throat. "The Blood Moon Rite *has* worked," he assured her, "but it does not prevent the fangs from descending whenever the need arises. Did you have the bloodlust when your fangs appeared?"

"Well, no. But—"

"Did you see a feeding frenzy in us here tonight when ours did?"

"N-no . . ."

"We are all still vampires, Cassandra," Milosh pointed out. "Nothing can change that. The fangs are part of it. But this is not all bad. They will always be at our disposal—at the ready if needs must—whenever we have a need to defend ourselves."

"I thought, I . . ." She trailed off.

Jon crushed her closer still. "You see, Cass?" he said. "It's going to be all right."

Were those tears in her eyes? He frowned at the strange glance that passed between his bride and Milosh. He couldn't read it, it was too fleeting, and her arms clutching him close called him back to the soft pressure of her embrace.

"Look!" Milosh said, turning toward the gaping hole where the door had been. "The sky is lightening. Come . . . move into the shadows, where we can wait and watch what the dawn brings. Our work is done down here."

The plan was to wait until the sun had risen before leaving the castle. Ideally, they would receive proof positive that Sebastian was dead. Cassandra was relieved about the fangs, but a greater press was weighing upon her now— the premonition. If she'd ever questioned, she questioned no longer. Milosh knew.

"Are you sure you are all right?" Jon said. "You're trembling, Cassandra."

She couldn't help herself. Her whole body was shaking in uncontrollable spasms.

"I will be once we leave this accursed place," she said. "I want to go home, Jon—back to England. Please . . . take me home."

They had reached the shadowy staircase at the end of the corridor, but they still had a perfect view of the flaming coffins. Milosh hung back in the shadows of the landing to give them privacy. From above, shafts of fractured sunlight beamed through the high-set windows, casting puddles of pink-gold sheen at their feet. Frowning, Jon stopped and turned his wife toward him, cupping her face in his hands. How strong they were, how comforting. She could not help but turn and kiss his palm. Its rough texture against the softness of her lips set her pulse racing. It tasted of salt, and of him, of his own true essence—of musk and lime, of leather, and of the earth—just as he had before the nightmare began, before the condition tainted all with the bitter, metallic taste of blood.

"The minute our work is done here, we shall leave for home," he said, rubbing his thumbs on her cheeks. "I promise you, Cassandra."

Her tears spilled down; she could not prevent them. She nodded her head in his hands. Drawing a ragged breath, she opened her mouth to speak, but a sudden chorus of blood-chilling shrieks and wails coming from the burning alcoves froze her, mouth agape, as the floor began to tremble. Milling bodies cloaked in smoke and flame swarmed through the corridor and were soon swallowed up as a great fissure rent the rocky floor in two, burying them beneath a mountain of slag and rubble. The buttress in that sector had collapsed, and the fissure was widening, spreading toward them.

Slipping his arm around her waist, Jon rushed her toward the landing and Milosh, who had come forward from the shadows as the walls began to shake.

"It is as I feared," the Gypsy said. "If this was the only staircase leading below, they would have had to pass us to reach it. There must be another way into that tunnel."

The shrieks still echoed from the tunnel, obscured now by great plumes of belching smoke, and Jon shoved Cassandra toward Milosh. "Take her up," he charged, "away from here. More come! I want to see where they come from . . . if Sebastian is among them! Stay up there, and keep her there. Do not let her out of your sight!"

"Jon!" Cassandra protested, but Milosh was rushing up the staircase, and Jon had already become one with the smoke and shadows.

"It is all right," Milosh said.

"Nothing is 'all right,'" she snapped.

"Well, *I* am all right, thanks to you," he returned. "I am in your debt, Cassandra. I was too weak to change back— just as you were down there. If you hadn't brought that trencher . . ."

Cassandra looked him in the eye. This was probably the only opportunity she would ever have to ask the one question that was tearing her up inside, the question only he could answer.

"What am I going to do, Milosh?" she murmured.

"You have to tell him, Cassandra."

"My God, will it be . . . as we are?" There! It was out. She held her breath, awaiting the answer she feared to hear.

"I honestly do not know," Milosh said. "But I do know this: If you were as Sebastian is—fully made vampires, undead—you would be sterile, unable to reproduce at all. As you are now, there is no way to know how the child in you will be affected. Not until it is born. I am sorry."

"The children!" she sobbed, her voice filled with despair. "The children that came in the night, that terrible knocking. Is *that* what is living inside me? Am I to give birth to a creature who will one day rap on doors in the night, bringing terror to the good people inside?"

"No, Cassandra," Milosh soothed. Gripping her upper arms, he gently shook her. "You must calm yourself. Those creatures were unfortunate urchins taken by vampires in their innocent youth."

"And mine is a child conceived of two vampires! What else could it be? How could it possibly be anything else?"

"Two *infected* by vampires," Milosh corrected her. "There is a difference, Cassandra."

"Milosh, I am not as strong as you. If it were infected, I could not bring myself to . . . to . . ."

"Stop now!" the Gypsy said through clenched teeth. "This sort of speculation will serve nothing. What is, *is*. I have seen several cases such as yours in my lifetime; all were different. Just as the gifts differ among us, so do the effects of the infection differ. Were you undead, you would not be carrying that child in your belly. That you have conceived is a good sign, Cassandra. The nature of its condition will make itself known as time passes, and you will deal with it then."

"The Blood Moon Rite . . . has that helped? Has it lessened the effect?" She was grasping. Her heart ached to give Jon a healthy, normal child.

Milosh hesitated. "From what I have observed, the child will neither be harmed, nor will it benefit from the Blood Moon Rite—that would only have been possible if it were conceived before you were infected. I am not an expert in these areas, but I will not lie to you. The Blood Moon Rite works as an antidote. The child will likely be immune to the rite, if he attempts it himself, because of the effect the herbal draught has upon the system."

"What am I to do?" she despaired.

"You must tell Jon," Milosh said. "He has a right to know, Cassandra. It is his child, too. You cannot wait until he guesses on his own."

Her eyes snapped at him. "Not until we are safely aboard a ship that has set sail for home," she said, and meant it. "I will not have my child born here in this god-forsaken place. I want it born in England. If I tell him now, he will fear for me to make the voyage. Coming, the passage was dreadful—terrible storms with horizontal rain and lashing winds— and that was early in summer, when the weather was warm and the winds were balmy and fair. Autumn soon gives way to winter. A voyage now would be treacherous. He will not want to risk it with me increasing, Milosh."

"That is, I fear, your coil to unwind," the Gypsy said. "He needs to know. The longer you wait, the worse it will be."

Cassandra nodded and said no more. He was right; it was her coil to unwind, and she would, in her own good and perfect time . . . When they were on the ship for home.

Jon reached the landing below as the walls began to tremble around him. The crack in the corridor floor was widening. Shielding his eyes, he stared through the flames and smoke and drifting ash for some sign of Sebastian among the mindless creatures falling into the gap; he had to destroy the vile monster, had to be sure. Sunlight had just begun to trickle in. Those vampires who did not sink into the fissure were disintegrating before it.

Loose rock dust began to sift down over Jon as he stood rooted to the threshold of the tunnel. He dared not stay much longer; the whole lower region was in danger of collapse. He'd almost given up when the wall moved behind one of the alcoves on the left side of the corridor, and Sebastian appeared. For a moment the vampire froze; then, shielding himself from the rays of the sun, he let loose a bloodcurdling shriek, teetering on the edge of the widening gap.

Jon's gaze was riveted to his nemesis. For a split second, their eyes met. Jon could not read the message in the vampire's deadly glare, but in a moment it was over: Sebastian spun and roared and spiraled down into the gap through the widening crevice, which swallowed him up in a rush of wind that ruffled Jon's hair and narrowed his eyes.

Yes. It was over.

Crumbling rock and debris sealed the fissure, and Jon rushed up the quaking staircase and reached Milosh and Cassandra by taking the steps two at a stride. "There are six burnt corpses below," he said. "Dozens fell through the rent in the floor. I saw them go down myself. Between the sunlight pouring in and the flames, it was as if the floor opened up and swallowed them."

"Sebastian?" Milosh asked.

Jon nodded. "Yes," he said. "He came at the last, through another entrance to the tunnel behind one of the alcoves. The sun was just streaming in when he arrived. He was swallowed up with the rest. There was no other way out of that corridor except through the open doorway into the sunlight or right past me, which he did not attempt. Go—see for yourself if you like, but hurry, the buttresses have collapsed. This whole section is going to go. We are no longer safe here."

Milosh disappeared over the edge of the landing, and Jon took Cassandra in his arms.

"I love you, Jon," she murmured. "Now will you take me home?"

He pulled her closer, the throbbing pressure of his sudden arousal leaning heavily against her, until her rapid heartbeat hammered against his own.

"Yes, my love," he said, showering her face with kisses. "We have much work to do there, and our whole lives to do it. It's finally time to go home."

Epilogue

It was difficult to bid Milosh good-bye. He would not be staying in the region, either. It would not be safe now that he had been found out; he would be hunted. This would not be a permanent exile, though. Once the current generation had passed on to their reward, he would return to his homeland, to this place where his beloved wife and unborn child were buried. It had happened before. It would happen again, and in the meanwhile there were other places for him to hunt down and destroy the undead. They'd heard that the condition had reached epidemic proportions on the far side of the mountains.

He had kept his promise not to divulge Cassandra's secret, and theirs was a tearful parting. She would not soon forget the sad look of loneliness in the Gypsy's eyes as he bade them farewell. That had occurred in the dead of night, a sennight ago, at a coaching inn on the far side of the river.

The final search of the castle had shown nothing else. Well hidden in the forest, they'd watched the mountain-

top for a week, looking for lights at night, and also monitored the villagers' comings and goings during the day,
but Castle Valentin remained shrouded in darkness,
hauntingly desolate and still. There was no sign of Sebastian, dead or undead. It was time to go home.

Now, fair but cooler winds blew upon the four-masted
privateer that would carry Cassandra and her beloved Jon
back to England. Sapphire waves buoyed the ship, and
whitecaps creamed against her prow like paper lace as
she pitched and rolled with the fickle rhythm of the autumn sea.

The crimson sun had almost set, but the sky still blazed
with streaks of rose and gold and purple that tinted the
clouds and the underbellies of the snowy-white waterfowl
that rode the wind. Cassandra could no longer see the
quay. She pulled her hooded cloak closer around her,
acutely aware of Jon's strong and pinioning arm. They
stood along the gunwales. Neither had spoken Sebastian's
name since they'd left the Carpathians. Neither had
mentioned the swarms of bats they'd seen sawing through
the night air silhouetted against the moon, even in the
forest, as their coach-and-four tooled ever closer to
Gdansk. Would she ever again see a bat in flight and not
be plagued with bone-chilling thoughts of Sebastian?

You cannot escape me. His malevolent voice and deep-
throated laughter ghosted across her memory, and she
shuddered. Was it only a memory, or was he speaking to
her mind from this side of the grave? The ghostly voice
faded, siphoned off on the wind as mysteriously as it had
come, and she cuddled close into Jon's strong embrace.

"Have I told you how much I love you?" Jon murmured,
gazing into her eyes. "If you hadn't set that creature's coat
afire on the mountain, we would not be standing here

like this. You saved our lives, my love. And I will never forget the sight of you as a panther doing battle, streaking through the air. I see it waking and sleeping."

Cassandra hesitated. "Do you trust me, Jon . . . I mean . . . *really* trust me?"

"Yes," he said, soothing her. "I trust you with my life. God knows you've saved it more than once on this mad ramble."

"No matter what?"

"Of course, no matter what," he said with a chuckle. "Look here, whatever is this?"

"And you won't deny me anymore when we make love?" she persisted, ignoring the question.

Jon's expression clouded suddenly. "Of course not," he said. "You know why that had to be until the blood moo—"

Cassandra laid a finger over his lips. "Shhh, I know," she said. "I just want to be sure that won't happen now . . . no matter what." She needed to be sure before she broke the news.

"Silly goose," he chided. Giving her a playful squeeze, he turned her away from the ship's rail. "Come," he said. "Let us go below so I can prove the point. I won't have to leave you this time to feed on cattle in steerage, nor will I fear feeding upon you. You can lie in my arms the whole voyage if you wish. We have much work ahead of us at home, and an eternity to do it, but this time is ours, Cassandra—all ours."

An eternity. That unfathomable concept of forever had haunted her as a child, and it had come back to haunt her again now more severely. She was still coming to grips with its vastness. The mere thought of living in Jon's strong arms throughout eternity made her heart race. This was not how it was supposed to be, certainly not what they had planned, but they were together; and with love, all else paled.

Cassandra had made peace with herself over the child she carried. Milosh was right; she would just have to wait and see, and deal with whatever happened when the time came. Whatever their fate, she and Jon would face it together. Right now, she was going home. England! Anticipation of that crowded all negative thoughts from her mind. How she had missed her home.

Through the slanted window that followed the contours of the ship's hull belowdecks, the waning moon threw fractured shafts of silver light on the bunk they would share. The scent of tar and salt was heavier here, pungent and evocative. One by one, Jon stripped away Cassandra's garments, and then his own. Staggering with the rolling swells that undermined his balance, he scooped her up in his arms and set her down on the bedding gleaming silver in the moonlight, then climbed in beside her.

"I am going to ravish you," he murmured. That deep, resonant voice set her afire from the inside out until she feared her bones would melt. In slow, tantalizing circles, his hands roamed her body, blazing a trail of icy heat from the notch below her arched throat to her breasts and the hardened buds of her nipples. They slid lazily along the curve of her waist to her belly and thighs, lingering on the soft, moist mound of her sex. "Would you like that, my love?" he whispered, nibbling on her ear, his hot breath puffing against her cheek. His hooded eyes were the color of mercury and dilated with desire.

Her pulse leapt, her body thrumming in anticipation. His voice crackled with smoldering fire. He had the power to penetrate her with that voice, with those eyes. And as the thick pressure of his arousal found her thigh, she melted.

"Yes, *please*," she murmured, taking his face in her hands. Her thumbs caressed his angular cheeks, the heels of those tiny hands reacting to the muscles along his jaw that had begun ticking a steady rhythm. "But first, my love," she murmured, "I have something wonderful to tell you. . . ."

DAWN THOMPSON
The Falcon's Bride

At twenty-one, after two Seasons with no takers, Theodosia Barrington should have been grateful to snare Nigel Cosgrove. The earl-to-be was a blue-eyed Adonis, a true catch. And yet, upon her arrival at Cashel Cosgrove, Thea found herself more intrigued by the Irish castle's legend, the tragic warrior Ros Drumcondra, than by her intended. "The Black Falcon" Drumcondra was called. His ghost was reputed to wander these halls, making women tremble with fear and desire. Hadn't he stolen away another's betrothed, made the woman his love slave? If only Thea herself could suffer such a fate. If only that Gypsy woman had spoken the truth, and Thea was a woman out of time, the one meant to be... *The Falcon's Bride.*

DORCHESTER PUBLISHING'S
GUARANTEED READ PROGRAM

If you are not fully satisfied with *Blood Moon* by Dawn Thompson, you may exchange it! Simply return the book with the required information below and your proof of purchase to:

Dorchester Publishing Co., Inc.
Guaranteed Read (*Blood Moon*)—BAB
P.O. Box 6640
Wayne, PA 19087

Name: _____

Mailing Address: _____

City: _____ State: _____ Zip: _____

Reason for return: _____
_____
_____
_____
_____

We will mail you another Dorchester romance immediately after the return has been processed.